# THOU SHALT NEVER TELL

P. J. MANN

ISBN 978-952-69294-3-9 (paperback)

ISBN 978-952-69294-4-6 (hardback)

ISBN 978-952-69294-5-3 (EPUB)

ISBN 978-952-69294-6-0 (MOBI)

# DEDICATION

This book is dedicated to my sister Elisabetta, to help her remember that we always need to look at the future with hope. Looking around, you will see, you're never alone.

## ACKNOWLEDGMENTS

I would like to thank first of all my editor, Tricia Drammeh, for her support and suggestions. My reader's team who gave great suggestions and supported me also for this novel. You guys are great!

# INTRO

The heat in the bar was almost unbearable; The fan on the roof creaked on its rusty rotor, lazily stirring the air in the bar, overheated by the constant humidity of the stretches along the border with the thick of the rain forest.

Jason slammed his empty glass on the scarred wooden table, scattering hardened food remnants from earlier patrons.

He glanced around and took a handkerchief from his pocket to wipe the sweat from his forehead. Omar, the bartender, watched with his dark eyes as he dried spotted glasses, fresh from the old dishwasher. From time to time, he flipped the dirty rag to shoo the flies and mosquitoes that had taken up residence.

Old programs ran on the television over the bar, the decades-old voices behind the din of the patrons.

"Bring me another one, Omar, will you?" Jason shook the empty glass in the direction of the barkeeper.

Omar arched an eyebrow. "Your mistress won't be pleased to have you drink so much. Besides, it won't be good for your health."

He placed the rag on the table, and as he grabbed the whiskey bottle, he walked to the table where Jason was seated.

"She is never pleased with me anyway, so why bother? Concerning my health, I am afraid death will not come soon enough," he observed as he watched Omar reaching his table and pouring the whiskey in the glass.

"Leave the bottle here, it will make things easier for you," Jason added.

"As you wish, boss. I am just giving a bit of friendly advice," Omar replied, walking away on the squeaking wooden floor, creaking at every step, threatening to fail any minute then. "The only suggestion I can give is that when things are desperate, you should do all it takes to avoid turning them into something worse."

"Ah, the old wisdom of the elders..." Jason mumbled, observing the color of the whiskey in his glass.

He never thought he would have been stuck in that God-forsaken spot in the heart of Africa. He never even considered it possible for a *mzungu* to be grounded there. *Where am I, by the way? This place is not even mentioned on any map. It's like being brought to another dimension or another nightmare.*

"She told me soon another guy will arrive. I hope he will be wise enough not to disappoint Her in any way. I will warn him about the dangers, but in the end, it will be all up to him."

Omar peered at him with a surprised expression, pausing from drying the glasses. "I really wish so too. One *mzungu* is enough to have in this bar."

He laughed heartily, showing his white teeth.

"I agree with you, but it's not because I wouldn't like to have some company, rather because I would never wish for anyone to have my same fate," Jason replied.

"Do you know already when he will come?"

"No, I have no idea, but she said he will soon be ready, and she is never wrong..."

# CHAPTER 1

Kaine stretched his back in the chair of his office, trying to ease the pain in the lower part of his spine.

It was the umpteenth time he switched positions. "I think I will take a walk; I need to move from this position before I scream in pain," he said, glancing at Nora on the other side of the room.

She raised her eyes to him, arched her eyebrows as if surprised to hear him speak. "Good idea. I should follow your example."

"Are you coming with me?"

"No, I'm going to walk to the cafeteria and get a coffee. With some luck, I'll also find someone to talk with for at least half an hour," Nora replied with a slight challenging tone in her voice.

Nora and Kaine were employed at the same private institution for anthropology studies. They'd worked together since Kaine started his career there, after a ridiculously long period spent on his doctoral thesis on African tribal cultures.

"How many years have we been sharing the same office?" Nora questioned, in an attempt to start a non-work-related chat as they walked to the exit. Kaine had never been talkative and they rarely shared the same research project.

"Uh... about three years," he replied, bringing one finger lightly touching his lower lip.

"And we basically don't know anything about each other."

Kaine laughed. "I am lousy at social relationships."

Sarcasm laced her voice. "You don't say?" In a softer tone, she continued, "I don't want to intrude in your private life, or nose into your business. I just... I just want to have a friendly relationship, more than 'good mornings' and 'bye-byes'."

Kaine cringed twisting his fingers. "I always feel uncomfortable when I meet new people. It takes time to get beyond general greetings."

Nora observed him for a second. "Isn't it time to go beyond that cold level of acquaintance? Before you came, your desk was occupied by Dr. Stevens. Despite having been a researcher with a long career, he was very social. When he retired, I knew I would miss his jokes and his brilliant mind.

"Then you arrived, and I felt so excited to have company until I realized that the only words, I would ever hear from you were 'Good morning, Nora... See you tomorrow, Nora.' I don't want to push you, but I'd like to know whether you are upset with me or you dislike me. I appreciate honesty, and I won't feel bitter if you would just tell me straight that you can't stand me."

Kaine gazed at her with wide-open eyes. "I owe you an apology if I made you believe I don't like you or find your presence annoying. I should have told you when I introduced myself that I am a bit shy, and it might take a long time for me to get acquainted. I think I..." he hesitated as they approached the cafeteria.

"Come have a coffee with me. I'll buy." she proposed.

Kaine smiled and considered. It would be an excellent chance to, first, learn some social skills, second, become familiar with his coworker, and, last but not least, do something different than walk thinking about his job. "Yes, but I would rather stand. My back needs to be far from a chair for at least half an hour."

Nora waived one of the waitresses as she came in. "So, what do you do in your life besides research?" She had to admit he was darn cute, but she couldn't even envision becoming more than a friend. *One secret for a happy life is to keep relationships and work separate.*

He squeezed his shoulders wondering what he was supposed to say to her. His life wasn't interesting, and he cringed at the thought of telling anything personal. Nevertheless, *if I keep everything for myself, I'll never develop any social skills.*

"What can I say? I do not have any particular interests or hobbies. I love to walk in nature, and most of the time, I bring a camera with me, but I am just an amateur. I find it relaxing and it helps me to de-stress," he commenced. "I don't follow any sport. It bores me to watch other people doing something."

"So, you are a get-into-the-action sort of guy," she played absentmindedly with a curl of her hair.

Kaine chuckled. "I wouldn't say that. I'd rather do things than watch others. yet, I do not practice any sport either. What do you like to do?"

"I am not a fan of any sport either, and I like to chat with friends, watch movies, or read. I go to the gym every now and then. It depends on how I feel at the moment. I don't like to have specific plans, but I'm always ready for suggestions, whether from friends or myself," she giggled.

"You seem popular," He closed his eyes to appreciate the scent of the coffee.

"Not at all," she said, casting a quick glimpse at the ceiling. "I have a few close friends. At college, I was considered a nerd because I always had my head buried in books, usually at the cafeteria or the library.

"In my senior year, I started to hang around with people more often and have fun. After graduating, my three best friends and I backpacked in South America for a year." She giggled lowering her gaze, recalling those times. "There I met Doctor Stevens. We connected immediately and he asked me to drop by his office once I returned home. That's my story in brief."

Kaine sipped his coffee then traced the handle of his mug. "I was also considered a nerd at college and had few friends. Being gay didn't help and I was often bullied because of it."

Of course, the cutest guys are all gay or married, she thought slightly disappointed.

Oblivious to her thoughts, his eyes lit up and he leaned so close she smelled the coffee on his breath. "I found documents about a tribe presumably hidden in the heart of Africa. Researchers have been looking for them for a long time, and I got the green lights from Dr. Luther to pursue the research. The exact location was never mentioned, and no photographic material was to be found. Yet, I assume the location should be on the stretch between Equatorial Guinea, Rwanda, and Uganda. Last time someone researched it was ten years ago, but that time there hasn't been any result."

Nora gasped, remaining open-mouthed. "That is a large territory to research. It could take your entire life to find."

"I don't have anything to lose, and if I find them, it could be the discovery of a lifetime. Think about it, an old civilization that has been hidden from the rest of the world for centuries." His face drew closer to hers, his passion palpable.

She thought about it and grimaced. "Have you thought about the possibility – assuming it is true and there is a civilization successfully hidden from the rest of the world for such a long time – that they would prefer to remain hidden?"

"Maybe yes or maybe not. I can't be sure of anything until I find them."

"Hmmm..."

"You don't seem convinced." Kaine frowned.

Nora placed a hand on her mouth and averted her gaze, looking at the big coffee machine behind the bar desk. "You know, I'm thinking about what you just said. Someone heard about this tribe and tried to track it down. Now, if he found them, why wouldn't he publish any pictures, location, and even – I don't know – collect some DNA samples to be analyzed? Why just a few words about their existence without any proof to sustain the thesis of the find?"

Kaine remained silent, pondering her words. His eyes lowered to the coffee cup. Perhaps she is right, am I being too impulsive?

He nodded, returning his gaze to her. "Maybe because he was requested not to publish any details?" Kaine dared, knowing that he had to find out more about this mysterious tribe, but also that he may need to guard any knowledge he gleaned, to protect them.

Nora smiled. "That's exactly my point. If those people are living in the middle of the thickest African rain forest, avoiding contact with the rest of the world, they have their reasons. The least we can do is respect their decision."

"I cannot blame them. We certainly aren't an example to follow. Perhaps we have more to learn from them than they have from us," Nora added.

A gleam of hope brightened his face. "Then, even better; let them be our guides. They can teach us about their natural world, and we can share some of our technology to benefit them, agricultural techniques, medicine... you name it."

Nora shook her head as a corvine curl followed her movements softly. "You don't get it, do you? What I mean is they probably already know what they need to about our culture to reach the conclusion that they do not want to have anything to do with us. Don't get me wrong! I believe that the research you are after is fascinating and deserves to be pursued, but this should not be for the glory of revealing a private civilization to the public. The meaning will just be keeping their secret... secret. If you engage in this search, you have to understand there will be boundaries you are not supposed to cross. I am afraid that exposing them to the rest of the world will lead to their demise, or at least destroy their culture."

Kaine took a deep breath. It was the first time he had shared his research with a colleague, other than the chief of the department, who had approved the search.

Was the chief of the department interested in the project only because he was expecting an economic return out of this research or because he really was engrossed in the find? Perhaps it had been a good idea to talk with Nora; her point of view opened interesting questions about the ethical implications of this find. Should we quit or continue, with the condition that we won't reveal anything about this tribe if they do not give us the explicit consent to do so?

"Are you thinking about it?" Nora asked, after a long silence.

Kaine startled as if awoken from a dream. He looked around and shook his head. "Yes, I have to admit that it makes sense. What I am wondering is whether the previous researchers were lacking information because they were asked not to say anything, or whether material got lost over time. Some of the articles I am referring to are dated over one hundred years ago, so..."

"One hundred years ago?" Nora asked in a loud voice. "The whole tribe might be extinct!"

Kaine turned around as other people seemed to notice Nora's loud comment. Then he returned his gaze at her, trying to contain the laughter.

"Not necessarily." Kaine continued with a lower tone of voice. "Humans are extremely resourceful. Alive or not, if they existed, they should have left traces of their civilization — a graveyard, artifacts. If they still exist, it would be interesting to know" — he counted on his fingers — "who they are, where they came from, their language, and so on."

"What if they never existed? What if this is just a myth?"

"Then we close the case, and maybe write an article debunking the previous find. A negative result is still a result, so I would be pleased with any outcome."

Nora noticed some people started to leave the cafeteria. "I guess we should return to our office. What do you think?"

"He glimpsed at his wristwatch. "Damn, we've spent a long time chatting. I might need to stay late this afternoon."

Nora raised her hand loosely in a nonchalant attitude. "Don't bother about it. We talked mostly about work. Consider our chat a consultation about the feasibility of this research, and an in-depth evaluation of the pros and cons."

Kaine laughed loud. "I have to admit that makes sense. Thank you. You gave me a lot to think about. I will use the rest of the day to consider your feedback, and how to apply your suggestions to the research."

"Glad to be helpful," Nora replied as they left the cafeteria and walked back to their office. "You see? It's not difficult to be more social, and it can help you see things from a different perspective."

"I know it, and I do not deny the power of sociality. My problem is starting a personal conversation with someone I don't know. In the professional sphere, it's easy to talk," Kaine said as they reached the office.

"So, you are a sort of Dr. Jekyll, shy and reserved on the general social relationship, who becomes a Mr. Hyde, self-confident and charming at professional events."

A laugh escaped Kaine's mouth. "I never thought about myself that way, but I guess that sums up my personality well. You should be a psychologist rather than an anthropologist."

"Sometimes, I believe the two disciplines meet."

"By the way what are you working on nowadays," Kaine asked.

"Oh, I am working at some computer reconstruction of bones fragments found in an archaeological site in Turkey. We received the images from the University, and I am trying to reconstruct the skulls and bone structures," She went to sit down at her computer desk.

"Oh..." Kaine exclaimed, interrupting Nora as he looked at his computer screen. He silently read the title of the newly-received email—"Your Research About the Lost Tribe. Listen to this," he said:

"'Dear Dr. Martin

I have been informed of your interest in the previous research of Dr. Cooks about a legendary tribe living in the stretches between Equatorial Guinea and Uganda. I have independently spent my career searching for it, and I presume you could benefit from the information I have gathered so far. I wish to invite you to meet me in my office in Fort Portal in Uganda.'

Blah...blah...blah... It appears that I am going to leave you alone for some time. This email was also forwarded to the chief of the department, so I expect him to come soon to discuss it."

His voice trembled with excitement, and his hands shook. He sensed he was close to the greatest discovery of his career. He wouldn't invite me just to tell me there isn't any tribe to be found or that I am wasting my time and the Organization's money on research that won't lead anywhere. If that were the case, he would have written a 'forget about it' email. Damn, I am so excited.

"Oh, no!" Nora exclaimed, "Just when I finally got you to speak to me This place will become lonely again, silent and boring."

"I will be back, you know? And you will have all the quiet you need to focus on your projects."

Kaine felt lightheaded and collapsed onto his chair, keeping his eyes on the monitor, considering whether he'd misinterpreted or misread any aspects of the email. After re-reading the text, it seemed clear that this man had found clues about the tribe and wanted to share the information with him.

Then doubt intruded, casting a dark shadow over his excitement. He raised his gaze to Nora as if to grasp a hope in the turmoil building up in his thoughts.

"Hold on a second..." His expression turned serious as he bit his lower lip. "Why is he giving me this information, when he could get all the initial glory and recognition for himself? He knows that if we find the tribe or any important information about them, the Organization will take credit for it. He will receive a mere honorable mention for his contribution."

Nora squeezed on her shoulders. "Perhaps he ran out of funds and needs to team up with someone who can take over the expedition or provide technical support. If he is based in Africa, it might be tricky to access the same technology we have here — sophisticated scanning radars and drones, powerful computers to process all the data and connected software. If I were him, I would also consider shared glory in exchange for access to better data and better chances to find out more about this ancient society."

"That makes sense." Nevertheless, a nagging voice in the back of his head grew louder. Could it be a trap? A scam to get money from us?

Kaine grinned tapping his fingertip against the desk. "I need to further research this man and talk to Dr. Luther about the proposal."

As if on cue, Dr. Luther appeared in the doorway. "We had the same idea. Come to my office to discuss this."

Kaine followed him to the lift, to reach the third floor, where Dr. Luther's office was. An uncomfortable silence between them.

"Did you have the same concerns as I do about this guy?" Kaine asked.

"Hmm," Dr. Luther growled. "I have a lot of questions and I am not going to offer any cooperation until I get a clear idea of who we are dealing with. He didn't leave a telephone number, so our only contact is by email. I don't mind that, but I am not going to send an expedition to Africa until I have something more tangible."

As they reached his office, Dr. Luther sat at his desk, inviting Kaine to take the seat opposite him.

"Jason Murdock..." Dr. Luther mumbled. "For some reason, that name sounds familiar; let's see what an internet search reveals."

His fingers flew over the keyboard, and he turned the computer so they both could see the screen. One link, in particular, captured their attention — an article about a missing researcher named Dr. Jason Murdock.

The men read about the mysterious disappearance of an anthropologist who reached Uganda, trying to follow the tracks of a tribe, the existence of which had been mentioned in many reports. It further stated nobody could determine its exact location.

He was supposed to return home after one year in Africa but never returned. The flight company recorded him boarding the plane, but his luggage wasn't collected at his destination and his passport wasn't recorded at immigration.

When they finished reading, their eyes reflected confusion.

"What the..." Kaine mumbled.

"...fuck," Dr. Luther finished.

"If this Jason Murdock is the same person who disappeared eight years ago, this could be a double find for our organization." Dr. Luther's eyes sparkled, thinking about the prospects.

He stood and paced around the room, as questions and doubts populated his mind. "How could a person go through the check-in at the airport with his passport, through the safety check and immigration, board a plane, then disappear during the flight? This doesn't make any sense!"

As Kaine watched his supervisor, he searched for a reasonable explanation. If someone stole Dr. Murdock's passport and forged it, changing the picture, there should have also been a record of this person reaching their final destination. With all the cameras at the terminal, surveillance would have noticed if someone had remained inside. The authorities would have known if a person with the same passport tried to board another flight.

Kaine spoke up. "We can discard the theory that he disappeared, but the mystery remains. How long can a person remain inside the terminal area before the surveillance starts to notice his presence day after day? Could it be that this person had another passport and used it to board another flight? But then what happened to Dr. Murdock, and why is he reaching out now to offer his help to the research?"

Dr. Luther raised his finger. "First of all, we need to gather all possible information about this Dr. Murdock, who disappeared eight years ago. Find out whether he has relatives, friends, and get pictures of him."

"I'll find out who sponsored his expedition, obtain information about his research," Kaine agreed. "I'll try to determine if he had any contact with the previous sponsor after his disappearance."

Kaine stood up from the chair to leave the room when doubt gripped him. "Should I reply to his email, or ignore it?"

"Good question. You can reply, requesting more details about the information he is willing to share with us. Propose him to come here and meet with us. Ask also for his telephone number or a video chat, something that allows us to see him or to hear his voice," suggested Dr. Luther.

"I will reply immediately and search for him. With your permission, I will also involve Nora; she is a talented researcher."

"Keep me updated." Dr. Luther returned his attention to his computer screen.

# CHAPTER 2

Unanswered questions multiplied in Kaine's mind as he walked back to his office, where Nora was immersed in her project.

The appeal of the loneliness he had preferred for so long dimmed. He entertained the idea that he should have engaged in a social relationship sooner.

Entering the room, he smiled. "I need your help, if you don't mind."

Nora looked up from her computer. *What do you know? It seems like he just needed a small push to become more social.*

"At your service, Sir..."

"When I was in Dr. Luther's office, we searched the internet for details of the person who sent us the email I told you about. Among all the links, there was an interesting article dated eight years ago, about an anthropologist who was missing in Uganda during one of his research trips. Now—"

"Wait a second, I think I remember it on the news. What was his name?" Nora interrupted.

"Jason Murdock..."

She smacked her palm against her forehead. "Of course. Murdock! I recall it. This is the man who contacted you?"

Kaine nodded. "So he claims. The email address confirms that he is a Jason Murdock, but this doesn't impress me. Anybody can create a new email using any name and surname. My biggest question is that, according to the article, his disappearance was connected to an unsolved mystery."

He sat down at his computer, glancing at the screen where the email awaited a reply.

Nora exhaled a deep breath. "That's a dilemma. Perhaps the only thing to do is go to the Police and seek their help to identify Dr. Murdock. Of course, you can ask him about his identity and an explanation about how he disappeared for eight years. I would love to know his story."

"Dr. Luther said this could be a double deal for us. We could make progress in the identification and location of this lost tribe and find Dr. Murdock. Think about the day we bring him back home."

With a lightness in his chest, he felt infected with the same eagerness of Dr. Luther and could not hide the wide grin reclaiming its place on Kaine's face.

"So, what's your next step?" she questioned.

"First, I will reply to him. I need more than just claims written in an email. I want proof of his finds, anything that can convince me he has something concrete in his hands, something that would justify the organization for sending an expedition to Africa."

He started to type a reply, trying to control his overexcited mind and focus on what he was doing.

*Is he the same Dr. Murdock? If he is, did he contact anyone before, his relatives and loved ones, to let them know he was alive?*

*** 

Sleep eluded Jason as he lay down on his bed, where a mosquito net hung from the ceiling. His thoughts wandered to the young researcher he'd just contacted. He didn't want anyone to approach the tribe, and he especially didn't want anyone getting close to Akuna-Ra.

"Why did She order me to contact that researcher if secrecy is so vital for them?"

His gaze followed the lazy spinning of the overhead fan. Outside, the voices of the people and the noises of their daily activities faded away, as they retreated to spend the night with their families, safe from wild animals.

"But what about those creatures not of this world? Will they feel safe from them as well? Will their amulets protect them from threats lurking in the darkness of the night?"

He stood up from the bed and peered through the curtain of his bedroom. The bonfires would have kept those shadows away, and hopefully, also the evil spirits the natives feared so much.

Finally, silence wrapped the whole village. One after another, the interior of the houses dimmed, lit only by a few candles to ensure extra protection for the youngest children.

According to superstition, the blood of innocents was preferred by the demons.

The wind soughed through the trees, carrying the bleating of the goats inside the barns.

The beep of an incoming email pulled him from his thoughts.

It wasn't difficult to guess who it was, as he'd lost all contact with the outside world since the day he was declared missing.

He turned his eyes to the bedside table, where his telephone blinked. Shaking his head, he walked toward it. "Tell me what you want to know, Dr. Martin. No doubt you have searched my name and have many questions."

He opened the email and, with a smirk, read:

*Dear Dr. Murdock,*

*I was surprised to receive your email, and as you can guess, I have been looking for more information about you. Unfortunately, what I found was more confusing than enlightening.*

*We need to speak with you before we can decide if our organization is interested in your offer.*

*Can you visit our headquarters in New York? We are prepared to pay for your plane ticket and accommodations. Bring the results of your independent research with you. If reasonable, we might set up an expedition where you will be the main leader, and we will agree upon your compensation.*

*The alternative is to video conference.*

*I hope you understand that it is not because of a lack of trust. You have been missing for over eight years and we must do our due diligence before committing funds and manpower to a project,*

*Best Regards,*

*Dr. Kaine Martin*

"I understand your feelings. Honestly, you've been too kind to even reply to my email."

Jason wiped his face with his hands. He could reach the nearby city and try to arrange the use of office space with a steady internet connection. He could share enough of his research to garner their interest.

He looked at his clock and, with a loud yawn, decided to wait until morning to begin the arrangements.

Suddenly, the door opened.

"Your mistress requests you," said Okumi, the messenger of Akuna-Ra.

His face contorted and glanced at the short figure of Okumi. He was perhaps the youngest of the tribe, apparently in his twenties or even less. His slim muscular structure revealed the physical activities he was carrying out. He wanted to tell him that she could go fuck herself, but he knew better. He would pay dearly his disrespect.

Without any reply, he followed Okumi, making sure to lock the door of his bungalow, to discourage snakes and other uninvited guests.

They walked in the darkness, led by Okumi's torch. After a few minutes, they reached the village and the shack where Akuna-Ra waited.

A fire in the center of the room barely illuminated the wooden walls. Sitting crossed-legged on the red soil in front of the flames was the thin almost ethereal figure of Akuna-Ra. The white pigment which decorated her face, stark above the ebony of her skin, imparted her a threatening appearance.

*Everything looks scarier in the darkness.*

Jason approached her, lowering his gaze. "You wanted to see me?"

Without removing her gaze from the flames, she shifted from her position "I can smell the whiskey from here."

"You sound like a bitter wife. But yes, I have been drinking, although I am not drunk... yet."

She raised her head and froze him with an angry stare. "You forget who owns you." Her voice hardened like the sharp edge of a knife

Jason's body contorted into a painful spasm and he fell to his knees. He could barely breathe. "What more do you want from me?" he cried. "Isn't taking away my life enough for you? How long...?" The pain sharpened, stabbed like a thousand spears.

"Obedience and loyalty," she said without moving from her position. Her voice escalated with every word, echoing in the room.

"Time..." she mumbled. "Time has no meaning here, and you should have learned this by now. Do you think eight years is a long time? How about eternity?"

The pain subsided, and his body remained hunched as he gasped to regain his breath. Fearful that his punishment would last for all of eternity he raised his gaze to the now-standing Akuna-Ra.

"I am not built for eternity. I am just a man, and I haven't forgotten that you own me," he replied, still kneeling.

"What I want to know is how can I obtain your forgiveness and be returned to my life."

Akuna-Ra opened into a half-smile, raising her chin. "I cannot set you free. I trusted you once, and you betrayed me." Her eyes flashed. "You don't understand, or you don't care about the importance of us remaining *undiscovered.*"

Jason lowered his gaze as tears filled his eyes. "Am I going to be yours for the rest of my life?" His voice was a whisper but, to him, it seemed to resound through the forest.

Returning to her seat by the fire, she asked, "What is left for you out there?"

"Perhaps nothing, but my freedom has more value than I ever imagined." He raised his eyes to meet hers. "Why do you need the other researcher? Why risk that he will tell about you and your people, and why risk cursing his life the way you cursed mine?"

"The reason why I want him doesn't concern you at all, let's just say that I am interested in his potential."

"Are you going to curse him anyway?" His voice turned bitter.

"What is this, a lesson in morality?" Her tone harshened. "Do I need to remind you why you are not free anymore? You have *no* right to talk about morality."

She closed her eyes. "I haven't called you here to indulge myself in an argument with you; the reason for my call was far more pleasant."

She stood and sauntered to a darker corner of the room. With an alluring movement of her hand, she invited to lie with her on a sleeping corner. "Come..."

Although she kept him as a slave, used him as she pleased, he could not deny his attraction to her. Even with the mask of paint on her face and her body, she was one of the most beautiful creatures he'd ever met, and she knew how to arouse him.

*Is it because of her magic power or because I find her truly beautiful?*

As he removed his clothes, a willing slave for the night, he coveted her body with his eyes.

***

Kaine reached his house in the suburbs at close to five o'clock. He had grown up in it and returned to care for his mother when cancer consumed her life away. The cost of medical equipment and a nurse twice a day ate into her pension and his salary, but he never griped. When she died a few years ago, he was the only mourner. He'd never met his father and didn't know who he was.

In an attempt to cope with his grief of having lost a piece of his soul, he had changed all the furniture and renovated the house, transforming it into something new.

Nevertheless, that day, as he closed the door behind him, he returned to his childhood, to coming home from school, to the aroma of his mother's cooking

He saw himself running from the entrance to the corridor that led to the kitchen, calling for her.

Then her voice, distinct in his ear, jolted him back to the present. "Remember not to talk to strangers…"

He gasped.

"M-Mum…" A lump formed in his throat.

"You heard me, remember not to talk to strangers," she repeated in his ear.

"I won't. I promise." His voice trembled and tears blurred his sight.

"Now look at you," her voice murmured. "Don't cry. I am here, and I am not going to leave you alone."

He wiped his eyes with his sleeve. When he opened them again, everything seemed to have returned to normal.

His mother was no longer there, and her voice was gone. The visions of the past had dissipated.

At a loss to explain what triggered that memory, so strong it seemed real, he started to doubt having heard his mother's voice. Even if it was her spirit returned, he didn't believe it could be powerful enough to talk to him.

"I don't believe in ghosts," he groaned as he grabbed his coat off the floor then strode to the kitchen to seek relief in a cold bottle of beer.

*And perhaps a good book.*

He chose a horror novel; his favorite genre, and found a comfortable position on the leather couch, the only piece of furniture he didn't change after the death of his mother.

At the end of the first chapter, the doorbell rang. He observed on the door, knowing he wasn't expecting visitors.

Leaning over the side of the couch for a better visual of the veranda, he recognized the silhouette of Mark, his neighbor. His heart thumped in his chest and he jumped up.

After a glimpse in the mirror, he took a deep breath and opened the door.

"Mark, what a surprise. Can I do anything for you?" he purred.

"I am terribly embarrassed to ask you something like this, but I just returned home from work to realize there is no water coming into my house. I am waiting for the plumber, it will be here in a couple of hours, and I'm in desperate need of a shower." He ducked his head and peered up. "May I use yours?"

For a moment, Kaine imagined Mark naked in the bathroom, water streaming down his muscular body. He'd had a crush on his friend since the first time he saw him, but Mark didn't seem interested.

Kaine shook his head, to cast away the image. "Of course, you can. You're welcome at any time. Get your clothes."

Mark's face relaxed, opening into a bright smile. "I knew I could count on you. You are the best!"

That said, he ran back to his house and returned with clean clothes slung over his arm.

"The bathroom is upstairs, first door on the left," Kaine said with a shy smile. He hoped his eagerness didn't transpire.

Mark said a fast thanks and turned toward the stairs

Kaine watched him take the steps two at a time. then imagined him slowly removing the clothes. The object of his desire stood naked on the floor above him, less than eight feet away. His breathing became shallow and his throat felt dry.

*Oh, c'mon, stop fantasizing. He is not within your reach, and it would be embarrassing if he came back downstairs to see you literally drooling over him.*

He went back to the couch, covered himself with a blanket, and grabbed his book, determined to be casual, to pretend he could not care less about having Mark in his house.

After reading another chapter, he realized that Mark had not reappeared yet.

*What if something happened to him?* "Mark! Are you still alive?" There was no answer, so he climbed the stairs, listening for sounds of activity.

At the bathroom door, he stood for a moment., No running water. No rustling. No human voice.

"Mark!"

He knocked at the door, but there wasn't any answer.

*Am I going crazy?*

His heart hammered in his chest and he remained frozen. Should he open the door or not?

He knocked again, louder this time.

Nobody answered. Unable to wait any longer, he mustered all the courage left in his body and opened the door.

Mark stood with one hand on his hip and the other against his cheek—and he was naked. "I wondered how long it would take you to open that door."

"W-what do you mean? I thought I needed to call an ambulance or, worse, that I imagined you coming to my house. I almost had a heart attack!"

Kaine wasn't sure whether he should feel angry, excited to see him in his full naked splendor, or wonder what it meant.

Mark walked toward him. "Look, I'm sorry I lied. I needed an excuse to be naked in your place—with you."

Open-mouthed, with dick throbbing in his trousers, Kaine froze as Mark's hand reached out to stroke his cheek. Kaine could not think of anything except Mark's face as it drew closer. Then his lips kissed him, soft as a feather.

Kaine melted into the embrace feeling the water dripping from Mark's hair to his shirt.

"Mark..." he whispered through the kisses.

Mark's tongue danced down Kaine's neck and reached his ear. "Show me your bed." His breath sending shivers along Kaine's spine

As they reached the bedroom, Mark lifted Kaine into his arms and threw him onto the bed. It protested with a creak. "I have waited far too long to have you in bed naked, and nothing is going to stop me now."

Lust coursing through him as he was breathless and unable to grab a steady thought. He so desperately wanted Mark to take him, wanted his fantasies to come true, here in his bed.

"Mark, take me...take me now. Please!"

"No need to beg me, baby," he said, removing every piece of clothing with tantalizing slowness. "You are delicious, and I am going to taste every single inch of you."

Urged by the caresses of Mark's tongue and gentle hands on his skin, Kaine rode the waves of ecstasy as his body responded desiring only to be taken.

"Oh, Mark, this is what Heaven must be like!" he said with closed eyes.

Mark's mouth reached his ear. "I hope this is how Hell looks like, because I am a bad boy, and I am not going to Heaven."

"Then you need to bring me to Hell with you..."

"I will turn you into a bad little devil, then, my little angel."

Mark's body blanketed Kaine, like an overwhelming presence caressing, arousing, and teasing his senses. He'd never felt the urge to be taken by any man like he did at that moment. Desire turned into need as Mark embarked on his quest to explore every part of Kaine's body with his hands and tongue.

When he finally reached Kaine's dick, a loud moan that seemed to shake the walls of the whole house escaped Kaine's mouth, as he tried to hold back from reaching the climax he needed so badly.

When they lay sated in each other's arms, Kaine found a peace he never thought he'd experience. It felt safe like nothing could touch him.

Time seemed to stop, and nothing outside of them and the bed was important. They fell asleep with limbs entwined and arms wrapped around each other

# CHAPTER 3

Awoken by the rays of light filtering through the curtains, Kaine turned on his side and the first thing he saw, was Mark, snoring at his side, his mouth open and his hair messy.

The appearance of a horny god he remembered from the previous evening faded away, but he loved every single detail of that noisy and funny image.

He thought he could never have enough of observing him sleeping or watching him in any situation.

"I'm hopelessly in love with you, and I hope you will never disappear from my life," his hands gently reaching for Mark's face.

With a sudden jolt, Mark opened his eyes and smiled at Kaine. "Good morning, my little devil in training." He yawned and stretched his body, hugging Kaine tightly to himself. "I wish I could stay like this forever."

Kaine held himself to his chest, to make sure he was no more dreaming. "I still can't believe what happened. I thought you weren't interested in me," Kaine gazed into Mark's deep green eyes. "I was also sure you were not gay..."

"And I'm not; I'm bi, but when I saw you for the first time, I needed to get to know you better. I couldn't reveal my feelings, so I pretended not to be interested until I reached the point when I couldn't stay away from you. You are everything I want in this world."

Mark's soft kisses brightened up his day, and Kaine wondered whether this could become his new life.

*Should I propose him to move in together? Is it too early for this? If I asked my mom, she would say at least I should wait to see how it goes, and she would be right. I'm too impulsive when it comes to relationships.*

Kaine stood up from the bed. "I think I'll go for a shower, but I wouldn't like to be left alone. I'm afraid to get back to being a good boy; I need a devil to supervise me." He winked at Mark.

"You definitely need supervision, and as a Master Devil, I will make sure you will follow me to Hell, where we can have fun for the rest of eternity." Mark held him from behind, whispering in his ear.

*** 

Going to work, he almost forgot about Jason Murdock and the lost tribe. His new boyfriend and the night they've spent together was the only thought he could focus on. He whistled for the whole journey, feeling like he wanted to sing for the rest of the day.

He reached the office and saw Nora, who seemed to have just arrived.

"Good morning!" he chirped happily.

Nora considered him and burst into loud laughter. "Well, someone is in an extraordinarily good mood. What happened, did you win the lottery?"

"Something like it, but much, much better," Kaine replied, still finding it hard to believe that he started a romantic relationship with the only object of his darkest sexual desires.

She wondered whether he would ever tell her the reason for his happiness, or if she would have to torture him.

"I'm in love!" he said with a dreamy voice, closing his eyes as he fell, seated into his chair.

"Does he know?"

"Not only does he know, but he loves me too!" he replied, opening his eyes and starting his computer.

Shifting his chair, he inched closer to her, drawing his hands together. "So, everything started yesterday afternoon after I came back home. You know, there is this guy, Mark, who looks like a GOD, and when he looks at me with his bright-green eyes, it makes me feel like melting."

He leaned on his chair. "I have been drooling after him since forever, but I was afraid he wasn't gay, so I never made my feelings evident.

"Yesterday, as I was reading a book, he rang my doorbell and told me his plumbing had some problems with the water pipes or so, and he asked to have a shower in my bathroom. Well, of course, I told him that he could, and so he went to the toilette, and I remained downstairs to read my book..."

"Hold on!" Nora interrupted, "You could really continue reading, knowing the man you adore is naked in your house?"

With a dismissive wave of his hand, he continued. "Believe me, that has been the most excruciating wait ever. Yet, not seeing him returning, I went to check, and he was waiting for me..."

Nora yelped, "Oh-my-god! I'm so happy for you. Do you have any pictures of him? I'm so curious to know what he looks like."

Kaine thought about it for a moment, wondering whether he had any photograph on his mobile phone.

Then he remembered Mark was quite active in posting his own images on social media. "I'm pretty sure I can find one for you; let me check."

After a second, his eyes brightened up, as he was sure he found the one that summarized his perfection.

"Here, Ladies and Gentlemen, Mark!" he announced, showing the image to her.

"Holy shit! He is indeed a God! But what about your journey to Africa?"

With a baffled stare, as he completely forgot about it, he looked at her. Slapping his forehead, he recalled the email and Dr. Murdock.

"Oh, that!" his expression relaxed. "Well, so far, I haven't received any answer from Dr. Murdock, and to figure out whether the lead is credible, to organize the expedition and gather the team, get all the authorizations and take care of the bureaucratical issues it might take more than half a year. During this period, I will also be able to consider the status of my bond with Mark. At the moment, we just got together, and there are no indications on whether this could be a long-term relationship or a couple of guys having some fun."

Nora turned her chair back to her desk. "You might be right. Enjoy what you have and don't overthink about the future. This is the kind of advice I should take more into consideration for myself as well."

Kaine returned to his computer, and as usual, he checked his email first.

That was almost a ritual for him. Before thinking about going and getting his first morning coffee, he needed to check that nothing important arrived, and only then would he consider going to the cafeteria.

The first email he saw was from Jason, and it was marked as 'urgent.'

He took a deep breath and opened it:

*Dear Dr. Martin,*

*Thank you for your kind answer and for the offer to visit you at your headquarters in New York. Although I would love to meet you in person, I'm afraid this couldn't be arranged for personal issues, which I will discuss in detail on another occasion.*

*I understand your concerns, and I accept the second offer of having a video chat with you. Since my schedule is relatively open, I would suggest you pick a date and time, taking into consideration the time difference between Uganda and the US.*

*I will be waiting for your reply.*

*Best Regards,*

*Jason Murdock*

"Any news?" Nora wondered, noticing his frown.

"Hmm... Dr. Murdock replied, and he agreed only to a video chat. I must admit I still find it strange that after having disappeared for many years, he refuses to return when the chance is offered to him." Kaine rested his head on the palm of his hand, without taking his eyes from the screen.

"Maybe he has some problems with the law?" Nora tried to guess.

"If so, there hasn't been any mention anywhere. Perhaps he thinks he had some troubles..." he suggested, rubbing his chin.

Since the email was sent to Dr. Luther too, Kaine decided not to go to his office. He would check his schedule and question him about the date he should give to Jason later. In the meantime, he also had other research projects to focus on.

Silence and focus fell, once again, between the two researchers, when, at half past eleven in the morning, his mobile phone started to ring.

Kaine smiled, thinking this could be Mark, but his smile faded almost immediately when he noticed an unknown number.

With a grimace on his face, he replied, "Dr. Martin."

"Good morning, Dr. Martin. This is Dr. Jason Murdock, and I believe you weren't expecting any call from me. Am I wrong?"

Kaine remained open-mouthed for a second, not sure about what he was supposed to say. Indeed, he was right, and he could have expected anything happening in his day – except being contacted by Dr. Murdock himself.

"Oh... Good morning," he mumbled confusedly. "This is a surprise, indeed. I-I... Well, I am taken aback by your call."

Jason laughed heartily and wondered about that young researcher. *What kind of use is She thinking to have with this one? He can hardly reply to a work call.*

"I appreciate your honest answer, it's something rare, nowadays. This also means we can cut the formalities and talk straight to each other, can't we?"

Kaine blushed, feeling like an idiot for what he'd said. He glanced at Nora, and considering that he might disturb her, he hurried away from the office.

"Of course, and I wish to apologize for my rude remark. I wasn't expecting any kind of phone call, and particularly from you. But satisfy my curiosity, if I may ask. How did you get my telephone number? I haven't set it up automatically in my email."

"I might have spent many years here in Africa, but I still remember how to search for a name inside an open organization like yours. You are not working for the CIA," Jason remarked.

He was walking to the common room when suddenly, he thought he had another hallucination. Kaine saw his mother one more time, and she was disappointed. She had that particular frown she used to display when he made mischief as a child.

Blankness painted in his mind.

"What did I tell you about talking to strangers?" She reproached.

"I-I well..." Kaine uttered, confused about whether to answer the hallucination of his mother or ignore her and go on with the phone call.

"Dr. Martin, are you there? Is there a problem?" Jason wondered, thinking about the possibility of interference on the line.

Her stare pierced his soul, his lips trembled. With the last vestiges of the same sanity he feared to lose, he decided to follow his instinct. "Can you hold on a second?" he asked, talking to Jason.

"Of course."

Kaine put the telephone on mute and stared at what appeared to be his mother standing in front of him. "I know I'm going insane, and I'm going to see a shrink immediately after this conversation. I know you told me not to talk to strangers, but this is a colleague," Kaine replied, pointing at the telephone.

"I warn you, Kaine; I warn you." With those words, she simply disappeared.

"I'm crazy; I'm even talking to my hallucinations." He stared at the phone and unmuted it. "Dr. Murdock, are you still there?"

"Yes, I am, but if this is a bad time, and you prefer me to call you later, you can tell me," he replied, concerned.

Kaine shook his head. "No, everything is fine now. I was having a sort of situation, and I couldn't concentrate on everything. Now we can talk, and please accept my apologies for this interruption. Apparently, I can't be anything but rude toward you."

Taking a deep breath, Jason nodded, wondering what was wrong with the new generations. "Apology accepted, and besides, I also should apologize for having called you so suddenly."

"It appears like we've started this call on the wrong foot. Let's start it again. I would like to understand the reason why you can't reach us here in New York," Kaine wondered.

"It's quite complicated to explain, and it concerns some personal matters I prefer not to reveal. What I would like to discuss, instead, is the possibility of having a video chat with you and when this would be possible. I have something to show you, and I guess you would also like to have some proof about my identity before even thinking about my offer."

A smile appeared on Kaine's face. He felt like Dr. Murdock didn't have any intention to hide anything, except the mystery behind his disappearance and his reluctance in returning home. *Maybe it was all a way to escape some demons he'd left here? Everyone has problems, and some of those can become so daunting as to force us to make drastic decisions. Perhaps I would never understand him.*

"I thought Dr. Luther, the director of the department, would have contacted you personally, or he would have informed me about his schedule. So far, he hasn't, so I can't give you an answer, unfortunately. What I can do is to go and ask him right after this call and inform you immediately after. Would this solution suit you?"

Jason didn't feel any urgency; he'd found the lost tribe indeed, and he was regretting that discovery every single day. *Perhaps I will continue to mourn my whole existence, which at this point, I hope to be short enough.*

"That would be more than fine for me. You will have to excuse my insistence, but discovering a lost civilization, which is still alive and well, it's to me the most extraordinary discovery ever. It's like finding out that the Mayans didn't die out, and they continued their existence in a hidden spot of the Amazon Jungle, far from the eyes of the world. Can you imagine?" Jason asked, recalling his enthusiasm when he finally tracked the exact location.

For one moment, it felt like coming back to those days when he still believed he could have reached the fame he was after with the discovery of the century.

He'd searched, queried, observed and followed any sort of tracks for years and years.

Even when the primary funder decided it was no longer practical to continue the search, he didn't give up. He knew he would find them; he felt it in his guts.

Every night he would dream about the next clue, and it was like someone was calling him, sending him hints on the location of the tribe. Then, on a bright morning, he was found by one of the hunters and guided to the camp.

I haven't reached the fame I was looking for, but I still hold the satisfaction of having been able to track it without any of the technologies available nowadays. That's something to be proud of in this story. At least at its beginning.

"Well, it sounds like we have a deal. May I call you at this same number?" Kaine asked.

"Oh... sure, I will always have this phone with me, so you can use it to give me your answer."

"Perfect, hear you later, then."

After he hung up the conversation with Jason, Kaine felt almost breathless. His mind went back to the vision of his mother and he wondered whether it was indeed a hallucination, or if she was really there.

*I'm more than sure she was talking to me, and she was also referring to the telephone call I was having with Dr. Murdock. But why did she have to come, telling me not to talk to strangers? Why was she so upset when I told her this was a job call? And what had she wanted to warn me about?*

Immersed in his considerations he strode to the office of Dr. Luther, trying at least to get one thing done: fixing the date for the video chat. "Afterward, I'm afraid I will need to get some answers, and this means getting an appointment with a doctor. Am I going crazy, or should I consult a medium?"

With his confidence regained, he knocked at the door of Dr. Luther's office.

"Come in."

Kaine peeked from the door. "Good morning, do you have a second?"

"Sure," he replied without taking his eyes from the monitor of his computer. "Please, have a seat."

Kaine did as he said and waited until he was ready to listen to the reason for his visit. Dr. Luther finally turned his face to Kaine. "So, Dr. Martin, what can I do for you?"

"I received a phone call from Dr. Murdock, or from someone who claimed to be him. He wanted to know whether we had an answer to his email. He can't come here, for personal reasons, but agreed to a video chat. He asked me to give him a date by today, or at least as soon as possible, so he could show us what he was able to find out. However, it's also prudent to ponder all the pros and cons before engaging in this research."

"Hmm..." Dr. Luther narrowed his eyes to consider what Kaine said. "Interesting that he called you. It seems like he is in a hurry. But why? He has been searching for his whole career. Why now this rush, can't he wait for a few days more?"

"That was exactly my same concern."

Dr. Luther turned the screen of his computer toward Kaine so that both of them could see what was there. "Look, I have searched for him, and I was able to track down one of his former colleagues. I was thinking of calling him to be present at the meeting so he could tell us whether this person is the real Dr. Murdock or an impostor looking for our money.

"I'm also excited about the find, and if we could confirm the existence of this tribe, that would be a turning

44

point. Nevertheless, I share the same concerns, and we need to be careful."

Kaine nodded in agreement, and with a smile, he replied, "Then we do not have anything else to do but to contact this person and ask him when he would be available..."

"I have sent him an email, and I hope we will receive an answer by this afternoon. But you look worried, or perhaps you are tired." Dr. Luther noticed Kaine's creased forehead.

Kaine brought a hand to his temple, massaging it as if to cast a lousy headache away. "I don't know whether I'm coming down with the flu or something similar; today is one of those days when I can't get anything done. I believe it would be reasonable for me to take the rest of the day off and relax. I will remain reachable and will check my email, waiting for your reply so I can call Dr. Murdock back and fix a date."

"Sure, take care of yourself, but if you need a few days off, we should maybe set the meeting for next week..."

"No!" Kaine exclaimed, unwilling to wait any longer. He wanted answers as soon as possible, regardless of his health status. Besides, it wasn't a question of having the flu, but perhaps something related to stress. "I would rather have the meeting set up. I can rest all the time I want afterward, but this is something I want to solve right away."

Dr. Luther chuckled at his enthusiasm; that was one of the main reasons why he wanted to have him on his team. "Of course, I will inform you as I have an answer."

Kaine stood up from his chair, not sure whether he wanted to go home. *Something must be done for those hallucinations.*

"Thank you, Dr. Luther. I will be back tomorrow morning, and I will be waiting for your call."

"Take care of yourself. See you, then."

***

Walking to his office, he wondered whether he should have asked Nora for advice. Although they'd shared the same working space for years, it was only one day since they'd started to interact with each other, if he didn't take into account work-related matters. *I wonder if I can speak to her about those hallucinations without fearing that she won't keep it confidential. Maybe I should speak to Mark about it.*

Kaine stopped in the middle of the corridor, not sure what he was supposed to do next, or with whom he should have talked with first. He wasn't sure he wanted to go to see a doctor.

The door of his office in front of him seemed an insurmountable obstacle.

Pursing his lips and grabbing all the courage he could find, he rushed his steps in its direction, trying to stop overthinking.

As he came inside the room, he scrutinized at Nora and closed the door behind himself.

"Nora, do you have time to talk?" His eyebrows drew together into a concerned expression.

She turned her eyes at him. "Wow, you don't look good. Are you okay?"

He shook his head and grabbed a chair to sit in front of her. "I'm not fine at all. It all started yesterday before Mark arrived..." Hoping to find the right words to explain the vision, the feelings, and the doubts daunting his soul, he told her what had happened the previous afternoon.

Kaine took a deep breath. "This is not all, unfortunately. The phone call I just received came from Dr. Murdock. He was able to find my telephone number and decided to contact me directly to speed up the procedure and have a video chat arranged. As we spoke, it happened again.

"My mother appeared in front of me. This time she was not concerned; she was almost angry, and she told me: 'What did I say about talking to strangers?'"

He grabbed his head between his hands. "I had to put the call with Dr. Murdock on hold and start to talk with what it appeared to be the ghost of my mother. Do you think I'm going insane?"

Nora watched him, with a baffled expression in her face.

Trying to understand what he blurted out, she put her hands in front of herself, as if to create a barrier between the flow of words and her thoughts.

"Hold on a second – so you're telling me you have started to see the ghost of your dead mother warning you about talking to strangers?" she wondered.

"Well, I guess... that sums it up," Kaine replied, confused. "But what makes me wonder, is why did she appear when I was on the phone with Dr. Murdock?"

Nora raised her shoulders. "Maybe she doesn't trust him. I don't know... However, I don't believe you are going insane. I mean, you're not the first one to see ghosts."

"Do you believe in ghosts?"

"I don't know. Many people seem to have seen them. As for me, I have never seen one, so I can't say whether I believe or not." She tugged a lobe of the ear. "This goes so much into a field I'm not familiar with, but again, you are not crazy."

47

Her voice was steady, as she wanted to assure him that whatever was the reason for those visions, hallucinations, or anything else it wasn't a symptom of insanity.

"Perhaps I should see a doctor or a medium?" Kaine scrutinized her, trying to understand her feelings about the topic.

Nora cocked her head, smiling. "Neither. If you want my opinion, it's not a question of a ghost or your sanity. I guess it's mostly about how you feel about this person who came, suddenly offering to help you in research you care so much about." She neared him and rubbed his shoulder. "I suppose it's your subconscious that wants to warn you about being careful about judging him, particularly about the risks of trusting someone when you have no idea who he is and what his real intent is. I guess that's all."

"But then..." Kaine protested. "But then, why is this hallucination about my mother? If it was true and it was only some stress about this new development in my research, I should have had dreams, not hallucinations or ghosts or whatever they are."

Nora didn't know what to say, but certainly, Kaine was not insane; he was a strange guy, but this didn't mean he was crazy.

"Why don't you take a day off and try to relax? You probably need time for yourself. I'm sure that once you allow your brain some rest and have the time to rationalize about the whole situation, these hallucinations will stop." A beeping sound distracted her from the chat and jerked her head in the direction of the mobile phone on her desk.

With a dismissive smirk, she turned to Kaine. "Why don't you spend time with your new boyfriend? You need to have more time at the beginning of your relationship, and this can be what you need to quit thinking about this project, Dr. Murdock, and your mother – and whatever the connection is between the three."

He exhaled and closed his eyes, focusing on his heartbeat and his feelings. *She's right; it's not a question of ghosts and insanity. It's a sign that I need to take it easy. I can't get so stressed over an email.*

He opened his eyes and smiled at Nora. Once again, he had to admit there were more advantages to being more social than disadvantages. "You're right," he snapped his fingers as he stood up from the chair.

"I will go home and try to relax. I might also take the rest of the week off and return only if Dr. Luther can arrange the video chat. He will get in touch with one former colleague of Dr. Murdock and invite him to participate in the meeting so as to make sure we are not dealing with an imposter."

"That is a great idea! But, now get out of here, before I kick you out," she giggled, amused.

# CHAPTER 4

It was about noon when Kaine reached his home. The first thing he thought to do was prepare a good lunch.

He wasn't a good cook, but perhaps his forced rest could have been an excuse to get more confident with the cooking process.

Kaine didn't want to admit it to himself, but secretly he hoped to have another hallucination and talk to his mother one more time.

Although she died years ago, he was still missing her. She had been a constant presence in his life, and suddenly, having her gone felt to him like having an empty space for which memories were not enough.

With a lighter feeling, he searched for something to cook. "I would like to understand whether you were a hallucination due to stress, or if you returned to warn me about something."

He started to talk to a hypothetical ghost, almost hoping to have her closer, and tell her how much he loved and missed her since she was gone.

"So, if you are here, somewhere, show me I'm not going crazy, and I'm not talking to an imaginary friend..."

He remained silent, listening to the slightest noise in the house as he tried his best to cook in silence. However, despite his efforts to sharpen his senses, nothing happened, and his home was as it always used to be.

The sudden ringing of his mobile phone caused him to jolt as he was slicing an onion, and he hurt his thumb.

"Damn!" He yelled as he went to get the telephone, answering without checking to see who was calling him.

"Hello." He was panting.

"Dr. Martin, this is Dr. Luther. I called to inform you about the date for the video chat. Are you sure everything is fine? You sound breathless."

Kaine observed his sliced finger; the wound was not deep, but it was bleeding copiously, and he needed to find a way to hand the conversation as soon as possible. "Yes, everything is okay; the telephone was in another room, and I was running to it. So, when can we have it?"

"We fixed it for Friday at half past eleven in the morning; in Uganda, it should be half past five in the afternoon, so I guess there shouldn't be any problem for Dr. Murdock. Are you going to call him today?" Dr. Luther wondered.

Kaine nodded, trying to find something to stop the bleeding. He grabbed a kitchen rag to help.

"Sure, I will do it immediately."

"Okay, then I will not keep you any longer. See you tomorrow?"

Kaine remained for a second to ponder whether he would prefer to take advantage of a couple of days off as Nora had suggested. "Oh, I was thinking of taking the rest of the week off, but I will come for the video chat if that's okay with you."

"Of course, take care of yourself, and see you on Friday, then."

"Thank you very much. See you."

He hung up the phone and yelled, "FUCK!" as he ran to the bathroom to see whether he could find something more appropriate in the first aid cabinet.

It took a few minutes to take care of the wound in a proper way, and when he considered himself satisfied, he took a deep breath, thinking about what to do next.

"The best thing to do is to call Dr. Murdock right away, and I would be grateful if my mother would keep her comments to herself," he said, raising his voice as if she could hear him.

With a grin of dismay, he grabbed the phone, dialing Dr. Murdock's number.

\*\*\*

Jason was sitting at the same table of the bar, lazily rolling the whiskey glass over the wooden surface. He wondered when Kaine would have called him.

He stared at Omar, who was following the soccer game on the TV, as he was cleaning the place. *I have to acknowledge his efforts at trying to keep this place as neat as possible; the problem is that he would need a miracle to fully clean up this place.*

*The sewage system is barely working, making the restroom the most uninviting place for humans, but the best place for mosquitoes, flies, and other unwanted guests. The whole structure should be torn apart and rebuilt...*

He smiled, amused as, despite all the odds, there were still customers coming either to eat something, to have a beer, or to watch the soccer game.

Local social life gravitated around the bar of Omar for those who were living there, either by choice or because they were born there and couldn't fathom any other place where to live.

The ringing of his mobile phone surprised him, and with a jolt, the little glass full of whiskey fell on the floor, spilling its precious content.

With a mumbled curse, Jason replied to the call.

"Dr. Murdock."

"Good afternoon, Dr. Murdock. This is Dr. Kaine Martin speaking. We spoke this morning, and as promised, I can give you the date for the video chat with the director of the department and myself."

He hesitated, wondering whether he should mention the presence of one of his former colleagues.

"Oh...Wow!" Jason exclaimed. "I was almost sure you wouldn't call until tomorrow."

"I wasn't sure either as I was waiting for the confirmation from the director of the department," Kaine replied, wondering whether it was only an impression, or if Dr. Murdock was slightly intoxicated. "He asked me to inform you that, for him, the best time would be this Friday at half past eleven in the morning local time. Do you think it's a good time for you?"

Jason smiled, arching his eyebrows. "It would be perfect. If you don't mind sending me the link for the video chat so I can synchronize my calendar, not to miss it."

"Of course. I will send it as soon as I can. I'm not at the office now because I got a little ill. Nevertheless, I will try to connect to my email account from home and sent the invitation to you and Dr. Luther so we all have our calendars set," Kaine assured.

"Fantastic. I will be waiting, and I'm looking forward to having a chat, virtually face-to-face with you. Take care of your health; if we are going to work together here in Africa, you will certainly need it."

Jason refilled the glass with whiskey, smiling at the sight of his poison.

"I do believe so. Well, I wish you a good day, and see you in a couple of days, even if only virtually."

"I can hardly wait. See you."

***

Jason placed his mobile phone back in his pocket and continued looking through the amber color of his whiskey. *Stay away from me, kid... and stay away from Her.*

He raised his hand to caress the stubble on his chin. "I suppose I'll have to clean myself up a bit before the meeting; if they see me this way, they'll never give a cent of credibility to my story, and if I were them, I wouldn't either."

He stood up from the chair, gulping his whiskey and slamming the glass on the table. "I'm leaving! I'm going to town," he announced.

Omar considering whether he was already too drunk to go anywhere. "Do you need a ride, Boss?"

"Are you worried I could kill myself?" Jason replied, wobbling to the exit.

"You and someone else who has no intention of dying so soon." Omar glimpsed at a young man at the end of the bar counter, signaling him to follow Jason.

The young man hurried to help Jason as he was exiting the place. "I will drive you wherever you need to go."

"Thank you, kid. I was thinking to go and have a haircut, but first, it would be wiser to have a shower, even just to sober up. What do you think?"

The young man smiled, amused, as he helped Jason reach the car. "That would be a wise choice, but maybe you would need to quit drinking so much."

He stopped and scrutinized the young man through narrowed eyelids. "What's your name?"

"My name is Akiki."

"Well, Akiki, I'll tell you one thing. I never got married to avoid having someone telling me what I should or should not do. Yet, also, in this case, I still find those who are in the position to manipulate my life. I don't need another one." Jason offered Akiki a glare, feeling too bitter and tired, to engage in an argument about what would have been better for him and his health.

"The only cure for all my troubles would be the chance to go home. Do you know how it feels being so far from home and not allowed to return?"

His face contorted into a painful grimace. "I'll tell you how it feels; it makes you wish you were already dead, and if that doesn't come naturally, you are ready to take your life by other means or hoping to reach insanity fast enough to escape the hell I have been confined to."

He wriggled from Akiki's hold and walked away toward his bungalow.

Tears started to well in his eyes. He missed home and wondered whether he would ever be allowed to return, or at least to die.

Nevertheless, he understood that what brought him to this condition was his fault. Had he been more considerate and trustworthy, this would never have happened.

"They are right, they are all right," he mumbled. "I should get a hold of myself, get over my bitterness and start to live my life once again. Getting drunk is not going to be of any help. Africa is not necessarily a terrible place to be, and to be honest, this stretch of rain forest holds more beauty than a concrete jungle... Yet, this is no home."

He resumed his walk and reached his bungalow in the heart of the small community that lived in the proximities to the tribe of Akuna-Ra.

She had been able to secure their loyalty to the tribe and keep their secret.

For the people of those communities, this was a great deal. They were guaranteed a certain level of wellness that wasn't so obvious for the other communities living in the country or on the whole continent.

Nevertheless, most of their loyalty came from the fear of Akuna-Ra's powers, which were unlimited on both sides, good and bad.

For those like Jason, who didn't believe in magic, she could become more dangerous, as their carelessness might have given them more troubles than they could ever imagine.

The touch of the cold water against his skin gave him a pleasurable, refreshing feeling from his thoughts and the oppressive heat of the forest. Also, the effects of the alcohol were slowly fading away, and his mind started getting clearer.

He looked at himself in the mirror. "I need a shave and a haircut, then I need to plan the rest of the week a little more in detail. There are three days left until Friday, and since today is almost gone, I should only count on Thursday and Friday morning," he considered as if he were talking to his own image.

"I resemble a hobo," he admitted, caressing the stubble on his chin.

*\*\*\**

Kaine remained for a while, thinking about the conversation he'd had with Jason.

The impression he'd been drinking took over his thoughts. Yet, unable to see his face, he hoped he might have misunderstood his tone.

"I wish I could get more information about him on the internet. I know he has been considered missing for eight years, but there must be something more about him. What I'm wondering is whether there are some details about his personal life," he said as he resumed his cooking.

His mother used to prepare braised salmon, and since he loved it, there would be some fillet to be found either in the fridge or in the refrigerator.

He forgot how relaxing and therapeutic cooking could be. "I should cook more often, and considering my relationship with Mark, I might consider bringing this activity to a new level. I should invite Mark for dinner today and see if we can keep our clothes on."

A chuckle amused him and wondered whether he should have called him at a certain point during the day to see if he was still interested in having a relationship with him.

Detached from the job and other worries, despite having had a call with Dr. Murdock, the vision of his mother didn't repeat.

"I'm starting to believe it was only a question of stress. I should take more time to recharge and focus on more relaxing activities. I can't live only for my job; regardless of how much I love it."

His life, once again, returned to be as carefree as it used to be when he was a kid, or as a student. The illusion of having all the time for himself brought a smile on his face.

"Also, I'm not going to poison my soul trying to find any information about Dr. Murdock. I will discover everything on Friday when we have the video conference," he promised to himself as he started to eat his salmon.

He spent such a long time in preparing his food, he couldn't call it a lunch; it was more accurate to define it an early dinner.

*** 

The rest of the afternoon invited him to engage in one of his favorite activities; reading. He'd recently bought a few books but had never had the time to read them, so his mission for that long weekend would be reading them all.

He brought the books into the living room and piled them on the table close to the couch. "Besides Mark, there is nothing that will take me away from my proposition," he got comfortable under the blanket.

He lost all cognition of time and felt surprised when his doorbell rang. He spent the whole afternoon reading and with a yawn, he stretched his body, as he went to open the door.

"I was waiting for you." Kaine smiled, as Mark came inside the house.

"Liar, liar pants on fire. If so, why do you still have your clothes on?" Mark closed the door behind him and pressed his lips against Kaine's.

"I told you I need supervision to be a bad boy," Kaine whispered through the kisses.

Mark grabbed Kaine's butt and raised him to his height, then pushed him against the door, as Kaine wrapped his legs around his lover's waist. "I was missing you the whole day, and I was waiting for this moment to fulfill all the fantasies I've been thinking about since I met you for the first time."

The warm breeze of Mark's breath on the base of his ear sent cold shivers down Kaine's spine, lightly creasing his skin like ripples on a calm lake.

"We've known each other already for five years..." Kaine urged, breathlessly.

"Hmmm... so you have an idea about the number of fantasies I have been thinking about."

Kaine parted to peer in Mark's eyes, licking his lips. "Show me... I want to see them all."

Mark allowed him to stand on the floor. "I can't. You know, I was so excited about having you in my life, that I forgot about them and booked a table at a nice restaurant to celebrate our new-born relationship. I hope you're not disappointed with this change of plans."

Kaine smiled; he was not at all upset. He felt special.

"Nobody ever brought me out for dinner simply to celebrate being together. Generally, when I started dating, the first two weeks were spent mostly in bed," Kaine chuckled.

"You know, I might appear to be a cocky asshole, but in reality, I have a romantic soul. Moreover, I don't consider you a one-night stand, so I want to spend some quality time with you. I want to flirt and talk; I want to dance, and I want to make love to you."

With an improvised dance move, he dipped Kaine. "This doesn't mean we're not going to have the wildest sex you can ever conceive of."

Kaine chuckled, recalling what they had the previous day and night. "I think you gave me an idea about the wild sex we might have."

"What?" Mark laughed. "You call what we had yesterday wild sex? Oh, my goodness, what kind of relationships have you had so far? That was hardly a taste!"

Kaine averted his gaze from him, shaking his head. He wished indeed to spend the night, exploring all the fantasies Mark could have thought of, but the original plan of going out for a romantic dinner was more appealing.

"We should go, or they won't keep the table reserved for us," Kaine chuckled, already regretting reminding him about the reservation.

"You're right." Mark noticed the conflicted expression Kaine had and raised his chin to gaze in his eyes. "Don't you worry, my little angel. We will have eternity to turn you into a little devil, I promise." He lightly kissed his lips.

Kaine didn't know what to say; he was feeling happier than he'd ever been before. All the troubles and concerns disappeared, and his life had never appeared brighter.

*\*\**

"So, how was your day?" Mark asked as they were having their dinner.

"I took the rest of the week off. I felt like I was overworking, and I might have accumulated some stress..." He wasn't sure whether he should tell him about the hallucinations he had and the possible connection with the new project and its development.

"Is there something upsetting you? You suddenly turned serious," Mark observed, gently holding his hand.

Kaine sighed and bit his lower lip. *If he is supposed to be my boyfriend, the man I trust with my own life, then he should be the one I can talk to about everything, and if this should be his reason to dump me, perhaps it's better if it happens now rather than later.*

Kaine turned his eyes to Mark and explained to him everything from the project he was following, to the contact email he received from Dr. Murdock, and his strange disappearance eight years ago, to the hallucinations he had.

Mark remained the whole time, severe and silent. Not a single emotion transpired from his expression, and Kaine started to fear he was trying to find an easy way to say it was over.

After a long pause of silence between them, Mark opened his mouth, trying to formulate something he couldn't put into words.

"I have to admit it; this sounds like a strange coincidence."

"Coincidence?" Kaine wondered, tilting his head.

"Yes, I mean, you have a hallucination or a vision of your mother telling you not to talk to strangers, and in the same moment, a stranger is calling you offering the solution to a mystery that had confounded scientists for centuries."

Up until now, Kaine hadn't made the connection between the two facts or the detail that his mother was probably referring specifically to Dr. Murdock. "You don't mean... Do you mean it wasn't a hallucination? Should I believe it was a ghost?"

With a light lift of his shoulder, Mark arched downward the corners of his lips. "I haven't said so, but you need to admit that it sounds like a warning from the person who loved you the most in her life. Some say at death, the soul leaves the body and passes to another dimension. Yet, there are cases when there is still something left of the immortal part, which remains bound here." He swung the fork he was holding in his hand. "For example, if your mother believed you still needed her, one part of her remained here to watch over you. I don't say I believe this; to be honest, I don't have an opinion about it. I think if this is true, then the warning should be taken more seriously."

"I don't know what I'm supposed to think. The only certain thing is that after a good rest, those hallucinations stopped." Kaine sipped his glass of wine and toured visually around at the other tables in the restaurant.

On the other side of the room, the band was preparing to start playing for the evening.

"You shouldn't stress too much but promise me something; when or if you need to travel to Africa, you will keep in mind those recommendations. You'll be watching over yourself. You will be too far from home, and whatever happened to Dr. Murdock, and impedes him to return home, might happen to you too. Keep safe and call me every day." Mark held tighter to Kaine's hand.

Kaine smiled, as he had never felt as loved and cared for as with Mark. He could tell the difference between him and all the other relationships he'd had. *Most of them were only for sex and if I did care for them, they didn't necessarily care about me the way Mark seems to do.*

Kaine blushed. "I love you, Mark. I will be careful, and I'll call you every day. Although I'm not sure whether we'll follow the lead proposed by Dr. Murdock. For all we know now, we can't be sure that the man who contacted us is Dr. Murdock himself. The fact that he's still considered missing casts a lot of doubt on his identity."

"Well, then let's not talk about it. How about a dance?" Mark proposed, standing up from the chair.

*** 

That evening was indeed the best in ages, for Kaine, and although they returned home a bit drunk, he felt more intoxicated by the presence of Mark than by the alcohol he'd been drinking.

"I'm going back to my home; tomorrow, I'll get up early to go to work, and I wouldn't want to wake you up. We need to rest, and I'm afraid I might not be able to simply fall asleep having you naked at my side," Mark purred, kissing Kaine's neck as he walked him to his door.

"I don't sleep naked..." Kaine corrected.

"That's why you're not going to Hell. You are a difficult devil in training," Mark laughed, amused. "Goodnight, little angel. I will call you tomorrow."

"Maybe you're right. I'm dead tired and too drunk for anything else but sleeping. See you," Kaine replied, opening the door.

Confronted with the loneliness of his house, Kaine remained for a moment to listen, as if he was trying to spot some little noise.

He wondered whether he was expecting to have his mother appearing again from the fog of his drunken state.

Had she seen him coming home drunk when she was still alive, it would have meant having a long argument about responsibility. It was challenging to upset her in any way, but if there was something that could infuriate her, it was people who couldn't keep themselves from drinking responsibly.

He felt relieved by her lack of communication, as he could go safely to sleep, hoping not to have a terrible hangover the morning after.

"I wonder whether I can avoid a hangover by not falling asleep." He felt amused by that thought and went to the kitchen and drink some water to rehydrate his body before heading to bed.

That night, he decided he would sleep naked. "Like a good devil in training..."

# CHAPTER 5

Finally, the day of the meeting arrived. Kaine reached his office a couple of hours in advance, so to have a chat with Dr. Murdock's former colleague.

He felt excited and relieved as the visions of his mother have stopped for good. He started to believe there wasn't anything supernatural about those events. *It was probably due to my overworking. Therefore, from this moment on, I will take it easy and enjoy my life. Mainly because now I have Mark to focus on, which is far more pleasant than working my butt off.*

He chuckled as he reached Dr. Luther's office, and without any hesitation, he knocked at the door.

"Come in," Dr. Luther invited.

As Kaine stepped inside, he noticed the presence of a middle-aged man, who stood up politely to greet him. He had short grizzled and curly hair and a well-cured goatee that gave him an aristocratic outlook.

"Good morning," Kaine greeted. "I'm Dr. Kaine Martin, it's a pleasure to meet you."

The man smiled kindly. "My pleasure, Dr. Martin, my name is Giuseppe Verrocchi. I was shocked when I was contacted by Dr. Luther with the news that perhaps Jason was not missing anymore. We had been working together for most of our careers, not always on the same projects, but I can say it was one of the saddest days in my life when I was informed of his sudden disappearance."

"We hope it's not the case of someone trying to take advantage of his name," replied Dr. Luther. "Is there anything you can tell us about Dr. Murdock?"

Dr. Verrocchi pursed his lips. "It depends on what you want to know, whether it's something about his career or him personally."

"I think we would need to know something concerning both aspects of his life, either on the professional level and on the personal one. What I would like to know is mostly related to his credibility," Kaine explained, getting comfortable on the chair.

"I understand," Dr. Verrocchi replied, returning to seat at his chair. "He has always been a controversial person. The only thing he used to follow was his passion and instinct. He never stopped just because something was not easily accessible to his research.

"Nothing appeared to stop him. The search of the tribe, mentioned in a few old documents, was a matter of life and death. He had the certainty of their existence, and with most probabilities, it was still hiding in the African forests." Giuseppe smiled recalling those times when they were working together.

It was difficult for him to accept the missing of one of his best friends, and still, those memories brought tears in his eyes. "He didn't have more than this clue, but for him, it was enough to leave and research on his own. In the beginning, the University was interested, and many other organizations agreed to fund the expedition.

"He started from Equatorial Guinea and searched, spending nights and days interviewing people, observing old maps, gathering information from satellites – you name it. Of course, we were also talking about the technology available over ten years ago. You can imagine how you needed to spend a considerable amount of time and effort to reach the results we might have today within weeks."

A bittersweet smile appeared on his face as Dr. Verrocchi took a short pause of silence, recalling those times. "Time passed by, and the data obtained were too few or inconclusive to justify the expenses.

"For this reason, with the withdrawal of the main funders, the University called Jason back. They had other research to focus their attention on, and he was mostly required as a teacher. He felt betrayed by their decision. We had the chance to have a phone call, and he expressed to me the bitterness of having to return home."

Dr. Verrocchi lowered his gaze to his hands crossed on his lap, frowning at the memory of his lost friend.

"Something strange, though, happened the day before he left Africa. I had a chat with him to find out if he needed a ride from the airport. We hadn't been just colleagues, but good friends, and I wanted to make things easy for him. He had obviously drunk one shot too much, and he started to weep. He asserted to have found the 'goddamn tribe' as he called it," Dr. Verrocchi continued. "Jason has never been a gentleman. He claimed to have been in contact with them, but he wasn't allowed to take any pictures. Jason had the proof, but he feared to show them to anyone. I had a strange impression that he was scared."

Kaine remained open-mouthed. "But if he got in touch with the tribe, why didn't he try to get an extended period to write a report about them? Many tribes do not allow being photographed, but even if he couldn't take pictures of the people, he could photograph the village or some artifacts. I don't get it."

"What I don't understand," intervened Dr. Luther, "is why he was worried. Do you think someone was threatening him? Perhaps this is the reason why he disappeared for eight years?"

Dr. Verrocchi shook his head. "There isn't any answer to your question, but if the man we are soon having a video chat with is Jason himself, then we can ask him all the questions we need. He is the only one who can bring some light to this mystery, and I can't wait for the time."

Dr. Luther glanced at his clock and stood up from the chair. "Let's move to the conference room. There, our IT technician should already have arranged the connection."

Without saying a word, they all followed Dr. Luther, all of them formulating questions in their minds about Dr. Jason Murdock.

***

Jason reached the office he rented for the morning. He needed to cross the border with Uganda to reach a city, which had business spaces to rent.

Everything was set up for the video chat, and as he was waiting online to be connected with Kaine, he quickly scanned his image on a mirror on the wall. He couldn't remember the last time when he had the same 'civilized' outlook and smiled at himself.

With a hammering heartbeat, butterflies seemed to populate his stomach. He wondered how he could reveal his finds without exposing the location. "This is the time to recall how to tell lies. You were a master in deception when it was time to get funding."

He smirked as if talking to himself. "You need to get back to your old touch..."

Grinning like a wounded beast, he felt still impossible to believe it all happened to him. "How did I get myself into this mess?"

The beeping sound of the video call brought him back to reality and he hurried to answer.

"I'll be damned," he mumbled when he saw a familiar face in the group of people he was connected to.

"Jason!" exclaimed Giuseppe, "I couldn't believe my ears when they told me it was you the one who reached out offering information about the tribe. I needed to see it for myself. What happened to you, and why did you disappear from the face of the Earth? We were almost sure you were dead. Why haven't you contacted anyone before?"

Jason shook his head. "You still sound like my mother. Nothing has changed. I haven't reached out to anyone because I couldn't do so. When I lost all the funding, I decided I couldn't simply turn my back on something for which I already had evidence, but no photographic material."

He took a seat and entwined his fingers together. "I called one of our major funders and explained everything I had found, requesting more time, but it was the biggest mistake I ever made, and I will suffer the consequences for the rest of my life." His breath got shallow, and he hoped he could keep himself from crying.

Never in his life did Jason conceived he'd reach the point he'd wish for death. Never did he believe he'd end up enslaved by something he could barely comprehend.

"Dr. Murdock, I'm sorry to interrupt you, but since you are claiming to have proof of the existence of the tribe, why you don't search for funding on your own without involving another partner to share the glory," Kaine wondered. There was no more doubt that the man talking to them was indeed Dr. Jason Murdock, the anthropologist gone missing eight years ago. "Don't misunderstand me, if you can show us your proof, but you need to have better equipment to reach them or to pinpoint the exact location, we would be ready to offer our assistance."

Jason observed the young researcher and figured out he was Kaine Martin, the one he had spoken with on the phone; the one She wanted to have there for a reason he couldn't grasp.

"Dr. Martin, I'm sorry for having rudely started this chat, without greeting you and Dr. Luther, who kindly gave me the chance to show you my results," Jason commenced. "I intended to obtain more funds, but mostly to have access to better technology. My finances are limited, and I'm not able to carry out the final research alone. Nevertheless, if I can share my screen with you, I will show you something I found indeed interesting."

He opened a file folder on his computer and displayed some images from satellites and aerial photographs. He knew they were old pictures, but since he got in touch with the tribe a few days before he was declared missing, he had been living under their strict surveillance and had never been allowed to leave.

He shared his screen and started with the first photo. "Apparently, this one doesn't show anything different from any other aerial pictures taken in the area, but when you take a closer look..."

He zoomed the high definition photograph to a particular detail on a minute clearance in the forest. "Here, on the place where I'm pointing, you can see something like a human figure. I tried to improve the resolution, and in the following image, you can see the decoration on its body doesn't match any other tribe known."

Dr. Luther, Kaine, and Dr. Verrocchi observed the picture carefully.

Nevertheless, in that room, the only person who had experience with African tribal heritage was Kaine, and he looked at the slightly blurry figure, trying to reconstruct it in his mind.

It took him one minute of close observation to understand that perhaps Jason was right, but there was still one question twirling in his mind.

"Dr. Murdock, I have an inquiry for you about this image. Where and when was this picture taken?" Kaine wondered without taking his eyes off the screen.

"The exact location is not certain, but I can pinpoint the area between Uganda and the Republic of Congo. Regarding when, I can't be sure, but no later than ten years ago." Jason replied.

"I see," Kaine mumbled, thinking about the known tribes and mentally comparing them with the figure. "Although the silhouette is a bit blurry, I agree with your statement; this kind of body decoration would be quite unusual for the groups we have already encountered in the same area. Also, it doesn't seem to match other tribes living on the continent, but to confirm this, I need better photos than this one. It would be good to have sharper images to understand the body features, which can only be guessed here and don't lead to anything conclusive."

Jason showed them a couple of more pictures, but Kaine was already persuaded by the idea that he might have just found a great reason to plan an expedition to Africa.

*He was right, and he has more information than we could even imagine. This means the tribe could be still there, and with the satellite imageries available nowadays, we could pinpoint the place where this picture was taken or where it's possible to find them.*

Kaine nodded, biting his lower lip, foretasting the adventure that would soon be starting. Suddenly, he considered his relationship with Mark.

The hallucinations he had about his mother didn't bother him anymore, and he hoped they wouldn't come once again to curse his life.

Dr. Luther observed Kaine, who was unable to take his eyes off of the picture Jason sent.

"What do you think?" he asked then.

With a sudden turn of his head, as if he was surprised to see he was not alone in the room, he averted his stare from the screen. "Oh... Well... I think we have at least something to ponder about, and the material you showed us is auspicious."

His eyes returned to focus on Dr. Luther and Dr. Verrocchi. "I would like to have these pictures in my computer. Dr. Murdock, could you send them by email, so I can study them at length?"

Jason smiled. "I have to deduce they have caught your attention, and in this case, yes. I will mail them right away, so if they fail to reach you, we can figure out another way to get them to you."

Kaine's face brightened up with a wide smile. "Thank you, I appreciate."

A few seconds after, Kaine's email blinked with a new message. "It seems like I have received the files safely," he replied as he opened them to make sure there wasn't any problem in any of them.

Jason looked down at his wristwatch and cringed. Soon, the time of his availability would expire, and he would be forced to leave the room to whoever booked it after.

"I'm afraid my time here is ticking, but we can arrange another video chat if you prefer."

Dr. Verrocchi frowned. "Will you call me another day? There are so many questions I wish to ask, and I'm also wondering whether you would be able to return home one of these days."

"I will see what I can do, but concerning my return to the States, I consider it fairly unfeasible, my friend. So many things have happened here, and perhaps this is my new home, after all. Here, I have started a sort of new career as a teacher, and I guess people need my teaching here more than they need me back in the civilized world."

Giuseppe nodded without saying anything else; he knew there would have been another time for personal chats, and he was only a guest there.

"Dr. Murdock," Dr. Luther interrupted. "We will remain in touch, and we will communicate with you our decision whether to engage in this expedition or not. Nevertheless, I am grateful for your kind offer in sharing your finds with us."

"I have to thank you for your attention. It has been quite a long time since someone listened to what I had to say. But now I need to go. Let's keep in touch, and I wish you a nice day."

*** 

As soon as the communication ended, Giuseppe peered at Dr. Luther. "I'm sorry if I wasted your time with personal questions to Jason. I feel better knowing he is not dead, and he's found another life in Africa. I know how much he loved that continent, and perhaps it's for his best if he'll remain there, where his passion and heart has always been."

Kaine smiled, shaking his head. "You don't need to apologize. We understand your feelings perfectly. If we were in your position, we would have taken the chance to have a personal chat and solve old questions that might have troubled our minds."

"Indeed," Dr. Luther added, switching off the computer and inviting them to follow him to his office. "We're grateful for your help in recognizing Dr. Murdock, and if you like, we will keep you informed whether we decide to organize an expedition to Africa, following the lead we just received."

Giuseppe's eyes filled with an inner glow, smiling gratefully. "I appreciate it, but now I need to go. I wish you a wonderful day."

They shook hands, and Kaine remained alone in the room with Dr. Luther.

"How do you feel today?" Dr. Luther asked, concerned about Kaine's health.

"I feel a bit better, thanks for asking. The pictures Dr. Murdock showed us were interesting. I do have to take my time to investigate them closely, but from what I could see now, there is a good chance that the person we have on film is a member of this lost tribe. I will have to compare any sort of description with those old texts, and only then will I be able to give you a clear answer."

"Will you come back to work on Monday?"

Kaine felt a bit guilty for having been absent for a few days, but he needed to recover fully as not to risk burnout. "Yes, I'm sorry for this unexpected absence, but I believe it was a wise decision to take some extra time. I will study the pictures from home anyway."

Dr. Luther went to take a seat at his desk and sighed. "Of course, there is no hurry, and the closer the look you take, the better it will be. But for Tuesday, I need to have a detailed report about your opinions and the grounds for the request for an expedition to search for this tribe."

"That sounds fair enough. Consider it already on your desk," Kaine replied.

"I wish you a good weekend, then, Dr. Martin."

"And to you too, Dr. Luther," Kaine smiled broadly.

***

Kaine was walking the streets and enjoying the fair weather, wondering how he should organize his time. He knew he would have spent the evening and the rest of the week, with Mark.

If he wanted to have some time in peace to examine the pictures, he had to go straight home and check them right away, writing down some draft notes for the report he promised to deliver on Tuesday.

He felt excited about the new find and called a taxi to reach home faster. He needed to start to work on it immediately. Only Mark could take him away from those images, and he felt grateful for having him in his life.

***

With a positive feeling about the outcome of the meeting, Jason left the business building where he had the video chat.

He could garner the trust of Kaine, but he was also gripped by the remorse of knowing he'd brought him a step closer to an eventual trap.

*Well, 'trap' is not the exact term. If he is wiser than I was back in the days, he will keep his promise and will never talk about what he will see. It will all be up to his commitment to being fair and honest. I wasn't sincere in the first place when I disregarded my commitment to Akuna-Ra. She is not wrong when she speaks about loyalty.*

Having the chance to talk to Kaine and warn him not to say a word, or even better, to forget about what he will see during his stay in Africa, could have allowed Kaine to return to his life as a researcher. He'd never have any sort of trouble with the cursed tribe, and their witch doctor.

The taxi driver was waiting outside. "We are ready to go back to the village," Jason said as he opened the door of the car.

Without any word spoken, the driver just nodded and lazily started up the engine.

The journey took about two hours, not counting the time he would need to cross the border. Nevertheless, with his long permanence in Africa and his new career as a teacher, the bureaucracy got slimmer, and he could travel through the two countries reasonably easily.

*I guess crossing the border is more difficult when you are a tourist or come here for a short trip. People who live here and have a job have some advantage in the bureaucratical practices.*

He leaned against the backseat and closed his eyes.

He couldn't wait to be back in his bungalow and rest. Traveling through the two countries was always stressful, and he wished to be already back home.

*Home - he thought - a word with so many meanings, I've begun to be confused about it. Indeed, Africa is no home for a mzungu, yet there are times when I feel like it's the only place in the world, I can call home. Sometimes, I wish so desperately to be back in my hometown. If I think about the place where I grew up, the university I frequented, which also became my working place, the people I have loved and cared for – then, this is home, and there is no place I desire to be.*

He took a deep breath and wondered what would have been his reaction if one day Akuna-Ra would have decided to forgive his lack of loyalty and allow him the freedom to go wherever he wished to.

*I'm not sure anymore if I will go back to the States, or if I will just settle somewhere else in Africa. One thing is certain--at least once, I would return to my previous home, and then decide whether to come back here permanently, or remain there. Freedom is a highly underrated concept.*

With that thought in his mind, he fell asleep, he knew the taxi driver would wake him up for the border passport check.

The sun had already set when he reached the village, and as the mother of one of his pupils saw him returning, she called him.

"Dr. Murdock," she yelled. "I was waiting for you to return."

"What's the matter?" he wondered. "Did you fear I was leaving the town?"

She shook her head with an amused smile on her face. "No, I know you won't leave without saying goodbye. I wanted to tell you my son got ill. We are going to bring him to the witch doctor..."

"Take proper care of him; health is the most important gift we have. He will catch up with school," Jason replied with a nod.

"Thanks, would you like to join us for dinner?" she proposed.

Jason knew some of them didn't have money to pay for tuition, and from them, he got either food or other sorts of goods. He didn't mind. His life didn't need any fanciness; he just needed to thrive, and so far, he couldn't be more satisfied with the outcome.

"It would be an honor; you are a better cook than I could ever become. Perhaps one day you could teach me to prepare food," he replied, and with a content smile on his face, he followed the young woman to her house.

# CHAPTER 6

Eagerness consumed Kaine, who couldn't wait to be home so he could start to study the pictures. Observing the aerial photographs without any particular tool was not going to yield good results.

Although the quality of the pictures was already at a high definition level, they could have been further improved.

From the University, he could install on his computer a sophisticated software to handle those kinds of images. Kaine was almost sure to get a sharp reconstruction of the figure in the middle of the clearance.

Upon entering the house, he dashed to his studio and started up the computer. Without looking at the clock, Kaine began to work on the pictures, knowing Mark would come to rescue him from overworking.

He opened the first picture he received and tried to isolate the figure in the middle. "Sure, it's blurred, and you can't recognize the features, but those white paintings on the body are so different from what I've seen before. I need to try and sharpen this figure, perhaps eliminating some of the background noise."

One after another, he applied all the possible resolution levels and filters. "It might take some time before it will give any result. Meanwhile, I might prepare myself another cup of coffee."

He stood up from his chair and walked toward the kitchen. He'd never felt so excited about a project before. His whole career started to open up to possibilities he'd never considered reachable. "I'm not sure this would ever mean becoming a famous anthropologist or having the cover of a dedicated print for myself. I feel this is something I'm finally doing for my personal growth, and not simply for the glory or the hunger of fame and fortune. This is going to enrich my soul with experiences I would never dare imagine," he said aloud as he started up the coffee machine.

As he was ready to return upstairs, the doorbell rang and glancing at his clock, there wouldn't have been the need of a clairvoyant to guess that the one who was on the other side of the door was Mark. "Great, I believe he would love to see what my work looks like," he chirped as he went to open the door.

"Hello, little angel," Mark replied with his charming smile.

Kaine felt like melting at his smile and the stare of his green eyes. He felt his dick stirring in his pants. *I still can't believe we are together; if this is a dream, nobody dare to pinch me!*

"I must have lost track of time; I thought you would have come later, "Kaine replied, inviting him inside. "Do you want coffee?"

"Yes, why not. Am I disturbing you?"

"Not at all. You came to rescue me from overworking," Kaine chuckled, walking to the kitchen, followed by Mark.

"I thought you took some days off from work. What happened, couldn't stand the guilt?"

"No, I couldn't endure the excitement. Today I had a meeting with Dr. Murdock, the scientist I have mentioned to you. He gave me a couple of pictures he had as a proof of the existence of that elusive tribe. I was too eager to wait until Monday, so I started to work on them, and if you want, I can also show them to you," Kaine replied, offering a cup of coffee to Mark.

"That would be interesting!"

"Great! Come with me. I left the software to work on the refinements while I came downstairs. If we're lucky, we can see the results right away."

"And if we are luckier, we will go wait in your bedroom," Mark replied, grabbing Kaine from behind. He turned him to face him and kissed him passionately, as his life depended on it, trying not to spill the cup he was holding in his hand.

Kaine felt like he could forget about the pictures and go straight toward the promised Hell, the place where they could enjoy each other for eternity.

"I have an idea," Kaine purred as their lips parted. "Why don't we get rid of those cups and go to my bedroom? I'm afraid I can't wait to have you."

"I see my lessons are bearing some fruits, and the little angel is turning into a little devil. I bet you have also started to sleep naked, ready to be taken..." Mark whispered in Kaine's ear, sending shivers like thousands of small electric shocks.

Kaine moaned as Mark took the cup from his hand and placed it on a dresser in the corridor. He lifted Kaine in his arms and walked to the bedroom, where he dropped him on the bed.

"I believe we've had enough time to get to know each other. We've been friends for a long time, enough to understand our attraction"

With a swift move, Mark pulled his shirt off, as Kaine felt himself almost drooling at the perfection revealed under the clothes and started to undress.

"Now, it's time to stop playing and be serious, my little devil in training." He unbuckled the belt of his jeans and slipped it away.

Kaine's heart was beating furiously in his chest as Mark reached him and with his belt tied his hands together, fastened to the bedhead. He was sure he wouldn't be able to say a word, not to make any sound more than his labored breathing.

With his trousers still on, Mark kneeled on the bed between Kaine's opened legs and slowly started to caress him from his calves to his thighs, reaching his crotch, where Kaine's dick was standing fully erect.

"M-Mark," was the only thing he could whisper.

"Now, I know you want me to take you right here and now, but I have better plans. And I'm going to show you what you have been missing all those years of flirting with the wrong lovers."

His hands moved on his dick slowly to tease, without allowing Kaine to reach his climax; *there will be time for it.*

A blissful expression painted Kaine's face, as Mark enjoyed his quest observing his every jolt and squirm at the different places he was going to stimulate.

For Mark, it was a discovery of what was going to drive his new boyfriend crazy, *and, baby, I'm going to take all the time it takes, because as I see it now, wherever I touch, I'm going to send you to heaven.*

82

With the picture, the tribe, Africa, and any other work-related matters, completely obliterated from Kaine's memory, he was in the only place he wanted to be for the rest of his life, on a bed with Mark playing with his body.

His head felt light, and if his heart continued to beat so furiously, he might pass out.

He lowered his gaze at Mark, slowly caressing him with his tongue as his hands moved to reach other parts of his body. *Oh My God, I'm sure soon I'm going to explode. I can't hold myself back for much longer.*

Mark raised his head from Kaine's crotch. "It seems like I have to hurry up or you will cum without me," he chuckled.

Without taking his jeans off, he lowered them enough to free his dick from that hellish restraint, which kept it away from Kaine's warmth.

He lifted Kaine's lower body and allowed himself to penetrate him. With slower movements, in the beginning, he reached the desired pace as moans grew louder, coming close to his climax at every thrust.

Mark intended to keep it going for as long as possible, but he underestimated his own arousal, and soon, he started to pound faster.

As they both lay in each other's arms, tender kisses were exchanged between the two lovers.

"I love you," Mark breathed after he removed all the clothing he was still wearing. "I love you more than I could even imagine I was able to. Never dare to go away from my life; I could never live without you."

His hand circled Kaine's hair in a soothing caress.

"I've never felt like this before and never had anything like this. Believe me, I'm not going away from you. At most,

I will go to Africa for a while, but I will come back as soon as possible. I will never be able to live without you." Slowly, his breath started to return to its normal rhythm, feeling calmed and comforted by Mark's tender caresses.

He held himself tightly to Mark's chest, wishing to keep him close to his heart and never let him go.

There was a short pause of silence between them, like their souls could talk to each other without any words, through the contact of the skin.

"Do you have any idea whether you will go to Africa, or when this might be?" Mark wondered, feeling concerned about his departure.

He wasn't worried about his safety; he knew the organization he was working for would never leave him on his own. *My actual concern is more selfish, as to how can I live without having him in my arms?*

Kaine sighed. "I have no idea. If something conclusive comes from these pictures, we will start planning for the expedition. Of course, this means a lot of bureaucratical steps, organizing the logistics, choosing the team. There are so many things to be considered and in the best-case scenario, we will be ready to leave in about six months.

This is when everything will go as smoothly as it can be. You shouldn't worry now, after all, we might also decide that the lead proposed is not sufficient to arrange an expedition."

Kaine parted from Mark and locked his eyes on him. "However, this is part of my work. Sometimes I need to leave for some research, but you can be sure you will be the first, if not the only one I will keep in contact with when I'm away."

Mark smiled. "I'm the luckiest man in the world." He caressed Kaine's soft hair.

Kaine took a deep breath and watched outside the window. The sun had already set, and the street started to become illuminated as people began to go out for their weekend celebrations. Yet, it seemed like, for the first time, nothing was attracting him out of his home, and particularly outside of his bedroom.

"I wish we could stay like this forever," Mark muttered, kissing Kaine's hand.

"We don't have to do anything else; we can also remain in this bed until Monday morning when we need to go to work."

Mark grabbed him and hugged him tightly to himself. "I suppose we made a deal about how to fill this weekend. We can order something to eat, and we'll spend as much time as possible, having a good time. This might be a taste of what is going to await us for eternity."

"You know I do have food here; we only need to cook it."

"Too much time wasted in doing something else but holding you." Mark dismissed with a chuckle. "One thing, though, I would like to do, and that is to have a check at the picture you wanted to show me. You can call me crazy, but I got curious about it, and besides, this was the main reason why we came upstairs."

Kaine sat up on the bed, trying to gather his clothes.

"What are you doing?" Mark wondered.

"I'm getting dressed; you told me you wanted to see the pictures..." Kaine replied, unsure about what he meant by that question.

"Tsk, tsk, no clothing for the whole weekend, my little devil in training." He started to put on his boxers.

"What are you doing, then?" Kaine wondered, baffled by seeing him getting dressed.

Mark pulled up his jeans and reached for Kaine, who was still sitting on the bed. He smirked, with a wicked expression on his face, and caressed Kaine's cheek, raising his chin to peer into his eyes.

"I mean, you are staying naked and ready for me." He collected his belt and kept it on his hand.

Kaine felt mesmerized by his green eyes and felt his dick twitching at his words. Mark noticed it and chuckled, forecasting a great weekend.

He reached Kaine's ear. "I promise you won't regret it. This is going to be one of the best weekends we will ever remember."

With his mind blanked by Mark's words, he simply nodded.

"Let's go and see whether your computer could run those filters to your picture. Now I'm starting to be curious, too, about the outcome." He grabbed Kaine's hand.

They reached the studio, where the computer had already gone on standby. Kaine felt a bit odd about being naked there. That was the place where he was also working from home. He felt like being undressed in his own office at work and wished he had something to cover himself.

Nevertheless, despite the strange feeling, Mark's presence made him feel better about his nudity.

*You will get used to it, and I can ensure you will enjoy every second.* – Mark considered – *I will make sure this weekend will be the best ever and will be a great reason to return home as soon as possible from Africa. Consider this a small incentive to make you feel homesick.*

Kaine sat on his chair and observed the result obtained. The definition indeed improved; the figure standing in the clearing became sharper, and the decorations on his or her body were better recognizable.

Yet, he wondered whether there was room for some improvements. Just to make sure, he saved a copy of the new picture, before trying another round of filtering.

Mark looked at the photograph, curious about that human figure. "Is this one of the people you were talking about?"

"I believe so. Dr. Murdock claimed this was one of the best proofs of the existence of the tribe, and at first sight, the statement seems to be correct," Kaine replied without turning his eyes to Mark and setting up the software.

"What makes you think this way?"

Kaine stood up and glanced at Mark with a smile. "You see, for every tribe, identity is everything. They use colors and decoration patterns and textiles to differentiate their members from other tribes. This is also important to recognize enemies from allies. Every group uses a different painting pattern on the bodies of their warriors, chiefs, witch doctors, and so on. Although I need to put in a deeper comparison level between the decoration patterns of other known African tribes, I can say this one appears to be totally new. I don't remember ever having seen anything like this before."

Mark felt caught by the undeniable passion driving his research. "This is so fascinating; I love the way you have explained it to me. Did you ever give lectures about anthropology?"

Kaine eyeballed at him, surprised. "Me?" He brought his hand to his chest. "No, never, but I have presented my papers to different symposia, to other experts."

"You would be a great teacher. As you explained it, I would love to hear and learn some more about the heritage of African tribes," Mark admitted.

"Thank you, that was a flattering compliment. I believe it's not an easy job, and I'm wondering about what kind of teacher Dr. Murdock was. There is something fascinating in him."

Mark pursed his lips and grabbed Kaine's chin. "I hope he's not too fascinating for you, or I will have to follow you to Africa."

Kaine laughed heartily. "Don't you worry, he's not my type, and I'm not sexually attracted to him. I find his story interesting, and the mystery of his missing is still bothering me. I suppose there's much more to it than a clear decision to stay there and continue the research independently. I can't believe a successful researcher and teacher at the university, all of a sudden, decides not to return home and plan his own disappearance. If he wanted to remain in Africa, there wasn't any need to pretend he went missing," Kaine explained.

"Hmm..." Mark mumbled. "Very interesting, but I warn you. Nobody shall touch you during your stay, or in any other circumstances. I can be very jealous."

Kaine pinched Mark's cheek. "Don't be. I'm very loyal when I commit to another man."

\*\*\*

For most of the night, Jason remained thinking inside his bungalow. He wondered about the plans of Akuna-Ra, and whether there would be an affirmative answer from Dr. Luther or Dr. Martin.

What made him wonder was the presence of his old colleague and friend Dr. Giuseppe Verrocchi.

"Beppe," he mumbled with a smile on his face. "I almost forgot about you, and I shouldn't have. I was convinced you're already retired. If I remember correctly, you were the one who couldn't wait to go and enjoy your golden years back in Sicily. I wish I could come and visit you. According to your descriptions, Italy must be an enchanting place."

Once again, he felt bitter about his captivity. Although it was fair to get the promised punishment for the lack of respect he showed to Akuna-Ra, he thought eight years should have been more than enough for something that hadn't brought any consequences.

"Nobody even believed me back in the days," he mumbled as he started to undress, ready to go to sleep.

As he was sitting on the bed, his attention was caught by the whiskey bottle he kept on the table of the kitchen.

He didn't plan on getting drunk, but he thought a shot would help him to fall asleep effortlessly. "There are so many thoughts going on in my mind at the moment, and all of them could keep me awake for the rest of the night. I know She doesn't like it, but if She intended to have me at her place, She would have called me earlier. I can consider myself free until tomorrow morning."

He sat at the table and poured a glass of whiskey, thinking about all the memories coming back to his mind after having spoken with Giuseppe. He felt homesick and wondered whether he would be allowed to at least call his old friend like he'd promised.

"I guess I should better ask Her. She hates it when I take too many initiatives, and the consequences can be more painful than I can endure."

He slowly sipped his whiskey, enjoying the feeling in his mouth and the smooth taste. That was one of the pleasures still allowed, and a recurrent payment for his daily poison was kindly offered by one of the families who had three children following his tuition.

"There are things here that can be more valuable than simple money. I have no idea where they get this whiskey. Here, around the only place to buy alcohol is the bar owned by Omar, but he doesn't keep this particular brand. I wonder whether they ask him to order this to pay me."

He laughed, amused at the typical African way to get things done, in one way or another. "Most of the time in a quite clumsy way, but still, if you don't care too much about the details, or if you aren't too picky, you can also say things work in a halfway decent way."

He stood up after the last sip and decided, without thinking any further, it would have been the time to say goodbye to that long day and fall asleep, hoping for a better day to come.

# CHAPTER 7

The morning after, Jason could barely open his eyes. Moving any part of his body was painful as if each of his muscles were cramping. He couldn't fathom what was going on, but he feared that whatever his pupil had, it was given to him as a gift when he went to have dinner the previous evening.

"Fuck!" he groaned, trying desperately to stand up, even to ask for help. *What kind of support I'm looking for, I have no idea. The only medical assistance I can have is from the witch doctor Akuna-Ra. Oh well, isn't it better than nothing?*

He rolled himself out of bed, falling on the creaking wooden floor with a heavy thump. "I don't know whether I should try to reach the restroom or the door and scream for help."

His voice sounded like a feeble whistle in the wind. "And who the fuck is going to hear me with this pathetic whisper?"

Trying to overcome the cramps, he crawled to the door, careless of wearing only his pajamas. *At least all the pain I had to endure all these years has served me to manage this one. I need to remember and thank Her.*

A wicked chuckle escaped him at his funny statement as he opened the door. "Help!"

His voice didn't go farther than his mouth.

Closing his eyes, he tried to scream with all the strength he still had left, when a woman who was passing by noticed him and ran to assist him.

"Mzungu, what happened to you? Are you ill?"

"Call the witch doctor, bring me to Akuna-Ra. I'm dying," he growled between clenched teeth.

She looked around, knowing she would never be able to carry him alone. "Don't move, Mzungu, I get you help!" She ran away.

"I was just thinking of going for a marathon, but I can wait for you," he replied sarcastically, letting his body fall on the logs, damp with the morning dew.

Soon after, a couple of men came to get him. "Don't you worry, Dr. Murdock, the witch doctor will take good care of you," one of them reassured as they eased him on a cart to bring him quickly to Akuna-Ra's shack.

Despite their caution in transporting him as fast and as comfortably as possible, the two concepts didn't go hand in hand, and the uneven ground of the path that cut through the forest made every step a painful jump for Jason, who reached the destination with his pants dirty with his stools.

Akuna-Ra was already waiting for them outside of her shack, standing tall with her usual grave expression that could pierce the hardest of men.

"Jason, I was expecting you." She leaned upon him. "Bring him inside," she ordered, glancing at the two men, who obeyed without a single word spoken.

They felt glad to discharge their stinky cargo and leave the place as soon as possible.

Akuna-Ra watched them running away with a disappointed glance, and entered the shack where Jason was moaning in pain.

The stench of his excrement made her cringe, and with a snap of her fingers, a couple of her servants appeared and undressed Jason completely naked. They took away his dirty clothes and returned to wash his body before their mistress could start examining him.

"I hope this won't be the beginning of an outbreak, as you are the third person, I've seen infected," she said calmly, walking to the center of the room, where the fire was burning.

The heat in the place was more intense than Jason could remember and wondered whether it was because of the fever.

He groaned in pain, unable to say anything. He was sure, she would have helped him; she still needed him.

"Save your breath, I know how you feel, and I can hear your thoughts. You're right, I'm not going to let you die, just like I won't let the rest of the village die."

She went to the pot boiling on the fire and got a bowl full of its contents.

Akuna-Ra reached his lips with the cup. "Now drink this, and things will get better quite soon."

"What..."

"Don't question and drink," she replied with a calm voice. He could almost say there was kindness in her expression.

He drank the thick fluid. He wasn't sure whether his excrement smelled worse than it, but he didn't question her orders and gulped the whole content of the bowl.

She spread her arms, and with a tone of voice that didn't resemble anything human, she intoned an ancient spell, aimed to, perhaps, implore the favor of the gods or to shoo the evil spirits from his body.

The monotonic tune echoed in the room, making it difficult to understand where it was coming from. Slowly her voice reached a higher pitch, and like the pain of a million needles, he felt as if it entered his body through each pore.

The soundwaves penetrated his skin, dancing rhythmically inside himself; everything blurred into a blissful unconsciousness.

He felt like his soul was leaving his body, suspended into the nothingness. He tried to open his eyes but couldn't say whether they were still closed, or the darkness surrounding him was so complete as not to allow any sort of light filtering through them.

As a distant echo, he could still hear the chant of Akuna-Ra, and a sense of peace pervaded his soul. "Is this the feeling of dying? Is this death?" he heard himself saying.

He had no idea where he was or whether this was just an effect of the healing drink he was offered. What he knew was that he could no longer feel pain, and there was nothing concerning him anymore.

"What kind of magic can do this?" he asked the darkness. He felt intrigued and needed to know more about it.

Traditional medicine couldn't find any place in those villages around the tribe of Akuna-Ra. People were more trusting of her healing practices, rather than sending their ill and injured people to the hospital.

Akuna-Ra was not the chief, but she was to be the one who held the power of magic. She knew past, present, and future; nothing was to her unknown. Yet, there were too many secrets about the origin of the tribe. She was the witch doctor, and together with the queen, they would have died keeping the secret.

For Jason, time and space no longer had any meaning.

He wasn't sure whether he was still alive; he didn't have any way to compare his condition with the one of the living.

It felt like he didn't have a mass anymore, and the suspicion of being already dead crawled into his mind, regardless of Akuna-Ra's reassurance of not letting him die.

With a tilt of his head he tried to dismiss his thoughts; either way, he wouldn't have been able to change anything regarding his condition. If it was right and he was dead, perhaps soon his immortal part would reach eternity; if instead, he was still alive, he needed to wait to wake up once again.

Despite the strange feeling of uncertainty, nothing perturbed his inner peace. To be honest, being far from earthly concerns felt almost good.

Into his comfortable timeless cocoon made of darkness, he finally thought he could hear something approaching. It was like a grinding noise that didn't make any sense to his ears.

He couldn't identify where it was coming from, nor whether it came from a machine, a beast, or a human. He tried to scan around himself and to open his eyes in case they were closed, and suddenly a light appeared in front of him.

"He's waking up!" a voice spoke. Finally, he could recognize some figures around him.

"Dr. Mzungu!" the trilling voice of a child yelled.

"Hmmm..." he growled, surprised at hearing his voice once again. *Obviously, I'm still alive.*

"Where am I? What happened?" he mumbled, looking around himself, recognizing Devina, the woman who'd invited him for dinner, and her son, Mahamadou.

"You are in your bungalow," Devina replied in a lower tone of voice, so as not to disturb him. "The witch doctor took care of you and of my son, together with what appeared to be the beginning of an outbreak of cholera. We are grateful for her help; without her, there might have been many other people infected or dead."

Jason nodded, still feeling perplexed. "How much time have I been laying on this bed?" he asked, trying to move his body, which felt stiff as a rusty gear.

"You have been unconscious for a week. The witch doctor made sure you would have not felt any pain or discomfort. She said you would have slept for a long time until your body would have been able to function on its own," Devina explained.

"It felt like ten years," he replied, trying desperately to move. "My body isn't ready to react..."

"She told us to give you this to drink." She took a bowl from the table and brought it close to his lips.

He wasn't sure he wanted to have anything coming from Akuna-Ra, but once again, he didn't have any other choice but to comply with her order.

Both taste and smell were neutral, and he didn't dare to question what was in the bowl; he was sure he wouldn't get an answer anyway.

"What happened during this week?" His mind started to get clearer with time, and a strange tingling all over his body was the beginning of the awakening of his motor capabilities.

"Your telephone rang several times. I have only replied once, and I hope you are not angry about it. There was a man who introduced himself as Dr. Martin, who tried to call you. I explained to him that you were ill and couldn't talk." Devina sat down on a chair beside the bed and caressed the sheets absentmindedly. "I asked him if he wanted to leave a message, and he mentioned your request was accepted, and they will start the bureaucratic... something... I don't recall everything, and he was speaking too fast."

Jason chuckled, amused. "Thank you. You helped me a lot by answering that phone call, and I will get in touch with him as soon as I can move my body. Do you know how much time it will take for my body to respond to my orders?"

She blushed and lowered her gaze. "The witch doctor forecasted it will not take too much time, perhaps already this evening you will be able to stand up."

"Dr. Mzungu, you need to come back and teach us!" Mahamadou yelled.

"My name is not Dr. Mzungu," he replied groggily. "I told you many times to call me Dr. Murdock or Teacher."

"Why don't you go to check whether your father is going to need you?" Devina hushed him away. With a huff, the boy left the bungalow, stomping his feet, and his mother sighed, relieved.

"He is a good kid," observed Jason.

His body slowly started to be more responsive, and he tried to sit on the bed. He would have never imagined the effort such an easy task would have required.

"I'm wondering what kind of potion Akuna-Ra gave me the day I was brought to her shack. The only thing I remember is being far away from here and from my body." He looked around himself as if he was in a new environment.

"When she gave the medicine to my son, she explained it was necessary to ensure that his body would be irresponsive to outside stimulations. This way, it would recover faster from the illness. I have no idea what was in that thing she made you drink, but we don't need to know everything when there is nothing we should worry about," she replied as she went to get some water.

"And it seems like you can read my mind. I feel like my throat is a desert. I wonder how I didn't get dehydrated by not having anything to drink during this week I have been asleep." He followed her movements as she searched for some water in the kitchen.

"You have only alcohol here; I will go and get some water from home. Don't try to get up; you are still too weak to move on your own," she warned, reaching the door. "I will be back in a moment."

She closed the door behind her, leaving him alone.

He started to collect his thoughts, and then he recalled she had mentioned Dr. Martin called him to tell him they accepted his request to organize an expedition to Africa.

"Did he send me an email as well?" he wondered.

His eyes toured the whole room, trying to figure out where his mobile phone was.

"I will have to ask her to give it to me when she is back with some water; I'm dying of curiosity. I also believe I should contact Beppe; if I can have a chat with him every now and then, perhaps my lack of freedom would feel less daunting."

The door opened after a few moments, and the girl appeared with a bottle of water. "I could only find this one, but I will get some more from the grocery shop as soon as possible. I'm wondering why you don't have any bottled water in your house."

She shook her head as she walked to the kitchen to pour the water in a glass.

"No, bring the whole bottle. I will drink it immediately," he pleaded. "Concerning the alcohol; it's highly unfeasible to have it contaminated with cholera or any other kind of virus. Moreover, it makes a great disinfectant."

She laughed and brought him the water, which he gulped entirely in a short while. He'd never felt so thirsty in his whole life and never had water tasted so good like it did in that exact moment.

Devina remained open-mouthed. "Well, you were right when you claimed to be thirsty. I will go and get you more water." She strode toward the exit.

"Before you go, I need a favor. I need to have my telephone. I will need to make one phone call to Dr. Martin; most likely he is waiting to find out if I'm still alive and well, and soon, I will be ready to escort him here."

She tilted her head, surprised to know he would have a visitor. "Is this man going to move here as you did?"

"I hope not. Certainly, I would enjoy having the presence of another guy from my same country but being here for the same reason would mean something terrible happened to him. Misery loves company, but I wish no harm to anyone," he replied as he lay once again on his bed.

She handed him the telephone. "We have charged it too..."

"You are angels. What would my life be without you all?" Jason smiled gratefully, grabbing his mobile phone.

"This is a community; we all work for the good of each other. You are teaching our children, educating them, they could never fathom. The least we can do to pay you back is taking care of you when you need it."

Jason nodded. *This is something my people forgot too long ago, the sense and the meaning of community. Nowadays, everybody thinks only of himself and his family at most, but when the shit hits the fan, these are the people who are going to thrive, not my people.*

***

Kaine reached his office a little later than usual that morning. He was wondering whether Dr. Murdock had recovered from cholera. He'd never thought about it, and he started to research if this could be something potentially lethal.

*Living in a country where sanitation is a top priority makes you forget about the deadly diseases its lack can bring. I hope Dr. Murdock had access, at least, to a hospital to treat the condition. It would be a real pity if he died before he could have considered returning home. Whatever the reason, which forced him to remain there, I believe he would have liked to have the chance to go back home one day.*

"Good morning," greeted Nora as she saw him coming inside the office.

He startled like he was just awakened from a dream. He glimpsed around, realizing he'd reached his working place.

"Good morning to you. I was so wrapped up in my thoughts that I didn't notice I'd arrived," he replied with an amused smile on his face.

"Yes, I noticed that," she giggled. "Any news from Dr. Murdock?"

"Not yet, at least. I was just thinking about him, and I hope he has access to proper medical care there. I understand he's living in a remote place, perhaps in Uganda or the Democratic Republic of Congo."

He sat down at his desk and, routinely, opened his computer. "I was pondering about how we take those services like sanitation and healthcare for granted. Yet, there are so many countries where even the basic amenities are not accessible to everyone."

"Well, if we talk about healthcare, neither here we have access to it properly. If you can't afford good insurance, you might also die for all they care," Nora grunted.

"You got a point." Kaine cringed.

"Hey! I got an email from Dr. Murdock!" he exclaimed.

"Awesome, read it aloud. I'm also wondering how he is doing," she replied, taking her eyes away from her screen.

Kaine cleared his throat and started to read:


*Dear Dr. Martin,*

*I apologize for this late reply, but as you know already, there have been some cases of cholera in the village where I'm living, and one of the patients to be treated was me. Luckily, now I feel much better, and I can at least write you back.*

*I would like to express my gratitude for your trust in my finds. I was sure those pictures were exciting and could give many clues to the eager eye of a researcher.*

*Concerning my health, I'm not yet fully functional, but give me a couple of weeks more, and I will be as good as new. Please, keep me updated with the news about your planned arrival here and the bureaucratical steps.*

*Please, get in touch with me by phone when you can.*

*Best Regards,*

*Jason Murdock.*


"I'm glad he could get the right care. Cholera can become a deadly disease, when poorly treated or not at all. I see this email was also sent to Dr. Luther, so I believe I should soon go there and talk about the details. He is handling, as usual, of all the paperwork, including finding the people who will participate in the expedition."

"You will need to take all sorts of vaccinations before you leave; you don't want to return home with more than a nice souvenir to decorate your house with," Nora warned, pointing a finger at him.

# CHAPTER 8

A few days after, when he was on his lunch break, Kaine decided to call Jason, hoping he was not disturbing him.

He hesitated for a while and wondered whether he should have waited a few more days instead. *There isn't any hurry, we can indeed have a chat another day.*

Pursing his mouth, as if to reproach himself for his indecision, he considered that if he didn't take the initiative, they wouldn't ever be in touch to discuss any of the vital details that needed their attention.

With a fast move, he grabbed his mobile phone and selected his contact. Fighting his growing hesitation and doubts pressed the 'call' button.

"Murdock," Jason answered as he was walking on his way to Omar's bar.

"Dr. Murdock, I hope I'm not disturbing you; this is Dr. Kaine Martin..."

"Oh, Dr. Martin. What a surprise. I almost feared you wouldn't contact me again. No, you are not disturbing me," he paused and sitting on a rock close by.

"I have been waiting for your health to improve, and I don't have any idea about the time required to recover from cholera."

"Well, you were right to be worried, but we have a good witch doctor here, and she was able to avoid a widespread outbreak."

Kaine cringed. "A witch doctor?"

He wondered whether Jason was joking, or he meant the healing priest, who would have evoked the spirits to clear the body of illness by expelling evil.

"Yes, I mean just that. I know it might sound crazy to rely on non-traditional and non-conventional healthcare, but as surprised as I'm, I'm here and healthy," Jason replied with a smirk. *You will understand better when you are here, kid.*

"Dr. Martin, Africa is a strange place, and nothing here works the same way as it does in the civilized world. As a researcher in African tribal heritage, you should know this detail, but sometimes we need to live in this reality to fully get what it means being part of a small village in the middle of the wilderness."

Kaine smiled, amused at his answer. "I will have a lot to learn. Perhaps I can plan a longer stay to have a better understanding of the lifestyle, in addition to the information we can obtain about the tribe."

"That might be a good idea because you'll have something to write about in your article in case we won't be able to gather enough data," Jason suggested, changing his position on the rock. His butt started to hurt, and he considered the possibility of resuming his walk to the bar to get more comfortable on a real chair.

"I'm not going away without any results about the tribe," Kaine objected.

Jason sighed, recalling he was once like him, and had the same eagerness and passion moving him. *Perhaps I should tell him there would never be any report, any paper or anything about it, or the consequences would be disastrous. Akuna-Ra can be extremely creative when she thinks about punishments, and her creativity can reach the level of cruelty. He should never cross her path.*

Jason fought with the need to warn him about the tribe, but he needed to be patient and wait for the right moment when Akuna-Ra would have given him the permission.

*I don't even dare to think about the consequences this confession will bring to my life. Although I don't wish my same disgrace to anyone else in the world, I prefer to care about my safety, not to mention keeping my promises from now on.*

"You need to remember no result is still a result. If we find out the tribe has been extinct, and only a few traces have remained of them, then you will have to write an article about their disappearance and whatever we can find about them," Jason warned.

"Oh, but of course," Kaine replied, understanding he had been too eager. "I feel so excited. I have been spending all my time trying to refine the pictures you have sent me. I was able to obtain an incredible amount of detail, particularly about the first picture, the one where a person can be spotted in a small clearing in the forest. I was comparing the decoration on the body with all the other known tribes, and I couldn't find anything similar in the whole continent. Something interesting was also the body structure, but this difference could be due to the definition of the image."

Waving his hand to Omar as he entered the bar, Jason went to sit down at his usual table. "That was the reason why I have sent them to you. I knew there was something there, which with better technology, could have been extrapolated to give a sort of support to my claim. I have been spending my whole career and life here, and I know what I'm talking about."

"Indeed. I can't give you any schedule for the expedition yet, and as a matter of fact, I was calling you to find out whether you were still ill, or if we could proceed with the paperwork. As soon as I finish this conversation with you, I will inform Dr. Luther, who is taking care of the organization and the team who will come with me." Kaine entered the cafeteria.

"What kind of team would you need here?" Jason wondered about the risk of having too many people coming to know the secret.

"I can't operate all the instrumentation to scan the area alone. We will need a group of at least five people, including me," Kaine explained as he found a free table.

"Of course," Jason uttered. "Well, I assume I'll have to let you go for now. Let me know when you have any news. I will be waiting here."

"Yes, I wish you a nice afternoon or evening," Kaine replied, not entirely sure about the time in the place where he was.

A waiter arrived to take his order. "Remember, people are not what they seem. You'll have to be careful when talking to strangers," he warned.

Kaine glanced at him, his jaw dropped. He wasn't sure whether he understood what he said, or if he was once again hallucinating.

"Excuse me... what did you say?"

"I said, have you already decided what you'd like to have?" He smiled, amused by Kaine's expression.

*That was definitely not what I heard.*

He perused the lunch menu and pointed at the first thing he saw. "I will take this large chicken salad."

"Perfect," he replied as he wrote the order. "Do you want some water, beer, soda...?"

"I will take orange juice with it, thank you." He placed the list back on the table, trying not to get fixated about the incident.

*There must be, for sure, an explanation for this. Maybe the music was so loud, and I misunderstood his words. I shouldn't be too worried about it; there is no need to get alarmed. Eventually, I was still thinking about what had happened with the hallucinations about my mother, and I mixed up everything.*

He opened up his mobile phone to check the news. Earlier in the morning, he hadn't had the time, so he thought this would help him to think about something else.

*Mark thought it might have been my mother coming to warn me about the journey.*

*Although I can understand an expedition to Africa has its risks, both from a health standpoint and on the safety level, this can be considered particularly true when we are talking about going into the heart of a conflict area.*

*The Democratic Republic of Congo, together with the stretches of the Virunga park, has been the playground of the rebel forces, and many tourists have been killed or kidnapped.*

He browsed the internet, searching for more specific information about safety-related issues.

He wondered whether this was the reason for the warnings. "Maybe they all want me to search and be prepared for any eventuality. But this should also be something my organization should provide. They have a duty to care for my health and safety in any circumstances. As an anthropologist, I'm traveling often, so a solid network to ensure my security is a must-have," he whispered as he searched for any information about The Democratic Republic of Congo and Uganda.

The food arrived soon, but he was so focused on his reading that he barely acknowledged it. He ate without interrupting his research about the internal conflicts and the danger for tourists or people traveling for business. Full-coverage insurance, together with the organization of armed guards, was considered the minimum to ensure a decent level of protection. Then, of course, keeping a GPS contact with people at the headquarters, who would be promptly alerted and ready to intervene in case of emergency, was highly recommended.

*I believe I will have to show this article to Dr. Luther. If we are going to have a team, there must be someone who remains at an established headquarters, keeping an eye on the position of the groups which will be on the field. Everyone, except me, will have turns, depending on the equipment we will need to operate.*

He was happy to have checked those suggestions. "This might be the reason for the hallucinations. Perhaps my brain wanted me to be careful and to plan everything to ensures a safe return home."

With a lighter state of mind, Kaine placed his mobile phone back in his pocket and continued to enjoy his lunch before returning to his work.

***

Life took a new comfortable routine. Dating Mark resembled a dream come true. He was everything he was looking for in a relationship; the perfect balance between sweet, tender love and hot sex like he couldn't dare to imagine. To be added to the package, he found in Mark a person who could engage in intelligent conversation about many topics and was grateful for his interest in his research and job. He also became interested in his role as a chemist in a pharmaceutical organization, and there had been many times when he loved to listen about his career, the struggles, the daily goals, and his achievements.

*I believe I have found the perfect match I was looking for, and I desperately wish he feels the same about our relationship. Soon we will face one of the hardest tests to go through, being away for a prolonged period. There might be days when we can't call each other, and I hope this kind of incident will only be restricted to the times I will be on a plane.*

A bright smile lightened up his face on his way back to the office. His relationship with Mark could perform miracles in his mood.

"It's good to see you in a good mood," Nora observed as she met him in front of the cafeteria.

Kaine sighed. "I was thinking about Mark. I was considering that I have never felt such a complete sense of happiness with any other of my former boyfriends, not even with my first one. Yet, I'm also concerned about the time we'll have to be away from each other."

Nora patted his shoulder, understanding his feelings. "If your love is as strong as you say, there will be no problems. If not, then this will be the ultimate test. After all, it's useless to waste your time in a relationship that's not meant to last."

With a groan, Kaine grimaced. "It would be a pity. With him, sex is amazing."

"But we don't live only for sex, do we?" Nora pointed out as they were climbing the stairs to reach their office.

"Of course not, but he is perfect in every aspect, or at least so he seems to me. You're right, though, if this relationship is not supposed to last, then it's better it ends before I become too attached to him. But do you want to know something bizarre that happened when I was having lunch at the cafeteria?"

His voice changed tone as he recalled the incident. "I was having a look at the menu when the waiter arrived to take my order. I have no idea if it was a question of me being focused on other issues, the music too loud, or something else. When he asked me whether I already knew what I wanted, I heard him distinctly saying something about being careful when talking to strangers."

"Oh!" she exclaimed, surprised, as she recalled the previous incidents he had. "I thought it was resolved."

"So I was thinking too, but then I understood what it meant. I'm going to travel to a place torn apart by civil wars and internal conflicts. The Democratic Republic of Congo has been at unrest for ages, and the LRA rebels continue their activity. The question of safety during my permanence in the area is vital, and perhaps this was the reason for my hallucinations and constant warnings. I needed to study the political situation, and I need to take my own measures to make sure this won't be my last trip anywhere," he explained, entering the office and grabbing a chair close to Nora's desk.

"I'm going through all the safety issues and will discuss them with Dr. Luther. Although this is not the first expedition we have organized in Africa, it's indeed the first one in the Democratic Republic of Congo, and perhaps we should get updated about the political situation before thinking of gathering the team and the equipment."

Nora sat down at her desk and switched on her computer. "That is so fascinating."

"What?" Kaine wondered.

"This sort of warning, coming from... I don't even know how to define it." She placed her elbows on the table and rested her chin on her entwined fingers.

Kaine considered it for a moment. "Hmm, so far, I was convinced it was due to stress or overworking, but do you believe there might be something supernatural about these incidents?" He moved closer to her, speaking in a lower tone of voice to avoid being overheard by anyone else.

She shook her head. "I'm generally skeptical about anything classified as 'paranormal,' but what happened to you is difficult to explain rationally."

"Mark, instead, believes that when people die, there is a part of them which remains here in this dimension. He believes that, perhaps, my mother felt like she still needed to be at my side, and now she is trying to warn me, forcing me to take care more closely of my safety." He leaned back on the chair, glancing outside the window, unsure about what he was supposed to think or believe.

He stood up. "I will go right away to talk to Dr. Luther. I need to make sure he will consider the risks of organizing an expedition in the Democratic Republic of Congo, and he won't leave anything unplanned."

Nora watched him as he dashed out of the room and smiled amusedly. What amazed her the most was the complete change in his attitude toward her. For many years he had been extremely reserved about his personal life. Then, after she asked him straight out whether his silence was due to antipathy toward her, their relationship transformed completely. "Sometimes, you need a little hint to make a friendship."

***

Kaine hesitated for a second in front of the closed door of Dr. Luther's office. *Would it be better simply to send him an email with all the links I could find about the political situation?*

He shook his head nervously, trying to shoo away all his indecision, and knocked at the door, fearing the hallucinations might continue until he could make sure that every risk was considered and taken care of.

For a moment, the threat posed by the numerous diseases still present in the area didn't sound as daunting as the threat of being kidnapped or killed.

*A disease can be cured, and if I'm going to be treated here, my chances of survival are quite high. However, a gun pointed at my head is far more deadly than most of the illnesses I could contract.*

"Come in..." Dr. Luther growled.

Kaine peeked gingerly from the door. Dr. Luther's tone of voice was not one he liked to hear. When he growled that way, it meant he was losing his temper.

He wondered whether he should reconsider the decision to bring to his attention some special safety issues connected to the expedition.

"May I disturb you for a moment?"

Dr. Luther raised his eyes from the pile of papers on his desk. "Yes, please. I need someone to distract me for a moment from this chaos."

Kaine came inside, took a seat on a chair in front of the desk and drew a deep breath. "If it concerns the organization of the expedition to Africa, I'm afraid I'm not going to help."

Dr. Luther narrowed his eyes, staring at Kaine with an icy glance. "Let's try anyway."

"Well, I was doing some research about the safety issues connected with any prolonged visit to The Democratic Republic of Congo. Our team will scan the area with drones and scanning radars, but at a certain point, we will have to enter the deep of the rain forest, either in or outside the perimeters of the national park. This means becoming an easy target for the LRA or other organized rebel groups..."

"I know that!" Dr. Luther spelled, through a threatening grin. He slammed the pencil he held in his hand and stood, pacing the room. "Do you think I'm not taking care of it?"

He was clearly stressed by a task that was more complicated than it appeared on paper.

"I have been spending two weeks trying to figure out a way to have a safe expedition, but whenever one hole is closed, another ten open. I'm wondering whether this means we should give it up," Dr. Luther wondered as he tried to calm down.

"Wouldn't it be more reasonable to ask Dr. Murdock for his advice? He is living there, and if he has been spending his career and life following the clues for the positioning of the tribe, he might have also spent a considerable amount of time in the forest."

Dr. Luther abruptly stopped his pacing around the room and remained still, thinking about Kaine's proposal.

He turned his glance to Kaine and smiled. "I consider it a great idea. I will call him immediately. Do you still have his number?"

Kaine searched his pockets, looking for his telephone. That was the only place where Jason's number was stored. "Of course, I can send it to your cellphone."

He browsed the directory, and when he found it, he sent the contact to Dr. Luther's phone.

"Here it is, it should arrive soon," he observed as a familiar beep informed them about the reception of the message.

"I will leave you to speak with Dr. Murdock in privacy." Kaine stood up from the chair. "Will you let me know about the outcome of the chat you have with him? I'm eager to understand how he managed for all these years to search the African rain forest without having more than a case of cholera."

Dr. Luther chuckled. "I will ask him about it. It sounds like an interesting and legitimate question."

Kaine left the office, wondering about the call Dr. Luther was having. *I should have stayed there. Now I can't focus on anything* - he huffed - *On the other hand, if he didn't invite me to stay, it also means he preferred to remain alone and have a chat in peace. It's not easy to concentrate on a phone call when you have an audience.*

He shoved his hands in his pockets and started walking to his office, feeling confident that Dr. Luther would have informed him about the result. "And if he doesn't, it means there is nothing I need to know. So better if you forget about it and start doing something more useful, like working, for example."

Although Dr. Luther didn't contact him, for the whole day, he could focus on his job hardly remembering the phone call.

When he saw Nora starting to prepare to leave the office, he realized his day was also over.

"So, see you tomorrow morning?" Nora grabbed her purse, ready to leave the office.

"Yes, have a nice evening. I will also leave quite soon."

"See you then. Take care of yourself and don't get too stressed about the expedition. There will be a right time to be excited and nervous, and this is not yet that time," she recommended, waving her hand to say goodbye.

He didn't reply; he simply smiled at her.

The streets started to get darker at sunset, and the artificial light in the room and corridors began to get brighter and brighter. His eyes returned to the computer's monitor, and his attention was caught by the clock.

"It's already half past five. I should also leave and focus on the time I will probably spend with Mark." He stood up from the chair, putting the computer in sleep mode.

Before leaving the room, he gave a final glimpse at the office. Seen in the evening on a winter day, it appeared quite sad, and he wondered about the weather in the DRC. "The rain forest is not an easy place to go. I have already experienced it, and it's not something I'm looking forward to, but on the other hand, this grey and melancholic weather doesn't appeal to me much either."

He switched off the light and started to walk toward the exit. Walking the streets to the metro station, he realized he'd never stopped for a second to carefully observe the place he was living and working. The city was not such an ugly place, not even on the depressing, rainy winter days.

Of course, nothing to do with the vibrancy of the green colors, the noise of the animals in the forest, at times, also deafening. Nevertheless, also the city had its attractiveness.

"I have never taken a moment to appraise the place where I live. The road goes by in front of me, and I don't pay attention to the people passing by, the effects of the streetlight on the wet asphalt."

He stopped trying to fix in his mind all the possible details of that evening. The sounds, the smells, the feelings, and the colors. "Two different types of jungle. So different, yet also so similar."

The ringing of his telephone brought him back to reality.

He struggled to find it in the inner pocket of his jacket, and recognizing Mark's number, he opened up into a bright smile.

"Hello, Hun!" Kaine replied, resuming his walk toward the station.

"I was wondering whether something had happened to you. Generally, at this time, you are already home."

"I know, I had something extra to take care of. The organization of the expedition is requiring a careful plan, particularly to ensure maximum safety. Concerning healthcare, it's sufficient to have the right vaccinations, but for other matters, I'm afraid we will need something more than a shot," Kaine explained.

Mark was standing in front of Kaine's door and wondered whether he should return home and wait for him there or not. "How long will it take for you to be back home?"

"It will take me a good half an hour. However, you can get inside the house with the spare key I keep under the second flowerpot on your right. I always keep an extra one, in case I forget it inside the house or at work, or I lose the one I have," Kaine suggested, hurrying his pace to reach the station earlier and get to the early train.

"Found it!" Mark exclaimed, opening the door. "I will be waiting for you here, and I will prepare you a drink to welcome you home."

He walked to the kitchen, trying to figure out what kind of beverage he was going to prepare for his little devil in training.

"Okay, see you soon. I love you," said Kaine.

"I love you too. Bye!"

Mark placed the telephone on the counter and searched for something to make a drink. "The liquor cabinet is well furnished; you have a real bar here," he observed, looking around.

"This will make my task much easier," he added. He grabbed a few bottles and thought about the proportions of alcohol and soft drinks. When he finally reached the taste he was looking for, he finalized the two glasses.

# CHAPTER 9

The organization of the expedition, the choice of the team, ensuring the contract for the security on-site, and the logistics took more time and effort than everyone could ever have predicted, but with the help of Dr. Murdock, many of the issues were simplified, as he was living there and could solve the majority of the safety-related problems, the local way.

This meant that within a period of eight months, Kaine and his team were ready to leave for one of the most critical expeditions in their whole careers.

"I can't believe it; tomorrow I will leave," Kaine purred as he rested on Mark's arms.

Mark didn't reply immediately. He felt torn between the need to beg him to stay and guilt for being selfish and thinking only about himself. If he could, he would have gone with him, but that was not an option.

"I-" he started to say, stopping and caressing Kaine's hair. "I will miss you. I will miss everything about being with you like I would miss the air I breathe."

Kaine held himself tightly to Mark's chest, feeling the same conflict in his soul.

For some long minutes, they remained in each other's arms, trying to figure out what they were supposed to say.

"This is not a farewell. I will be back," Kaine tried to rationalize.

With a deep sigh, Mark moved from his position to peek into Kaine's eyes. "I know, and it feels quite stupid to create such a drama. I know you will be back, although we don't have a steady schedule for your return. You know what? I believe this is the problem."

"We don't have an exact date for the end of the project?" Kaine wondered, lowering his gaze, caressing Mark's hand.

"Yes, I don't have a countdown to set, but you know what? We can make one. Let's say you will be back in twelve months. Most likely, this would be a reasonably long period for your research, and I guess you will also have the chance to take a holiday from your job. So, we can say that next year, on the 21st of June, your project will reach an end. If you will be back earlier, then this will be even better news," Mark proposed, raising Kaine's chin peering into his eyes.

A bright smile appeared on Kaine's face. "This is one of the things I love about you, the fact that you always see things from a positive point of view. You never give up and dwell on negativity."

"I owe this to you; you are my happy thought. However, I wish for the time you're away, you will resume being my little angel, as I wouldn't like you to fall into temptation when you're away from me."

A long laugh relieved the heavy curtain of sadness that had fallen between them. "I will be a good boy, I promise, and I will call you every day from now on. Unfortunately, I have no idea when this will be possible, and with the time difference, this means it can be virtually at any time of the day or night," Kaine warned.

"I know, don't you worry. There won't be any chance I would feel annoyed if you call me in the middle of the night or during my workday. There, I will constantly keep the handsfree on, and whenever you call me, regardless of what I'm doing, I will be able to answer."

Kaine stretched his body and yawned loudly. He glared at the clock on the bedside table and pouted. "Tomorrow I have to wake up early, so it's better if I go to sleep."

"And since I'm going to drive you to the airport, I guess I also need to rest, or we'll never reach it safely," Mark observed, holding Kaine tightly against him, hoping to be able to fall asleep for the whole night in each other's arms.

*** 

The morning after, at three o'clock in the morning, the alarm mercilessly rang, announcing a new day and perhaps one of the most stressful, exciting, and also sad in many ways. With a loud groan, Mark opened his eyes, mumbling a curse against the clock.

His expression melted when he saw Kaine at his side, and once again, a deep sadness pervaded his soul as his eyes opened to a new day.

"Good morning!" Kaine greeted groggily, stretching his body on the bed. It felt too good to wake up with Mark at his side.

"You know what I think?" Kaine held himself tightly to Mark's chest.

"You are no longer leaving for Africa?"

"No, but it's a tempting thought," Kaine chuckled. "I was thinking that, once I'm back from my journey, we might start planning on living together. I love waking up by your side."

"Hmm..." mumbled Mark, kissing his forehead tenderly. "That's indeed a great idea. Once you're back, we'll think about who is moving where, or whether it would be better to move toward a neutral ground and buy a new house."

Kaine stood up and took a fast visual tour around. He would feel sorry to leave the house of his mother; he had too many memories connected to it. Departing felt like betraying her.

*I can't live my life depending on her memory, and besides, she would be happy if I move away because I have found the love of my life. Maybe I can rent this one just in case.*

"What are you thinking?" Mark wondered. He noticed the frown on Kaine's face as he collected his clothes to go for a shower.

"I was contemplating the possibility of renting this house instead of selling it away. It might be good to have it as an investment."

Mark shook his head. "Don't bother your mind with those questions; we'll have time to think about it when you're back. Now, let's focus on what's coming up soon. And, more specifically, about reaching the airport in time for your flight."

As Kaine was going for a shower, Mark decided to save time and prepare breakfast. *Starting with a strong coffee or I will fall asleep driving the car.*

He liked Kaine's house and perhaps he could move in with him. "This would be a better solution. At least there will only be me who has to relocate, rather than both of us."

"Were you saying something?" Kaine wondered as he reached the kitchen.

"I was thinking aloud, and I was considering it would be better if I come to live here."

Mark placed the plate with scrambled eggs and some toast on the table, pouring coffee for them.

" I can't wait to return and start living together. This looks great, generally, I don't even have the time to eat at home, and I have something fast from the cafeteria on the ground floor of the building where I work. Do you always make breakfast at home for yourself?" Kaine wondered munching his toast.

"I do, and I prepare something more than this. I believe you'll need someone to take care of your nutritional needs. You can't always eat '*something fast*' to save time."

Kaine was impressed. He'd rediscovered the pleasures of cooking, but he still considered breakfast something overrated.

"You're right, and things will change once we're living together."

Within another half an hour, they were ready to leave the house. "I will take care of your house during your absence. I've noticed you have some flowerpots which will need to be watered or they will die. Do you need me to collect your mail too?" Mark wondered.

"Uh... sure, I'd almost forgotten about it. I would appreciate it if you could do that. I'm sorry I didn't even remember to ask you about it."

"No problem. I asked because I was ready to take care of it. Besides, if I move here to live with you, I'll also need to start getting familiar with the house."

Kaine looked at him without reply. *I can't find the words to express my gratitude for having found a man like Mark in my life. Whatever I have done to deserve him, I wish I could repeat it for eternity.*

A sudden silence fell between them. Perhaps it was because it was early in the morning and the sun hadn't yet risen, or maybe it was because there were too many things to be said, and a little time to tell them all. Whatever the reason, they continued driving for the rest of the trip in silence until they reached the parking garage of the airport.

Kaine peered at the clock; there were still three hours until the departure of the plane. "At least I won't be late." He unbuckled the seatbelt.

"I would have never allowed you to miss this adventure. I know how passionate you are about your career. Despite our relationship is also important, we both need to fulfill our personal goals and aspirations." Mark held Kaine's hand.

"I love you so much," Kaine purred, reaching Mark's mouth, living only for the second their lips would touch and melt together in a kiss that meant everything for them.

Mark could taste Kaine's tears through their lips. "Why are you crying, baby?"

"Because I'm sure I won't be able to stay away from you for such a long time. Because I have never felt so happy in my life, and I tremble at the sole thought that something could keep us apart."

Wiping his tears away Mark parted from him. "Nothing will divide us. Nothing and no one. Now get on the plane, call me when you arrive at your destination, and you will see everything will be fine. This period of separation will help us to cope with all the issues that might happen in our relationship. We will be stronger."

"I already miss you so much," Kaine replied, holding himself to Mark.

"So do I, but now, you need to hurry, or you will be late for the plane."

***

As they reached the check-in area, Kaine could spot almost immediately the rest of the team who was supposed to travel with him to Africa. They all were still sleepy, when instead, he was so excited he feared he wouldn't be able to fall asleep for a single second.

He turned his gaze to Mark. "I think this is the time we have to part..." He bit his lower lip.

"I guess this is it. But you remember I will be waiting for you here. Just focus on your job and think about me only in your free time." Mark kissed his lips for the last time.

Kaine hugged him, wishing he could pack him and bring him wherever he would go. "Take care of yourself. I will call you later tomorrow, I guess."

"Call me at whatever time you can. As you know, I will be expecting your phone call 24/7. Have a safe trip!" Mark hushed, parting from him.

He watched Kaine walking to his colleagues, who greeted him with their tired expressions.

With a melancholic smile, he turned himself and walked to the car, ready to return home and to his work. *I wonder whether I will have time for a small nap.*

He reached Kaine's house at sunrise. He glanced at his wristwatch; he could sleep for at least another hour. "I'll set the alarm on my phone and take the opportunity to go and rest on his bed, where I can still find Kaine's scent."

He didn't have time to undress, but he still wrapped himself in the sheets where he'd spent last night with his boyfriend. He wasn't sure he could fall asleep, but he wanted to enjoy the illusion of having him still there for a while.

When the alarm clock finally rang, he realized he hadn't only been able to take a nap, but also to dream. He couldn't remember exactly what he dreamt, but he was sure it was about Kaine and his journey.

"I hope everything will go smoothly. I already miss him badly," he moaned as he stood up. He brought a change of clothes for the night and, before going to work, he indulged himself in a long shower. He still felt tired due to the little time he'd slept and was almost tempted to call his supervisor and take the day off.

"No, if I don't go and think about something else, I'll go crazy," he considered as he went to prepare a stronger coffee.

He took a round of the house to ensure everything was fine and left. "I'll be back tomorrow to water the plants and make a general check of the house, but I won't sleep here."

He closed the door and went to his car, ready for another working day and a whole year without Kaine.

*** 

125

As time passed by, and the boarding time got closer, the crew began to feel excited. Perhaps they didn't yet realize or even believe they would track a lost tribe that was possibly still alive and hiding in the middle of the Congolese side of the African rain forest.

"When Dr. Luther told me I was chosen to be part of the expedition to Africa, I thought I was going to die." Jenna smiled from ear to ear. "I have never been there, and it has always been a place I promised myself to visit."

"I have been to Africa several times, but never in this same area. I'm thrilled. Perhaps not to be visiting Africa itself, but because of this tribe. For centuries researchers and adventurers have been searching for it. Those who claimed to have found it weren't ever able to take pictures of anything belonging to them – not artifacts or camps, or people. Some others simply disappeared in their search, yet there are also people like Dr. Murdock who returned from a presumed disappearance," Kaine explained.

"Obviously we are going, not only to search for a lost civilization, but we might get swept up into an ancient curse," Lawrence replied, keeping his voice slightly lower than usual as if he didn't want to concede believing in curses.

"Oh, come on!" Jenna yelled, pushing him. "You can't believe this mumbo jumbo!"

"Well, no... it's not that I believe, but whether it's a question of magic, or because people have been kept prisoners or killed, the whole situation is to quite mysterious," Lawrence protested.

"In my opinion, there are indeed a lot of rumors about them. Not everything is true, and I think we should avoid falling into the trap of an easy scapegoat, like that of an ancient curse or ruthless killers. We will get better information about everything the day we find them or by talking to Dr. Murdock. He will certainly reassure you about any hidden threat." Kaine chuckled at Lawrence's hypersensitivity.

Nevertheless, he was still thinking about the strange hallucinations he'd had recently. *To be honest, if I have to connect all the legends and the visions I had, I could almost believe those tales about a cursed tribe are not all fantasy. Besides, even in the craziest story, there is a foundation of truth.*

He suddenly turned grave as he started to consider the warnings he received from the ghost of his mother.

"Hey, why are you now so serious?" Jenna wondered.

"Oh... I was thinking about something else that popped into my mind. Something about the management of my house," Kaine lied, considering there wasn't any good reason to spread panic through the team.

They needed to be reassured that there would be nothing to fear besides getting malaria or other diseases not covered by the vaccinations they'd received. *Supernatural and paranormal are banned on this journey. Everything must be based on truth and scientific evidence.*

"Haven't you given your house keys to someone you trust to take care of it from time to time? We will be away for a prolonged period, and anything can happen. As for me, I left them to my sister. She lives nearby, and she will go there every weekend to check everything is in order and to empty the mailbox," Lawrence said.

"I gave them to my boyfriend, but I'm not sure I have explained to him everything that needs to be checked regularly. I will have to send him an email as soon as I reach the hotel."

"Talking about technology," Jenna wondered. "Is there a place to be used as a headquarters? We will need a minimum of steady electricity flow, a reliable internet, and satellite connection. I'm not sure whether these things can be arranged in Africa, but if we're going to stay there for an undefined period, they should already be set up."

"Don't you worry, Dr. Luther and Dr. Murdock have thought about the logistics and the requirements, and I believe they have organized all the necessary arrangements. We will meet Dr. Murdock at the airport. He promised to plan our pickup in case he won't be able to come personally." Kaine observed the departure screen. "We need to start heading to the gate, or we will never board the plane."

"I've never traveled first-class. Do we have the financial support of other organizations?" Lawrence wondered as he looked at his flight ticket.

"I believe so, besides this tribe has been sought for centuries without any conclusive results. As I mentioned before, many clues give us a strong idea of their existence, yet nobody before could either return or convince the members of the tribe to be photographed. I am sure many organizations would pay a lot to be able to finally get the credit for the discovery. This is going to be huge!" Kaine exclaimed.

"What if those people do not want intruders in their territory?" Jenna wondered.

"Then we kindly get the fuck out of their sight." Lawrence walked back a couple of meters with his hands in front of him.

They all laughed and reached the gate, ready to leave for the longest journey of their lives.

*** 

Jason was sitting at the bar as usual, but this time, he was not drinking whiskey. Omar scrutinized him, caught up entirely in his thoughts and considerations. He'd never seen Jason in such a state.

Since he walked into his bar the first time, he had the careless expression of a man who had lost everything and didn't have any chance of getting anything back. He was resigned to his destiny like a ship at the whim of a storm.

"Boss, what's wrong?" he wondered.

Jason caressed his chin and gave a fast stare at Omar. He was freshly shaved, and his hair well-combed, like he had an important meeting. Yet, it seemed like he wasn't in a hurry to go anywhere. "Nothing and everything, my friend," he answered vaguely.

"Do you want a glass?" Omar proposed, taking the bottle of whiskey.

Jason raised his hand. "No, not this time. I have a meeting, and I need to be sober; things are going to change, and I'm not sure they are going to change for the best."

"Is the guy you were talking about coming soon?"

"Yes, he will be here tonight. I have promised to go and get him from the airport." He stood up as if he was leaving the place. "I don't like this situation; I don't like it at all."

Omar narrowed his eyes, smirking as if Jason had said some sort of nonsense, but then he remembered who was behind the whole story of Jason's life, and turned suddenly serious. "I hope you are overreacting, or we will all have to be worried."

"You have no reason to be concerned; this is a matter between Her and me, and eventually this guy who is arriving soon with his team of researchers." He started walking toward the exit, and without turning his eyes to

Omar, he waved his hand. "I hope to be your only white customer here, at least on a steady basis."

"Take care, Mzungu!" Omar replied, lazily cleaning the counter.

Jason reached the door and snapped his fingers to Azizi. "I need someone to drive me to the airport in Beni."

Azizi smiled, grabbing the AK-47, lying on an old barrel on the veranda. "You got the right man, Boss. Do you need to go right now?"

"I need to be there in seven hours; I guess we have plenty of time. What are the road conditions?" Jason wondered, hoping to reach the destination without risking being stuck in the middle of nowhere. *As if I'm somewhere here!*

"All the ways are in decent condition, as it hasn't rained much recently, but we'd better go now. Are you expecting guests?"

"At least a team of five people..." Jason replied, uncertain whether there would be the need for another car.

Azizi opened his mouth, surprised. "I might not be enough; if you give me one hour, I can gather two jeeps and a few other guys. There has been some activity in the Ituri region, and we don't want to risk the safety of none of those people."

Jason nodded. "Great, I will be waiting for you here. Don't be late. I need to get those people in seven hours and bring them to the village."

"Don't you worry, within one hour we will be leaving, and we also reach the airport well in advance to take care of the route back to the village safely."

Azizi left the place and started up the engine of his jeep, moving as fast as he could.

Jason smiled. "I might miss this place and those people if I ever get my freedom and decide to return home."

He sat on the barrel where the AK-47 was. He grabbed a napkin from his pocket and wiped the sweat from his forehead. "This heat and humidity are the things I will never miss if I have the chance to leave. For once, I wish I could once again experience the chill of the snowy environment, breathing the crisp thin air of the mountains."

He closed his eyes with a slight smile on his face, trying to bring back to his memory the feelings that seemed lost in a faraway time. "It doesn't even feel like ten years. It feels like centuries ago," he whispered, still glancing at those memories behind his closed eyes.

# CHAPTER 10

Kaine and the rest of the team reached the civil airport of Beni in the Democratic Republic of Congo after quite a turbulent one-hour flight from the International airport of Goma.

The first thing they noticed was the complete difference between the two airports. This one, appeared to be an unofficial one used mostly by the United Nation's mission, as the presence of the white vehicles with the UN letters testified.

The landing lanes were not paved, and the process was not smooth, making them also wonder about the condition of the equipment they were carrying in the cargo.

"Gosh, here is hot indeed," complained Jenna as they got out of the plane and started walking to the terminal for the immigration routine.

"Get used to it, since depending on the place we will be lodged, we might find it a luxury to have running water, let alone AC," Kaine warned.

"If we're not going to have water, how are we supposed to wash ourselves?" Lawrence wondered with a disgusted grin.

Kaine smirked. "You will get creative about it, I'm sure."

Jenna shook her head, wondering why she'd ever agreed to come to that place on the planet.

When they finally could collect all their luggage and equipment, they reached the hall where the only white man waiting was Dr. Murdock.

Jason took a general glimpse of the team and wondered how they would be able to stand the Congolese lifestyle. *And when I'm talking about it, I'm not referring to the one in the largest cities; I'm talking about the villages scattered at the border with the National Park, in the rain forest.*

He shook his head hopelessly, and wearing his best smile, he walked toward them.

"Good afternoon, you must be Dr. Kaine Martin, am I wrong?" Jason greeted. "Welcome to Africa, your home for the next few months."

Kaine smiled and shook his hand. "It's a pleasure to meet you in person."

"Did you have a good trip? I know the flight between Goma and here is probably not what you expected. I hope the one from New York was at least better."

Jenna beamed with a sarcastic grin. "The first leg went fine, but this last hour was a real nightmare. I'm still wondering how we landed alive."

Jason was amused at that naivety of the first-time traveler to Africa. "You will have many other occasions to wonder how you were able to survive, believe me, but let's go to our cars. I have arranged for three jeeps, considering the equipment you are carrying. I hope I calculated it right."

As he saw Jason coming out from the terminal building, Azizi gestured for the others to help them to get their luggage and help the travelers on the vehicles. "It's not the best thing to drive night-time, but the route I was considering should be safer, although a bit longer. We might be there in three hours, compared to one and a half, but at least we will make it alive."

"A-alive?" Jenna wondered, concerned.

"We are in the Ituri territories, and the conflicts have never ended. Then, when we are safe from their possible attacks, we will be in the territory where the LRA rebels are operating. Fortunately, the latter hasn't been recently active in this area, so we might get lucky after all."

"Where in this world have you brought us?" Lawrence started to become alarmed.

"Welcome to Africa, and most of all, welcome to The Democratic Republic of Congo!" Jason chuckled, amused.

Kaine knew perfectly what the deal was when traveling in Africa, and safety was always going to be the first concern. Although he'd never traveled to the DRC, he had been reading enough to get a good idea about the place they were going to stay. So far, everything was exactly the way he expected it to be.

He observed Jason and each of his moves. He was a reasonably good-looking man of an undefined age. His addiction to alcohol was apparent by the slight shake of his hands, but it was something he could control. He appeared to be amused by the team of researchers who resembled aliens coming from another planet. Nevertheless, there was something in his way of observing them that revealed a sort of concern, something worrying him on a deeper level and which he tried his best to hide.

*I have no idea what bothers you so much, but something tells me I will come to know about it soon, and*

*I'm not even sure I'm eager to discover what it is.* "Well, let's not waste time; the earlier we leave, the earlier we'll arrive," proposed Kaine.

"Sure, let's go," Jason urged, glancing at Azizi.

The journey was quite bumpy, as the roads they had to take were not the most comfortable, but Azizi chose the route to safety, not the one to comfort, and although extremely tired and wishing only to have a hot shower, they reached a village close by the one where Jason had his own house.

There he had organized one bungalow for each of them, to make them feel more like home. He provided them with the most basic needs for a westerner, which was running water, toilette, and some sort of working kitchen, equipped already with water and beers.

"Here we are," exclaimed Jason as they finally reached the village and the group of cabins.

"These are the bungalows that have been reserved for you guys. The people here did their best to provide you with the best service they could offer, and I hope you will be grateful for the help. Remember where we are, the fact that this is not a leisure trip, and that we couldn't arrange you a stay at the Kempinski."

They all scrutinize their accommodations, and they all were satisfied with the result, but the one who appeared to be the happiest, was Kaine. He knew what it meant to have proper sanitation in a place in the middle of nowhere.

He turned his eyes at Jason. "I'm impressed; these bungalows are simply perfect. More than I could expect."

"Glad to see you like it. You can choose the one you want; they are all the same," Jason agreed. "Did you have any dinner before arriving here?"

"Yes, we had something fast at Goma's airport. For today, we can call it quits, and we can retire to our cabins. Now, I'm not sure at what time we will be able to wake up tomorrow to start settling our camp, but perhaps we should meet at noon, to make sure we are all awake by then." Kaine observed the other members of the team, who was already half asleep.

"Please, can we go to sleep now? I'm not sure I'm still awake at this point. All I need is a bed to collapse in," Jenna wept, her voice almost trembling from exhaustion.

Jason nodded with a smile. "Of course, goodnight."

He started to walk away, when he considered it perhaps wise to talk with Kaine, who seemed to be, despite his age, a man who had more experience in Africa than many others.

"Dr. Martin," he called, turning toward Kaine.

"Yes?"

"May I have a chat with you? I understand you might be dead tired, but I need to talk to you in private." He held his own hands together, feeling almost guilty for keeping Kaine from his rightful rest.

"Is it indispensable? Can't we wait for tomorrow?" Kaine wanted only to fall on his bed, and besides, he needed to call Mark, as he promised.

"It won't take long, but there are a couple of things I believe you would like to know right away, before starting the planning for the research."

Kaine grimaced, but he understood by the tone of Jason's voice, he had something very important to tell.

With a long huff, Kaine walked toward Jason. "So, what's so important you need to tell me?"

"I will be fast, I promise," Jason assured, walking away from the others toward one of the bonfires that were kept to light the village. He invited Kaine to sit down with him and admired the flames dancing in front of him.

"I know you believe, or at least you hope this expedition will bring your name to the center of the scientific community. Nevertheless, I need to warn you, this might not be what is going to happen. Finding the lost tribe might mean that whatever you'll see, witness and hear shall remain within yourself, and nobody in this world should come to know about it."

Kaine scrutinized him, wondering whether he was trying to scare him, discourage him, or simply because he was drunk. "I don't know what you're talking about. We haven't yet found the tribe. We haven't even started the search for it."

Jason brought his hands to his head as if he was struggling to prevent it from exploding. "More than hundreds of years of research have lead many researchers here to this exact place where we are standing. They began a long time ago; you are continuing an endless and perhaps hopeless search. You need to concentrate on different goals than the glory and fame you will get, in case you will find it. You need to focus your attention on what you can learn from them, and your contribution to their lives. You can't consider your research selfishly one-way. This is not about you; this is also about the future of a tribe that might want to keep themselves away from the rest of the world."

"This was exactly what Nora warned me about..."

"Then, if you don't want to listen to me, at least listen to this girl who seems to be your friend. She gave you a bit of great advice," Jason suggested.

137

"I feel like you know more than you want to tell. Am I wrong?"

"I know something, but less than you think I do. Yet, there will be a time when I will tell you what happened to me and why I decided to remain here in Africa. For now, I needed only to warn you about the possibility of returning home with no results, regardless of the outcome of this expedition..." Jason replied, standing up from the rock. "To be honest, I wasn't expecting more people than you to come here. The presence of the rest of the team wasn't something I was forecasting."

With an amused chuckle, Kaine stood up as well, ready to go to sleep. "Times have changed. Nowadays, the technology requires more than one single man. But you might be right if you mean that things also got more complicated. I wasn't counting on the fact that the rest of the team envisaged something so radically different from what they were familiar with. Some of them never traveled to Africa, and I feel a bit responsible for their difficulty in adapting to the primitive lifestyle we are going to experience here. Nevertheless, it's good for them to see what's going on outside their perfect world."

Jason patted Kaine's shoulder. "I will see you tomorrow at noon," he said, walking away.

"Where are you going?" Kaine thought Jason was also going to stay in the same place as them.

"My home is in another village, and in the morning, I need to teach the kids. I will be back here to help you organize the search."

Kaine nodded. He felt his question was silly. *Of course, he has his own house and not necessarily here in the same place. I have forgotten he made a new life here in Africa. I wonder whether I will ever know what happened to him, or*

138

*if there will be many things I will have to guess. Dr. Murdock is a living mystery.*

Slightly tilting his head, he left, striding in the other direction toward his bungalow. All the other members of the team were already inside their own, judging by the lights filtering from the windows.

He grabbed his suitcase and walked into the cabin reserved for him. He switched on the light and remained for a moment to observe the place, which would become his home for an undefined period.

"That is not bad at all. Basic but cozy."

After a small tour, he grabbed his mobile phone and dialed Mark's telephone number. He guessed he was still at work, but he gave him permission to call him at whatever time of the day or night.

"Hello." Mark's familiar voice felt immediately at home, but also gave Kaine an unspeakable sense of homesickness. He was missing him too much.

"Hi there, baby! How are you?" Kaine greeted.

"Kaine!" Mark exclaimed happily. He was using his headphones and replied without even checking who was calling him. "That's the voice I was wanting to hear. How are you? Are you already at the hotel?"

Kaine chuckled. "I'm far from any kind of civilization. We have been organized with bungalows in a local community living at the border with the National Park, so no hotels whatsoever. Nevertheless, the cabins are quite cozy and functional with all the basic needs. I'm impressed and satisfied."

"You will have to take pictures and send them to me; I'm so curious to see what Africa looks like. The only places I have seen it was on the documentaries and the images of the travel agencies or blogs," Mark pleaded, as he went to sit on a chair of the laboratory where he was working.

"I will, for sure, take as many photographs as possible, but one day we will have to come together here. Images can't give a complete idea of what Africa looks like. Perhaps, next year, when I take a long holiday from my work, we might return here, but this time not in a conflict area and in a good hotel," Kaine chuckled, leaning on the bed.

"I'm waiting for that, but mostly I'm waiting for you to come back. The journey was pretty long. How do you feel?"

Kaine stretched his body on the bed, glancing at the fan on the ceiling. "I feel like I could sleep for another year. Nevertheless, tomorrow we will start working at noon, just to give everybody the chance to recover from the jet-lag and the tiredness."

"What time is it there now?"

"It's almost eight in the evening, and I'm already on my bed."

Mark smiled at the image of Kaine sleepy on the bed in a place lost in Africa. "I will let you sleep then. This can be the time we can call each other, as it might be the time you have quit your working day and we can have a chat. Generally, at this time, my day is almost over, and I can take it a bit easy."

Kaine yawned loudly. "Let's do so, baby. You can expect my call between eight and ten in the evening, local time. I also miss you terribly. There isn't another place I wish to be now but in your arms. It won't be an easy test for our relationship, but I'm sure we can make it."

With a nod, Mark considered the challenge of being away from each other for a prolonged and undefined period. *One year is a long time...*

"Of course, we can make it. But now you'd better sleep. I'm sure you will need all your energy to carry out your job there. I'll be taking care of your home and waiting for your call. Everything will be fine; don't you worry. I love you."

It felt so good to hear those last three words; he felt like he could endure everything just for their sake. "I love you too, Mark, but now, my eyes are closing."

"Good night," Mark replied, hanging up.

Mark remained staring at the phone with a sad smile on his face. It felt good to hear his voice again and knowing that everything went smoothly. That was at least a sort of consolation, and it felt like it could be enough.

He had been looking for some information about the place Kaine was going to research, and nothing was good news.

Although there wasn't an open conflict, the war wasn't over. The rebels considered tourists an excellent way to finance their arsenal and the continuing of their belligerent actions. *Most of them don't even know or remember what they are fighting for... This is such nonsense!*

Kaine lazily undressed, getting ready for the night. He was a bit hungry, but the tiredness won over any other feelings, and as he switched off the lights, he fell immediately asleep, hoping not to be disturbed for the additional fifteen hours left before the meeting with Jason.

***

Jason reached the village of the tribe. He wasn't sure Akuna-Ra was expecting him, or if she'd already sensed his arrival, but he needed to know what he was supposed to do with the team of researchers.

He greeted a couple of girls who were passing by and faltered in front of the shack.

"What are you waiting for?" She asked, knowing he was hesitating outside.

With a smirk, Jason entered the shack and saw her facing the fire. "I guess you already know the reason for my visit."

He remained holding on at the entrance, observing her slender figure standing in front of the dancing flames, as if to interpret an ancient message coming from the spirits or other worlds.

"I haven't called you, so I presume you came on your free will. What peculiar behavior from a man who wishes to be as far as possible from here," she sneered, almost smiling.

"This is not a courtesy visit." He walked shyly toward the fire, wondering whether this was a good idea at all.

"So, the researchers have arrived. But I wish you to keep them searching and scanning the forest for some time. I will tell you when the young researcher will be ready to be introduced to the tribe." She raised her eyes to him. "I'm not inclined to take risks the way I risked with you. For this reason, I need to better understand his nature, whether he is a deceptive snake like you or a trustworthy person."

Jason narrowed his eyes, wishing nothing else but to kill her. He clenched his fists, trying to control his breathing.

Without saying a word, he turned his shoulders to her and started to walk away.

"Where are you going? "She calmly asked.

"Where I can still find some appreciation and better company than a lousy witch," he hissed through his grinning teeth.

"This lousy witch saved your life," she remarked.

"You could have spared yourself. I have never asked to live this long." He turned to face her, pointing his finger toward her.

She could have smashed him like an unwelcome bug, and she felt like his insults were utterly inappropriate. "I might remember it next time."

He spread his arms apart. "Why not right now?"

"You lost your sense of sarcasm." She walked toward him; his face relaxed like she might have granted his wish.

*After all, she might not need me anymore. The kids are the only ones who still need me as a teacher, and the people of the village still find me useful.*

She grabbed his fists and unclenched them. Her eyes pierced his soul like a knife stabbing through a light curtain.

His eyes filled with pain and tears.

"What makes you cry?" she asked with a softer tone in her voice. "I seriously doubt it was my remark over your lack of loyalty."

"You will never understand, so I'm not going to bother trying to explain to you. Besides, you know your answer already, you can read through me..."

He averted his eyes from her without leaving her hands. He still felt attracted to her.

*Am I falling in love with her? Do I do what she wants to avoid useless pain or because I want her to be pleased with me? What do I want?*

She remained silent, listening to his thoughts. "I want to listen to it from your mouth. I want you to hear it too because I know you are not even able to say out loud what makes you bitter or cry." She kept holding his hands, already relaxed in hers.

"Maybe I don't want to hear it. Maybe I'm afraid it will make me suffer further, and that's something I'm trying desperately to avoid." He raised his glance at her. "I have enough troubles in my life to add something more."

She nodded with a strange smile he couldn't decipher.

"You're right, and I might not need you anymore. You might wonder why I keep you, not just alive, but around."

With a puzzled expression, he frowned, still keeping his eyes fixed on hers. He reluctantly released her hands and moved closer to reach her mouth. He didn't want her that night; he needed her.

His lips reached hers, and slowly they fused into a tender kiss, the first one they shared.

He knew he would regret kissing her and showing what his feelings were, but most of all, he was scared to admit to himself that even with the freedom to leave, Jason would have chosen to remain there close to her.

He held her tighter to himself. As their kisses become more passionate, he felt her arms crossing around his shoulders. She brought him back inside the shack, and as their lips parted, their eyes met, and what he could see appeared to be a different person.

"I hate myself for loving you the way I do," he uttered, hurt.

She opened her mouth as if to say something, but for the first time in her existence, words failed her and wished for once he could have the same gift of reading the minds of people, so to avoid telling him what she was feeling in her heart.

"Why should you hate yourself for that?" she asked in a lower tone of voice.

For the first time in her life, she felt like she should belong together with the soul of another man. And particularly a man who didn't belong to the same race, a man not built for eternity.

"I-I believe I should return to my bungalow," he murmured without moving as if to wait for her to stop him.

Instead, she turned her eyes to look at the fire and considered that perhaps it would be better if both of them reconsidered everything on their own.

"I guess it's a good idea; we need time..." she said in a hushed voice as if she wanted to talk only to herself or maybe to the spirits she was consulting before he arrived.

He smiled at her, and after one last caress on her face, he left.

# CHAPTER 11

At eight o'clock in the morning, Kaine's opened his eyes. The fan was still, and the heat was already oppressive. He wondered why he'd forgotten the previous evening to turn it on, and mainly how he could have slept the whole night without it.

"I might have been too tired to even think about it," he claimed, standing up from the bed. He realized he was drenched in sweat.

Slipping away the damp shirt he was wearing, he switched on the fan and walked toward the kitchen. "I'm wondering how I can still be alive after having sweated so many fluids."

The fan started to move the air in the bungalow, and although there was a lot of room for improvement, the breeze felt like being in heaven.

He changed the sheets on his bed, and lay back under the fan, enjoying the feeling of that whiff caressing his body.

He wasn't in any hurry to wake up, have breakfast, or take a shower; there were still four hours until the appointment with Jason, and he had every intention to rest as much as necessary.

"I didn't remember how badly jet-lag can hit," he said aloud. "I wonder if it's because of the conditions or because it has been quite some time since I've been traveling."

He hadn't had any time to check the night before whether there was a sort of starting package of food, at least to cover the breakfast for that day, or until they could figure out a way to get some groceries done.

He stood up from the bed and went to the kitchen. With some relief, the fridge was working and there he could find some bottles with water, a tetra pack of milk and some bread. He was curious to see what else he could find.

He felt like a child engaged in a treasure hunt, only in this case, he was looking for something to survive.

"I have to admit Dr. Murdock organized everything down to the littlest detail. I will have to thank him for his invaluable help." He closed the door of the kitchen cabinet and looked around, being able to find in his hunt a box of cereal, instant coffee, sugar, and bread.

He didn't need to eat lunch, mostly because he didn't feel hungry. Milk and cereal were enough for him, but most of all, he was constantly thirsty.

"I'm afraid the only thing I will need will be water, and for the moment, I have enough of it, but some grocery shopping will be the first thing we all should think about."

After a shower, he went once again to lie on the bed. He glimpsed the clock and decided he could have another two hours of napping. To be sure, he also set the alarm of his phone to ring, and as soon as he closed his eyes, he fell asleep.

After some time, he was awakened by an insistent knocking on his door.

Kaine peeked at the clock on his bedside table and realized that indeed, it had rung, but he ignored it completely. "I'm coming!" he yelled, jumping from his bed.

A smiling Jason appeared on the other side of the door. "Wake up!"

The other people of his team were waiting for him, but since he was already dressed and ready to leave, he stuffed his equipment in his rucksack and closed the door of his bungalow.

"I woke up this morning at eight o'clock, and after having a shower and breakfast, I thought I still had some time to have another nap..." Kaine tried to justify his delay.

Jenna shook her head. "Don't even try!"

"So, what's the plan?" Jason wondered, cutting the small talk.

"I believe we first need to get some groceries. I have no idea about the others, but at least in my bungalow, there was enough to cover a few breakfasts, and that's it. I guess the most important thing we should think about is water. Last night I sweated my life out of myself," Kaine proposed.

"Did you remember to turn on the fan on the ceiling? It might appear barely sufficient to move the air in the room, but in this case, it makes the difference between good night sleep and a bath of sweat," Jason pointed out, bending his head slightly to one side.

"No," Kaine replied seriously. "I just fell asleep on the bed, without noticing there was a fan on the ceiling or that I started feeling hot."

A burst of laughter raised louder among the small group, and the worries, tiredness and bad feelings of the previous day, were finally forgotten.

"Okay." Jason tried to recover from his laughter. "Let's do it this way. We are laughing, but you are indeed right, and the priority here is water. I will drive you to a small grocery shop not too far from here, where we can buy food and water. Then, we might want to set up a sort of headquarters. I have no idea about your equipment, so we might sit down for lunch somewhere and discuss everything we need to be ready to start. Afterward, I suggest we make a list and organize the work for the whole week."

They all glanced at him, unable to say anything. Evidently, having a person with his experience offered them a significant advantage. Although they knew these were the necessary steps, they could have never put them on a list as fast as he did.

"Well, what are we waiting for? Let's move!" Kaine rushed, interrupting the silence between them.

The whole organizational process took them the entire day, and only later, at about seven in the evening, did they settle on the best solution. Lawrence and Josh would share the same bungalow and use the empty one as a headquarters, where they could set up all the equipment, including computers, screens, drones, and scanners. They organized the schedule for the whole week, planning the area to be scanned with drones and on foot.

Jason made sure that the searched location was quite far from the place where Akuna-Ra's tribe was located.

"We might already start scanning tomorrow morning. I would suggest moving to the position where we can operate the drone in the morning. Therefore, we should leave from here before sunrise," Kaine suggested.

Jason nodded in agreement, keeping his eyes on the map.

"If we reach this position at six o'clock, we might have a chance to explore this whole area by noon," he proposed, drawing a circle on the map with his pencil.

"If you want to cover most of it, I suggest we split into two groups. One goes to scan with the drones in this part, which is the one covered by the thickest forest. And the other covers by foot this place, which is a bit clearer," Lawrence suggested.

"At noon, my team will return to the headquarters to prepare the drone-scanning images so the next day, we might spend it pinpointing the places that require a better exploration by the trekkers. I suggest to alternate days of reconnaissance with data interpretation," Jenna proposed.

Kaine nodded slowly, considering the plan. "Thinking about the climatic conditions, this makes a lot of sense. Being in the field every day might be too stressful, and without a clear analysis, we might miss much useful information."

"Not to mention that we need to be as effective as possible; we are not supposed to stay here for the rest of our lives. We have a restricted time to obtain results, whether positive or negative," Josh added.

"How much time do you have at your availability?" Jason wondered, trying to figure out a schedule between the search and the real finding of the tribe.

Kaine took a deep breath and held it for a few long seconds, narrowing his eyes to peer at Jason.

He exhaled. "I have no idea. We were talking with Dr. Luther about a period stretching between a few months to one year. But I believe the latter will be the time we are expected to have already returned home with our reports ready to be shown to him and the Organization. I think they want to have results, rather than 'no result.'"

Jason wiped his face with his hands. "It's always about money and time. For once, I would like to see someone interested more in what we can learn from our discoveries, than what we can earn."

He toured visually around the group of researchers in front of him. "That's one of the reasons why I decided to remain here. Your society is focused only on material gain, and never on intellectual growth..."

"If I don't recall it wrongly, you are also receiving generous compensation for your cooperation..." Josh pointed out.

"And of course, you think this reward will be spent on a better lifestyle, fancy clothes, a car. I have a school here; believe me, I will spend my allowance on their education, rather than on my personal gain. I wouldn't even know what to do with a bigger house or clothes... look around yourself." Jason turned and pointed with his fingers to the village they were in. "What would I need more money for, if not to share with this community?"

He felt calm and was not at all upset at what could have sounded like a rude remark. He understood that coming from western society, where individualism was worshipped to the extreme, they might have received a huge cultural shock.

*You will all understand it better once you've spent a few months here, and if any of you remain stuck as I did, it will be for your own good. I wonder whether this was a punishment or a chance to see the world from a different perspective. I should have taken it as a lesson since the beginning instead of crying over my misery.*

"Let's not start arguing over who is better. I am sure Dr. Murdock was not criticizing any of us in particular, but the way our society has developed." Jenna sensed the tension in the air. "We should all take this chance to experience other cultures and to learn something. Dr. Murdock is right; we should prioritize learning over earning."

Jason smiled at her. "I didn't mean to be rude to anyone."

***

In the evening, after having called Mark, Kaine walked to the window of his bungalow. The bonfires were burning bright, and he considered having some time to think about his life in front of the fire. He opened the door, paced toward one of the bonfires, and sat down, observing the dance of the flames.

He always liked to watch them; it felt almost mesmerizing, and in the night, in the proximity of the forest, without the noise pollution of the city, the sounds of the animals in the jungle became clear to his ears. He beheld the sky and couldn't recall having seen anything like that.

"I should absolutely bring Mark to see this beauty. Jason is right when he talks about cultural differences. Indeed, the lack of sanitation, of commodities that make our lives the way we know it, might sound like a nightmare. Yet, this is how we all were supposed to be, a part of nature, being ruled by it, and nothing else."

He closed his eyes and focused on the noises.

"Mzungu!" a quiet voice came to interrupt his thoughts.

Kaine turned his head to the direction of the voice and saw a man wearing only a pair of old jeans standing behind him.

"It's dangerous to stay out at night; you should return to your bungalow," he suggested, throwing more wood in the fire.

"Won't the wild animals be afraid of the flames?" Kaine wondered.

The man smiled and sat down at his side.

"The beasts in the forest are not the only reason why we keep the fires. The evil spirits are more dangerous, and those who wander endlessly in the forest won't be scared by a few gunshots," the man replied, glancing at him with a grave expression.

"What about you? Aren't you afraid?"

A broad smile creased his face marked by the age. "I am, but I also carry something that is going to protect me. I know the spells... Return to your bungalow and try to sleep."

Despite his smiling face, the stare in his eyes betrayed a particular concern for having someone who was not protected against the forces of the night.

Kaine stood up from the rock in front of the fire. "Thanks, and goodnight." He wasn't sure he could believe what the man said, but there was something in his voice that made him less doubtful.

"Remember to keep one candle lit during the night. The spirits won't come to bother your sleep," the man recommended as Kaine walked away.

*This is only mumbo jumbo. However, after the hallucinations I had and all the strange things that happened in my life since Dr. Murdock appeared, I feel the need to be more cautious.*

He reached his bungalow and closed the door behind him.

The air inside was already suffocating, and he wondered whether it would have been better, to keep the fan on at least starting from sunset.

153

A fast visual tour revealed the presence of a candle and a matchbox on the dresser in front of the window. "They obviously take seriously the threat posed by the supernatural forces of the night."

He chuckled as he lit the candle. He gazed outside and observed the man who had spoken to him, performing some sort of rituals in front of the fire. He considered it intriguing and found it difficult to tear his sight away from him.

"I need to remember to ask more about this ritual. Every legend and magical practice is born from some tragic happening in the past. I wish to understand what terrified them so much to keep them performing these rites."

*There are perhaps no records, but they still feel horrified, and the magic they brought stopped the curse...* A voice seemed to say as he was focused on following the man outside.

It was a tiny voice, like something carried by the whistle of the wind, but he was sure he could hear it and understood what it said.

He turned himself to face the room, to see whether there was someone, but he couldn't see anyone.

"Well, now I'm starting to become a bit worried; either I'm not completely alone in this room, or I'm going insane." He walked away from the window, feeling watched by whatever was in or out.

"This is ridiculous!" He grinned; his heart started racing in his chest. The only noises in the room were his shallow breathing and the soft swoosh of the blades of the fan.

His knees felt weak like he was soon going to fall on the floor, and his hands were shaking.

"What the heck is going on?" he questioned aloud as if expecting an answer from the ghost in the bungalow. "Why are you following me? Is it you, Mom?"

At that question, he was even more worried about his sanity, and when nothing answered him, he felt threatened.

He reached the kitchen to get some water; he hoped the reason for his state of mind was a lack of fluids. He started to drink, not knowing how much was enough to stop the restless feeling in his soul.

He sat down at the table and lit another candle. He felt like there was something genuine in the words of the man who was in charge of keeping the fires on at night.

He grabbed his head between his hands, knowing there wouldn't be any sort of sleep to be found.

He stared at the telephone on his bed and wondered whether it would be too late to call Mark once again.

"Well, it should be something like four o'clock in the afternoon or so. I doubt he's already sleeping, unless he's with someone else." He chuckled and considered that perhaps he would be the best person to talk to.

With his eyes steady on the telephone, he walked to the bed without any sustained thought in his mind, besides the desire of not being alone with his paranoia.

"Well, it seems like you're starting to miss me," Mark chuckled, amused and flattered at that unexpected call.

"I'm sorry to disturb you, baby. I just..." His voice started to tremble as if he was on the verge of a nervous breakdown.

"Kaine, sweetheart, what is going on there? Did something bad happen? Are you hurt?"

Mark was driving home and tried to speed up to reach his house as fast as possible, to be able to focus on whatever happened to Kaine.

"No, I- I think I'm just tired, and perhaps being in the middle of the forest, out of the civilized world..." he started to explain, as if losing the grip with his feelings.

"Kaine, now get a hold of yourself. Calm down and tell me what makes you so upset. I can't help you if I can't understand what's the problem!"

Kaine took a deep breath and closed his eyes. "I have heard something... okay, I will start from the beginning," he tried to collect his thoughts.

"During the night, here in the village, people are lighting bonfires. The reason is most probably to keep the wild animals away and to have some sort of illumination, in case anything happens. I thought it was a good idea to take a moment in front of the fire and listen to the noises coming from the forest, but then a man came, warning me about those evil spirits roaming in the night, looking for prey. He convinced me to return to my bungalow and remain there until the morning."

Mark relaxed, as he thought he understood where the discussion was going to lead.

After a short pause, Kaine resumed his story. "I returned to my cabin and lit a candle, which is what everyone does here during the night. As I watched outside the window, wondering about their superstitions, I could hear a tiny voice telling me about something that happened many years ago. Even before anyone can recall.

"I know I sound stupid, but I felt so scared that I absolutely needed to hear your voice to calm down."

"Kaine, you did the right thing, and in those circumstances, it's easy to get overwhelmed by the

156

conditions around you. You might have heard the whistle of the wind filtering through a crack and allowed your mind to reconstruct it in a way to fit with the local superstitions," he explained.

"Do you think so?" Kaine wondered, hoping to find comfort in his explanation.

"I know so," Mark assured as he opened the door of his house. "Now, I want you to get undressed and ready for the night if you haven't already. Then I want you to close your eyes and think about positive things. Think about how you have spent one day there, and that is one day less dividing us."

Kaine smiled and did as Mark suggested. When he was in his bed with the slight breeze offered by the ceiling fan, bringing some sort of relief to his senses, everything started to get better. The presence of the spirits he felt before he called Mark disappeared, and he was calmer.

"I feel like a fool," Kaine said.

"Don't feel that way. You're tired, in a foreign environment, far from my arms... Of course, you have nightmares, my poor thing!"

Kaine laughed and felt immediately better. He missed Mark terribly and was almost ready to quit everything and return home on the first flight he could book.

"I wish I could give up this expedition and run to your arms," Kaine muttered, keeping his eyes closed.

"Time will fly, don't you worry. Just try to focus on your job, and remember the earlier you get your results, the sooner you can come back home."

Kaine started to feel tired and looked at the clock with a loud and long yawn. "I think I'll go to sleep. I'll call you tomorrow evening after work."

"I'll be waiting. I love you," Mark replied.

"I love you too. Goodnight, babe."

As soon as he hung up the phone call, Kaine fell asleep like a baby, without caring about switching off the lights in the bungalow.

## CHAPTER 12

The morning after, the real work could finally start. The two teams split; one of them was guided by Azizi and the other three guards, armed to the teeth.

"What's your name again?" Jenna asked as they were driving to the destination they set up on the map.

The young man admired her with a bright smile. "My name is Azizi, and what's yours?"

"My name is Jenna," she averted her glance, shyly shaking his hand. "Let me ask you a question: why do we need so many armed guards? Are we going to some sort of dangerous territory?"

Azizi laughed. "Miss Jenna, DRC is dangerous territory; there isn't a place safer than another. The only thing, though, I can say for sure is that we have never been attacked by any militia in the villages in our area, but this is mostly a coincidence, I guess."

She felt flattered by being called 'Miss' and also a bit awkward. Everybody she had introduced herself to addressed her merely by name.

"You can just call me Jenna. What does your name mean?" she wondered curiously.

"It's a Swahili name, and it means 'precious treasure.' I'm not sure, though, if I have ever been such to anyone. What about your name?"

"I have no idea. I guess my parents just gave me this name because they liked how it sounded." She felt like blushing in front of his kindness.

"Well, Jenna, I can help you with that. Your name means 'white shadow;' it has a British origin."

She remained frozen and didn't know what she was supposed to say. "Thank you. Where did you learn the meanings of the names?"

"It's just curiosity, I suppose. I believe when a person receives his or her name, the whole character will shape to fit it," he replied, his expression turning grave, as from time to time, he observed outside to keep his eyes on the bushes.

"You will stay long enough to learn a lot about the people of Congo. This is the real heart of Africa, and some say you will fall in love once you visit it."

He turned his eyes suddenly as the car took a deeper hole on the road. Although he was talking casually with Jenna, his attention was never averted from what was happening around him. He turned himself to check on the map. "We are almost there. Omari, be careful there at that turn," he urged, navigating the driver.

Omari simply nodded, always keeping his eyes on the road.

***

After half an hour, they reached a clearance on the top of a hill. From there, they could efficiently operate their drones and scan a considerable area. As soon as the car stopped, the whole team got out and started to prepare for the scanning, while Jenna took a peek at the valley around.

The sun was rising on the emerald green forest, covered by a light veil of mist. From there, everything seemed peaceful, and the beauty of the scenery was simply breathtaking.

It was nothing like what she saw on television about African documentaries. The smell of the iron-rich earth, of the damp wood, the scent of the trees, with their contrasting harmony, brought tears to her eyes like she witnessed a sunrise after an eternal night.

With the starting of a new day, the jungle came back to a different kind of life. From the chirping of the night creatures that withdrew to its darker heart to sleep, the buzzing sound of insects, the dawn chorus of birds, and the whooping call of the monkeys rose to the sky. It echoed through rocks, trees, and bushes, reaching every little corner, louder and louder in an almost deafening orchestra. The mighty rain forest was awakening.

As the air became brighter, the light spread from the tops of the woods, fighting its battle against the night. The green color of the valley gleamed at the touch with the sun rays.

The night dew evaporated as the weather grew warmer, like a ghost gradually fading away in a puff of smoke with a final glow in the air.

Jenna felt overwhelmed by the richness of sounds and scents; she didn't even acknowledge the presence of Azizi coming closer. "I told you, you would fall in love with this country," he whispered.

She jolted as she returned to her reality. "This is so amazing. I feel like I have been blind for my whole life, and now I can finally open my eyes," she said, wiping her tears, unable to find any word to describe the richness of feelings she was experiencing with such a breathtaking view.

"If we have time, I will show you the mountain gorillas. Those are such amazing animals, and among all, the ones I respect the most. Of course, there isn't an animal I do not appreciate, but they are indeed my favorites," he explained.

"I so wish to see them. I hope to have some free time to also enjoy this stay here in Congo." With a pout she recalled her duties, glancing at her team that was ready to start the scanning.

"Jenna!" Josh yelled. "Are you going to help us or not?"

"Got to go!" she squeezed in her shoulders, returning to her work. "I'm sorry, I was caught in the admiration of the forest."

"Yeah, now get tangled in the exploration of what is under it and see whether we can get something done," He replied, his arms crossed over his chest.

As soon as the equipment was set up, the drone started its flight, silently gliding over the forest, taking imageries from the radar.

***

Jason was leading the group of anthropologists and guards on the more open stretches of the forest, where walking was more comfortable, and the observation of the different patterns on the ground could reveal the presence of something buried, which could have hinted an ancient civilization's ruins. The possibility that they had to deal with something already extinct, was something to be taken into consideration and every track should be followed.

Jason observed the equipment they used to scan the forest using thermal scanning and remote sensing radars.

*Anthropology is no longer the same as I remember when I started my career.*

He shook his head, wishing to have those toys at his availability when he was younger.

"Interesting gadgets you have," Jason chuckled.

"Yeah, with the advance of technology, our job has become much faster and easier, not to mention the level of precision we can reach. 3D modeling, the use of drones and scanning radars, has been a blessing for those who work in the field. Both archaeologists and anthropologists have found plenty of advantages to this," Kaine admitted, as they continued to walk on the uneven terrain. "Yet, I can see how being accustomed to walking in this kind of place is advantageous. I feel like all my joints are screaming in pain."

Jason explored around himself, and observing the whole team, he noticed how *those city folks will have a long way to go before they get used to trek for long distances on uneven terrain like those stretches of forest. Yet, they have no idea what actually advancing in the deep of the woods looks and feels like. It's nothing like the fancy movies where there's always a clear way through the trees. At least here you won't even be able to touch the ground; the roots and bushes create a continuous pattern over the earth.*

From time to time, he peered at the map to make sure they would stay outside the reach of the territory of the tribe of Akuna-Ra. *There will be time for them to get there, and to be honest, I might also make sure that only Kaine will remain here and have contact with them. The fewer who know about their existence and location, the safest it would be for everybody.*

Kaine followed the preliminary results of the scanning arriving in real-time on his tablet. Those were just raw images and needed to be analyzed, but they could give an idea of whether there was something that stood out immediately.

He stopped for a moment to regain his breath, with the humidity of the forest it felt like breathing water.

He sat on a log and gasped for air. "This heat is a killer!"

Lawrence didn't appear any better, and neither did the other guys, except for the guards and Jason.

"Let's have a rest; you're not used to walking in these climate conditions. It took me over ten years of living in this area to get accustomed to it. I don't pretend you to stand the heat and humidity so easily," Jason replied, glancing at the guards who were escorting them.

Jason peeked at his wristwatch and hummed. "We might think of having our lunch here and now. We've been walking for three hours; we all need to rest. Let's take an hour's break, and then we'll continue for another three hours before moving to the village. I suggest as soon as you return to the camp, you stretch your body if you don't want to cramp overnight. Tomorrow you will have a headquarter day, but if you don't do it properly, you will find yourselves unable to move for weeks. Trust me, I speak from experience."

He took a bottle of water and began to drink as much as possible. He knew that although the body wouldn't complain, it was too easy to get dehydrated.

He was glad to have some people around from the same country. He had started to feel a bit lonely in his forced exile.

Kaine and the other members of his team felt already exhausted. The deafening buzzing of the insects in the forest, the heat, and the humidity took their toll on their nerves. Yet, they tried to keep calm and focus on their job.

"I shouldn't have underestimated the physical challenges we were going to face. I'm afraid I approached this expedition like a trek in the park," Lawrence admitted, breaking the silence between them.

With a frustrated huff, Kaine wiped his forehead with his sleeve. "We all did. I've been to Africa other times, but mostly it was around Kenya and Tanzania and in better seasons. This time we didn't consider the fact that avoiding the rainy season meant only dealing with intense heat and the high humidity of the rain forest."

"Keep drinking, you have no idea how much you're sweating," Jason remarked, handing the bottle to him.

Allison, the technician who was there with them, didn't say a word. She was suffering a lot without complaining and considered it would be better to save her energy instead and keep drinking like Jason was suggesting.

Nevertheless, she was already dreaming of being on the airplane back home. *It's useless. I should stop thinking about home to avoid making things even more difficult. Perhaps if I believe that there won't be any return, I will start to react, and my survival instinct will kick in.*

She shook her head. *No, it doesn't work. If I had to be here for the rest of my life, I might consider suicide.*

Suddenly, she felt something crawling on her hand. Petrified, and terrified she didn't dare to peer at what it was, fearing it was some sort of poisonous spider or worse.

"Sorry, guys," her voice trembling. "Could you check what is climbing on my arm?"

Jason hurried over. "Ooh!" he marveled. "You should see this, it's magnificent." He tried to take the insect.

"Look!" He showed her a giant beetle.

Allison jolted, releasing a scream of terror at the sight of such a disgusting creature. "Throw it away, far from me!"

"Why? Don't be scared. Do you know what it is?" Jason asked.

The others became curious and gathered around him to have a better look.

"It's a Goliath Beetle. It's not easy to spot it. Well done, Allison!" he cheered.

Allison watched it from a due distance; that was the largest insect she'd ever seen, even in her wildest nightmares. Yet she also had to admit it was somehow fascinating. Perhaps its size and the fact that she couldn't see anything threatening calmed her racing heartbeat.

They all wanted to touch it, to understand how it felt, that shiny striped beetle.

"Come on, Allison, try to touch it," Lawrence dared.

She got closer, but as soon as she stretched out her hand, it spread its wings and started to fly, prompting a long high-pitched scream from Allison.

"You sound like a screeching monkey," one of the guards laughed.

She brought a hand over her mouth, feeling scared, still recalling the flying monster.

"Well, I guess it's time for us to resume our journey. We'd better focus on something else, and as usual, watch where you're stepping. You won't mind killing a spider, but you don't want to piss off a black mamba."

With a long sigh, they all prepared their gear and resumed their trek again, following the lead of Jason, who had the area to be covered on the map.

*** 

Akuna-Ra had just come out of her shack when Okumi came running to her.

"Mistress, I was sent by our queen to bring you to her place. She needs to talk to you," he panted, after having run as fast as he could.

"I know," she whispered, concerned, glancing at the direction where the queen, Kaiphindi, was.

Okumi scrutinized her, wondering why Akuna-Ra didn't already go there if she knew she was waiting. He lowered his gaze and remained silent, holding on for any command.

Without saying a word, Akuna-Ra started walking. She knew there was an open issue that needed to be solved, *and the sooner, the better.*


Kaiphindi was seated on her throne inside the shack where she received her people, sensing the arrival of her witch doctor and friend, Akuna-Ra. Their souls had been connected by a tight bond since they were born. They were both chosen ones for the delicate task in the tribe they were called to undertake.

Akuna-Ra entered the shack. "My soul sister!"

Kaiphindi stood up from the throne and walked toward her. "I could feel the turmoil in your heart. I believe we needed to talk about what is happening."

With a lowered gaze Akuna-Ra, unable to face the stare of her queen, waited.

"What is going on with the people you have summoned here? I thought only one was supposed to get in touch with us?" Kaiphindi asked, holding Akuna-Ra by her shoulders.

With a slight shake of her head, Akuna-Ra raised her eyes to peer into hers. "There will be only one who will be brought here. I was also expecting to have one person arriving. I'm afraid we have underestimated the changes of the times. Technology advances, and this might require more people than we could have fathomed."

Their hands held each other's, and Kaiphindi smiled at her. "Do you think this young researcher can be trusted?"

"I'm taking my time to evaluate him. So far, it appears as if he could be more trustworthy than Jason, or any other we needed to stop..."

"We need to be sure; we can't risk anymore. The more people who get to know about our location, the more difficult it's to convince them to keep the secret."

Akuna-Ra walked away from her, looking around the room. She recalled all the memories brought back by the place, and smiled at them. *Yet, this is not home...*

Scanning her thoughts and feelings, Kaiphindi observed her every movement. "There is something you are not telling me. I'm wondering whether you have been hiding this secret also from yourself."

Afraid of her queen's possible reaction, Akuna-Ra's heart started to race in her chest. She didn't shift from her position and closed her eyes.

The gentle touch of Kaiphindi's hand on her shoulder seemed to calm her spirit. "You might have been too harsh on yourself for too long."

"No, I can't pollute the connection with the spirits of the forest with human feelings; I'm not allowed..." Akuna-Ra whimpered as tears welled in her eyes, and her face contorted into a sad mask.

"To fall in love?" Kaiphindi guessed.

At those words, Akuna-Ra toughened her expression, clenching her fists. "NO!" she yelled, turning her eyes to her. "I can't allow human foolishness on me; I'm not supposed to endanger the strength of my connection with the spirits for a single man. Regardless of whether he is Jason or anyone else. I'm the bridge between the two worlds!" She pounded her fist against her chest.

"Have you questioned the wraiths?"

"I don't need to..."

"You might have misunderstood the nature of your connection. My soul sister, my heart is bleeding seeing you so unhappy and fighting against yourself. You are too mighty an opponent to fight against. There will come a day when we might leave, and you need to have a clearer knowledge about what you want to do and how to deal with your heart." Kaiphindi embraced Akuna-Ra tightly to herself.

Akuna-Ra felt once again relieved in his embrace and wished to stay longer in her arms. She held her soul sister to herself and allowed the positive feelings to spread all around her body and soul.

She didn't feel any hurry to return to her duties; the spirits were better summoned and communicative at dusk and in the middle of the night. She might have asked them one more time, and perhaps she would have been surprised by their answer.

For centuries she had denied herself any human feelings, as she believed they would have created an interruption to the bridge between the underworld and her. She feared this would have contaminated her, and having her power diminished was something she couldn't afford. Her magic was all her tribe could rely on to remain safe and secret.

Akuna-Ra parted from Kaiphindi. "I will question the spirits once again, as you suggested. But I'm already expecting a negative outcome. I rarely fail when I interpret their messages and requests, and to my understanding, they were quite clear."

"This is something which happened centuries ago. Perhaps it was due to your inexperience that you might have misunderstood. You have questioned them only once, and maybe it would be wise to ask about your happiness one more time," Kaiphindi insisted.

Pursing her lips, Akuna-Ra nodded and turned herself to walk in the direction of the door, ready to think about herself in the silence of her shack. She felt she could better concentrate in front of the fire.

"Thank you for your words, my soul sister. I appreciate your love and be sure I do exchange it with equal intensity."

Without waiting for any reply, Akuna-Ra left the shack of Kaiphindi, and with a hopeful smile on her face, she walked toward her place.

# CHAPTER 13

At dusk, Kaine returned to his shack from the one they used as headquarters. They had spent the whole evening trying to organize the data to be analyzed the next day.

A strong wind seemed to be willing to wipe out the forest, and people closed themselves inside their shacks. Kaine glanced at the man who was taking care of keeping the bonfires on and wondered how he could manage with such a storm.

Suddenly the wind stopped, and the place was immersed in an unnatural stillness.

The man noticed Kaine and walked toward him. "Hurry to your bungalow, Mzungu. The spirits have been summoned; it's not safe to be outside."

Kaine shook his head and hurried back to his place, sensing the intensity in the silence, as if there was indeed some supernatural force gathering there.

He wondered who was summoning the wraiths, for which reason, and what kind of entities they were. "This place gets weirder and weirder. I have been in touch with many African tribes and beliefs, but never in my life have I felt something so strong as in this place," he talked to himself as he entered the bungalow.

He smiled when he realized he was locking his door more carefully than the previous day.

"I have been here only for two days, and I already feel influenced by their mumbo jumbo nonsense," he laughed as he lit the candle.

He tried to laugh at himself, but he couldn't deny feeling uneasy. There was a storm in his soul matching the one going on outside. He listened to the noises of the night, but it was like every single insect, animal, and sound was cast away from that particular spot of the Earth. The silence was complete, and only his heartbeat and his breath were to be heard.

"This is unnatural. If the animals feel so threatened not to make any noise it might easily mean that man wasn't lying. Does magic really exists and in this place it's so strong it influences every single living being?"

He sat down on his bed and glimpsed the clock. It was late, and the strain he was feeling in his muscles reminded him of Jason's recommendations.

Therefore, not willing to risk being sore and immobile for an entire week, he stood up and started to stretch his body. The first attempt felt like his joints and muscles had lost all flexibility, and they hurt like hell.

Kaine didn't allow this to stop him and insisted on stretching every single muscle for as long as it took to feel some elasticity blessing his body.

"The next step, I suppose, is to drink more water. In this heat, there is no such thing as drinking too much. My body will certainly sweat it away quite soon."

He reached the kitchen and lit a candle there before getting some water. He turned to face the table, and although there wasn't any draft, the flame started dancing like crazy.

He remained for a while, observing, and wondering about it. He tried to reach it with his hand to see whether there was indeed some sort of whiff coming, perhaps from the window or some other part of the log wall.

Carefully, as if he was catching a butterfly, he reached the flame with his hand, surrounding it to find an explanation for such a phenomenon. The air around the candle was still, but he retreated immediately when he felt it almost freezing.

His heart started to race.

"I-is there anyone here?" he asked in a feeble, barely audible whisper.

There was no answer, but the flame began dancing faster as if to reply to him with some sort of sign.

"Okay, there is somebody." His breath was short, and his head felt light, but he tried by all possible means to keep calm. "Do you mean any harm to me?"

At his question, the fire danced slower into a wavy dance. "I'm not sure whether I can interpret this as a confirmation of your good intentions. If you don't mean to harm me, as I believe and hope, could you, please, stop the movement of the flame?"

The light of the candle doubled its length, and then it stopped completely remaining stationary as usual.

"Thanks... I guess I'm just going to my bed and try to fall asleep. I appreciate your willingness not to hurt me."

That said, he walked back to his bed and undressed himself to get ready to sleep. He remained looking at the fan on the ceiling, feeling comforted by its movement and by the slight relief it gave to his body.

Almost mesmerized by the rotation of the blades, the buzzing of the motor, and the tiredness he'd accumulated during the day, he fell asleep.

***

At the shack of Akuna-Ra, the spirits answered her summoning and gathered around the fire burning in the middle of the room.

Her eyes were closed, and in an ancient language, she formulated the questions for the future of her tribe, of the villages they were protecting, and last, but not least, also for herself.

She had no idea what she was supposed to do, and as a servant to the main forces of the night, as a bridge to connect the underworld and the world of the living, she needed an answer.

It wasn't just asking about whether she was allowed to have human feelings she had duly denied herself for centuries. She wanted the ancient spirits to clarify what was the warmth she felt when she was kissed by Jason. He didn't belong to her tribe nor to her world, and indeed, he wouldn't be granted the chance to come with them once their task was over.

"What is the meaning for me to have those feelings? Why bother if I need to say goodbye?"

The air in the shack suddenly went still for a moment, and an abrupt vortex roaring from the flames, and with the fury of a wild blaze, it engulfed the whole room, burning everything without consuming.

Like eyes of fire, they glared at her.

She remained composedly seated in front of the flames, patiently waiting for an answer, hoping perhaps for a negative response to make her decision easier and her pain milder.

174

"What do you want?" The blaze breathed.

"I'm humbly requesting to see my heart, to understand what I feel," she calmly answered, keeping her head lowered without opening her eyes.

"Do you want to see your heart? Then open your eyes and see through the flame, my daughter."

Akuna-Ra was not prepared for such an answer. Being brought in front of her heart was something she had always been scared of, although that was her request. She knew from experience those who could have seen their own soul through the sacred flames would have lost their mind discovering the truth they preferred to ignore.

"Open your eyes and look at it," the voice repeated.

She inhaled deeply and slowly opened her eyes. The flames took shape, and she saw all the times she had been following what she considered her duty of purity from human feelings.

*I could have killed Jason like all the others...*

"That was not what you were supposed to do," the voice replied. "My daughter, if I wished you to avoid those feelings, I wouldn't give you a soul able to experience them. He deserved to die for his broken promise, for his lack of loyalty to his word, but you needed him to understand the purpose why I gave you a heart."

Akuna-Ra shook her head. "I don't get it. I can't love him. He is not one of us."

"He came into your life for a reason, and you shall find it out, either by listening more often to your inner self or by looking deeper into his eyes."

"What is the meaning?" Akuna-Ra asked impatiently as her voice trembled in frustration, and her fists clenched, grabbing the red sand under her legs.

"You already know the answer. Why ask me?" the voice sneered, trying to open her eyes to the truth.

Akuna-Ra unclenched her fists and closed her eyes, feeling defeated. "I don't want to fall in love..."

Her voice was hardly a whisper.

"I don't want to compromise the connection with the underworld or with you."

"You are the connection; you are the bridge. Whether your heart loves or hates, you will always remain the same. Your fate can't be changed, but you are the master of your feelings, whether they be love, hate, or nothing at all."

The spirit of the night returned to the flames and from there, back to the underworld.

In the silence of the shack, Akuna-Ra seated still, with the only noises being her sobs.

"Then it shall be nothing at all."

\*\*\*

"My soul sister..." Kaiphindi greeted as she appeared at her door.

When there was no reply from Akuna-Ra, she walked toward her and seated herself in front of the fire at her side.

She grabbed her hand and pulled it into her lap.

"What was the answer of the spirit?"

"I was right. I can't compromise my magic..." she lied.

Kaiphindi smiled, recognizing when Akuna-Ra was lying. She didn't understand the reason for her lies, although she already had an idea about it.

"So, it shall be, my soul sister, but I believe, once again, you have misinterpreted their message, and I'm afraid you prefer this way."

Akuna-Ra turned her gaze at Kaiphindi. She drew a long and deep breath and waited until she could focus her mind once again to the level of clarity required of a witch doctor. "You were listening?"

"It wasn't my intention, but obviously the spirit you summoned wanted me to hear too. I'm the queen of this tribe. I need to know the struggles of every single member, including you.

"You and I have essential tasks, and we carry great responsibilities," Kaiphindi reminded her. "Nevertheless, we all need to accept this new nature we obtained when we reached this planet. Remember the reason why we were sent here. This was not just a random choice; the spirits never make arbitrary decisions... Do you remember?"

Akuna-Ra nodded. "I do; I haven't forgotten, but..."

Kaiphindi held her tightly to herself. "You have mighty powers, but you need to learn, also, other gifts that do not come from magic."

She stood from the ground. "You will find your answers only when your heart will make a decision. At the moment, I don't see you ready for them, so don't rush, and take your time. But this time, don't summon the spirits, summon your feelings."

She turned her shoulders and walked away.

For the rest of the night, Akuna-Ra didn't find any peace, but as the sun started to rise, she decided to keep her questions for a better time.

"There are more important issues, and I prefer to choose the path I have followed so far. I'm not going to fall in love with anyone. I won't confuse my thoughts and mind with foolish love, and no one shall cross me without finding the deserved punishment. There is a long way home, there is almost an eternity to fulfill. Only when my duty is accomplished, I might consider other feelings."

A slight smirk appeared on her face as she saw the people of her tribe preparing for another day.

***

Kaine woke up at the sound of his alarm clock. He would have rather slept for the whole day, and as soon as he tried to stand up, his muscles felt like they were made of wood, sending stinging pain all over his body. He wondered whether he should have stretched more the previous day.

"Well, it's useless to think about what I was supposed to do yesterday, as there is no way I can go back in time," he said, sitting up on the bed.

"The best thing to do is try to stretch my muscles today as much as possible. Maybe tomorrow I'll feel well enough to continue the trek from where we left it."

With a loud moan of pain, he stood up on his feet and approached the kitchen, not even knowing how his legs found the strength to support him.

"I will never be able to walk again," he cried as he reached the fridge. He grabbed the bottle of water and drank like his life depended on it. The desert in his throat made him wonder about how much he'd been sweating.

With a slow jerking movement, he leaned to check whether the fan was on.

The lazy movement of the blade gave him a reassuring feeling, and he prepared breakfast before washing himself and starting to work on the data they'd gathered the previous day.

He reached the shack dedicated as a headquarters, walking like a one-hundred-year-old man. He felt every joint painfully moving like rusty gears, and he wondered whether there was a spell known to the people of that village that could perform some sort of miracle to heal his muscles.

"Good morning," he said, coming inside the bungalow, grimacing at every step he took. Lawrence, Allison, and Josh peered at him understanding the feeling he was experiencing in his body.

The rest of the team, who had been mostly moved by car, felt less empathetic and found the situation a little amusing. Jason was the only one of the group of the trekkers who didn't have any problem with his muscles.

He walked to the door and helped Kaine to reach the long table, where all the computers were placed. The electricity generated by solar panels was able to provide for more than they could need.

"Come on, Grandpa, let me help you," Jason chuckled. "Did you do as I suggested and stretch your muscles yesterday?"

"I did!" Kaine protested with a groan as he sat down. "I might have underestimated the fact that my walking sessions are generally on an even pedestrian path back home. This sort of pattern requires a different level of training."

"I agree," Lawrence added. "Going to the gym is not enough when this is the kind of hiking you need to be prepared for. Yesterday we walked for six hours; perhaps we should have started with a more relaxed schedule... who knew?"

Jason grinned, feeling responsible for their pains. "I have to take my part of responsibility in this. I should have known that you might have needed more time to get used to this terrain before trekking for the whole day."

"Well, I guess there is nothing we can do now, and debating on the past is useless." Jenna urged them to quit the small-talk and begin working. "Let's get started. I can't wait to see the results of the data we obtained yesterday. Tomorrow we might be in better shape."

Finally, they could start their day, having the chance to remain seated with some breaks to stretch or have lunch.

***

After the first three months of exploration around the area, their initial excitement about the possibility to find any evidence about the tribe began to fade. Concern about not having any conclusive results to present in the preliminary report cursed Kaine's thoughts. He wondered if this would be the end of their adventure.

"I don't know what I should say or write in the paper," Kaine admitted when he was talking with Mark on the phone in the evening. "I have so many mixed feelings about it. I would gladly return home and resume my life together with you. On the other hand, regardless of the lack of results, I feel like we might soon find some sort of evidence. You might also call me a fool, and perhaps this was the same mistake that brought Dr. Murdock to be jammed here."

"I wouldn't want you to be stuck there. Particularly, not without me," Mark replied, chuckling. "But I understand your feelings. It feels disheartening when you reach such a far destination like Africa, you work on promising clues, but then... they all seem to fade in front of your eyes."

Kaine kept thinking about what he said: *Maybe some magic trick is the reason why we can't find anything.*

"Did you have other hallucinations?" Mark wondered when Kaine remained silent for a moment.

"No, I haven't had any since we started to get into the project. Eventually, I got so busy and I didn't have time to even think about them."

He didn't want to talk about the magical practices he had been witnessing during the period of living in the village. Nor about the presence of spirits who never meant to harm anyone.

*I have no idea whether it's just me who's going crazy or if there is indeed something strange going on in this place, but for the sake of my relationship with Mark, it might be better if I don't tell anything about all the things I've seen here.*

"You shouldn't get too stressed about it. You said it yourself that 'no result' is also a result. Besides, if I recall correctly, Dr. Murdock warned about this possibility. I believe nobody will ever blame you for not having found the tribe. Moreover, some tribes lead a nomadic life, so perhaps they migrated a long time ago."

Mark sensed Kaine's stressed tone of voice and wondered whether it was just because they couldn't find anything conclusive, because he was missing home, or there was something more he preferred not to tell.

"I wish you were here. Right at this moment, I need to be in your arms so badly!" Kaine's voice flickered as he tried his best to keep himself from crying.

"Kaine, what's wrong? Are you sure you're only missing me, or is there something bothering you?" Mark wondered. "You know you can talk to me. If you don't trust me, then who?"

Tears glowed in his eyes. "I believe I'm just getting tired of this heat, of the physical and the mental stress. I

181

just wish I could take the first flight, return home and remain in bed for one entire year."

He started to sob desperately.

"You're close to a burn-out. Can't you just take a break? I understand you're in one of the most beautiful places on Earth. At least, according to the pictures you've sent, I couldn't imagine a more breathtaking place. Nevertheless, you're not there to enjoy yourself. You're constantly working, and even when you're on a free day, your brain is still handling this free-time as work."

Mark walked to the window and watched outside. Despite the fair weather, everything was dull without Kaine.

"I wish I could take the first flight..." he kept repeating, pausing for a second, trying to regain the strength willing to escape him. "I love you. You are the only thought that keeps me sane here. I guess you're right, and we all should be allowed to have a pause from this journey. I will try to have a talk with the rest of the team and propose a break to Dr. Luther. I'm not sure whether he'll say that since we're coming back, we can also return for good because he doesn't believe we can find anything..."

Mark smiled. "Admit it, this is your biggest fear, what keeps you from taking any sort of vacation. You're scared you won't be allowed to continue your research, isn't it?"

Kaine remained open-mouthed. "I have never considered this... You know, this might be the real reason. Every day I feel like this will be the day when we'll find something, some clue that can change the direction of our expedition completely. Then when we return to camp without anything accomplished, I feel my hopes crashed against the hard wall of reality. I feel like I'm constantly failing, and soon I'll also lose my job."

"Nobody will be fired, and particularly not you. Now, I can almost feel your tears falling, so wipe your eyes and go to bed. Close your eyes, and tomorrow have a chat with the other members of the team. You all need to recharge."

There was only one wish in Mark's heart, and it was Kaine's happiness. At that moment, he wasn't happy, and the worst was he was also too far for Mark to take care of his boyfriend. There was nothing he could do, and the feeling of impotence drove him crazy.

"You might be right," Kaine considered as if he was talking mostly to himself.

"I'm right, baby, and the only thing I wish is to have you back home safe and sound," Mark assured. "This also means the safety of your beautiful mind and soul. Take good care of everything that belongs to you. I miss you too much already."

Kaine felt a deep stinging pain in his heart. "I don't want to give you any trouble, and believe me there isn't any other thing I desire more than returning where I belong - in your arms."

With a smile, Mark returned to sit down on his chair, glancing at the screen of his computer. "Remember, I love you and even if I'm far away, I'm always close to your heart. Now just rest and call me again tomorrow. But then I want to have great news about your next vacation, okay?"

Kaine laughed. "I will do my best... I love you too. Good night, babe. I will see you in my dreams!"

"See you there."

# CHAPTER 14

That morning, waking up felt more difficult. Kaine had no idea what he was supposed to do or whether he needed to call someone and ask to be brought to the nearest hospital.

His head pounded painfully, and the rest of his body didn't have any intention in following his orders.

He groaned, turning on his side, hoping to be able to roll over and at least sit on the bed. Managing that simple task felt like the most challenging goal in the world. "What the hell is going on with me this morning?"

Feeling breathless, the pain was spreading along his body like a patch of oil on the calm water.

He hoped he didn't contract any kind of disease, which was not included in the vaccinations. Mentally, he went through all the possibilities and all the risky situations he had been exposed to during the previous week or so, but he couldn't think of anything, which might have caused the pain he was feeling.

He closed his eyes and took a deep breath, trying not to become overwhelmed by panic. He wondered whether it would have been better to wait for someone to come, or if he should try to walk to the headquarters bungalow.

He felt lucky, as there wasn't any sort of trekking scheduled that day.

"What am I supposed to do?"

He tried to stand up from the bed when a sudden movement of his bowels forced him to dart to the bathroom.

When he got out, he felt better.

"Perhaps there was just something I ate yesterday that was not completely fresh." He walked to the kitchen to drink some water.

The door opened, and Jason appeared, glancing around and looking for Kaine. "Dr. Martin, are you here?" he called without coming inside the bungalow.

"I'm in the kitchen," Kaine replied, inviting him to come in. "I know I'm late. I was a bit unwell this morning. I'm afraid I ate something I shouldn't yesterday."

Jason came in and reached him, glad to see him awake and obviously in good shape. "Well, it's like you were not the only one. At least half of the team had some problems too. I was wondering whether it would be better if I drive you all to the nearest hospital for a checkup, just to make sure there isn't anything worse going on."

Kaine gulped another glass of water to make sure he got rehydrated. "That might be the wisest thing to do. Losing one day of work is what bothers me the most..."

Jason grabbed the bottle of water and poured some water for himself. "If you don't take care of your health, this might also be the last day of your stay here. Why risk it? Losing one day of work won't be as bad as compromising the entire expedition."

Even though Kaine had been already been in Africa several times, he had never been in the situation of really caring about his health.

*It seems to me as if he'd been in places where he could count on a five-star hotel to sleep in and carefully prepared meals,* Jason thought.

Kaine considered the way he was feeling and ignoring the conditions of the other members of the team, he decided to avoid the risk of having the whole group sent back home for something that wasn't adequately treated.

"I guess we should be checked at the hospital. You're right when you say it's better to waste one working day than to compromise the health of every member of my team. I will never forgive myself if something happens to them because of my careless behavior."

Jason stood up from his chair and smiled at Kaine. "I will arrange the ride. Be prepared to leave in about one hour. I'll go inform the others, so they'll be ready."

"Is the hospital far from here?" Kaine wondered.

He recalled the time when Jason had been treated for cholera by a sort of shaman, and he was curious to meet him or her too.

"It's nearby to the airport where you arrived. I don't know whether you can consider it close or not."

"Once you were talking about a witch doctor who healed you."

Jason chuckled. "Would you like to be cured by her?"

"I'm not sure, but one day I would like to meet her. Which tribe does this healer belong to?"

"I will tell you everything when you return, now, you all need professional healthcare."

Jason felt cornered by Kaine's questions, and perhaps it was his fault when he mentioned being treated by the local shaman.

*The best thing is to send them to the hospital and get in touch with Akuna-Ra. If she gives me permission, I might also bring him to meet the tribe quite soon.*

Jason averted his gaze from Kaine, pursing his lips to avoid telling too much and revealing the turmoil agitating his soul.

"You're right. Call us a ride, and when we're back, we'll talk more about it. Now we all have to think about our health, and forget about all work-related matters," Kaine reasoned. He'd noticed the tense expression on Jason's face and understood he was putting him into a difficult situation with all his requests.

"I'll be back in one hour with the ride to escort you to the hospital. I won't be able to come with you because I have to attend to my duties as a teacher today, but I can assure you'll be in good hands."

He left the bungalow as fast as he could and went to inform the other members of the team about the change in schedule.

They all seemed extremely glad to have the chance to reach a real hospital, not only to check the reason for their sickness, but also to have a complete check-up on their general health status, and perhaps even obtain more malaria medications and refill their first-aid supplies.

Jason took his leave and agreed with Azizi to gather the necessary people to drive the whole team to the closest hospital, taking care that they would be cared for as soon as possible, and they would be returned to the village safe and sound.

"Don't you worry, Boss, the Mzungus are in good hands," Azizi reassured with a bright smile on his face, as he left to gather the rest of the security team to escort the *mzungus* to the hospital.

With a nod, Jason turned around and went to check on the conditions of the patients. Jenna was one of those who didn't have any symptoms and was outside on the veranda of her bungalow. When she saw Jason returning, she walked toward him.

"You have been here in Africa for a long time. Do you have any idea what happened to Lawrence, Kaine, and Josh?" she wondered, anxious to get to the hospital.

With a smile, Jason placed a hand on her shoulder. "Don't you worry, if it was a case of salmonella, they would feel much worse than they do now; the same with other deadly or semi-deadly diseases too. Most likely, what they ate yesterday was not as fresh as it should have been. It's good to bring them to the hospital and have them checked, just to be sure to have the right medications."

"Hmm." Jenna nodded, bringing a hand to her mouth. "I guess it would be good to have us all going for a checkup..."

"Take this as a well-deserved holiday. You all have been overworked, and now it's time to slow down a bit. This might also be a reaction to the stress you've accumulated."

Jason turned his shoulders and walked away, determined to return to his village for the lesson he had with the kids.

"Where are you going?" Jenna wondered, surprised to see him walking away.

"I'm not coming with you. I have class with the kids today. Remember I'm making my living here, giving basic education to the children. I'll be waiting for you later this afternoon." He turned at her without stopping.

"Call me when you're ready to return so I'll know when to be here."

Jenna didn't know whether to be worried or not, but she felt almost happy at the knowing Azizi would be traveling with them. She liked him, although she understood they belonged to two different worlds and it wouldn't be easy to combine them together.

She sighed with a slight whine, like a pouting kid who just discovered the world is not running the way she wants.

She walked back to the headquarters to see whether the others were already there, ready to leave for the hospital.

The first person she met was Allison. "Hey, there!" she lazily greeted, still thinking about Azizi.

"Good morning. I was checking up on our patients. They don't seem to be about to die, which is a good sign, but for sure they aren't in the condition to work either," Allison replied, pouring some coffee in a cup. "Do you want some?" She grabbed the pot.

"Sure."

Jenna took a cup and poured some coffee for herself. "To be honest, I'm almost glad for this small break. I wonder if we should agree on a holiday. Not necessarily to return home, but at least to have some rest in another city where we can indulge in some civilization. I miss the comfort of a good hotel."

"That would be a great idea. As soon as we have our patients treated, we need to negotiate some regular breaks. I would suggest a week out of four," Allison proposed.

"I'm afraid we were all so excited about this new adventure and we forgot to take some time to recharge. Dr. Murdock said this overworking could be the reason for their sickness, and he might not be completely wrong." Jenna sipped her coffee, with a satisfied expression on her face for that little enjoyment.

Kaine entered the bungalow. His face was pale, and he walked stumbling like he wasn't sure his legs could support him. Grabbing everything on his way to the table to get better stability, he finally reached the chair, and with a loud groan, he collapsed, seated.

"I'm going to die today!" he protested, closing his eyes.

"Drama queen!" Allison dismissed him. "Nobody is going to die; we are soon getting you and the others to the hospital."

"I hope whatever you have is nothing contagious." Jenna stood up and walked farther from him.

Allison glanced at her and back at Kaine, frowning. She reached Jenna on the other side of the room. "Let's make sure they travel in a separate car. Now that you mention it, I wouldn't want to risk it."

Kaine stared at them and grimaced. "Fear not! If this was some sort of virus, we would all be infected. Obviously, this was a bacterium found in something a few of us were eating yesterday or in the previous days."

They remained silent for a moment; then, Jenna turned her glance outside the window. When she saw Azizi coming out of the car, her heart skipped a beat. *Stop thinking about him; you don't belong together. Soon this expedition will be over, and you will return to your country where everything is working fine, and no deadly diseases are waiting for you at every meal.*

They gathered in the yard, and using two jeeps, they drove away to the hospital.

\*\*\*

After the lesson with the children of the village, Jason checked the clock. It was already time to have lunch, but he wanted, first of all, to talk with Akuna-Ra.

*I need to understand how much more time she needs in order to know whether she can trust Kaine or not. The questions he started to ask about the witch doctor who cured me can be answered, and surely, I can find one of the villagers to pretend to be the healer. Nevertheless, I have a strange feeling he wants to know more.*

He walked away, taking a hidden path through the jungle, the same crossing Omar's bar. There were many questions in his mind, and not all concerned the reason why Kaine was there.

Something started to trouble his soul, and the feelings he began to admit having toward Akuna-Ra confused him.

In his life, he was sure he would have never got his heart mixed up with any of the tribe's members he had been in touch with.

They were the *job.*

Yet, his connection with the tribe and particularly with Akuna-Ra – the one resembling more like a tale of slavery and possession – had started to become something more profound than he could have ever feared.

Hesitation grabbed his soul as he looked at the village from the outer border of the forest. There he could spot the shack of Akuna-Ra, his mistress.

His heartbeat began to drum faster and faster. Feeling almost breathless, he closed his eyes, trying to focus on getting its pace back to the normal rhythm.

With a smirk, he resumed his walk toward the village, looking for his mistress.

Akuna-Ra was in her shack when she sensed Jason approaching. She clenched her fists to overcome her feelings. *There is no way he is going to take my focus away from my duties.*

Toughening her expression, she walked toward him.

"What are you looking for here? You haven't been called."

The tone of her voice was as rough as an uncut stone and sharp as a knife. Somehow, he wasn't expecting anything more than that reception, and she was also right; he wasn't summoned at her presence.

Nevertheless, he could swear there had been some sort of tenderness in the kiss she'd exchanged with him. It would be like pretending a stone had feelings. She is a witch doctor.

"I came uninvited," he replied dryly. "I needed to know whether you have made your decision, or you need more time to investigate Dr. Martin's intentions. Soon I will have to lead him outside of the country to avoid reaching your tribe."

She narrowed her eyes at his sarcasm. "I need more time..."

"How much time do you need?" he pursued.

"I will let you know. Now disappear," she growled, turning her shoulders and leaving him alone.

Jason watched her walk away. Under other circumstances, perhaps with another human being, he would have run behind her and insisted on having an explanation for her cold behavior. *In this case, if I care about my life, it's better to leave her be and do precisely as she orders. Next time if she gets the chance to save my life or kill me, she might choose the second option.*

With a resented grin, he walked away, trying to hide the pain in his heart.

"Mzungu!" Okumi called.

Jason turned his eyes to him without a reply.

"My queen wished to see you," he urged keeping his hand on the door. "Please, follow me."

"I hope I'm not in trouble with her too. I think I have enough of it," Jason replied, following Okumi, glancing around at the activity of the tribe as they walked.

Kaiphindi was waiting for him, and as soon as she saw him brought by Okumi, she smiled.

"My queen," Jason greeted with a bow.

"Dr. Murdock, I came to know about some difficulties you had with Akuna-Ra," she commenced, tilting her head and scrutinizing him.

Jason raised his hands to cover his face, and with a slow movement, he moved them back to his hair. He had no idea about what he was supposed to say, or what she already knew.

"Your highness, I'm afraid there is no way I can avoid disappointing Akuna-Ra. Although I try my best, I end up always doing something wrong, like today."

Kaiphindi nodded, knowing she needed to find a solution. She agreed with Akuna-Ra and allowing him to leave would be a risk they couldn't afford taking.

Nevertheless, if she had to trust her power of reading people's hearts, she was sure that even if he had the chance, he might not have left the village, nor would he have betrayed them.

*I believe you have learned to respect the people of this tribe, our need not to be discovered, and to be revealed only to chosen ones. But I'm afraid the trouble is no longer about the trust we have for you, it's something more complicated than we could have ever forecast. You fell in love with each other.*

Her brows knitted. "Dr. Murdock, I do believe you don't need me to understand where the problem is. For this reason, you will agree with me to keep your distance from this tribe and Akuna-Ra, unless she is summoning you. For us, it's imperative that she maintains her connections with other worlds, and your presence might interrupt her focus on her duties."

Kaiphindi didn't want to go into the details of the feelings troubling her soul sister and hoped Jason could understand what she meant when she asked him to leave them alone.

"I see, I'm going to keep my distance, but why can't I be set free?" he wondered, knowing perfectly he would have never left the village.

"Dr. Murdock, you certainly remember the reason why you are not allowed to leave is because of your lack of loyalty. We can't risk anymore. It was difficult enough to eliminate all the evidence you had gathered and were able to send outside this tribe," Kaiphindi explained with a calm tone of voice. "This punishment didn't have any expiration date. It was not like being in jail for a certain period to allow you to think about your actions and the possible consequences. Short term imprisonment is for those crimes that are harmless if repeated."

Jason lowered his gaze, noticing a big lizard walking across the room.

"I know. I haven't forgotten. It has been my curse and a blessing. I will do as you suggest and won't return to this place unless summoned here. I would just like you to grant my plea; try and convince Akuna-Ra to make a faster decision over the young researcher she asked me to bring here. It has become difficult to keep him from this part of the forest. Therefore, either I will have to persuade him to return home empty-handed, perhaps creating some sort of clue about your demise, or he will soon be allowed to meet you."

"I will do that," she assured. "I will make sure by the time the young researcher and his team are healed; Akuna-Ra would have made her decision."

Jason smiled, wondering how it would feel to be able to know everything that's going on around him.

"Thank you, your highness, and if I'm allowed, I will now return to the village where I will be waiting for the researchers to come back from the hospital and for an answer from Akuna-Ra."

"Of course, Dr. Murdock, you are dismissed and free to go wherever you need to be," she replied.

# CHAPTER 15

Heartbroken, Jason returned to the bar where Omar was, as usual, taking care of the place and some customers.

He waved at him, and without saying anything, he went to take a seat at his favorite table, in a corner of the room, from where he could have a view of the whole place and was close enough to the secondary exit that would give him a safe escape route.

Omar scrutinized him, and by the expression on Jason's face, he understood the reason he came there – to forget.

Without asking, he grabbed the bottle of his favorite whiskey, one glass, and walked to him. "You look like you need this," Omar sneered, locking his eyes on Jason's.

"I don't know what I need, my friend," Jason replied. "Perhaps the best thing would be just to be able to disappear forever."

He poured a small shot and gulped it as fast as he could. With a grimace, he slammed the glass on the table.

"It looks like troubles with a lady," Omar wondered.

"I wish it was only a *lady*. I could have forgotten about her and jumped on to the next one, but this is something different. I have trouble with God himself."

Omar frowned, feeling sorry to see his best customer in such a state. "Boss, you need to take care of yourself; life is too short to waste it complaining."

Jason avoided looking at Omar, he poured another glass. "Life is too long..." He tried to hold back his tears.

He remained alone, glancing at the amber color of his drink, rolling the glass between his fingers to see the light reflected through it. The only wish he had was to go back in time.

*Even a couple of weeks before, it would have been enough. Any time before I kissed her, for there is nothing I regret the most but having discovered and admitted being in love with her.*

Sipping his whiskey, he found in the burning warmth and the smooth taste an easy, temporary escape to his sadness.

*I know I will not find the solution in this bottle, but in all honesty, there is no way out of this problem. Again, we are not talking about a woman to which I can explain and try to reason. We are talking about a creature able to kill me with a glance...Literally.*

He didn't know what he was supposed to do, and perhaps the proposal of Kaiphindi was the most reasonable. She was the wisdom of the tribe, the heart, and the soul.

About one hour had passed when his mobile phone started to ring.

Jason grabbed it and tried to think clearly. "Hello," he mumbled.

197

"Dr. Murdock?" Jenna wondered.

"Yes, it's me," he sighed, wagging his head as if to shake away his light drunken state. "So, what's the condition of the patients?"

"Oh, well, nothing serious, as you suspected. It was a bacterium that caused their sickness. They have been given some antibiotics and prescribed a few days of rest. Let's say, in a week, we can resume all the research," she replied hesitatingly, wondering whether it was as it seemed, and Dr. Murdock was drunk, or the connection was a bit disturbed.

She didn't want to investigate and preferred to pretend everything was fine.

"Perfect, a few days of rest will be beneficial to everybody, and perhaps you should also plan a vacation for the future. I suppose you will be back in the village this evening, so we might agree to meet tomorrow morning at the headquarters to check on the condition of the patients, and consider a new schedule," he proposed. He didn't want to be seen by anyone as drunk as he was, or as he could become in the next few hours.

"That sounds like a plan. At what time do we meet?" she asked.

"There's no hurry. Let's say at about ten o'clock in the morning." He proposed, trying to dismiss her as soon as possible. "I need to leave you. See you tomorrow."

"Yes, bye." Jenna hung up the conversation and remained to stare at the phone, puzzled.

"What did he say?" Allison wondered, noticing her expression.

"We will meet tomorrow morning again at ten o'clock." She raised her face. "I... Just... I think he was drunk," she whispered to avoid being heard by the others.

"Are you sure?"

"Well, it could also be that there was some interference on the line, and I might have misunderstood it. I mean, he seemed to be able to talk and to make plans, but... How can I explain the feeling I had when I was talking to him?" Her forehead creased, as she played nervously with a string of her rucksack.

"I think I understand," Allison replied. "Nevertheless, he's in his free time, and it's not up to us to judge how he prefers to spend it. So far, he has been more than useful for our expedition."

"I know, and you're right. It felt strange."

\*\*\*

Kaine fell asleep during the journey back home. He wasn't sure whether the excessive tiredness was caused by the travel, the illness, or the medications he'd received. Something he noticed when he woke up was that he wasn't the only one who felt that way, and all the others were sleeping.

"Where are we?" he asked, stretching his body. Outside was already dark, and he couldn't orient himself.

"We are close to the village," the driver replied. "How do you feel?"

"I feel like I need to fall asleep for another year. Thanks for asking." Kaine chuckled, trying to see something from the window of the car.

"Generally, the medication they give at the hospital puts people to sleep. It's the best way to get rid of the infection. Probably within a couple of days, you will all feel better."

"I hope so. Nevertheless, we won't resume any expedition or trekking before next week," Kaine replied. "It's wise to get some rest."

He looked down at his wristwatch and considered he might be a bit late on his usual call to Mark. *I miss him so much! Maybe it's a good idea if I send him a message informing about the possibility of a delay.*

He searched his pockets for his mobile phone, but as he switched it on, he realized there wasn't any service available. With a silent huff, he placed the phone back inside his pocket. All the others were still sleeping, and he started to feel bored.

He considered himself lucky when he could finally step out of the car. He briefly bade goodnight to the rest of the team, and headed back to his bungalow, with the intention of having something to eat, calling Mark, and falling immediately to sleep.

"I can't wait until this infection is over. There is nothing worse than being sick far from home and away from proper healthcare," he said aloud as he reached the kitchen.

As he ate something, he felt like he couldn't even talk to Mark. He was exhausted. He sent him a message explaining to him the situation and went immediately to his bed, where without undressing, he fell into a deep sleep until the morning after.

*** 

Jason was also thinking about going to bed, and after having lit the candles in the kitchen and bedroom, he started to undress. His movements were a bit slowed by the effects of the alcohol, but he wouldn't have considered himself as drunk as usual.

"This only means that I might have milder nightmares, but I'm not expecting any good dreams either," he protested, mumbling.

Suddenly the door opened and Okumi appeared.

Jason scowl at him with a stare of pure hatred, wanting only for him to disappear. "Let me guess, your Mistress is asking for my presence."

His tone of voice was bitter, and he wondered why she had to request him when he was drunk. *Call it coincidence, but I'm starting to believe she's doing it on purpose.*

"Do you need me to help you reaching her?" Okumi proposed as he observed Jason trying to put on the clothes he'd taken off.

"I guess I will..."

As they were walking to the path leading to the shack of Akuna-Ra, Jason started to feel restless. After the last encounter with her and the chat with Kaiphindi, the last thing he wanted to do was meet her again.

It was not the fear of her volatile mood and the consequences he preferred to avoid. Much more, what worried him was the certainty that he couldn't hide his feelings any longer. He wanted her with every fiber of his being.

Akuna-Ra was, as usual, waiting for him in front of the fire, and when he saw her, his attraction and desire to have her, felt irresistible.

"I'm wondering what makes you drink so much..." Akuna-Ra spelled without raising her face at him and signaling Okumi to leave.

"It's you, and you should know it, but I don't think this was the reason why you wanted to see me," he replied.

"Tell me why you called me, and then I will return to the village, where I will go to sleep, finally."

She didn't like the tone of his voice, but after the chat she had with Kaiphindi, she understood he had his reasons to be upset.

"You can bring the young researcher."

"When?"

"Whenever he feels better. At this point, you should make clear that he will be the only one allowed to reach us, and perhaps the rest of his team might return home if they please."

They both avoided looking at each other.

"Should I tell him that I found the tribe? Should I..." He wasn't sure what he was supposed to say. He felt tired and intoxicated. His mind couldn't think straight, and the heat in her shack was more oppressing than he remembered. Yet, he was unable to leave as he was determined to.

"You tell him what you know. At this point, you can also tell him what happened to you, as he is supposed to get in touch with us. Now you can go if this is what you want."

Jason quivered his head a little. "This is not what I want, but I promised Kaiphindi to stay away from you to avoid interfering with your connection with the spirits."

"What do you want?" she asked.

"It doesn't make any difference, does it?"

Without waiting for any reply, he turned and left the shack. He needed some time to think and to plan how he would start the conversation with Kaine. He needed to make sure he would be alone. *But how?*

*I believe the best thing of all would be to go there to meet the team and inform them I will continue the research on my own. They will need to remain there at the headquarters, caring for those who need to recover. When I return, after one week, I will talk to Kaine and explain to him the situation.*

He considered that plan, and with a satisfied smile, he returned to his bungalow, ready to finally call it a day and rest.

*** 

For the whole week, Jason kept himself as far as possible from both Akuna-Ra, Kaine and his team. He needed to create a credible alibi for the lie he was going to tell.

Kaine wondered about Jason's absence, but perhaps this was the best way to take care of the expedition. If the whole team had to be inactive for one entire week, then it was more than reasonable to have, one person who knew both the area and the target of the mission to continue independently, also without any technological backup.

"This has been his job for more than a decade. He might have found more clues to follow and went on without us," he said aloud as he lay on his bed, following the directions the doctor gave them at the hospital.

For a couple of days, he was weak and tired and the most he could do was stand up to reach the kitchen or the restroom. The communications with Mark were only through messaging, where he tried to reassure his boyfriend of his health status.

"For him, it must be difficult to withstand. I would die with worry if he had been away from home and infected with a disease that doesn't allow him to speak on the phone," he admitted, and he decided it was perhaps a good idea to let Mark hear by his own voice that he was still alive and well.

He grabbed the phone, and without any hesitation, he dialed Mark's number.

"Sweetheart! Is it really you?" Mark answered, surprised to hear Kaine's voice. "You sound terrible, poor little angel."

"I know, I feel like a piece of junk. I needed to call you and hear your voice. I wanted to let you know that I'm still alive, and although I'm not well yet, things are slowly getting better," he replied as he walked to his bed.

"I was distraught. The evening when you wrote me a message, telling me you were a bit unwell and you preferred to go straight to sleep, I understood there was something more than tiredness."

Mark prepared to leave the laboratory, he switched off his computer and grabbed his jacket.

"I'm sorry if I made you worry. I could barely keep myself awake. The medications we received were keeping me completely dizzy."

Mark chuckled. "I wonder what kind of medicine they gave you, but on the other hand, with tropical diseases, those kinds of strong drugs are required to make sure the virus or the bacteria are eliminated from the organism."

"That's exactly what one of the local people said to me. According to the doctor, this kind of infection was also facilitated by our levels of stress. Therefore, we decided to propose another schedule to include a vacation rotation for each member of the team. You were right when you warned me about risking burnout, and this illness opened our eyes to the seriousness of the threat."

Kaine rolled on his side on the bed to get more comfortable.

"That sounds reasonable. Do you think you'll get to return home, or will you be granted some vacation time in a better place on the same continent?"

"I don't know. Jenna sent a request to Dr. Luther, but I haven't yet had the chance to ask her about it. I guess she's waiting for us all to have recovered to tell us the outcome of the negotiation."

Mark entered his car and remained for a moment, thinking about it. "Well, it's your right to have breaks. Nobody can force you to work seven days a week for one entire year without any pause."

He waited for a moment before starting the engine, and from the window, he watched outside, observing the cars driving by.

"I know, and if we don't have it granted, we are ready to return home and give up the whole expedition. After all the money invested, they don't want to risk having us coming back with the resignation letters in our hands."

Mark peeked at the clock of the car. During the evening, he thought he needed to focus on driving rather than talking to Kaine. Of course, he preferred the second option, but the car was starting to get cold. "I'm in the car now. Would you mind calling me later?"

"I'm already in bed. I think I'll switch off the lights and try to rest until tomorrow morning. If you prefer, I can call you later from now on."

"That's probably the best solution. Call me an hour later than the usual time."

Kaine smiled weakly, feeling his eyes closing and his body switching off for the night. "I will. Have a good night. I'm going to dream about you," he said groggily.

"Good night, baby, and sleep well. I will be there in your dreams and always in your heart."

Kaine fell asleep, and the telephone fell from his hand.

Mark chuckled. "Good night, little angel. Sleep well and get better soon," he whispered, hanging up the conversation.

# CHAPTER 16

The following week, Jason returned to the village in the morning and walked into the bungalow, where he was sure he'd find all the others gathered to discuss the next schedule for the exploration.

"Good morning," he greeted with a bright smile on his face.

"Look who's here!" Jenna cheered. "We thought we'd lost you for good. Where have you been?"

Jason walked over to take a seat on a chair, getting comfortable. "I've been around, but I might have found something interesting."

Kaine's eyes opened brightly. "And we're all ears!" He sat down in front of him, waiting for some good news.

Jason approached his face with a wicked grin. "I need to talk to you in private first." He lowered his voice as if to reveal a big secret.

Kaine got even closer to the kind of distance he would have called generally, *the boundary.*

That was the distance to be able, almost to kiss each other. "What would it be?" Kaine muttered.

"Not here, kid; in private," Jason spelled, unimpressed.

All the others were just watching what was going on between Kaine and Jason, wondering whether something was going on between them.

Jason stood up from the chair with a rapid movement and turned his shoulders to Kaine as if he was going to walk away.

He turned his glance to Kaine. "Are you coming or not?"

"N-Now?"

"When? Tomorrow?"

Kaine glimpsed the rest of the team who remained speechless at his unexpected behavior. They all wondered what was going on between them.

As they were outside, Jason continued to walk toward Kaine's bungalow, expecting him to follow.

"What was so urgent and private you need to tell me?"

"I've found it." Jason tried to figure out a way to tell him about the whole story behind the tribe and his forced stay in that God-forsaken place in the heart of Africa.

"What?" Kaine mumbled, surprised at his words. He hoped Jason meant to say he found the tribe, so their search was finally over.

"I know where the tribe is, and I had some contact with them, but you need to listen to my story because you need to work with me for the sake of our lives. I wanted to talk to you in private because no one else besides you and I should know about this find. Not even your team. NOBODY!"

Jason walked to the kitchen where there was a table they could both sit down at.

"It all began eight years ago, five months before I legally disappeared..."

"Hold on a second, you knew about this tribe since then, and you didn't tell anyone? Why?"

Kaine's heart started to race, and an uncomfortable feeling rose from the innermost part of his soul.

"Let me finish," Jason reproached. "I was able to meet one of their hunters, and by following him, I reached their location. I was welcomed and introduced to the queen and the major figures of their society, in particular, their spiritual guide and healer. I was forbidden to take any pictures of the people and the camp; anything concerning their culture should have remained a secret between them and me."

He sighed, recalling those times and his foolish behavior.

"I promised them, but I did not truly intend to keep my word. I thought there wouldn't be any harm to anybody if I disclosed a few details about them, so I secretly gathered some evidence and wrote a nice article. I spent a few months with them, and when it was time to say goodbye, I sent the report to the University, foretasting the glory I would have gained."

Kaine eyeballed at him, open-mouthed. His mind was blank, and he had absolutely no idea what to say. What he knew was that there was more to be said, and he was waiting to listen to the reason he decided to remain there.

"In a hurry, I left to reach the airport and bought the first ticket to the US. I couldn't wait to return home, unaware that this would never happen. I boarded the plane, and during the night flight from Goma to the States, I fell asleep.

When I woke up, though, I found myself in the shack of the spiritual guide of the tribe. She was staring at me with a glare of pure hatred, and I realized that when she said I would regret it if I revealed their secret, she was not joking."

Kaine gasped.

"What? How could you wake up back in her shack? I-I don't understand. It doesn't make sense!" he exclaimed as his hands started to shake.

"Akuna-Ra has magic beyond any imagination. She commands time and space. Nothing is impossible for her, and this is the reason why I can't return home. I'm condemned to be her slave, here in this village. She owns me." He clenched his teeth and closed his eyes, feeling on the verge of crying.

"I have tried several times to escape, and the result was always the same. The morning after, I have woken up, still in this village. I don't want to scare you, but you need to understand that this expedition is something you will have to use for your personal growth, for something that can give you a better understanding of the Universe we are living in. If you follow the rules and will be loyal to the promise you will have to make to them of keeping the secret, nothing will ever happen to you. On the other hand, I have no idea what kind of punishments she can think about, and, believe me, neither do you."

Kaine covered his mouth with one palm. "Are you serious? Are you sure you haven't been drinking too much?"

Jason toughened his expression and slammed his fist on the table. "Fuck, do I look drunk?"

He stood up and brought his hands to his head, turning his back to Kaine. *I know I drink too much, but if I do it's to escape this nightmare, even if for a few hours.*

Closing his eyes, Jason focused on his heartbeat, trying hard to control his emotions. Taking a couple of deep breaths, he returned to sit on the chair.

"You have no idea, kid, but you'd better listen to me. I would have loved to have had someone to tell me what I was going to get myself into when I started my search. I might have been more considerate and spared myself from all this mess."

"I-I'm sorry, I didn't mean to offend you. I have been rude." Kaine mumbled apologetically. "Let me ask you one thing. Why, then, did you contact me? Why did you give me those clues and lure me here? Why me?"

"It was not my choice, I'm afraid. She wanted you here. You will know the reason why in due time when you meet her, but at this point, you can also say you are not interested, and you're returning home. You will have to write a non-conclusive report about it, but perhaps we can make sure that your results will end up with an extinct civilization. We can make up some traces of their past existence for the eager reader out in the world. Please, let me be the only one cursed in this place."

There was a long pause of silence between them, and Kaine pondered carefully all the options he had on his hands. *If what he says is true and this priestess is so dangerous, it would be wiser to leave. Nevertheless, I'm also curious to know what she wants from me and why she forced Jason to call me here. I'm afraid I can't just go back without having an explanation about her choice.*

He peered around, avoiding looking at Jason, who, understanding his need to think about it, waited silently.

*This would be the time when the appearance of my mother would be highly appreciated. I have no idea what I'm supposed to do in this case. Indeed, she warned me not to talk to strangers, but did she refer to Dr. Murdock, this priestess, or both? Fuck! I can't even ask for advice from Mark.*

"I'm not sure about what should I say. I know I would die with curiosity if I leave without having asked this woman about her reason for calling me here. On the other hand, after what you have told me, I can't avoid feeling threatened," Kaine admitted, glancing finally at Jason.

With a slight nod, Jason remained silent for a moment to consider how he could help him with his decision. "I understand your dilemma. And I would feel the same if I were you. If you need to take some time to think about it..."

"Could you give me until tomorrow?"

"Of course, there isn't any hurry. However, you're not supposed to talk about this with anyone, so if you're thinking about calling someone to help you make the decision, I suggest you don't do that. This is like already revealing their existence, something they are trying to avoid by any means. Unfortunately, it's a choice you need to make on your own. Or, if you need to ask me anything, I will answer all your questions."

The sound of somebody knocking on his door made Kaine literally jump in the chair. He focused his attention on the door with his eyes wide open, like a scared puppy.

Slowly, the door opened, and Lawrence peeked gingerly inside the house. "Are you still alive?" he asked, chuckling.

Jason understood the situation required fast action to divert their attention from the tribe, and grabbing Kaine, holding him tightly to himself, he kissed him.

Lawrence remained open-mouthed as he spotted them kissing in the kitchen, and slowly closed the door, feeling embarrassed.

As he left, Jason parted from Kaine. "I'm sorry. I didn't mean... that was the first thing I could figure out to divert his attention to the fact that I might have had something to tell you about the tribe. Now they will think I just wanted an excuse to be alone with you..."

Kaine was also taken by surprise. "Are you..."

"No, I'm not gay. I needed to find a diversion," Jason replied with a chuckle.

"I'm sure you fooled him because you also fooled me, and I'm gay," Kaine mumbled.

He had to admit he almost felt aroused by Jason's kiss.

"We'd better go back. They already have enough to speculate about." Kaine growled and turning his shoulders to Jason he paced to the exit.

*** 

Lawrence returned to the bungalow, chuckling. "You have no idea what I saw!"

"What?" Allison wondered.

"Well, the reason why Dr. Murdock wanted to talk with Kaine was just to reveal to him his feelings. I caught them kissing passionately in the kitchen."

"What?!" Jenna exclaimed, surprised. "I didn't know Dr. Murdock was gay."

"I have never felt so embarrassed in my life. I mean, it's my fault for having come in without waiting for any reply to my knocking, but we all needed to start doing something..." Lawrence added, trying to make himself feel slightly better about his intrusion.

"Shut up, they're coming, and please try to act like nothing has happened," Allison warned.

As they entered the bungalow, Kaine felt the questioning gazes of the rest of his team upon him. He wasn't sure whether that kiss was a good idea. *On the other hand, if it's so important to hide the existence of the tribe, this might be the best explanation and diversion ever. I presume this should be a detail I'm supposed to keep hidden from Mark.*

"So, are we ready to continue planning the next week of explorations?" Josh asked, trying to release the tense atmosphere created by Lawrence's revelation.

With a quick nod, Kaine replied, "Yes, indeed..."

Jason reached the table where the map was unfolded and observed the places that had been scanned and explored by walking. "We might start searching this area on the southeast." He grabbed a pencil and drew a couple of circles.

"This will be the place we should better scan with a drone, and this other will be the one we might want to check by foot. What do you think?" He pointed at both circles and visually toured around for any sort of agreement or objection.

Josh came closer and observed the places. "This area could easily be scanned from this hill. What would be the condition of the roads leading to the top?"

"There shouldn't be any problem to reach it. I know this road is always kept in good condition because it's the one used by the farmers to get to their fields on the other side," Jason replied. "Nevertheless, there's something we might start taking into consideration, and that is the weather factor. Soon enough, the rainy season will begin, probably operating the drone might become, for most of the time, impossible."

"Moreover, some of the roads will be flooded. What I suggest is to use this last dry period to cover the most critical areas, so as to save the easiest ones for later."

Soon the incident between Kaine and Jason was forgotten, and everybody returned their focus on the exploration and the reason why they were in Africa.

"The drone will be completely useless once the rainy season starts. It isn't affected by a few drops of light rain, but I'm afraid this won't be the case, would it?"

Jenna gazed at Jason with a frown.

"No, there might be some days when it won't rain, but as you've already noticed, we don't have any paved roads around, so those running along the valleys are likely to be inaccessible for the season. Alternative routes are possible, but only to reach the most important places."

"How long does it take for the roads and paths to get back to the conditions they are in now?" Kaine wondered, considering the possibility of having a break.

"Let's say that the beginning of the rainy season is next month, but the rain will be milder, and some exploration can still be done. October and November are the worst, but until February, you can expect wet weather..."

"A dream come true," Allison complained.

"We might ask for a vacation. We can't perform most of the job, anyway," Kaine suggested. "My best proposal is that we try to gather as much data as possible within these two months and leave the analysis and planning for the next season."

Jenna smiled, nodding approvingly. "Brilliant idea! In this case, if we all agree, we should get in the cars and start moving. How about it?"

She jumped, standing from the chair, ready to leave. They all agreed with the plan, feeling eager to have their flight tickets back home already in their hands.

***

In the evening, when he was alone in his bungalow, after the call with Mark, Kaine started to consider the chat he'd had with Jason.

He still didn't have time to figure out what he wanted to do or what would be the best thing to do – whether to leave the continent, never to return, or accept the invitation of the priestess and discover the reason why she wanted to meet him.

"Once again, Mom or whoever is listening," he said aloud, hoping to find someone who could give him some sort of advice, warning, or whatever hint that could help him to decide. "If there is something, I should be aware of, please let me know."

He remained in silence to listen to every single noise coming either from inside or outside the house. He held his breath.

The whole bungalow seemed more silent than it had ever been. Not even the slight whistle of the evening wind blew through the cracks of the wooden structure.

It felt like the entire world remained there, holding its breath together with him. Neither his hallucinations dared to move in the stillness of the night.

Kaine exhaled again. "It seems like every single creature in the world, whether alive or not, fears this priestess. Perhaps I should take this as a strong enough invitation to start packing my things and leave this place."

He observed the little flame of the candle, burning on the table of the kitchen and on the small dresser in front of the window in the bedroom.

As it burned, keeping a steady movement, he recalled the way the fire danced furiously in the evening when he was rushed back home by the man who was taking care of the bonfires in the yard.

"I wonder whether I could ask him the reason why the ghosts refuse to talk to me tonight," Kaine wondered, walking to the window to watch outside.

The man was sitting by the fire, and it was like he was speaking with a sort of imaginary friend. "Maybe the spirits are busy talking to him."

He turned his back to the window. "I have never believed in ghosts, and now after only a few months, I also consider asking them for advice. I must have become crazy!"

Slowly, he undressed, considering that there wasn't any conclusive decision to be made. "I will sleep on it, and maybe the night will bring me some sort of wisdom. If not, tomorrow I will have to give my answer to Jason and... Oh, fuck it, we will see. I feel already too tired to think about the tribe."

He turned over on his bed and closed his eyes, hoping at least to be able to fall asleep.

\*\*\*

The insistent knocking on the door of his bungalow woke him up before the sunrise. He turned his eyes at the clock and wondered what kind of emergency could have happened to wake him up.

When he opened the door, he saw Jason standing in front of him. "What the hell is going on with you? Do you have any idea of the time?"

A vein on Kaine's temple began to pulse, but Jason came inside anyway, closing the door carefully behind him. "I know, and I'm sorry to wake you up before the sunrise. However, as you can guess, I came to get an answer from you. I have to admit I couldn't fall asleep last night."

He walked to the kitchen and grabbed a chair.

Still sleepy and wondering whether he was still dreaming or not, Kaine followed Jason. "I haven't yet made any kind of decision. I was waiting to wake up in three hours, and with a clearer mind, I would have made my choice. Technically, at least from my point of view and according to my concept of day and night, we are still far from tomorrow. So, now, I'm going back to sleep. If you want, you can join me, as there is a couch in the other room where you can rest your troubled spirits. Then, when I wake up, we will talk in front of a good cup of coffee."

Without waiting for any answer from Jason, Kaine returned to his bed, trying to fall asleep once again.

Jason looked at his retreating back, his mind blank, feeling surprised by his unexpected behavior.

*I must admit he's also right. It's no later than four, and we can still consider ourselves far from the morning. What am I going to do?*

He had no intention of walking back to his bungalow and decided that the best option would be to fall asleep on the couch.

With a slight groan, he stood up from the chair and went to his makeshift bed for the next few hours.

Pushing a hand on the cushions, he tested the softness and the general comfort. When he realized that the other option was represented by the bed where Kaine was also sleeping, he felt more than satisfied, and with a smile, he lay on the couch and fell almost immediately asleep.

# CHAPTER 17

The morning after, Kaine woke up earlier, and at six o'clock, he felt sharper than usual. As he sat up on his bed, the sleeping presence of Jason on the couch reminded him about a decision he had to make.

*I promised him I'd give him an answer, but night gave no wisdom this time, and I still don't know what I'm supposed to do.*

He stood up and put on his jeans, walking to the kitchen to prepare the coffee for both of them. He had no idea what kind of breakfast Jason usually ate, so he decided to wake him up and let him help himself with whatever he could find.

"Good morning," Jason growled as he reached the kitchen. "Look, I'm sorry for having barged into your place in the middle of the night. I don't know what happened to me and why I was in such a hurry."

Kaine turned to him and smiled at the ruffled hair on his head. "I see, and if you told me the truth about your connection with the priestess, I could understand your turmoil. If you want, you can go and have a shower, comb your hair, and even shave. I still have a few razors left from the last grocery trip I made."

Jason peered down at himself and caressed his chin. He couldn't see himself, but he knew he must have been a mess.

Kaine walked toward a dresser and grabbed a couple of clean towels. "Here you are. I'm sure you will feel better after it."

"Thanks, you're a kind person. It would be a pity if you're also stuck here the way I am," Jason replied, walking to the shower room.

In the bungalows, there wasn't a real shower, but a bucket to be filled with the water coming from a tap. Yet, there was at least a mirror, and as his eyes met his image, he wondered how Kaine wasn't scared when he saw him. "I'm like a zombie!" he mumbled as he started to undress.

He returned to the kitchen, feeling like a different man.

"Good morning, Sir. Do we know each other?" Kaine chuckled as he saw him reappearing, shaved combed and, to be honest, quite attractive.

Jason smiled, lowering his gaze, flattered by the peek Kaine gave him. "I guess we do, and once again, thank you for welcoming me here. Is there some coffee?"

"Yes, sure." Kaine poured a cup for him. "I have no idea what you generally eat for breakfast, but you can help yourself."

Kaine sat down and scrutinized Jason as he started to cut some bread. "Tell me more about what happened to you. I-I still can't understand how a person can command time, space, and bring back someone from thousands of kilometers away, just in the blink of an eye."

"It's a mystery to me as well," he replied, munching on his bread. "I don't belong to their tribe except as a captive.

Therefore, their secrets are not shared with me. What I believe is they might not belong to this planet. I can't say."

"Do you mean they could be some sort of aliens?" Kaine wondered with a grin.

"Aliens, demons, spirits... I have no idea. What I know, and I have witnessed with my own eyes are their powers. Nevertheless, the priestess is the one who holds the strongest ones," Jason explained, sipping his coffee. "So, what's your decision?"

Kaine averted his gaze from Jason and stared at his empty cup. Lazily, he poured some more coffee and continued to think.

"It's a difficult choice, and anyway, I'm afraid I already know enough to be included on the list of the people to be watched, so there is no chance for me to avoid the risk of the curse."

He raised his gaze to Jason. "I'll come to meet them. I'm curious to know everything about them, even if it will be something, I need to keep to myself."

Jason nodded. "I would have done the same... well, I did the same, as a matter of fact."

"One thing we will now have to figure out is how to create an alternative story, some evidence to confirm the extinction of the tribe. We might figure out a disease, famine, war with other tribes. I will invent something with the help of the people of the villages around here." Jason stood up from the chair and was ready to leave.

"What's the deal with those people? Do they know about this tribe?"

Jason turned his eyes to Kaine, "They know, and they've created a sort of symbiotic relationship with the tribe. They won't suffer diseases or any attack from the rebels or any organized army, and they keep their secret...secret."

He then turned back and walked to the door, determined to start creating the proof to make sure the rest of the team would be dismissed as soon as possible.

"I believe it won't be easy to produce convincing evidence, but I'm confident in the skills developed by Jason." Kaine grabbed his head between his hands, feeling trapped already.

"I should have listened to the hallucination of my mother and forgot about the search for this tribe. But why did she have to be so mysterious? Couldn't she say it clearly not to get involved with this expedition?"

He stood up and walked to the window in front of his bed, and still sipping his coffee, he looked at the sky getting clearer with the sunrise. The woods surrounding the clearance created for the village seemed to glow with the first rays of light, and the air filled with the sounds of birds and the far call of the monkeys.

*The mighty rain forest is waking up. I wonder whether they are also aware of the magic in this place.*

He smirked, caressing the rough surface of the dresser in front of the window. *I needed to come to Africa to start believing in magic, but this is no longer a question of believing in something or not; this is what I have witnessed, beginning with the presence warning me...*

"Better if I stop thinking about those things now, and focus on the report I will have to write, the explorations we had scheduled yesterday, and the fact that soon enough, I will be meeting the tribe I have been searching for, for quite a long time. Although I can't tell this to anyone, it's personally a great achievement."

With a satisfied smile on his face, he went to get ready for the day to come, knowing that, in all likelihood, they would have to start trekking without Jason.

***

It took about another month to collect the evidence and bring the whole team to agree to a likely extinction of the tribe. Therefore, also their permanence in the heart of Africa was coming to an end.

It wasn't difficult to inform Dr. Luther about the outcome, as he was delighted to be the first organization to bring an end to an ongoing search that lasted for centuries. So far, nobody before was able to find the semblance of an artifact belonging to them.

Kaine would remain for a couple of extra months there in the village to collect all the possible evidence and write the report, which would be compiled together with Dr. Jason Murdock.

There was only one person who wasn't completely happy about returning home: Jenna.

There was some sort of attraction between her and Azizi, the young guard. He kept his due distance, but with unspoken words, they both knew it would be an awkward goodbye.

"So, this is the time when people generally say goodbye and wish each other a happy life for the future, I guess," she said, trying to keep herself from showing her feelings.

"I'm not sure I believe in goodbyes, Jenna," he replied with a soft tone of voice.

"Then we are in trouble, I'm afraid. I don't believe in them either."

"Should we then say, see you? Or maybe we should say something different." His voice was shaking; he'd never fallen in love with anyone before, and particularly not with a *mzungu.*

"Like what...?"

He took her hands in his. "Like, don't go."

"Or come with me?"

They both laughed at the ridiculous situation.

He reached her lips and slowly kissed her, not even sure what he was doing, or whether it was the worst thing to do for two people who didn't belong to the same world.

Jenna hugged him tightly. "Azizi, what are we supposed to do?"

He held her, feeling the warmth of her cheeks against his own, wishing to have her in his arms for the rest of his life.

"I have no idea. But here is a suggestion. You take that plane, go back to your home. Let's try to live our lives the way we knew before, and if we think we should get back together, we will contact each other." He parted from her, locking his eyes on hers.

"I don't know how to get in touch with you."

"How about by phone?" he proposed, taking his phone out from his pocket.

She giggled. "Of course."

As they exchanged telephone numbers, there wasn't anything else to do but to start driving to the airport, hoping to make it in time, without any useless delays.

Kaine felt alone like he'd been left behind for the rest of his life. Seeing his team going away, and knowing what was waiting for him, both excited and scared him.

Jason put a hand on his shoulder. "Everything will be fine as long as you keep their secret."

"I really don't know. I'm still wondering how I could have gotten myself into this." He turned to face Jason.

"If this makes you feel better, when Akuna-Ra gets an idea into her head, she will never give up until she reaches her goal, and as you can see, generally, she does."

Kaine's eyes narrowed as he wondered about the meaning of his words. "Do you mean to say, she wanted me to be here so, besides ordering you to contact me, she made sure everything would be resolved in her favor?"

With a slight nod, Jason replied, "More or less, this is what happened. I can't be one hundred percent sure, but I'm ready to bet my life that she did."

"But this is the time. Come with me; she is waiting for you, together with the tribe."

They started to walk as the people of the village watched them leaving. They all knew where they were going, and some of them prayed for the safety of the young researcher.

For the whole journey, neither of them had anything to say. Kaine was immersed in his thoughts and toured visually around, trying to figure out the route to their village. He realized how carefully their research had been diverted to other locations to avoid that they would have accidentally spotted their position with the drones or by walking.

*It's incredible to see how those people have been able to avoid civilization for so many centuries. One thing I would like to know is whether they recall, or if they have any record of their ancestors, those who reached this place before them. Oh, I have so many questions, I have no idea where I'm supposed to start.*

After a while, they arrived at the location of the tribe and, besides the general appearance, of a typical tribe in the middle of the forest, Kaine immediately had the strange feeling that they were hiding something more than simply their existence.

They reached the place where Akuna-Ra was expecting them.

She was waiting in front of her shack, as few people were allowed to enter her personal space.

Kaine remained open-mouthed at the haughty posture she kept.

"Dr. Martin," she greeted with a slight smile on her face. "It's a pleasure to meet you."

"I was anxious to meet you, and I consider it an honor to be allowed where many others would never be able to come," Kaine replied kindly.

"You were granted the privilege to reach us because I could trust you. I know what Dr. Murdock told you about this tribe, and it's all true."

Her eyes pierced his soul, reaching the depth of its core. Kaine felt naked in front of her, and a sudden shiver of fear crawled along his spine, like the skittering of a thousand spiders.

"Our people conducted a nomadic life until we found this part of the rain forest. This was the perfect place to establish and settle. During our journey, we strengthened the bonds with the forces of the underworld and the spirits of the forests. During the centuries, those skills have been improved."

She walked away in the direction of the shack, where Kaiphindi was waiting for him. "You will have the time to learn about us, as much as we will have the time to learn from you." Her eyes continued to scrutinize him and his intentions.

"You are the priestess of this tribe?" Kaine asked, wondering why he wasn't first introduced to their king.

"Yes, and I know what you are thinking. You have been introduced to me first because I'm the one who has summoned you to reach us. I'm the spiritual leader, and if there is a threat or a potential gain to our community, I will be the only one to deal with it. I could never risk the safety of our queen."

Kaine was impressed by her ability to read his mind. "I wonder whether there is any need for me to ask any questions if you can guess my thoughts so easily."

Akuna-Ra smiled, amused. "You will get used to it, and I'm sorry if this might sound impolite toward you, but it's also the best way to understand people's real intentions. What we have learned is that what people speak does not necessarily reflect what they really think."

As they walked, Kaine observed the activity of the tribe. At first glance, they all were intent on the regular activities he had studied in other tribes. *But there is something different I can't grasp.*

Jason remained silent the whole time, wondering whether he was supposed to leave them alone or wait there. With a side stare, he observed Kaine, who looked around at the people.

*That might have been me the day I first reached this place. I was so young and eager to know everything.*

"When did you become established here in this part of Africa?" Kaine wondered.

Akuna-Ra glanced around as if she was looking for an answer written somewhere. "It should be a few centuries ago; we don't keep track of time in the same obsessive way you do. Time is just a concept, and one year, one hundred years, compared to eternity, it doesn't matter."

"But thinking about the life of a human, it does make a difference. However, you have a point about the tracking of time we keep," Kaine objected. "Just satisfy my curiosity: why do you want to keep your tribe secret from the rest of the world?"

Akuna-Ra turned serious, and her expression tensed. "We have our reasons. You will know about them with time, and I hope you will be our guest for more than just one day. I am sure we both will have our benefits in getting to know each other more closely, and with this, we will come to the reason why you were allowed to reach us."

There was a pause where Kaine hoped he didn't upset the priestess.

"If you keep an open mind, you will have a lot to gain too, and it will not just be a sterile exchange of knowledge," Akuna-Ra continued, her tone of voice returning calm, and her face relaxing.

"What kind of society have you developed?"

"Our society is a matriarchal kind; women are the keepers of spiritual magic. The Queen is our leader, the one who organizes and regulates the whole tribe. We don't have a king, and although our queen does have a companion, there is no political or decisional power transferred to her mate. Hunting and Defense are equally shared between males and females, and everyone takes care of their households.

"As you can imagine, we do not have any use for money or any other currency like you do, except services. We share what we have and help each other."

As Akuna-Ra went on to explain how their civilization worked, Kaine observed what the people were doing. It appeared that many people were out either hunting, gathering, or... "Where is the rest of the tribe now?"

"As you can imagine, some are searching for food; others, instead, are patrolling the surrounding areas to make sure no threat will reach us," she replied.

They reached a larger wooden building, where he imagined the Queen was living.

"Here is where our Queen receives guests; this is not the place where she lives," Akuna-Ra explained. "Kaiphindi is waiting for you."

That said, she guided Kaine to enter and, to his surprise, there was only one large room, barely furnished, except for a fireplace in the middle of the room surrounded with pillows to allow people to sit down. A sort of throne was placed at one side, facing the fire.

Kaiphindi was waiting for them in front of the fire and with a gentle smile, she opened her arms to welcome her guests.

"Dr. Martin, I have heard about you for such a long time I was eager to meet you."

Kaine felt slightly embarrassed by that kind reception and wondered how he was supposed to address her or talk to her. Jason hadn't ever talked about any sort of etiquette.

He peered at Jason to get an idea about his behavior; there wasn't any formal sort of bowing, kneeling or whatever else.

He shyly smiled. "It's an honor for me to be allowed in your presence and to be introduced to know your tribe, heritage, and customs. I wish to express my gratitude for being welcomed here to learn about you."

With a nod Kaiphindi invited him. "Please, come and have a seat at the fireplace. We consider the fire as a divine force, as the spirits talk through it."

She showed him the way to the fireplace, inviting him to have a seat on the pillows. "Our priestess, Akuna-Ra, must have already given you a small introduction to our tribe, showing you around. You will find many similarities to your own culture, but also profound differences. I hope we both, after this period of getting to know each other, will part enriched, with a better understanding of these two different worlds."

She spoke with a calm tone, and he felt enticed by their willingness to show him their way of life.

"Your highness," Kaine commenced when they were all seated around the fireplace. "I have so many questions about the mystery around the existence of your tribe, that I do not have any idea about where I should start. I hope you will not take my eagerness and curiosity as an offense."

Akuna-Ra approached them, and reciting an ancient spell, she glimpsed the fireplace where nothing was burning. Kaine observed her, fascinated by the rite, and wondered what the meaning of those strange words was. In a trice a fire started from the center of the fireplace, dancing with wavy movements. Kaine marveled at her trick.

What came first into his mind was the resemblance of the movement of the flames with that of the candle in his bungalow.

He remained open-mouthed, wondering whether the same spirit was there moving the fire.

*Something is definitely not right; this is not a trick. This is the same dance the flame of the candle performed.*

Kaine scrutinized at Jason with a questioning expression. Then at Akuna-Ra. "How...?" He didn't know what to say.

"The spirits are listening," she replied, glancing at him with an expression that resembled the stare of a predator who observes his prey before attacking.

She took a seat beside Kaiphindi in front of Kaine and Jason.

Kaine observed the flames, mesmerized. *Do you mean to harm me?* He formulated the same question he'd asked to the spirit that moved the candle, and just like in the previous case, the flames, as if they remembered what had happened in the bungalow, stopped their undulating movement and stood still.

Kaine's heart started racing and he felt almost like fainting yet felt relieved that there wasn't any intention to hurt him or anyone else.

# CHAPTER 18

Kaine spent more than another month getting to know the tribe and their customs, and it was difficult to lie to Mark and everybody else about them. "I guess the most important thing is to divert the interest of the scientific society from them. Yet, they are so insistent about keeping their secret for myself, that makes me think twice before saying anything even to the spirits."

He walked to the kitchen to get another glass of water before going to sleep. He visually toured the bungalow and took a seat at the table, grabbing his head between his hands, wondering about the feelings he had. "Why do I sense there's something they're hiding from me? Why is Jason always so silent when we are there, and why does he seem to know everything, but he's either not willing or not allowed to share the secret with me?"

He remained in silence for a long time, listening to the noises coming from the outside the bungalow. Suddenly, he thought he heard something different than the previous evening. It was like footsteps approaching his cottage.

He stood up and walked to the window in the bedroom when someone knocked at the door. He felt petrified and breathless.

Even though he knew there was nothing to fear, he peeked outside the window and drew a relieved sigh when he saw Jason standing in front of his door.

"Jason, you almost gave me a heart attack!"

Jason was serious. "You need to come with me. Your time in this country is almost coming to an end, and I believe this is the time when they will tell you what they would like you to give them."

Kaine cringed. "I don't have anything to give them...I don't understand, I still have so many questions."

"Then this is the best time to ask whatever you want," Jason replied, forcing a smile on his face.

"Is there anything I should be warned or worried about?" Kaine didn't want to step outside the bungalow, as he felt threatened even by his own shadow.

"Nobody is going to harm you, don't you worry. The same thing happened to me when the time arrived for me to go back," he explained. "They decided when you were ready to meet them, and they decide when it's time for you to leave the tribe. There isn't anything that's left to your decision, besides whether or not to leave the country."

Kaine swallowed hard. "And then you tell me not to be afraid?"

They started to walk under the brightest moonlight Kaine had ever seen. It was like it was closer than ever, and it had a light of its own.

The chirping of the night insects was louder, and as they approached the camp, the pounding of the drums felt like it was echoing inside their bodies, until Jason brought Kaine to its center, where the queen Kaiphindi was waiting together with Akuna-Ra, and the rest of the tribe seated in a circle.

There, the drums stopped, and the chirping sound of the night creatures faded away as if someone closed a window.

Jason brought Kaine to the center of the circle and left to sit with the others.

"You don't have to fear, Dr. Martin," reassured Kaiphindi, sensing his discomfort and apprehension. "This is going to be a goodbye celebration, and we have no reason to be hostile toward you. Nevertheless, as much as we offer you the knowledge of our heritage, sharing our traditions and culture with you, we are now going to ask something in return."

Akuna-Ra walked toward him, and when she was close enough, she pointed at the moon. "It was far before the memory of this forest when we reached this place. It was a long journey to survey and to expand our knowledge. Nevertheless, differently than all the other places we have explored, this was the one that offered better chances for its diversity."

"What do you mean? You certainly..."

With a kind smile, Akuna-Ra raised her gaze back to the sky, and then once again to Kaine. "This is not home; not for us, at least. One day we shall resume our exploration and eventually return home, but I will miss this planet."

She averted her eyes from Kaine and glanced at Jason. She would have never said it out loud, and mainly she would have never admitted her feelings. Nevertheless, there would have been a time when she might have explained to him the reason why their destinies were never supposed to meet, and that was the imminent planned departure.

As their eyes met, Jason understood what she meant and let his arms fall limp beside his body. He felt heartbroken, and indeed he missed her already, even if the time between the present day and the day of their departure would take hundreds of years.

"What we are asking you in return for our welcoming is a promise – a vow of silence, if you please. We are collecting data to resume our journey, and it's vital for us to remain undiscovered."

Kaine gasped.

He'd never thought he could have ever gotten in touch with a civilization coming from another world. "Our people could cooperate with yours if we knew about your existence."

"You really think we are so naïve?" Kaiphindi intervened. "We have been observing you, and not just here in this stretch of Africa; we have observers around the world. Your people believe in their supremacy over the whole Universe. Your leaders would engage in a devastating conflict, which aftermath would be nothing else but death and destruction. We prefer you to stay away from a possible annihilation; we have no intention to start a war. This was not in our plans, but if defending ourselves will become necessary, we won't step back. Don't judge us based on our lifestyle; you might be surprised to understand the level of our technological advancement."

Kaine lowered his gaze. *Unfortunately, they are right; we will engage not just into a war against them, but against each other to obtain their secrets.*

"I will do my best to keep your secret..." His voice trembling.

Jason kept his head lowered, and a slight smile brightened his face. His eyes stared into the nothingness, and his soul found peace.

Kaine observed him and felt like Jason was far away, and what he was seeing was an image transmitted from another dimension.

Akuna-Ra grabbed his chin and forced him to peek into her eyes. "Dr. Martin, I hope you are not going to break your promise. There have been many people who failed our trust; some of them are dead, some others..." she pointed at Jason. "Some others were not so lucky. This is a warning, a promise I will never fail to fulfill."

His heart started to race as her eyes burned like flames, promising nothing good for those who would have crossed her path.

He had the chance to experience her magic. She was not just playing tricks; she could command the forces of nature. Under her spell, time and space didn't have any meaning, and he started to regret the decision of coming to meet them.

Akuna-Ra let him go gently and walked away, leaving him drained from the fear that almost caused him to wet his pants.

"But this is a celebrative moment, so we should not spoil it with resentful feelings," Kaiphindi clapped her hands, interrupting the awkward silence brought by the words of Akuna-Ra.

As Kaiphindi was the most respected person, worshipped as a living goddess, Akuna-Ra was the most feared. Like Kaiphindi, she didn't have an age, whether she had ever been born, or if she had always existed, regenerating herself like a Phoenix.

Whenever she spoke, the forces of the underworld woke up and gathered at her side, ready to answer to her summoning. Nobody wanted to disappoint her and face the punishments she would have considered appropriate. Kaiphindi and Akuna-Ra were the two main powers, the creation, and destruction, the balance that kept their people together and thriving.

The drums started to play once again, and the dancers commenced their performance to say goodbye to a welcomed guest and friend.

"Tomorrow, you should start to book the flight to return home," Jason said, approaching him. His face was relaxed, giving the impression of being relieved of Kaine's departure.

"Are you happy to see me going?"

"What I hope the most is to be the only white guy condemned here for the rest of my life. You might believe this is the sort of place you can get used to and even find a new purpose that gives you happiness. Remember, a golden cage still remains a cage, and there is not a single day when I don't think about what I have left back home, or the chance to have the freedom to leave this place." His voice was full of pain and regret, and he lowered his gaze to look at the ground.

Kaine felt his sorrow and wished he could help him. Yet, knowing the powers of Akuna-Ra, not even death could be an escape for him; she might not allow him to die.

He looked at the camp and the celebrations offered in front of his eyes as he sat beside Kaiphindi. The food provided was delicious, but he couldn't stop thinking about the threat posed by Akuna-Ra.

He turned his gaze toward her, and with a wicked smile, she nodded at him. *Does she already know that regardless of my efforts, I will say something? But this is impossible. I will never say a word about what happened here. I'm not going to betray their trust, but most of all, I'm not going to risk my life.*

With a bright smile he replied to her, and trusting her ability to read his mind, he felt confident she already knew his intentions not to betray them.

She nodded, satisfied, but she was aware that humans were never to be trusted. Indeed, she could have wiped away his memory of what he saw, but the reason why he, like all the others, was called, was the hope that they would have used the shared knowledge of the Universe to build and improve themselves and the society they had grown so far.

*The only people who could avail themselves of our teaching proficiently are those people living in the close-by village. Those who keep our secret and gain a better understanding of their planet and how to use it sustainably,* Akuna-Ra considered, observing every move Kaine made.

*I could sense your ability to communicate with the spirits. I wish you would remain here and become one of the spiritual leaders of the village you are living in now. Your potential might be wasted in your society.*

\*\*\*

The celebrations went on for most of the night, and at about three o'clock in the morning, they all retired to their shacks and bungalows. Jason was walking away with Kaine toward their villages when Okumi called them.

"I will guide Dr. Martin to his bungalow; you are requested to present to your mistress," Okumi said glancing Jason.

With an uncertain nod and a nervous smile on his face, Jason turned his eyes at Kaine. Without saying a word, he parted from them and walked in the opposite direction to the shack of Akuna-Ra.

If he had to be honest, he was glad to be called to her presence. He had some questions bothering his mind, and perhaps she summoned him because she was going to satisfy his curiosity, or maybe it was to quench her appetite.

As he went inside her shack, he saw her standing in front of the fire. She appeared concerned, and as she noticed him, without saying a word, she gestured for him to come closer.

"You wanted to see me..."

"You wanted answers," she replied, inhaling deeply.

Jason licked his lips, hoping that the time had arrived for him to solve all the questions that had bothered his mind for such a long time.

"And will you give them to me?" He kept a lower tone of voice, wishing she wouldn't bother listening to his heartbeat.

Her eyes locking into his felt like the pain of a million blades slashing his soul.

He smiled.

"You said you are going to leave. Is there any scheduled departure?"

Her expression relaxed into a smile. "You forget what time means to us. If I tell you in a couple of thousand years, we will resume our journey, would it make any difference to you?"

"It would if you keep me alive. I have no idea about your powers. The more I know you, the more you surprise me. Nevertheless, I can sense something more than a punishment behind your willingness to keep me around. Either you are getting used to me, like an annoying pet, or you enjoy teasing me, or maybe..." He grinned. "...nobody can satisfy your appetite the way I do."

She looked at him, puzzled, and then burst into laughter. "I have to admit it, you have convincing arguments when I call you for pleasure, and perhaps it's a bit of everything; taunting you, or also getting used to your presence, so much that maybe I might miss it one day when you aren't here. To answer your question, there isn't a scheduled departure. But I forecast it to be soon."

Jason averted his gaze, trying to hide his feelings. "What would happen if I ask to come with you?"

"No human is allowed with us. We are not going to take a specimen of any sort of living creature from the places we are visiting. The journey is only for our people..." She turned her eyes to the fire as if to ask a question to the spirits, or as if she heard something coming from there.

"Then promise me one thing," Jason pleaded, almost fearing what he was going to ask. "Promise me, if I'm still alive, you will end my life the day you leave. I'm not sure I want to live, knowing I have lost you forever."

The corners of her mouth lowered into a light frown; she didn't want to see him dying. Although she decided not to love anyone, she wasn't sure she could ever comply with his request. *The day we will depart, I might be strong enough to love...*

"So it shall be. Now, go away," she replied curtly, hoping he would go away without any other questions.

"You said you would answer my doubts. I still have many others, but I understand your desire to be alone..." He turned away, and without waiting for any reaction from her, he left the shack and the camp.

He was exhausted. He was sure he had never been that tired in his whole life, and the only thing he wanted was to be in solitude, and possibly have a drink or two to forget about the bad feelings welling from the deepest part of his soul.

*Do I really want to die if she leaves?* he wondered as he was walking the path back home. There wasn't a clear idea in his mind, and perhaps it was just the tiredness he'd accumulated during the exploration.

He hoped his soul would have regained some peace, once he would have returned to his everyday routine.

He reached the kitchen and lit the candles that were supposed to burn for the night. "I'm not sure why I'm fighting them now; within three hours or so, the sun will rise, and the evil spirits will return to the darkness from where they came," he said, opening the cabinet to take the whiskey bottle and a glass.

He sat down in the chair and, unhurriedly, he poured a half glass. Since his captive life, he started to appreciate the scattering of the flame's brightness filtering through the amber liquid.

The light danced with the creation of thousands of reflections like many little stars dancing on the tiny waves created inside the glass.

He felt mesmerized by the plays of light, and a smile appeared on his face as he started to sip his whiskey.

***

As Kaine returned to the bungalow, he felt so excited to return home, that he didn't even think about calling Mark. The very first thing he thought he would take care of was getting the flight ticket from Goma to New York as soon as possible. He started up his laptop and immediately checked the first available flights.

The best opportunity was offered within four days, which gave him time to organize his transfer to Goma, whether by the same plane from Beni airport or by road, taking a longer route to have the chance to enjoy the scenery.

When he received the confirmation for the ticket, he switched off the computer and let himself collapse on the bed.

The wooden frame protested noisily with a couple of loud cracks, but the frame was solid enough to withstand his careless treatment.

"I can't believe in only five days I will be back home." He stared at the fan, thinking about the comforts of his house, and the fact that soon, he would once again be held by Mark.

He stood up, as sleep wouldn't come to relieve his stirred soul. "I'm wondering whether I can call him."

He glimpsed the clock on the bedside table and realized it would be too late to wake him up.

"I can certainly wait until tomorrow. I'm sure he understood the reason why I couldn't call him last evening."

He watched around the whole place. Although it was a rough building and was furnished with just the bare necessities, he didn't need anything more.

"I'm not sure whether this is going to influence me to the point of deciding to move to the countryside and live a simpler life. Nevertheless, it will certainly give me the chance to think about what I need and what I don't."

He switched off the lights and observed from his bed the dancing flame of the candle. This time, there wasn't anything strange in its movement. The only thing he noticed was how mesmerizing it was, and soon enough, before he realized it, he fell asleep without even undressing.

\*\*\*

The sun started to rise, and Jason was still on the chair in the kitchen, glancing at the whiskey from the clear glass he rolled between his fingers.

Either because of the alcohol, the tiredness, or the many thoughts swirling in his mind, he couldn't grab a steady idea and simply remained to stare at the glass, waiting for something he couldn't fathom.

He tried to stand up from the chair, and wobbling, he reached his bed.

"I love you, and for this reason, I wish to die tonight. We are obviously not meant to be together, and you've started to become an obsession," he mumbled as he lay down, hoping to fall asleep.

A terrible hangover and a severe headache welcomed Jason to a new day. He regretted his decision not to keep any analgesic in his house. Even though hangovers like the one he was experiencing were quite seldom, and he rarely suffered from headaches, there was nothing he needed more than a painkiller to get rid of it.

He tried to stand up, but his legs didn't have any intention to keep him up, and he collapsed back on the bed.

"At least I don't have a class with the children today, and I don't have to guide Kaine. Nevertheless, if I don't reach the door to ask for someone to drive me to town and get some medicine, my wish for dying will be granted real soon."

He gathered all his strength and started to walk outside to ask for help from whoever would listen to the cries of a poor drunkard.

# CHAPTER 19

The final five days went by slowly, but at least Kaine had time to enjoy the nature and the surroundings of the place.

He was as excited as a little child as he walked outside the bungalow with his luggage packed. *Only hours are dividing me from Mark and our life together. I can't describe how thrilled I am.*

"So, are you ready?" Jason smiled, opening the door of the jeep for him, where Azizi was ready to drive.

"I am, indeed. I'm so electrified, I could even fly without an airplane," Kaine replied as he placed his luggage in the leg space of the backseat.

He remained for a moment to observe the village as if he wanted to memorize everything that had been his life for more than eight months. It felt like losing a piece of his heart, as he'd started to like it.

"Don't think about how much you would love to stay in a place like this. I can tell you from experience if you would have been forced, the way I am, you wouldn't find it fascinating and beautiful anymore," Jason replied, interrupting his contemplation of the details he wanted to be imprinted in his memory forever.

With a chuckle, Kaine shook his head. When they were all inside the jeep, Azizi started up the engine and commenced his ride to the airport of Beni.

The road went by smoothly, but it was like each of them wanted desperately to find something to say, without the possibility to find the right words. As soon as they reached the airport, Azizi got out of the car and approached him. "Dr. Martin, may I ask you a favor?"

"Of course, you can."

"Do you have any chance to meet Miss Jenna?"

Arching his eyebrows, Kaine replied: "Yes, I think I can reach her."

Azizi searched for something he was keeping in the pocket of his shirt and handed Kaine a small figurine carved in wood with a little envelope. "Would you please give this to her? I wish she won't forget about this country and the reasons why she liked it so much," he explained. "I have never been in the US, and I'm sure it's also a beautiful place, but it's good not to lose memories, even when they seem to be so far you can't grab them anymore."

Kaine observed the finely carved artwork. "Oh... a gorilla. It's amazing. Where did you get it?"

He raised his gaze to Azizi.

"I made it. Here, time is something you don't miss, and if you use it to learn new skills or to perfect the ones you have been born with, then your time was wisely spent," he replied proudly.

Kaine remained open-mouthed. He never saw anything so beautifully carved. "It looks almost alive. I will give it to her as soon as I reach my workplace. You can be sure of it."

Azizi bowed his head slightly. "Thanks, I appreciate it."

"So, this is goodbye," Jason stretched his arms after the long road trip.

"That's what it seems." Kaine shook his hand. "I wish to thank you for your assistance and for guiding me to visit the tribe. Most of all, I am thankful for helping me write a story about an extinct civilization and to have gathered some handicrafts to confirm the claim. I would have never been able to do it alone."

Jason nodded, feeling satisfied that he could save Kaine's life from a curse far beyond anything the young researcher could imagine. "Now it will be up to you never to talk about the tribe to anyone. Remember always the power of Akuna-Ra. Her promise is not to be underestimated, and if you don't trust my empty words, just take a look at me. You don't want to be next."

Kaine still found it crazy. He wasn't a person who could have been easily persuaded to believe in magic or paranormal activities. Mainly, it was challenging to make him admit the existence of creatures able to perform things beyond the rules of nature.

*Nevertheless, if I think they are not even from this planet, I need to reconsider what is possible and what is not, particularly in a universal vision.*

"I will try my best," Kaine chuckled.

A sudden shadow crossed Jason's expression and he grabbed Kaine by his shoulders. "I'm not joking, kid, and you should take it more seriously."

Kaine froze at the swift change in Jason's attitude. "I-I didn't mean..."

"It doesn't matter what you meant or not. Don't think it was just a joke or that they will never be able to reach you. There isn't a safe place where you can be in this universe, once you have triggered Akuna-Ra's rage."

Jason's voice trembled, fearing that, just like he did when he was younger, Kaine didn't believe in the promise made by Akuna-Ra.

"I-I will remember," Kaine mumbled uncertainly.

He gathered his luggage and turned his back to Jason and Azizi and walked away, hoping never to return for his whole life.

Jason remained there and watched him entering the small building where he would take care of immigration and passport control. He prayed all the entities he knew that this was the last time he saw Kaine.

"You seem to be concerned, Boss," Azizi observed.

"I'm not worried. I'm terrified, Azizi. The kid doesn't understand who he is dealing with; I hope he'll be smarter than I was and will keep the secret." He closed his eyes and leaned on his seat.

"The kid, as you call him, is a grown-up man. Perhaps you should give more credit to him..."

"I wish you were right, my friend; I wish you were right."

\*\*\*

As soon as he arrived at the airport of Goma, Kaine couldn't wait any longer; he needed to hear Mark's voice one more time.

"I don't care whether I'll see him again tomorrow. I just need to hear him."

He grabbed the mobile phone and dialed his number.

"Good morning!" Mark greeted excitedly. "Are you at the airport already?"

247

"Yes, I'm at the international airport in Goma now, and within a couple of hours I will leave Africa to come home. I can't tell you how much I've been missing you, my house, my life... Everything, even those things that, before leaving, annoyed me so much."

His voice trembled in anticipation. He wished he were already there, and those few hours were like torture than an exciting wait.

Mark laughed, amused. "This means that soon you can resume your little devil-in-training attitude. Are you ready?"

"I can't wait. I want to spend the first two days in the bedroom with you," he said, taking a seat at one of the cafeterias in the gates area.

"I will tie you there!"

They both laughed, and all the stress, the hallucinations, the magic, and paranormal activities were far away and forgotten. Kaine didn't wish anything else but to forget about the whole expedition and resume his life the way he used to know it.

"I will call you as soon as my plane lands. Will you come to pick me up?"

"I'm not sure whether I can make it. I will do my best, but don't be disappointed if I won't be there. I'll be waiting for you at home with one of my cocktails to welcome you home," Mark smirked as an idea began swirling in his mind.

"That's no problem. I can understand you might still be at work at the time my plane lands. We can see each other back at home."

When they hung up, Kaine visually toured his surroundings at the airport. He thought he would never see that moment. He started to feel like he had been cursed the same way Jason was.

He felt comforted by the people around him preparing to leave either for a business trip, or to meet some relatives abroad, or to return home.

There weren't many white people there, and in a place like the International airport of Goma, a white person wouldn't have fallen between the cracks.

He ordered a coffee and something small to eat. He was sure that during the flight, he would be served, at least, with dinner and breakfast, and thinking about the meals he was going to have, he considered it wise not to have a full meal before the flight.

He thought about the months he'd spent there and all the natural marvels he had seen. *I'm certainly going to return to Africa, and next time, I don't intend to listen to anything about magic, tribes, and anything else but savanna and wild animals.*

*It's funny, thinking about the last time I was in Africa for work. It didn't impress me the way it did this time. Congo and the rain forest indeed have something special, which fascinates the soul and makes you feel homesick as soon as you are at the airport.*

His thoughts went immediately to Jason. Most likely, he didn't have anyone left back at home. Everyone, starting with his family and then all his friends, thought he was dead.

*It must feel terrible being alive and be forced to let your beloved ones think you are dead. I wonder how he coped with that feeling... Thinking about it, I'm not surprised he abuses alcohol. It must be the only way to remain sane.*

He considered what would have happened if something similar happened to him. He knew if he had disappeared from the face of the Earth the same way Jason did, Mark would have suffered unbearable pain.

"Now I understand what Akuna-Ra meant when she pointed at Jason and said that some others weren't as lucky as those who found real death for not having kept the secret," he thought.

He shook his head and started to walk toward his gate. "From this point on, I'm not going to think about Jason, or anything connected to the expedition. There are more urgent things to focus on, and the first is to establish my life together with Mark. Then there will be other projects to follow at work, and this story will soon be buried in the past."

***

Akuna-Ra was walking back to her shack, fully immersed in her thoughts. She couldn't take her mind off the power she'd sensed in Kaine.

"What bothers your soul?" Kaiphindi wondered, approaching her from behind.

Akuna-Ra turned her head slightly and observed her out of the corner of her eyes. "That man; the researcher," she commenced, bringing her hand to her mouth. "Did you notice the behavior of the fire when he was introduced to our tribe? I didn't pay attention at the beginning, and only now I recall what happened and how it behaved. He could communicate with the spirits; he could understand them..."

Kaiphindi closed her eyes, trying to remember whether she noticed the same particular incident Akuna-Ra did. However, despite her efforts, she had to admit not having paid attention to that detail.

"When I told him the spirits were listening, he turned his eyes at the flames, and suddenly the movement stopped as if to obey an order or a request."

Questioning her mind and twisting her fingers, Akuna-Ra paced around the yard in the middle of the camp.

"We know there are also humans who have the capability to communicate with the spirits. Their abilities are certainly raw and can't compare with those of our people. Nevertheless, they have potential. It might be this young man was one of them," Kaiphindi tried to reason, recalling her understanding about human nature.

"I'm afraid that, despite his potential, he has no idea of his powers..."

"Why are you concerned?"

"Because I have a strong feeling, he will betray the promise he made." She glanced at Kaiphindi, toughening her expression.

Kaiphindi didn't seem impressed by her revelation. "Then he will meet his fate."

Without waiting for an answer, she left, walking in the other direction.

\*\*\*

The airplane finally landed at the JFK International airport. Kaine felt tired, regardless of the comfortable first-class flight. He needed to move his legs and breathe some fresh air, which he hoped to be able to do quite soon.

His feet were swollen, and he feared he would fall immediately asleep as he reached his house.

*I wonder whether it's a good idea to see Mark right away. Perhaps it would be better to call him and ask him to meet tomorrow –* he pondered *– No, I can't wait so long to*

251

*see him again. After all, what's better than falling asleep in his arms?*

He rushed to the baggage claim, from where he called Mark to inform him about his arrival safe and sound.

After an endless number of rings, he wondered whether he would be there waiting for him or not. He hung up the phone, and as he was going to put it away, a message beeped.

*"I'm still at work, sorry baby, I'll be late. See you this evening at home."*

Kaine cringed, admitting his disappointment, but on the other hand, he knew this was something that could have happened. "I guess there's nothing else to do but grab my luggage and call a taxi..." he whispered as he fetched the last suitcase.

He didn't have time to turn around before a couple of officers came to him.

"Dr. Martin?" one of them asked.

"Y-Yes, but..." Kaine couldn't understand what was going on. He was not transporting any prohibited items, and besides, that would have been noticed on the scan at the airport.

"You will need to come with us," one of them said, grabbing him by the arm and guiding him toward a service exit.

Kaine's heart started to pound, wondering whether there had been a moment when he left the luggage unattended and someone might have hidden something inside it. Mentally, he went through all sorts of souvenirs he had purchased in Africa.

"Is there anything wrong? What's the matter?" he wondered as they walked through the corridor.

One of them, who was firmly guiding him, almost squeezing his arm, replied, "We have been informed you are carrying illegal substances, and we need to verify the contents of your luggage and perform a scan of your body."

Kaine's blood froze in his veins. "No, I-I... there must have been a misunderstanding...Who...? Why would they lie?"

His mind started to race with the millions of possibilities, considering that perhaps the checked-in suitcases were stolen, and something was inserted by drug traffickers. He had no idea how he would have been able to defend himself, or what would be the consequences for having smuggled drugs inside the country.

They reached a room where they placed all his luggage on a table and started to open them one by one, exchanging glances and smirking at each other as they were going through his belongings.

Then, suddenly, one of them grabbed a package. "That's what we were looking for!"

Kaine was sure he was going to have a heart attack. He felt his heart racing in his chest, his hands were shaking uncontrollably, and his knees failed him. He collapsed, sitting on a chair behind him, glancing at the unknown package one of the officers had taken out of his suitcase.

His head felt light, and he couldn't speak a single word. He just eyeballed the officer and had no idea how he would get out of such a mess. *How am I ever going to prove this is not any of my belongings? How do I convince them that someone has placed this package in my suitcase after the check-in?*

The officers started to laugh, and one of them grabbed him by the arm and forced him on his feet. "We're going for a ride," he sneered.

They walked him to a secondary exit, where a black van was waiting. The first thing he noticed was that it wasn't a Police vehicle, nor did it belong to any official authority, whether US Customs or anything. It was just an anonymous black van.

*Something is wrong here.*

He started to fear that perhaps those were not real officers, but instead the drug dealers who were waiting for the package, and if that was the case, he believed he was in deeper trouble than with the law.

They brought him inside the van, and as soon as the door closed, they allowed him to sit down, blindfolded him, and cuffed his wrists.

"Where are we going?" Kaine mumbled with the feeble voice he could gather from his lungs.

"We are going for a ride, like I told you," one of the officers sneered.

The van started to move, and Kaine's mind got foggier trying to understand what in the world was going on and who those people might have been. It was clear to him that they might not be real officers, or they would have brought him to a Police van and wouldn't have made any secret about the place they were going to.

It took about forty-five minutes to reach the location, and when the car stopped, the door opened, and he was guided outside. They walked for a few meters before he could hear the noise of a door opening.

He was pushed to enter inside the building, and the door slammed after him. The blindfold was removed, and he started to understand everything.

As he recognized his home and Mark there, yelling, "Welcome home!" he began to laugh hysterically.

"I will kill you," Kaine yelled through his laughter.

Mark reached him and kissed his lips gently. "Then I'm afraid I'm not going to remove your cuffs."

He scrutinized the two men dressed as officers. "Thank you, guys, you have been amazing!"

"It was a blast," one of them chuckled. "You should have seen his face when we got the package out of his suitcase. It was priceless!"

"Now I believe you owe me some explanation, and if you uncuff me, I promise I won't kill you," Kaine replied as, finally, his heart returned to beat at a regular pace.

"What do you say, Officers? Is it safe to release him?"

"I believe he's telling the truth, but I would be a bit wary just in case. Those 'devils-in-training' might be deceitful," one of them chuckled as he went to remove the cuffs from Kaine's wrists.

"So, it's time for some explanations and also introductions," Mark said as Kaine rubbed his wrists, which started to hurt. "Those are Greg and Tim; they are old friends of mine, and they really work at customs control at the airport. When you asked me if I would come to pick you up, one idea began to twirl in my mind. I made a couple of phone calls to see whether they could help me with a fun plan to make your return home more thrilling. They came up with the idea, and they knew how to make sure they would find a package inside your suitcase."

"Well, indeed it was quite exciting. I was already forecasting my life behind bars, and how I would have explained to my supervisor and all the people who know me that I've been framed." Kaine peered at Greg and Tim. "Now I understand why you were laughing and chuckling the whole time. I should have guessed it was something like that."

"It was a pleasure, but now we need to return to our duties. Our shift starts in about an hour," Greg grimaced, glancing his wristwatch. "We should get together one of these weekends when we all have more time to get to know each other."

"Of course, it would be great, and you have been amazing!" Kaine replied.

***

Once they were alone in the house, Mark walked to the kitchen and returned with a couple of cocktails. "I guess this is the time when we can finally celebrate your return back home. I have been missing you so much."

Kaine took the glass in his hand and looked around at his house. The wooden frame was gone, together with the evil spirits and the fear of curses. He felt comforted by the familiar smell of his own home. That kind of scent that tells your heart not to be worried any longer, as you are finally in the place where you are safe: Your home.

He closed his eyes, inhaling deeply, listening to the sounds of his safe haven: the ticking of the clock, the muffled noises of the cars passing by. The smell of the paint and the wooden furniture.

*This is home.*

He opened his eyes and smiled at everything familiar to him, and as his eyes met Mark, his heart knew there was nothing he could have desired more.

*I have everything I need in this world; my life is brilliant.*

"You have no idea how it feels to return home after such a long time spent in the middle of nowhere, and most of all, I'm extremely thankful to have you here at my side. Although you almost caused me a heart attack, I can tell you I have never been happier in my life as I am now."

Mark smiled tenderly. "I didn't remember how it felt having you in front of me; you are so beautiful."

He took the glass from Kaine's hand and placed them on a small table in front of the couch. The only thing he cared about was having him in his arms, at last, feeling the contact with his skin and, just as Kaine said on the phone the previous day, staying in bed for the whole weekend, just to enjoy the warmth of each other's bodies.

Their lips locked together in a tender kiss, able to stop time, and for a moment, Kaine thought of being in a place suspended within one second and another. Their souls could talk to each other in a language nobody could decipher, in a whisper only they could hear.

The tiredness that seemed to be winning over his senses when he went to get the luggage, vanished like the African mist at the first rays of light, and there was only the feeling of growing arousal that led them to the bedroom.

Nevertheless, as soon as they were naked on the bed, Mark's sweet caresses soothed him, and before he could even realize it, he fell asleep in the place he would like to rest for eternity. Mark's arms.

# CHAPTER 20

Within a couple of months, Kaine's life seemed to have returned to its old routine, and perhaps he thought he could archive the expedition. Also, the gorilla figurine he was supposed to give to Jenna remained forgotten in his pocket.

One day, when looking for his mobile phone, he found it together with the envelope Azizi had given him.

"Damn!" he mumbled as he hurried to the part of the building where she was working. He didn't know exactly on which floor her office was, and it took him almost the whole morning to locate her.

Before going to lunch, he went to see whether she was still there or if he could leave the gift on her desk.

"Look who's here!" Jenna greeted as she was coming out of her room. "Long time no see. How are you doing?"

"I'm fine, thanks. How about you?"

"I can't complain. Were you looking for me, or someone else?" she wondered, giggling.

"I came to search for you. First of all, I need to apologize, as I completely forgot to give you something Azizi asked me to give you. I was so absorbed by the fact of returning to my regular life that I disregarded everything else," he felt like a real jerk for giving her the gift two months later than he was supposed to.

Her jaw dropped, and as Kaine mentioned Azizi, her expression brightened with a broad smile.

With a trembling hand, she took the gorilla figurine and observed it in detail. "It's such beautiful handiwork."

"He carved it himself. He is incredibly skilled; it's almost alive," he said, admiring it one more time.

"I thought he forgot about me. I tried to call him, but his telephone was never to be reached. I thought he didn't mean to stay in touch..." she replied without taking her eyes off of the little gorilla.

"I hope in the letter, he gave you an alternative way to contact him or an explanation for that problem. Remember, in Africa, and particularly in the middle of the rain forest, technology is not strong enough to reach everybody."

She placed the gift in her pocket together with the envelope, which she was planning to read in private, perhaps at her lunch break.

She raised her gaze to Kaine and smiled. "And what about your boyfriend, Dr. Murdock?"

With a slight jolt, Kaine recalled the incident and perhaps everybody thought they had an affair. "No, we are not together. I have a companion here. What happened there was a big misunderstanding."

"Well, you said it right. It was big because Lawrence talked and speculated about it for the whole journey back. He was sure you would move there and live your life in the middle of the rain forest, looking for ancient and actual civilizations," she giggled.

"Then someone has to tell him I'm back and there hadn't been anything between us. What he saw was a mistake that shouldn't have happened."

Kaine blushed embarrassed at the thought of what everybody was speculating about; *although it was not what it seemed, it was still a private matter.*

"So, I have to presume the whole building now knows about it." His tone changed from embarrassed to upset.

"Don't you worry, me and Allison made sure he wouldn't talk about it anymore," she assured, winking at him.

"How? Did you threaten him?"

"Kind of; we blackmailed him. You are not the only one who has secrets. Allison and I know hot secrets about him." She giggled amused adjusting the ponytail that bond her auburn hair. "We promised we would have made them all public, ruining his whole social life, if he ever mentioned it. I also considered he was thoughtless when he told us about what he saw. He is not a bad guy, but sometimes he behaves like a little brat and needs the firm hand of an adult to make him behave."

Kaine smiled, relieved to hear his reputation was still safe.

"Thanks," he chuckled.

"You're welcome. Are you going to lunch?" she asked, not sure whether she wanted to be alone and read the letter during the break or wait to be at home where she could think of calling Azizi right away.

"Yes, I was going for lunch as soon as I talked to you. Do you want to join me?" Kaine asked politely.

Generally, he would have preferred to have some time alone, so he could read the news and get updated with

260

what was going on in the world, but since she had been kind enough to defend him from an embarrassing situation at work, he considered being polite and asking her to join him, the least he could do.

"Why not? So, you can tell me more about the lost tribe? After all, it was truly gone, and we were there for nothing."

They started to walk toward the restaurant where he usually went to eat. He felt a bit uncertain about what he was supposed to say about it. Even talking about it made him feel uncomfortable.

"In our job, having no result is as conclusive as a positive one. In this case, it meant we could prove the existence of the tribe and record their passage. Also, we could gather some interesting artifacts, which could be linked to their culture and beliefs. Of course, it would have been better to have met them in person, but we might need an Ouija board to do so."

A nervous chuckle escaped his mouth, and he hoped she wouldn't notice it.

"That might be the case..." she replied thoughtfully.

"If you haven't yet read the report I have written, you can have a check it out; Dr. Luther must have forwarded you all the link to its location."

"Yes, he sent it, but I was so busy that I haven't had the chance to read it. I'm sorry." She opened the door of the restaurant, smiling at the welcoming scent of the food and the warm atmosphere of the place. It was a popular place to have lunch; it felt so cozy and friendly to give the impression of being back at home. It was one of those places capable of bringing back childhood memories.

Kaine loved it. It was one of the few restaurants where he could unwind from his work, at least for half an hour.

Not to mention the quality of the food was far superior to that of other places in the neighborhood.

"You remained there in Africa for more than a month after we left. I thought you would have returned after one or two weeks, at most. Did you gather many artifacts?" she wondered as she started to study the menu to decide what she would eat.

"Not many to tell the truth. I was writing the report with Dr. Murdock, as I thought he could also combine what he found out independently..." He tried to find a reasonable excuse to close any discussion that might lead to a confession of the actual existence of the tribe.

*But what if I tell her about it? It's not like she would go and write an article for the world to read that I found the tribe, but I prefer not to say. Moreover, if I tell her the truth and the reason why they need to keep their secrecy, she will understand... NO! You can't tell anyone, can't you remember?*

There was a real battle inside his soul. There was a part of him that needed to tell someone what he had found out and the fantastic experience it had been to meet those people. On the other side, there was a scared side of himself recalling the curse that made it impossible for Jason to come back home.

Jenna observed him as he was reading the menu. His eyes were fixed on one place, and his mind was far away even from the planet.

She noticed how his fingers grasped the corner of the menu as if he was trying to grab onto his last hope before falling into an abyss.

262

"Are you okay?" she wondered, gently touching his hand.

With a sudden jolt, like he'd been tasered, he dropped the list on the floor.

"I'm sorry, I was thinking of something else." He tried to apologize for not being with her. "I've been rude by allowing my thoughts to carry me away."

Jenna shook her head with a concerned expression. "You don't need to excuse yourself. I was worried whether there was something wrong, or you had some problems. If you need someone to talk to, I can listen."

Kaine turned his eyes at her, and it felt like his mind suddenly went blank. The approaching of the waitress arrived like a lifesaver in that awkward situation.

"May I take your orders?" she asked.

Kaine exhaled and looked at her with a thankful expression. "I will take a large chicken salad and a glass of water," he replied.

Among all the dishes served that was his favorite. The chicken was always perfectly cooked and juicy, the salad fresh, and the special vinaigrette sauce, the recipe for which they kept a secret, was something to die for.

"I will take a Greek salad and some orange juice," Jenna replied, still observing every move Kaine made.

The waitress left with the orders, and Kaine regretted dearly having invited her to join him for lunch. *I should have come here by myself like I do every day. Why did I have to ask her to go with me?*

"Kaine..." she said. "If you prefer to be alone, I can move to another table."

Kaine shook his head. "No, please, just... Can we talk about something else besides work?"

"Of course, if this makes you feel uncomfortable, or if you have some troubles there, we can change the topic. Why didn't you say so before?" she giggled.

For a moment, he considered himself safe, and he shook his head, trying to relax. Soon the tension between them dissipated, and they started to chat about everything else, which wasn't connected with Africa.

\*\*\*

Nevertheless, in the evening, as he was lying on the bed with Mark, he recalled the feeling he had during the lunch break with Jenna. He was still aware of the promise he made to Akuna-Ra; however maybe he needed to discharge his stress, or it was the extra drink offered by Mark, but the words started to flow from his mouth, revealing all the secrets he was not supposed to tell.

"So, do you mean to say this tribe is still actually in existence, but they do not want to have anyone nosing around?" Mark wondered after he listened to Kaine's story.

"Yes, and I can understand their willingness to stay away from our civilization. So far, we haven't brought anything good to those tribes we have '*discovered*,'" Kaine admitted.

Mark nodded. "You're right, and you can count on my silence. I have no idea what you're talking about, because I believe we've both drunk a bit too much, so I will forget everything you tell me by tomorrow morning. The secret of the tribe is safe with me."

"I needed to release the tension I had today during the lunch break. I can't even put into words the discomfort I had when Jenna was observing my every single move. I was sweating myself to death." He held himself to Mark. "Will you stay the night? I don't want to fall asleep alone."

Mark parted from him and locked his eyes on Kaine's. "Tomorrow, I will have to wake up earlier, so it's better if I go back to my place. According to the contract, I can leave the house in a couple of months, and then I will come here to live with you for the rest of my life. I can wait until you fall asleep if this will make you feel better."

"I know this might sound a bit foolish, but can I ask you to get a candle?" Kaine pleaded, remembering the evil spirits wouldn't intrude into a place where there was still light. They lived in the shadows, and the smallest beam of light was a deterrent for them to enter a room.

"You are letting those superstitions influence your life too much, but if this little thing makes you feel better and safer, then I'm going right away to get you a candle."

He poked the tip of Kaine's nose and left the bedroom to reach the kitchen.

"Here you are, my little angel. Nobody will ever touch you, because angels can't be touched, particularly when a Master Devil is watching over them." He placed the candle on the dresser and lit it.

As soon as Mark left, Kaine felt a deep sense of loneliness. It was like he had been alone in the dark without any light to guide him home. He wasn't sure whether what he did could count as revealing their secret, as Mark would keep a high level of confidentiality, and there wasn't any threat connected to his revelation.

Slowly he fell asleep, forgetting all the bad feelings and the strange day he left behind.

*** 

He was awakened by a loud thump on the floor.

He opened his eyes. The candle was still burning on top of the dresser. The sun hadn't risen yet, but he could clearly see a shadow cast by the feeble light against the wall.

He turned to face the source of the shadow, and his heart stopped for a second when his eyes met the wrathful expression in Akuna-Ra's face. She was standing in front of his bed, holding the ceremonial stick he saw her using during the farewell ceremony.

"What was the promise you made us?" Her tone was calm, but he could feel the rage hardly contained inside her.

"W-What? How...?" Kaine mumbled, trying to regain some breath, hoping he wouldn't die that day, or perhaps wishing exactly for that.

"It doesn't matter how, or what." She grinned. "You have broken the promise you made us. Sure, you were warned, but yet you needed to tell your boyfriend about the tribe and the secret we try to keep for ourselves."

"H-He won't tell..."

"Silence!" she thundered. "It doesn't matter if he will tell or not; the issue is another; you have broken a vital promise. Moreover, you can't say whether he will be able to keep the knowledge to himself or if he will go and tell it to another trusted person until the wrong one knows about us."

Kaine tried to sit up on the bed. He had to find a way to make it up to her and her tribe. *She's right; I should have kept my mouth shut, but after what happened yesterday with Jenna, I felt the necessity to release my tension, and I needed to have someone who knew about what happened to back me up with this story.*

As she heard his thoughts, her eyes narrowed. "This is not working as an excuse, and you shall indeed face the consequences..."

At the same moment, the flame of the candle started to dance furiously as if there was something that desperately tried to talk in Kaine's defense.

Akuna-Ra jolted as she turned her gaze toward it. *You know he deserves punishment; stay out of this –* she thought, recognizing a presence different from the one she was in touch with.

Suddenly, the flame stopped its movement, as Kaine observed the situation, wondering what was going on in his room, and whether he was still dreaming, or he was awake.

"Back to you," she said, turning to face him. "We should eliminate you right here and now like we did with many others. Yet, like Jason, you seem to have something that can save your life. For this reason, I give you a gift. The gift of death."

"What do you mean? Are you going to kill me or not?"

Akuna-Ra smirked wickedly. "From this moment on, whoever your eyes will see, will die within seconds. I suggest you blindfold yourself for the rest of your life, or at least until Okumi will arrive to bring you back to Africa. There you will have your chance to be redeemed..."

Without another word, she shook the ceremonial stick and pronounced an ancient spell. The room was immersed in a thick fog.

When finally, the room was cleared, Akuna-Ra was gone.

"No...No...NO!" Kaine yelled, fearing she was dead serious, and he would become a killing machine.

Once again, his heart pounded in his chest, and his head felt empty. Tears of terror filled his eyes and started to fall like rain, dripping on his legs. He covered his face, sobbing desperately as the first rays of the morning sun began to light the room.

He wished he was already dead because he could never stand the guilt of killing other innocent people. Suddenly he thought about Mark; if he looked at him, he would also die.

"There is only one thing to do, go to look at myself and kill me. If it's true and I have this gift, then I should be able to take away my own life."

He stood up from the bed and walked to the bathroom, took a deep breath, and opened his eyes, looking at his reflected image, hoping it would work to end himself.

To his surprise, he didn't die, nor did he even feel hurt.

The conviction that everything had been a dream or a hallucination took form in the fog of his thoughts, giving him a hope. "I must have dreamt it..."

A hysterical laugh filled his mouth and he felt relieved, but also a fool for his stupidity.

Still feeling amused, he went for a shower and prepared for another day at work.

He returned to his bedroom to snuff out the candle, so it wouldn't burn the whole place down. Anyway, the candle was no longer burning, and he didn't remember having done anything to it.

A bewildered grin flashed across his face. It was earlier than usual, and he indulged himself in sipping that first cup in complete calm, enjoying the sunrise and the city that was waking up.

With a gentle gesture, he moved the curtain in the window slightly open to see outside. A teenage girl was walking on the other side of the road, and as he watched her, he realized how foolish he was to believe that with a stare he could have killed a person.

Suddenly, coming out of nowhere, a car came from behind and, as if it were out of control, hit the girl, who probably died instantly.

Kaine's breath failed. He dropped the coffee cup and fell to the floor. He tried to scream, but there was no air in his lungs, and only a pathetic whistle came from his mouth.

The words of Akuna-Ra echoed in the room, together with her laughter.

He had no idea what he was supposed to do or to believe. One thing was for sure, the girl died, and the real killer was probably him, not the man who lost control of the car he was driving.

Kaine remained paralyzed on the floor, unable to move a single muscle. He tried to recall the words of Akuna-Ra before she left, perhaps even to rationalize what had happened. The accident wasn't necessarily caused by the curse.

"That could be a coincidence..." he said aloud, regaining control of his own breathing. But it didn't matter how much he tried to convince himself about the possibility that there wasn't any curse on him.

As tears welled once again in his eyes, and the sound of the sirens of an ambulance drew closer, he felt himself sinking into a hopeless abyss from where there wouldn't be any coming back, unless by the mercy of Akuna-Ra.

# CHAPTER 21

The sudden ringing of the doorbell brought his soul to a new level of fright.

*I can't open the door to anyone. If it's true and I'm cursed, I will kill another person, and that's something I can't accept. What happened to this girl can't happen again.*

He crawled to the living room, trying to keep his eyes on the floor, afraid to accidentally peek out the window that opened onto the veranda.

Nevertheless, whoever was at the door was determined not to leave without having talked to him. He continued to ring the bell without minding that if nobody answered, it meant the place was empty.

"Dr. Martin, open the door. I know you are there." He could recognize the voice of Okumi and the particular accent the people of the tribe had.

"Okumi, is it you?" Kaine yelled from behind the door.

"Yes, it's me. You need to let me in."

"I can't. I have been cursed..." At his sentence, he felt ridiculous.

"I know, but it won't affect me. Now open the door before I tear it down."

He could barely recognize Okumi by the tone of voice. He was Akuna-Ra's servant, and he always had a kind voice. This time, he sounded almost menacing, and Kaine wasn't sure he even wanted to be near him. Suddenly he felt vulnerable and lost.

Yet, he stood up from the floor, and with a deep breath, he opened the door. In front of him was undoubtedly Okumi, but he was wearing a dark suit. He also appeared to be older and taller than he remembered.

Okumi peered at him through narrowed eyelids with a disdainful expression, considering him from head to feet. "You need to follow me; there is no time to waste," he said, grabbing Kaine by his arm and pulling him out.

"Let me at least get dressed!" Kaine protested, regaining his strength. He left the door open and hurried to the upper floor to gather clean clothes to change and be ready to leave.

He also grabbed his telephone and battery charger. He wasn't sure whether he would be allowed to have them, but he needed to try. He had to tell Mark about what happened, and perhaps he could help somehow. He was desperate and couldn't think clearly. One thing he knew for sure, his life was about to change drastically, and it would be all his fault.

"Are you ready now?" Okumi wondered, out of patience, as he saw Kaine returning downstairs.

"I will never be ready, but let's say I can follow you now, and I wish to have some explanations on our way."

"I don't owe you any sort of explanation. You should already know everything you need to know," he sneered, pulling him roughly by his arm.

"I need to inform Mark about the fact that I won't be back... He will be worried."

"No need to. I have taken care of him."

Kaine stopped for a moment, fearing the worst. "What the fuck is that supposed to mean? What have you done to him?" he yelled, grabbing Okumi by his blazer, ready to punch him as hard as he could.

Okumi narrowed his eyes and grabbed him by the neck, raising him at the level with his eyes. "Don't dare to do it again. I haven't been ordered to bring you back to the camp in a good state."

Kaine felt suffocated by his grip and wondered how Okumi could suddenly appear so big when he remembered him to be shorter than himself when he was back in Africa.

Okumi let him down on the ground. "I haven't killed him, if this is what you are afraid of. I made sure he didn't remember anything about what has happened. As a matter of fact, like everyone informed of your return, he doesn't recall that you came back from Africa. Soon you will be declared missing, and he will go on with his life."

The cruelty of those words reached him like a punch in the nose. Kaine's face turned into a mask of sorrow, and without any hope left, he lowered his head and silently followed Okumi to a car waiting for them.

He'd lost everything. He was turned into a nobody, something that would exist only in the little stretch of the rain forest at the edge of the national park.

Kaine glanced at his hands as the car started to run. He wasn't sure about what he was supposed to do to be finally forgiven. His thoughts went to Jason, who would have been the only connection with reality and the only chance to feel as if he was alive.

He tried to glimpse outside the window to guess where they were going. He thought they were going to the airport, as he mentioned returning to the camp in Africa, and wondered how he was supposed to leave the country without his passport or any flight ticket.

The windows were darkened entirely, and he couldn't follow the direction they were driving to or where they were.

"You said we are going back to Africa. How are we going to fly there? I don't have any ID with me."

Okumi smirked. It was like he was enjoying teasing Kaine, who was left wondering about his fate and almost everything else concerning his life, present, and future.

"If we would have needed any passport, I would have asked you to get it. Differently than you, I know what I'm supposed to do, and I do my best not to make any mistakes."

***

It was almost midday when Mark finally opened his eyes. He felt like he had the biggest hangover of his entire life, and failed to understand where he was, or what was going on. The only thing he could feel was the headache and the buzzing in his ears.

Gradually, the fog in his mind faded away, and from the blurred images, he could recognize the face of a nurse who was there taking care of his IV.

"Where...What..." he mumbled, trying to get a steady thought in the confusion of his mind, and why he couldn't recall anything.

"Oh, you're awake." The nurse smiled. "You were brought here this morning after your employer tried to reach you by phone."

Mark groaned. "What happened? I can't recall anything..."

"Do you at least remember your name?"

"Yes, yes," he assured her. "My name is Mark. What I wanted to say is I can't remember anything about what happened this morning. The only thing I know is that I woke up early because I needed to go to work, but after I stood up from the bed, everything seemed like a black hole."

"I'll inform the doctor that you're awake. He'll come to visit you later and explain to you in detail what happened to you," she replied.

Mark remained alone in the room and started to recollect his thoughts. He thought about Kaine... *I need to call him, or do I have to wait until he calls me? I feel so confused, and I can't say what I'm supposed to do.*

He tried to sit up on his bed, but his head felt light, and everything started spinning around him. He grabbed his head between his hands and collapsed back on the bed.

After a few minutes, the doctor arrived in the room. "How do you feel now, Mr. Donovan?" he asked, barely glancing at him and still keeping an eye on a folder where all the test results were listed.

He closed the door of the room to have some privacy and walked toward Mark's bed.

"I have no idea. I woke up, and I felt like I had the biggest hangover ever. I can't remember anything about what happened after, so if you need to ask me anything about it, you can spare yourself," Mark said, still feeling woozy.

"All the tests we have performed seem to be normal, and nothing is wrong. Do you have a stressful job? Troubles in the family? Financial problems?" he asked, trying to understand whether the reason he lost consciousness was caused by an overload of stress, or if there was something that needed to be discussed more thoroughly with a psychiatrist.

"Well, this is something I was somewhat expecting. Recently, my job is requiring me to work at the lab for longer days, and also, my partner is now working in a remote area of the Democratic Republic of Congo. There hasn't been good news coming from there, and I'm constantly waiting for his calls to be reassured he's not hurt or missing."

The doctor nodded, frowning, and remained silent for a few moments, thinking about the situation. It was clear to him that the problem was a stressful condition he was living in and pondered what kind of therapy he could suggest.

He raised his glance to him and smiled. "You need to learn to understand when you are overdoing. I can give you the contact information for a good psychotherapist who can help you with your stress problem. I'm also giving you a couple of weeks of sick leave. You will have to rest before you can think about returning to work. At the same time, I will prescribe you a restorative therapy, and I suggest you take this time off work to relax and unwind from your job."

Mark nodded. "When can I leave the hospital?"

"You can go right now, but I would like to keep you here at least until tomorrow so if this fainting episode repeats, we might have the chance to test your condition immediately. We have informed your employer already, so you don't need to worry about it. The less you stress yourself, the better it will be. I'm afraid if this was caused by overworking, you might be close to a burnout," the doctor warned, turning serious.

"Thank you. I will stay here for whatever amount of time you consider appropriate. I'm wondering where my telephone might be. I'm waiting for a call from my partner, and I'm afraid that not having my phone with me might stress me further," Mark pleaded, unwilling to be far from his only means of contact with Kaine.

With a quick nod, the doctor turned his back to Mark, ready to leave the room. "The nurse put your mobile together with your clothes, I will ask her to bring it to you, you try to relax."

Without waiting for a reply, he left the room, and Mark allowed himself to sink back on the bed, trying not to think about anything else but his own health. "I'm not going and force myself to remember what happened this morning."

He closed his eyes, hoping the nurse would have brought him soon the mobile phone.

***

Kaine had no idea anymore about where he was or where he was going. They should have already reached the airport if that was the direction they were taking. *But where else, if not to the airport, to reach Africa? I can't believe they are going to use another means of transportation.*

Nevertheless, the sensation of being transported into a vortex where time and space didn't exist grew stronger and stronger. He had no idea what time it was and where he was, but he felt like his strength faded away. It was like falling into a trance, but the feeling was that of being wide awake into complete darkness, suspended between one breath and another.

Keeping his eyes closed, he inhaled and exhaled, letting himself go into that impression of peaceful existence.

He didn't know how long he'd been in that condition, but when he woke up, it was by being slammed on the floor inside the shack where Akuna-Ra was waiting for him. He opened his eyes and saw her sitting in front of the fire dividing them.

The feeling that any word he had said would have been considered inappropriate stopped him from wanting to say anything.

"How could you?" she said, with an apparently calm tone of voice. She continued to stare at the flames without turning at him.

Kaine wasn't sure it was a question he was supposed to answer and felt like there was something more to come. Therefore, he waited for her to finish what she was going to say.

"You have been warned not once, but many times, either by me, by Jason, or by our Queen. I'm wondering what you didn't understand."

Kaine took a deep breath, trying to move from the ground to a seated position. "I'm sure Mark would have never spoken about your tribe with anyone. I can trust him with my whole life. Besides, he wouldn't have any interest in revealing what I told him. I know you warned me not to say anything about your people, and I understand that spreading this news would have been harmful. Nevertheless, I beg you to reconsider the fact that in this case, there wouldn't have been any trouble whatsoever."

"SILENCE!" she thundered, finally glancing at him. Her eyes were burning like the flames of the fire, and her voice echoed around the walls of the shack.

Kaine lowered his gaze, unable to stand her stare.

"You have been welcomed by our tribe and had the privilege to see things and witness our powers. You were trusted enough to be aware of our origins and identity. We only asked you one favor in return: your silence."

She stood up from her position and paced toward him. Her shadow engulfed him, and it felt like he was once again a prisoner of the darkness surrounding his body during the journey.

She grabbed him by his shirt and forced him to stand up.

"I'm sorry. I didn't mean to put your existence in danger, nor did I wish to harm anyone. Please, believe me when I say there hasn't been a moment when I haven't considered the risks." Kaine tried to regain his confidence.

He couldn't meekly accept the same fate as Jason without trying to redeem himself. "I would have never revealed anything to Mark if I knew I couldn't trust him. Besides, the fact that his memory has been erased should be a warranty to your need for secrecy. Why do you need to punish me for something that will never have any consequence?"

Akuna-Ra frowned and threw her hands in the air. "What about proof of loyalty? What about honoring a promise? Is it really so, and for you, a word is only a combination of letters? Don't you have any concept of honor? Do you know the meaning?"

Her voice started to rise, as she felt frustrated at the lack of understanding humans have.

"You deserved your punishment, and I should bring you back to your home to deal with your brand-new gift. Perhaps the day you will kill the person you love the most, you might also find the meaning of the word honor." She pointed a finger against his chest.

She was furious. *How could I be fooled so easily by the way they can deceive themselves with the conviction of being righteous and honorable people? I should have been more careful, particularly after the previous experiences. Yet, the spirits have plans for him.*

"You are right; like most of the people living on this planet, I have used the word *promise* too lightly. I should have been more considerate, and if I thought I couldn't grant you secrecy, I should have told you." He bit his lower lip, as it was hard to admit how disrespectful he had been toward them.

He turned his gaze to Akuna-Ra. "You are right, and I do deserve your punishment indeed. I-I wish to make it up to you and your people, but I also hope to have the chance to return to my life, to the place where I belong, with the people who would suffer for my presumed death."

He sincerely regretted having told Mark about the tribe. *After having spoken with Jenna, my mind was in such confusion that the only way to release it was to talk with someone.*

Akuna-Ra scrutinized him, trying to listen to his soul. And she felt surprised in feeling that there wasn't any lie in his words; he was sincerely sorry for his behavior.

"That is the reason why I haven't killed you; I could sense something that needed to be investigated in you. Yet, your punishment remains until I have consulted the spirits and our Queen."

"Wouldn't I meet her?" Kaine was surprised about their hierarchy.

*Obviously, Kaiphindi is the queen and leader of the whole tribe, the one who keeps the order and also the one everybody follows. Yet, Akuna-Ra went over her authority and act at her own will. Their society is quite fascinating, and I wonder whether it would be wiser to wish to remain here and learn more about them, or simply want to return to my life back home.*

"This is not something up to you, but exclusively up to Kaiphindi, the spirits and me. You have no power to influence our final decision," Akuna-Ra replied to his thoughts.

Kaine shivered at that remark. "If you can read my mind, then you should have also been able to see my intentions, and you should know I had spoken the truth when I said I didn't mean any harm."

Akuna-Ra shook her head, trying to keep her temper. She didn't like it when someone tried to mock her abilities.

"You still fail to understand what I have explained to you a few minutes before. I hate being forced to repeat myself. I'm used to dealing with intelligent forms of life." She grinned, baring her teeth.

Kaine lowered his head, unwilling to fight against an opponent who was unbeatable under many aspects. He exhaled, closing his eyes. "So, what is going to become of me?"

"For the moment, you are going to stay here. Don't you worry about the people of the village. You won't kill any of them, nor will you be able to kill Jason, so you will be in good company - two snakes in the same pit. You might want to find a way to be useful like Jason already is." She turned her back to him, walking back to the fire. "I will consult with Kaiphindi, and the spirits will give the final response. Don't fill yourself with foolish illusions of a mild treatment. You are no longer a guest; you are nothing but a captive slave here."

Those words reached his soul with a roar, shaking him like a peal of thunder. He didn't have anything to say anymore, and perhaps it would have been wiser to find Jason, hoping to have some empathy at least from him.

He'd had enough reprimands for that day. He would have liked to know how to get out of such a situation, and he wasn't sure there would have been anyone, Jason included, who could have helped him.

He started to walk in the direction of the village where he was lodged when suddenly he wondered whether there would still be a place for him. "I'm behaving like I never left this place, and there is my bungalow waiting for me." He considered his clothes. "I don't even have anything to change myself with. I have only what I'm wearing now... Where in this world am I going?" he said aloud, knowing that there wouldn't be anyone who could have listened to him in the middle of the forest path.

"You are going to come with me, kid."

Recognizing the voice, Kaine turned himself in its direction and noticed Jason coming his way.

"Where are we going?"

"Home..." he said with a tired expression in his eyes.

# CHAPTER 22

That evening, just before sunset, Kaiphindi walked to Akuna-Ra's place. Once again, the forest was silent, as soon the spirits would be summoned for a final verdict.

The question was not about what to do with Kaine, or with Jason. There was much more at stake; the whole future of the team that reached that place centuries before needed to be cleared, and the teaching was to be tested.

The fires burned brightly at the camp, and Kaiphindi arrived at Akuna-Ra's shack, who was waiting for her outside of it.

"My soul sister," Kaiphindi greeted Akuna-Ra.

"My queen. I feel like I have failed in interpreting the goodwill of the young researcher." Akuna-Ra answered her with grief weighing heavily in her voice.

Kaiphindi approached her and placed a hand on her shoulder. "There was a different call for him, rather than his loyalty to us. He is not like Jason or anyone like him; he might be the one who could end our permanence here."

Akuna-Ra invited her to come inside the shack and offered her the seat beside her at the holy fire.

Without any further explanation, she commenced her summoning to the ancient spirits and the powers that guided them there.

Kaiphindi closed her eyes, listening to the spell, feeling comforted in hearing the old language she knew as their own, something so far in time and space as to become almost foreign. Yet, as soon as she could listen to it from the voice of Akuna-Ra, her heart felt at ease, as she was finally brought back to the place they called home.

As flames engulfed the shack, and the spirits took form in front of them, Akuna-Ra drew a couple of deep breaths, ready to consult the wraiths.

*** 

Jason guided Kaine back to his bungalow. "Here we are, kid. We'll need to fit into this one, at least temporarily," he said, opening the door.

"You might want to stop calling me *kid.* It's fairly annoying," Kaine protested.

Jason sneered at him. "I'll quit the day you behave like an adult. So far, you've shown yourself to be as foolish and arrogant as a spoiled child."

"Do I have to remind you of the reason why you're stuck here? If I have been acting like a fool, and I admit I have, then you're no better." He walked to the kitchen to drink some water, feeling already that his throat was like sandpaper.

"I'm guilty of the same sin, but I didn't have the same warnings you had. There wasn't someone here who had been cursed and warned about the fate that was waiting for me. I have been in touch with many tribes in my life before reaching this one. All of them were warning me about not upsetting the gods and spirits, or they would

283

curse my soul and me. None of them ever came true." He followed Kaine to the kitchen, grabbing a bottle of whiskey and two glasses. "At that time, I thought they were talking the same mumbo jumbo as all the others. I had been arrogant toward them all; I admit it, but the reason I fell into this curse was more understandable than yours."

Kaine opened the fridge, looking for a bottle of water. "Don't you have any water here in your place?"

"No, I have whiskey, though. Have a seat and join me."

Kaine cringed. "You can't be serious and drink only booze..."

"Last time I drank water, I got cholera. It wasn't the most pleasant experience, and believe me, you won't like it," he replied, pouring the whiskey for them both and pushing one glass toward Kaine.

Kaine shook his head. Perhaps that was the best idea, at least for that night.

"I'll need some clothes," Kaine mumbled as he started sipping his whiskey.

"We'll take care of it tomorrow. We'll also have to find a way to make you useful in this community. As you already know, here, there isn't much use for money. We got some, but mostly we exchange services, at least for the basic needs. I have no idea if, perhaps, the kids in the other communities might need a teacher, if maybe you are strong enough to help with the building or in the fields, or whether you have some hunting skills to join the hunters."

The sudden rise of the wind seemed to have the will to destroy every bungalow in the village, and perhaps to wipe away the whole rain forest.

Kaine felt his heart jumping in his chest and remained breathless for a moment. He felt like invisible hands were grasping his soul, choking every breath. "The spirits are summoned..." he whispered as if he was in trance.

Jason stared at him with a puzzled expression on his face. He had no idea whether Kaine was already drunk, or if he had some extra powers.

Kaine gasped for air, and with a heavy breath, he looked at the window. "They are going to decide about us."

"What...?" Jason wondered. "Do you hear them?"

"Yes. I can't say I can really hear, but I know at least why they have been summoned." He shook his head, turning his gaze to Jason. "A couple of months before your first email, I started to have what I thought were hallucinations. Now I believe they were real, and the ghosts that came back from the grave warning me about never talking to strangers were just trying to warn me about this possible outcome. If I would have listened more carefully, I might have never come here. I might have given up the expedition and ignored your email."

"Are you telling me that you can talk to the spirits? That's the reason why Akuna-Ra wanted you here. She might need your ability." Jason remained open-mouthed at his own comment. He was persuaded the tribe possessed paranormal abilities, yet he still considered those attributes something peculiar to them, and not accessible to regular people.

Although it sounded like nonsense to Kaine, he believed Jason was right. In that optic, his interest in that particular lost tribe, Jason's email, the warning from the ghost of his mother, it all started to make sense.

He thought about Mark. "I will need to make a phone call. When Okumi came to get me from my home, he said that he erased my return from Mark's memory. I believe he still thinks I never returned, so I should at least call him."

Jason smiled, shaking his head. "Not without your Mistress's permission, my friend. She won't allow you to connect with anyone to tell what has happened to you, risking compromising everything."

"He'll be worried!" Kaine protested.

"As if she gives a shit," Jason chuckled and sprawled out.

Kaine frowned, fearing the worst, and grabbed his mobile phone. He tried to dial Mark's number, but as opposed to the times he was there in the past, now it seemed dead and there was no service to be found.

He felt gripped by a terrible sense of urgency and despair at being completely isolated from the rest of the world.

"What sort of punishment would it be? What kind of captivity would it be if you had the freedom to call for help? This is something you should have considered since the beginning." Jason sipped his whiskey. "I know how you feel. It would have been great if I could have told my family that I wasn't going to come back home, but at least I was still alive. I have lost everything, and even though I will be allowed to return to my town, I won't find anything left. She took everything from me, and although it was something I deserved, maybe it was a price too high to pay."

He gulped the last sip of whiskey and filled another glass.

Kaine was on the verge of crying desperately. Nevertheless, also that was something that wouldn't have helped in any way, so he grabbed the glass and drank the entire content.

*It might not help, but I'm starting to understand the reason why Jason is drinking; it makes it easier to cope with the pain. With time, I hope it will begin to feel better than it feels now.*

They remained for a long time in silence, each of them trying to deal with their misery.

***

The morning after, Mark got out of the hospital and wondered why Kaine didn't call. It certainly happened before that he was too tired or in a place where there was no coverage. Yet, in those cases, he always sent him a message, even in the middle of the night, to reassure him.

"I hope that everything's okay. I couldn't stand losing him forever if he went missing in the middle of the rain forest. If he doesn't call by the end of this week, I swear to God I'm taking the first flight, even risking getting lost myself there. I'm not going to give up on him for any reason in the world," he said as he opened the door of his car.

As he was driving, he recalled that perhaps it would be a good idea to go and take a look at the plants in Kaine's house. *I can't remember whether I watered them yesterday, or the last time I did. I still feel confused after what happened.*

He turned on the radio so he wouldn't feel alone with the confusing thoughts twirling in his mind, hoping to find his favorite station.

As the music started filling the car, he already felt distracted from his problems and worries, and soon enough, he found himself singing along with a smile on his face.

After a good forty-five minutes, he reached his house, and for the rest of the day, he tried to relax without thinking about his work and anything that could have caused him any stress.

Only in the evening, he arrived at Kaine's house and he started to search for the key. It baffled him that they weren't in his pocket; that's the place where he kept it generally, together with the keys for his house.

The suspicion that the previous day, or whenever he was last there, he might have put it back in the original place, rose in his mind. He turned on the flashlight on his phone and crouched down to move the pot.

*Why in the world did I place it back there?* He thought, staring at the keys in his hand.

Refusing to think about it too much, he opened the door and switched on the lights. He turned his eyes to his left where he could have a visual of the open kitchen and the living room.

Open-mouthed, he remained to look at the kitchen, where he saw a cup broken on the floor and coffee spilled. It was like someone had been there. "But who?"

He walked carefully toward the kitchen as if he didn't want to make any noise. "Well, I think I'm overreacting a bit," he said, collecting the pieces of ceramic from the ground. "If there had been a thief, he wouldn't have come in to make coffee..." he said, pondering about what had happened there.

Wondering whether he could find some more clues, he toured the ground floor. *This couldn't have been me. I was found unconscious in my house, not here.*

Feeling his heartbeat starting to increase its pace, he crept toward the stairs. He hesitated for a moment, looking at the darkness upstairs.

With trembling hands, he switched on the lights and carefully started to climb. At every step, he felt the adrenaline rush. It was like he was waiting for a monster or a ghost, or a thief to appear from one moment to another, causing him to fall and kill himself.

"Fuck, this only happens in horror movies. Stop this bullshit!" He reproached himself for his sensitivity.

He walked to the bedroom, and his knees gave out when he saw Kaine's clothes on the floor. Breathless and gasping for air, he couldn't keep his eyes off the pants stained with coffee.

*It can't be... He couldn't be here. I-I know he's in Africa...*

His mind seemed to go blank once again, and he feared he was going insane. "What is going on here? Who has been here, wearing Kaine's clothes...? This doesn't make any sense!"

The bed was still undone like someone had been recently sleeping there, and he sat down to get a hold of himself.

There wasn't a steady thought in his mind, and every memory blurred into an incoherent mass, and started to cry, not even knowing the reason for his tears.

Was he frightened? Confused? Puzzled? Everything and nothing at all. Staring at the clothes from the bed, he tried to find a reason that could have explained what happened.

Why, after months of absence, and after he regularly went to check that house, now, suddenly, everything suggested that Kaine had returned, stained his trousers, and disappeared one more time.

Determined to understand what was going on, he grabbed his mobile phone and tried to dial Kaine's number, hoping he would answer.

After the first ring, the call was diverted to voicemail.

His hands trembled in frustration, but he decided to leave a message anyway. If he was going to switch it on at any point, or if he went to a place with better service, he would at least listen to it.

Still feeling dumbfounded at the view of the clothes, the broken mug, and the bed undone, he switched off the phone and remained seated.

With a raging grin, he stood up and tried to reconstruct what had happened.

"I have no idea who it was, the person who came inside this house, but let's consider for a moment that Kaine arrived the night before I was taken to the hospital." Mark went to bed and lay there.

"Kaine woke up in the morning, and probably, I was already brought to the hospital."

He stood up and went to the bathroom, where he noticed the towel on the floor. "He took a shower."

His attention was caught by the toothpaste and the bottle of cologne lying on the tiles. *There is something that might have scared him, or the ringing of the phone startled him.*

"At this point I presume he dressed and went to get his coffee," Mark pondered, walking downstairs to reach the kitchen.

"Much probably he was at the window when he dropped the cup. Could it be that he saw the accident that happened here?" he mumbled.

"That's the reason why he went to change his clothes, but why in this world didn't he put them in the laundry to be washed?"

Failing to make sense of that reconstruction, he huffed.

*He was taken* - a voice whispered in his ear.

Mark jolted, turning himself in the direction of the voice. There wasn't anyone, but he was sure he'd heard a female voice telling him that Kaine was perhaps kidnapped.

"I don't believe in ghosts. I'm still under the effects of the drugs they treated me with at the hospital," he mumbled.

For a moment, he remained to listen to whether the voice would come to persuade him that it wasn't something he imagined, and it knew what had happened to Kaine.

"He was taken..." Mark repeated. "By whom? Why? Where did they bring him?"

Fearing for his sanity, he considered going home to rest. "This is my home... this is the place we were supposed to live together, and I'm not going to leave it until he returns or until I find out what has happened to him."

"Fuck! Answer me! When did he return home? Why didn't he even call me?" His voice started to sound more and more desperate, and from the original steady tone, now it trembled as if close to a nervous breakdown.

He grabbed his head between his hands and moved them toward the back of his head, glancing around, almost fearful of being alone.

A light touch on his shoulder startled him and tried his best not to turn to look, afraid to be faced with some scary monster.

*You need to remember what happened, and only then can you help Kaine. I tried, but they are more powerful than I can ever be* – the voice whispered again.

Mark closed his eyes. "Is he in danger?"

*No, they need him, and they do not have ill intentions. They are not going to harm him, but he might be trapped forever* – she replied.

"Where am I supposed to go? I have no idea where he's being kept. The world is not that small, and he could be every..."

*I will guide you* – she interrupted, with an urgent tone.

Mark opened his eyes and, not caring whether he was talking to himself or to an imaginary friend, he started walking toward the door. "Then, let's go."

\*\*\*

It was already midnight, and Kaine looked at his wristwatch. He was tired, but he felt like he still had so many questions to ask.

"What is the worst thing about being stuck in this place? I mean, besides having to give up any relationship you had back at home, of course."

Jason thought about it for a moment. It was a relatively straightforward question, yet it was so difficult to answer. "Everything is bad about not being able to move freely. The worst part is perhaps the fact that if I had the chance to choose where to go, being free to decide the final place where to live, I would probably remain here in this exact place."

He continued to stare at the glass filled with whiskey as if he was mesmerized by the light scattered through it.

"Why? I mean, if this is a place where you feel like you're in prison, why would you stay here?"

Jason smiled bitterly, still keeping his eyes on the whiskey.

"There are many reasons behind this choice." He raised his gaze to Kaine. "One is because those children need me as an educator. Without me, they will never get access to any kind of education. So at least they will have some basic knowledge to move into the world. Another, and perhaps this is the most complicated one, is that I'm in love with Akuna-Ra. I love her deeply, passionately, and with every fiber of my being. I could never be far from her."

Kaine remained open-mouthed at that confession.

"I know it sounds absurd, and it's not a case of Stockholm syndrome, believe me. We both started sharing the same kind of emotions, and her position as high priestess doesn't allow her to share any sort of feelings, but we know what we do feel deep inside."

Kaine lowered his gaze. "It must be terrible..."

"We will get used to this too. But now we should go and get some sleep." He stood up, trying to manage and not fall on the floor.

"Where am I supposed to sleep?" Kaine said groggily, struggling to stand up.

"If you don't mind sleeping in the same bed as me, you are more than welcome there. But don't even think of getting any sort of tenderness. I'm already taken."

# CHAPTER 23

"The spirits have spoken," Akuna-Ra said as the flames of the fire withdrew.

Kaiphindi nodded lightly, feeling concerned about their response. The possibility of being able to resume their journey and return home gave her mixed feelings, and maybe she couldn't yet cope with them all.

"There isn't any further destination..." Kaiphindi exclaimed excitedly.

"Perhaps this is the time we can think about home. Do you still remember it?" Akuna-Ra grabbed Kaiphindi's hand, holding it tightly to her own.

"I do... How could I ever forget about it? Not even a whole eternity will ever be able to wipe it away from my mind. But one question remains open, and that is when? Would it be one year, a hundred, a thousand?"

Akuna-Ra stood up from her position. "They are going to tell us when everything will be set. We need to make sure that those who have shown loyalty to us will remain protected."

"What about the others?" She almost feared the answer.

"At that point, we won't need them anymore..."

Kaiphindi bent her head with a questioning glance. "None of them?"

Akuna-Ra turned her back to her, knowing that sometimes there is a need to make difficult decisions, and even if it hurt her, she said, "None of them..."

"Then we will have to set them free. Once we are away, our secret doesn't mean anything anymore. Not even the vow of loyalty or their broken promises." Kaiphindi stood up, ready to leave the place. She sensed Akuna-Ra needed to take some time for herself to think about what she was supposed to do.

In the loneliness of her shack, with the crackling sound of the fire and the noises coming from the forest, she thought about the possibility of returning home. There wasn't any specific date or time for them to get ready for, and besides, time was not of any interest to them. Yet, as Jason pointed out, for those who are not built for eternity, time had a significant meaning.

*I need to focus on more critical issues. The young researcher, for example. I need to know more about him and about his ability to connect with the spirits. If he proves to be cooperative enough, I might even think about coming to a deal with him. Yet, before removing the gift from him, I need to make sure about his willingness to commit to us. I need to make sure that we can leave safely with the same confidentiality we had when we arrived here.*

She sighed and walked outside to glance at the sky. The blinking of satellites passing by made her frown, knowing that her skills to command time, space, and matter was something she needed to maintain, and if possible, to strengthen.

"One single me..." She kept her gaze on the stars. "I fear I might not be enough to elude the surveillance humans have created around this planet."

The light breeze coming from the north brought the scents of the forest to her nostrils. She closed her eyes and inhaled deeply, still formulating the questions in her mind, hoping to receive an answer as soon as possible.

The voices arriving from the woods started to rise, and when they reached her ears, she thought she finally had a response.

Okumi walked cautiously toward her. "Mistress..." he said in a whisper.

Akuna-Ra suddenly turned her eyes to him, and with a disappointed grin, she noticed that Okumi was not alone, but he had brought one of the shamans of the village.

"You have not been summoned. What brings you here?" she wondered, gesturing for Okumi to leave.

"I heard the voices of the spirits. I know your intention to abandon us," the shaman commenced, concerned about the fate of the villagers who lived around the tribe, taking advantage of the protective powers Akuna-Ra had. "What will happen to us once we don't have your protection anymore? How am I or my warriors supposed to front the possible attacks from the rebels and other tribes? How are we going to thrive?"

He spoke in a lower tone of voice as if he was talking to the gods. And indeed, for the people of the villages, Akuna-Ra was a goddess, and her protection was far beyond that offered by any governmental institution or army.

She kept their village thriving in peace, and if they were going to leave, they might be plagued by diseases, wars, and famine. He had to find a solution to protect his people.

She sighed. *Their loyalty deserves a reward. Among all the people who came to know about us, those were the only ones who truly understood our mission and were willing to cooperate. Indeed, they needed our magic, or at least this is what they believe in.*

"You know, you should trust more in your abilities. You are not as helpless as you think you are."

The shaman scrutinized her, wondering what she meant by that.

"The day we are going to resume our journey, we won't leave you alone. Your commitment and cooperation have been beneficial for us both, and we won't forget about it. We are going to give you the means to remain safe and thrive for the centuries to come."

Her voice seemed to hide a sense of turmoil, and the shaman noticed it.

"We feel honored and grateful for your kindness, but we would like you to reconsider your decision to leave the place. We don't talk just about the benefits we have obtained, but also a sort of attachment the people of my village have developed with some of yours. I wish you to know about the deeper relationships that have been created. Despite your apparent immortality, the youngest have sympathies for each other..."

Akuna-Ra smiled and considered that as much as she refused any human feelings, this might have not been a followed rule for all the others. "When we will leave, whoever wants to remain here will be free to go where they please. Yet, I need you to understand that this is not our home. Although we have been here before the memory of the forest, we never forgot the place where we come from, our mission and our journey."

She inhaled deeply, thinking one more time about the past and the reason why they started the exploration.

"Eons ago, a chosen group left our home, far away from here. The task was simple: gathering understanding of the Universe and its boundaries, wherever they are. We knew about other planets where similar forms of life developed, and we were sure that during our quest we would have found many more. We wanted their knowledge and to learn about their powers, so we left."

She started to pace as the shaman began to stroll at her side. "When we reached your planet, we couldn't believe the diversity of life and the potential. For this reason, we decided to spend more time here to get to know all the forms of life, from the basic to the most evolved. Your world fascinated us, but we needed to remember that once our understanding would have been fulfilled, our journey had to resume, and eventually, we would return home. The technological advances of your species gave us the chance to expand our knowledge without even moving away from here. We gathered the information about your solar system and a big part of the Universe. Considering the place where we came from and the data we have collected, staying here gave us much more than we could ever know... Yet, this is not home."

She turned her eyes to the shaman, who kept his gaze to the ground, listening, and understanding what she was saying.

"Will your people be free to remain if they want? Will you unveil to us more secrets and powers to keep us safe and in peace?"

"Yes, whoever believes this is going to be their new home will be allowed to stay. Although this is not included in the plans, we do understand their needs. As a gift of long-term friendship and cooperation between our worlds, we will also provide a solution to your concerns.

We will have to figure out something." She smiled at him, sensing the importance of keeping a balanced relationship with the populations of the planets they were going to interact with.

"I'm deeply grateful for your cooperation, and I hope you will never forget us. We will keep you in our tales so that the generations to come will never lose the memory of you. Many times, I wish the rest of the world would reach the level of development and wisdom you have reached, but then, we are made different, and learning is not included in our proud nature."

The shaman shook his head, trying to hide the concerns for the whole human race that bothered his soul.

With a bow, he dismissed himself from the presence of Akuna-Ra and returned to his village. He couldn't save the world, but at least he could guarantee the continued thriving for his people and of the neighboring communities.

***

The morning after, Okumi arrived at the bungalow where Jason and Kaine were still sleeping.

Kaine was already awake, but he was seated on the bed, his head felt light from the hangover. As the door opened and Okumi appeared, Kaine cringed, recalling the day before when he had been taken from his home.

This time, he wasn't menacing anymore; he was the Okumi he used to know. "Your Mistress is waiting for you. Come," he urged.

"I'm afraid that she will have to wait a bit. I'm not in the condition to hurry."

Okumi grinned. "Do you need any help to reach the camp?"

"That would be much appreciated." He tried to stand up, feeling the whole world spinning around him.

He glimpsed Jason, who was still sleeping, and obviously, he didn't even notice that someone had opened the door. Kaine shook his head, and helped by Okumi, he started to walk outside.

The sun was about to rise, and the light morning dew covered the plants and grass. The man who was watching over the fires for the night stared at them with curious eyes, following them until they disappeared from his sight.

Kaine remained silent for the whole trip to the camp, wondering what the reason for her call was. *On the other hand, I'm glad she did. Perhaps, after a night's sleep, we might talk more reasonably, and Akuna-Ra can explain to me better what is expected of Jason and me. She could have killed us both since the beginning instead of bothering having us around.*

She was waiting for them outside her shack and watched them coming without saying a word. She could sense that Kaine had been drinking and grimaced with a disconcerted expression on her face.

*Is it possible that people of this planet can't stay away from alcohol?*

She clenched her fists, trying to get a grip on her temper.

"Either there is a problem in dealing with reality, or booze is something you can't avoid consuming," she observed sarcastically.

"Bring him inside. I need to talk to him in private and with calm," she added addressing Okumi, entering the shack.

She walked to the fire and grabbed from behind it a jar and a cup. She poured their contents into a bowl and offered it to Kaine.

"Drink it; it will take away your hangover and the stench of the whiskey from your breath," she ordered.

Generally, he would have questioned the ingredients, but since she assured him that it would wipe away that horrible feeling, he was practically ready to drink blood.

He grabbed the bowl and without even thinking twice, he gulped the entire contents. The taste was terrible, as he would have expected, but there was a sort of aromatic aftertaste that softened the primary bitterness. *On second thought, it's almost tasty.*

He stared at the empty bowl before returning it to Akuna-Ra.

It was a matter of a few seconds, and his mind started to feel sharper. His body felt energized, and reasonably soon, his hangover was miraculously gone.

"How... What kind of potion did you give me?" he marveled.

"Feeling better?" Akuna-Ra sneered. "It's an old recipe, a mix of herbs; I have found it beneficial for many things, and one of those is the toxic effects of alcohol."

"Well thanks, it worked like a charm. I know it would make a best seller in my country. Nevertheless, I don't believe you called me at this time of the morning to help me with a hangover. Am I wrong?"

She indicated the place in front of the fire where he was supposed to take a seat, and without speaking another word, she walked to the other side of the fireplace and waited for him to be ready to listen to what she was going to tell him.

"You are certainly wondering whether the reason for having you back here has something to do with the chance to have your curse lifted." She took a short pause, observing every single move Kaine was making to understand his thoughts and feelings.

"There is something I noticed the last day you spent here before returning to your home. I could sense that you could communicate with the spirits. It appeared to me like you had powers uncommon to other humans. You can feel them, hear them, and talk to them. Am I wrong? Are you aware of this capability you have?"

Kaine nodded slightly, recalling the ghost of his mother and the presence in his bungalow. "I have no idea whether I have some mediumistic powers or not." He squeezed into his shoulders, glancing around, trying to avert his gaze from hers. "To be honest, before being contacted by Jason, I had never even considered the existence of paranormal forces. I never believed in ghosts or magic. Yet, the first time I saw what I thought was a hallucination of my mother warning me about talking to a stranger, I started to reconsider everything."

Akuna-Ra was listening carefully to his story and was sure that there was something else she might need to know.

"However, something even more bizarre happened one night when I was returning from the cabin we used as headquarters. That night, the wind was blowing like it intended to wipe away the whole forest, and I was urged by the shaman to return to my bungalow, as the spirits were summoned." Kaine shook his head, still finding it impossible to believe his memory. "I didn't know what that meant until I reached home and lit a couple of candles. One of those flames started to dance furiously, and I asked it whether there was someone I couldn't see and if he intended to hurt me. The flame's dance followed a wavy pattern, and so I asked that if he didn't want to harm me, it should stop moving the flame. And so, it did."

A silent whisper escaped Akuna-Ra's mouth, but she kept quiet, not just to wait for Kaine to finish his tale, but to process the information and connect it with the behavior of the flames of the bonfire.

"I doubt it was a coincidence. Some of the spirits wanted to protect you, but they were minor ones and still obeying the main force dominating in this forest."

She locked her stare on him, ready to read his deepest thoughts. "I'm almost sure that with some exercise, your power can be amplified."

"What if I don't want to?" he protested.

"What if you don't have the luxury of choice?" She toughened her expression.

Kaine shook his head. "Why do you want me to develop skills I'm scared of? Isn't the punishment you inflicted on me enough? Why tease me this way?"

"You don't understand." Akuna-Ra bent her head, relaxing her facial features. "If you cooperate with us, you might get the possibility to return home and back to your life."

She started to explain to him the story of her team, from the time when they left their planet to the present moment.

"The technological advances of your civilization offered us a great opportunity to get to know more about the universe without even traveling. Yet, this also means that we won't pass through the cracks if we want to leave."

"So, you will need me to...interfere with our monitoring system?" he puzzled, uncertain of what he was saying.

She giggled, amused at his naïve answer. "Something like that. Once we are out of your atmosphere, you will be able to return home."

"What about Jason?" he wondered, not sure whether he needed to question what would become of him.

She straightened her back and recoiled her face, wondering what he meant by that.

"I mean, he loves you..."

She inhaled deeply, glancing at the movement of the curtain that closed the door of the shack with the morning breeze.

"I know, but he will survive even without me. One day he will be able to rebuild his life, whether here in Africa, or back in his hometown."

"What about you?" Kaine dared.

She narrowed her eyes and scrutinized him. "It's none of your business."

Kaine lowered his gaze. "I understand, and you're right, my comment was inappropriate. Nevertheless, you might consider this as a way to start thinking about what you want to happen. Humans are a foolish race, and for this reason, I hope you will behave more wisely than we do."

He peeked her from his lowered eyes, hoping to have given her a way to think, and perhaps also reconsider. *Probably there's a way to put you two together for the rest of eternity. I know Jason will not be able to just go on with his life after having lost her.*

# CHAPTER 24

Mark moved his stuff to Kaine's house. He still kept renting the place where he was living, just in case Kaine was declared missing and his belongings would have to be divided with his heirs. That thought killed him and, in the morning, as he was preparing breakfast, he reconsidered everything that happened and the big hole he had in his memory.

"If Kaine returned and then he had been taken as the voice said, I need to understand whether there is something I'm missing and how to recall it. He would have told me about his return."

He moved aside the curtain from the window of the kitchen and observed the sunny sky. He had a couple of weeks available for his sick leave, but if he needed to go to Africa and find Kaine, he would require at least a month, if not a year.

"Although I know the place where he was going to, this doesn't mean it would be easy to find a man. Regardless of whether it's a white man who won't go unnoticed, the rain forest offers a great place to hide someone from the eyes of the people."

He sipped his coffee and closed the curtain.

The house was silent and calm, and Mark remained thinking about what had happened and how it could be that he forgot everything.

*But what have I forgotten? What am I missing?*

Suddenly, like a flashback, he thought he could recall the presence of a man ringing his doorbell the morning when he was brought to the hospital. He closed his eyes, focusing on Kaine and the image of his house.

He gasped and opened his eyes.

"Kaine had indeed returned; he came back one month ago! I remember it now!"

He looked around, and it was like he could see what happened, like in a movie made of flashbacks. "The same man...The same man who rang my bell in the morning took Kaine away!"

"Jenna..." he said feverishly.

He had no idea how her name popped into his mind. Did Kaine mention her? Was she one of the team's experts who left with him to Africa?

He needed answers, so he rushed to the door, grabbing his jacket, determined to reach the place where Kaine was working. He had to find out if there was someone called Jenna, and whether she could have given him some hint about what happened.

"If I need to go to Africa, she might give me the exact location of the place where they were lodging. That should be the best starting point."

He felt excited and surprised that he could recall at least the name of those who were involved in the expedition. He was aware a simple name didn't mean much of anything, because there would have been perhaps more than one Jenna. Yet, he was sure there was only one of those who was working with Dr. Kaine Martin.

He tried to speed up in his car to reach the place as fast as he could. He couldn't wait a single second more. The seat of his car felt like burning under him and he needed to get out of it.

As he reached the building of the organization for which Kaine worked, all his determination disappeared, and he felt overwhelmed by hesitation and doubts.

He wondered whether this was the best way to find out where Kaine was and was tempted to turn back and walk away, maybe to reconsider what to do.

Toughening his expression and clenching his fists, he walked inside, ignoring all those fears. There wasn't any room for hesitation, time was not a luxury he had.

If it was true, and Kaine had been taken by someone back to Africa, he needed to know where he was and perhaps plan a way to reach him. *I can't afford to lose him, now that I found him.*

It wasn't easy to find the right department where Kaine worked, but after a good forty minutes, he reached it and arrived in front of a room where his name was still on the door together with the name of a certain Nora Morris.

He gently knocked at the door, and gingerly peeked inside where he saw a young woman working.

Nora observed at him and remained open-mouthed when she recognized him from the photograph Kaine showed her.

"Oh my God," she exclaimed. "You must be...Mark?"

Acknowledging the picture didn't give any justice to such an incredibly handsome man, standing there looking like an Adonis, she stood up.

She nervously adjusted her hair, fearing that it must have been a mess, and as usual, she resembled a porcupine.

"Do we know each other?" Mark wondered.

"Kaine showed me one of your pictures once. He told me you are a couple now, and he was so excited."

Mark came inside the room, feeling more relaxed. "The reason why I came here is to understand what has happened to Kaine, or whether you have had any news about him."

She sighed, and a worried expression darkened her face. "It has been some time since we've had any message from him. We couldn't get in touch by phone or by email. We all hope he is still... Oh, my God."

She brought a hand over her mouth, regretting even the thought that Kaine could have been dead.

"I'm going to find this out. I'm going to leave for DRC, and I need some information about his latest location. Kaine had been talking about a certain Jenna, who was in the same expedition with him. I'm wondering if you know where I can find her."

She scratched her forehead and searched on her computer. "You might be referring to Jenna Weeks. You can find her on the fifth floor. Try asking around there, and whether she is the one or not. They might know who was in the same team with Kaine."

She stood up and guided him to the corridor. "There are the elevators," she added, pointing her finger to her left side.

Mark smiled. "Thank you for your help. I hope I can find her and at least try to figure out what has happened to Kaine."

"Please, if you happen to have any news once you are there in Africa, could you also inform us?" She turned to reach her desk and grabbed a business card. "Here is my telephone number and email."

Mark took the card in his hands and gently placed it in the pocket of his jacket. "I will. If I find him, I will let you know."

He resumed his walk toward the elevators, hoping to find Jenna, *whoever she is.*

It didn't take much to find her, and she was quite surprised to have Kaine's boyfriend there, looking for information. "I have no idea about where he might be, or what has happened to him. The only thing I know is this a rumor according to which he might be missing."

*If we listen to Lawrence's speculations, he fled with his new date, but I don't think a person like Kaine would ever leave without informing Dr. Luther about his resignation and intention to remain in Africa for the rest of his life. Moreover, he was so keen to return home, that I will never believe he decided to disappear willingly.*

Mark nodded thoughtfully. "Can you give me any geographical indication of the last place where he had been seen? For example, the place where you had your camp. That might be a good starting point. People must have seen him."

Jenna thought about it for a moment. "Yes, of course, I can give you the exact location with all the coordinates, but perhaps I can even do better. You know there was a young man who was one of the guards who escorted us during our expedition. I have his contact information, and you might want to ask him for help. Do you mean to go there?"

"That's at least my intention. Do you think this guy can also agree to be my guide?"

Jenna nodded swiftly. "Without any doubt. If you don't mind, I would like to join you." She blushed as she proposed to leave with him.

"It would be dangerous," Mark warned. In reality, he didn't want to have anyone go with him, as he believed having someone like Jenna meant also having to watch out for her.

"Azizi and I, the man you are going to meet, have a sort of long-distance relationship. I might take the chance to come with you and remain there. He will certainly agree more eagerly to help you if he knows I will be there too."

Mark cringed.

"Please..." she said, making her puppy eyes.

Mark tightened his upper lip and snorted. "Fine, but I'm nobody's babysitter. I'm not going to slow down my pace waiting for you."

She grinned. "It might be the other way 'round, buster. I have been there walking on the rain forest's terrain for six months. You have no idea what is it like." She pushed him with the tip of her finger.

"Perfect! So, will you take care of contacting this Azizi?"

"I will handle everything: logistics, housing, and safety. You get ready to leave with your luggage. Get all the necessary vaccinations, if you haven't already. Go and buy the flight ticket for yourself; I will take care of mine."

He was surprised by her preparedness and thought that perhaps having someone who had been there would have been more an advantage, rather than something that would slow down his search.

He shook her hand. "You got a deal. I wish we will find him safe and sound."

"Let's hope so," she replied. "I will call Azizi immediately. Now should be a good time for him to talk." She hesitated with the phone in her hand. "I wonder whether it would be better first to send a message."

She shook her head and sent him a message about the possibility of returning to Africa.

A few seconds after her telephone started to ring, Azizi was calling her. "Hi Azizi, sorry to disturb you, maybe you were busy and..." She blushed.

"Are you joking? When I read your message about your possible journey back to Africa, I thought I was dreaming!" he exclaimed excitedly.

Quickly, she tried to explain to him the main reason for her visit and her intention to eventually remain there. She was afraid he would think she was using him to find out where Kaine was, but she grabbed the chance offered by Mark to meet him again.

"I would gladly help you to reach the village safely, and I believe there will still be the same bungalow available."


He suddenly remembered the community would be quite close to the tribe that was supposed to remain secret.

Moreover, the man they were looking for was still there. It would be challenging to ensure they wouldn't find him until he could get to talk with the shaman of the village. *He is undoubtedly going to give me the answer I'm looking for. There is no way I'm going to fail their trust.*

"I will have to check it out. But in case these won't be available anymore, I will find out a place where you and your friend can stay," he tried to explain.

"There won't be any problems," Jenna assured him, knowing that in those communities, one place was like any other, and the choices weren't many.

"So, when do I have to come to pick you up from the airport in Beni?" Azizi wondered.

Jenna glanced at Mark and asked him silently, simply moving her lips *when?*

Mark wasn't sure what to reply. He certainly had the passport, and the flight ticket wouldn't be a problem. Yet for the vaccinations and the visa, it would require a week or two, if not more, considering those shots, which needed to be taken in advance. He wrote the answer on his mobile phone.

With a nod, she resumed her chat. "I'm not sure, but two or three weeks; we need the vaccinations and visas."

"Okay, let me know one week before your arrival with the time you will arrive in Goma. I will calculate the time you will need to reach Beni from there."

She was glad to hear his voice once again and couldn't wait until she would be with him.

"I will let you know, but maybe I can call you at other times, just to say hello." Her voice trembled, and she wasn't sure she was overexposing her feelings, or if it was precisely what she was supposed to do.

"Your voice is the most welcome to be heard. Even if you would call me every minute, I would feel lonely between them." His voice was tender and warm, and she wondered if she had to leave everything or perhaps find a way to work from Africa. *From an anthropological point of view, it's such an enticing place for research. I might ask Dr. Luther about the possibility. In the meantime, I will go there and see what my feelings are once I'm with him.*

After she ended the conversation, she turned her eyes at Mark. "What I can suggest to you now is to make an appointment to get your shots. Then control the requirements for the visa. Mine should still be valid, as we made it for one year, and I should still have at least a few months...I will have to check that too."

He wrote his telephone number on a piece of paper and handed it to her. "This is my number. Let's keep in touch."

She took a business card she kept in her wallet. "I will let you know about the progress. See you then."

"Yes, have a nice day."

When he was back in his car, he tried to call Kaine, but once again, it went straight to voicemail. He was frustrated but tried to remain calm.

"I'm an idiot!" he said aloud. "I'm listening to a ghost telling me to go to find Kaine in the middle of the rain forest without even having the necessary knowledge. Just because a voice told me she would guide me. Fuck, I'm a massive idiot! God thanks, I've found Jenna."

He grabbed his head between his hands and felt like it was going to explode. *I have made a fool of myself in front of her. And if she's now laughing at me, she is quite right.*

He let his hands fall on his lap and leaned on the seat of the parked car. "Whoever you are, if you're listening to what I'm saying, let me tell you if you aimed to humiliate me, then you have succeeded."

313

*I'm sorry, I tried to help* – that time the voice came louder and more distinct.

So loud that he turned around in the car to see whether there was someone with him.

His heartbeat started to race when he realized he was alone, probably talking to the beginning of his insanity or to a real ghost.

He closed his eyes, focusing on the voice. "Who are you, by the way?"

*It doesn't matter. I'm glad you have found the right travel mate to reach Africa. I also know the location, but for once, I have forgotten you still belong to the world of the living and need to follow their rules. Once you die, you forget almost immediately about them* – the voice continued to explain.

"How can be sure I'm not going crazy, and you are not the product of my illness?" Mark kept his eyes closed. He hoped this would ha protected himself from seeing a horrible monster.

*People do not go insane from one moment to another* – She was amused at Mark's concern, but it was also true that having a chat with a ghost was not something generally accepted as *'normal.'*

Mark chuckled as he started to review what had happened over the past two days. He grabbed his mobile phone and found the number of the psychiatrist he was supposed to get in touch with. "You can say whatever you want, ghost, but I need to find out from a professional. I'm not going to trust a voice trying to convince me I'm not insane."

He felt immediately better as soon as the consultation was set, and having all the time at his disposal, he also booked an appointment to get the necessary vaccinations to leave for Africa.

***

When he returned to Kaine's place, he felt exhausted. It was already half past six in the evening, and he had barely eaten anything during the whole day.

"And I'm the one who is supposed to recover from stress, overwork, and possible burnout. No wonder I hear voices!"

He put his coat away and went to relax on the couch. There, on the small table beside it, there was a book. He grabbed it, wondering what Kaine was reading before.

It was a horror book written by an author he had never heard of before. "No, I'm sorry, after all, I have experienced these past two days, the only reading for me would be at the level of a fairy tale."

He placed the book back on the table and started to consider what he was supposed to eat for dinner.

# CHAPTER 25

Azizi returned to the village in the late evening. The shaman had already lit the fires for the night and was about to start the rites to ensure the wellness of the people of the community.

"Nganga!" Azizi called as he approached him.

The man turned his face to Azizi, and with a kind smile, walked to him. "You should be at your home with your family," he said warningly.

"I need to talk to you. One of the people who came here months ago is searching for the researcher who returned – Dr. Martin," he said, hoping there wouldn't be any problems if he helped her.

"That's not good. The witch doctor Akuna-Ra won't appreciate any intrusion from them."

Azizi cringed. "That is also what I feared, but one of them is the girl I wish so dearly to have back. Isn't there a way to have them coming, but making sure they won't find the tribe or Dr. Martin? Can't you try and talk with the witch doctor?"

The shaman took Azizi's hands in his. "So, it's all for the love of this girl?"

Glancing back at the flames dancing on the bonfire, the shaman walked toward it as if to ask for permission from the ancient wraiths of the forest. He knew Azizi like he knew every single member of the village. He had a pure heart, and now it was aching from being away from the girl.

Azizi remained to observe him. He barely dared to breathe or blink an eye. He knew the spirits had their way to judge situations, and they could come to a painful decision when it came to the wellbeing of the community they were protecting.

The shaman opened his arms and started an ancient chant, using a language Azizi had never heard before.

His voice seemed to rise to the sky, and the flames followed a spiral pattern to reach double the average height.

*The spirits are listening.*

Azizi's heart was racing furiously in his chest, and he hoped from the depths of his soul that their response was not to forget about Jenna.

After an endless amount of time, which felt for Azizi like an eternity, the flames withdrew back to the original shape and height. The shaman remained for a moment, observing the fire and taking some time to interpret their message.

He turned to face Azizi, who was almost paralyzed in the same position and paced toward him. With a deep breath, he stared at him with a grave expression. "The presence of the two strangers is not welcome. Yet, the spirits look with a positive eye at the union you expect to have with this girl, and if this is a consolation to you, there is no need to forget about her."

"But then..."

"Then," the shaman resumed his speech. "Then, I'm going to speak to the witch doctor. I will bring her the response of the spirits, although she might already know about it, and beg for her understanding."

The old man put a hand on Azizi's shoulder. "Go home, it's late."

Azizi didn't know what he was supposed to feel, or how to interpret the message of the shaman. On one side, he felt ecstatic because he hoped one day to marry his beloved Jenna. On the other hand, the fact that the spirits didn't want any intrusion from the two foreigners meant perhaps he had to wait for better times.

*They make it easy to talk about time; they have eternity...but what about me? I do not have anything but this lifetime. I'm mortal, and I don't have patience.*

The old shaman observed Azizi walking away and followed him until he saw the door closing behind him. With the people of his village in the safety of their homes, he exhaled.

***

Kaine was waiting in Akuna-Ra's shack. He had no idea what he was supposed to do or choose. "Before coming to Africa, I didn't even believe in ghosts!" He shook his head.

Nevertheless, the chance of being able to communicate with spiritual entities, to have a better understanding of life and death, was something fascinating him, and for that reason, he began to consider accepting Akuna-Ra's proposal. Besides, he didn't want to bear his curse for the rest of his life.

He took a visual tour around the shack. The place was barely furnished, considering it was the home of a witch doctor, but the fire burning at the center of the room cast long shadows on the walls and objects, keeping the light quite dim. He didn't know what time it was, but on the other hand, he was not in a hurry.

Suddenly, the curtain used as a door opened, and Akuna-Ra entered. Her figure, barely illuminated by the fire against the darkness of the night, cast a long shadow, making her seem omnipotent.

"Have you thought about my proposal?" She remained at the door as if trying to block any sort of escape attempt.

He felt trapped, and with a long exhalation, he nodded. "I accept it and would like to cooperate with you, but you will have to answer any question I find important to know."

With an amused smirk, Akuna-Ra entered the shack. "I admire your bravery. Yet, I suggest you not dare your luck. My patience has a limit, and generally, I don't like it when people who disappointed me put conditions on my kind requests."

"Although your request was not truly kind, I do agree and if I'm in this situation, it's due to my poor judgment."

Akuna-Ra walked to the fireplace.

Her expression toughened as if she'd received a message from the spirits. She turned at Kaine. "The shaman is arriving, and you will not be allowed to listen to what he needs to tell me. You can return to your bungalow, where you are going to wait for the shaman to call you. He will train you for the task. There is no time to waste."

Kaine noticed the change of expression on Akuna-Ra's face and guessed something serious had just happened. Although he wanted to know, he decided it would be better not to investigate any further, supposing if there was anything, she needed to tell him, he would be informed about it.

Just as she ordered, he stood up, and without saying a word, he left, walking back to the bungalow he was temporarily sharing with Jason.

As he walked away, he saw the shaman arriving, just like she said. He shook his head, still failing to understand or grasp all her powers.

The old man saw him and greeted him with a quick smile and a wave of his hand.

When he also saw Okumi running in the direction of Akuna-Ra's shack, Kaine realized there could be something quite important going on.

Knowing that this wasn't a good sign, he hurried back to his bungalow, hoping to reach it before whatever was going to happen would have started.

\*\*\*

Akuna-Ra waited until both men were in her presence. She stared first at the shaman and then at Okumi, who already began to fear the wrath of his mistress. He didn't dare to ask anything, but he could feel the fires burning in Akuna-Ra, consuming his soul.

"I was almost certain you had erased the memory of Dr. Martin from everyone who knew about his return." Her voice sounded steady, but there was a slight flicker of rage that meant a storm was about to start.

Okumi didn't know how to reply. He was sure nobody would have recalled it, not his companion, nor his colleagues.

"Yet, his boyfriend and one of the members of his team are coming here to find out what happened to him. He was not supposed to engage any search!"

Her voice began to thunder.

"Mistress, I had erased the whole period from their memories..."

"His boyfriend recalled what happened, particularly because he found the house the way Kaine left it. You were not only asked to delete their memories but also to clear up his house to make sure it appeared like nothing had ever happened. How could this have escaped your attention?"

Okumi's heart sank and he fell to his knees. "Mistress, please forgive me."

His voice was shaking in fear as he waited for her rage to consume him. "Akuna-Ra, there must be a way to fix the problem. Now we don't have time for revenge or punishment. We have a situation that is getting more complicated than we think."

The shaman interrupted Akuna-Ra's anger, wanting, first of all, to solve Azizi's concerns about his girlfriend.

Akuna-Ra got calmer and nodded. "You are right. I sensed the question you have proposed to the spirits, and I know their answer. The relationship between the girl and Azizi is well seen, and personally, I wouldn't have any problem if she hadn't come to find Kaine and would have come alone."

"I know." The shaman felt confused and didn't want any trouble. "Azizi proposed to keep them far from here as they search for Kaine. Like Jason did, he can do the same with them. They certainly won't doubt his willingness to help, particularly because they will trust him, in the light of his feelings for the girl."

She turned her gaze to the fireplace as if looking to find inspiration, and with a smirk, she turned at Okumi. "Go and bring Jason here!" she ordered dryly.

Okumi stood up, and without any hesitation, he rushed to reach Jason's bungalow.

"I believe if he can convince them that Kaine is missing, they will feel satisfied enough, and they might leave the place."

The old shaman lowered his gaze. "It seems to me fairly cruel. His boyfriend will grieve the hell, knowing the man he loves has disappeared."

He raised his eyes at Akuna-Ra's with a pleading expression. "Isn't there any other solution? Can't we give them hope that he is still alive and...?"

"They will both suffer if they find him."

The shaman nodded lightly. He hoped there would have been another possibility. "Couldn't they come to know about the tribe Dr. Martin was looking for? If his boyfriend started to recall things, most likely, he would also remember the revelation Dr. Martin told."

That solution could have saved them all, but she needed to consult the spirits once again. She felt reluctant to make that decision on her own anymore, particularly after centuries of fixing humanity's deceptive behavior.

"Your faith in humanity is commendable. Nevertheless, I need to remind you about the trouble your species has caused, not just to the people of your tribe, but to those who are now protected by us. You don't have predators, and this planet is plentiful in resources. But this doesn't stop you from fighting each other for nonsense." She shook her head with a bitter grimace, distorting the regular features of her face.

"We need to search for the good in everyone. There isn't perfection in nature, and particularly in humanity. Despite this knowledge, I still search for something good in each of them. Take Azizi, for example," the shaman said, pointing his finger in the direction of the village. "A child soldier raised to fight a war against his own people. If I didn't bother to find the good in him and brought it to the surface, he would have been lost and perhaps also dead. He has a kind soul and deserves to find love."

Akuna-Ra preferred not to answer. "The spirits need to be summoned once again before they reach Africa. Meanwhile, as Kaine has accepted to become your pupil, you are going to start training him right away. The nights are the best times to initiate."

Feeling dismissed and having an important role to fulfill, the old shaman bowed his head and left the shack, at the same moment as Jason arrived with Okumi.

"Did I come late to the party?" Jason asked as he noticed the shaman leaving the place.

Akuna-Ra grimaced at the lousy joke. "No, I haven't asked you for this party, but you were at a better one, considering the alcohol I can smell from here."

"Had you informed me about this one, I would have tried and kept myself sober." He came inside, walking to the fireplace. "You always summon me in the middle of the night, when it's clear I will have to spend the night alone. Well, actually with my new roommate."

Akuna-Ra observed him, considering his presence and figure against the light of the fire. She had a new task for him, but she needed to unwind from the worries poisoning her soul, and if there was something Jason excelled in, it was taking her fears away.

She slowly walked to the corner of the shack where she used to sleep, and lay there, sensing his hungry eyes on her body, feeling his heart increasing its pace in his chest.

"Come here, come be with me." She smiled at him alluringly.

Jason stared at her, and still, he couldn't think of anything more arousing and beautiful than that dominating, at times cruel, but needy creature.

He slowly undressed and went to lay by her side, gently caressing her painted body, uncovering it from the clothing she wore.

His only desire was to give her as much pleasure as her sole presence was able to offer to him, hoping there wouldn't be any interruption that night they would spend together.

"How many nights can I hope for before you'll be gone?" he whispered, holding her tightly in his arms.

Sensing his urgency, she realized the need to have him embracing her, feeling the warmth of his body, and the passion of his words. "Don't think about time, think about now."

She adjusted herself, cuddling with him on the bed made of furs and hay. That was something she would miss. Despite her efforts to deny them to overcome her heart, she felt she'd failed in her proposition to avoid foolish human feelings.

*Was this also the meaning of our quest? Were we supposed to get acquainted with the inner soul of the civilization we were going to meet to further enrich our understanding?*

She started to reconsider what the spirits told her. *Probably Kaiphindi was right.*

She sighed.

"What makes you thoughtful, my mistress?" Jason asked with a soft tone in his voice, caressing her hair.

"It's too complicated to tell. Maybe one day you will be ready to understand us better. Who knows?"

"Then let's enjoy this night and try to find some rest. I will be here for as long as you wish."

He was deeply in love with her, and it was not something connected to any kind of syndrome, as a psychiatrist would have suggested. He didn't feel the same toward Kaiphindi, who would have been the one to order his release and the end of his captivity.

He was in love only and exclusively with his beloved Akuna-Ra.

***

Kaine was just getting ready to fall asleep when someone knocked at his door. He wasn't expecting any visitors, and he knew that generally people were told to remain inside their homes during the night hours.

He stood up, but hesitated, wondering whether it could have been an evil spirit... *Oh, bullshit!*

He shook his head and walked to the door. The old shaman didn't let him say anything and urged him to follow. "Come with me. Akuna-Ra ordered your training would start now."

Kaine looked at him, puzzled and full of doubts and questions in his mind. Yet, he followed him, closing the door of the bungalow behind him.

"Akuna-Ra is sure you can connect with the spirits, but also you need to be guided to master and use these powers," the shaman spoke, walking toward one of the fires burning in the center of the village. "She said they speak to you. One thing I have learned in my whole life is the wraiths will always try to connect with everyone, but when they find the one who can listen and grasp what they say, then they become more insistent. The

325

underworld and the world of the living are like two rooms separated by many doors. You can consider humans like the doors to our world, and the spirits are those trying to open them. Do you understand?"

Kaine found the idea of people seen as gates fascinating, and simply nodded to reply to the shaman. "One thing I wonder. I believe there are many kinds of entities coming from the underworld, and if there are the good ones, there must also be those others who mean to harm..."

"That is the job of the shaman," he replied. "He can recognize those entities and will keep the door closed for the evil ones, and they will open for the good ones. We can let them in and out at our will. We can summon them when there is a question we can't answer, and we will use their message to guide our people."

From his neck, he took a necklace which bore a little bag, probably made of some animal's leather, and containing something Kaine felt he didn't want to ask about.

"This is for you. It's a powerful amulet and will help you control the forces."

The shaman put the necklace around Kaine's neck. "Never take it off. Now the spirits know you are a possible open door, and they will try harder to pass through you. From today on, every night, we will go through different spells, and I will test your power. One thing you should learn is, first of all, to dominate your emotions. Before being able to command the spirits, you need to control yourself."

Kaine listened to what he was saying and hoped from the deepest part of his soul that Akuna-Ra knew what she was doing, and her judgment was, for once, correct.

"One thing, though," Kaine wondered, as the man seemed to be willing to make a shaman out of him as soon as possible. "How do you know I have the power to become a shaman?"

The old man's face crinkled into a smile. "I don't. I will find out. My son, I have seen a lot in this world, and my time has started to get short. This tribe needs another shaman..."

"Hold on!" Kaine interrupted, fearing what he meant to say. "I don't mean to remain here for the rest of my life. Akuna-Ra promised to take away the curse from me and allow me to return home if I helped them... She... She never said anything about remaining here forever and becoming the new shaman."

He didn't want to offend anyone, but his life was not supposed to be there. He had a home, a boyfriend, a job, or whatever would remain of it once he returned.

He had no idea what Akuna-Ra had in mind, or what their agreement was. One thing for sure was he had no intention of remaining there stuck in the middle of nowhere, particularly not without Mark.

The shaman remained silent for a moment, wondering whether he might have understood it wrong and Akuna-Ra meant to train him for a different purpose.

*This is something we will have to figure out, and perhaps Akuna-Ra will help to find another candidate for the role. As a general rule, the shaman's son should become the next one to take charge of the spiritual world, but when my son died...*A lump formed in his throat.

He turned his eyes at Kaine, and with a smile, tried to forget about it. "We shall think about a solution, don't you worry. Now let's focus on understanding what your potential is.

# CHAPTER 26

With the help of Jenna, who could use the same contacts she gathered for the previous journey, they were able to reach the airport of Beni on a bright afternoon in March.

The air already felt suffocating to Mark, who had never traveled abroad and particularly never in different climates. The humidity, which made the warm heat feeling more intense, was the first thing he noticed as they stepped off the plane.

Then he started to peer the environment surrounding that small airport. The other detail, which immediately caught his attention, was the smell of the iron-rich soil and its bright color under the scorching early afternoon sun.

He lowered the hand-luggage on the ground and took a napkin to wipe the sweat that started to drip from his forehead.

Jenna watched him and recalled how it felt the first time she reached that airport. "You'll soon get accustomed to it," she giggled.

"If I don't die before..."

He picked up his luggage, adjusted the rucksack on his shoulders, and resumed his walk to the building, following Jenna.

"It seems like this airport is mostly used by the military forces," Mark said, noticing the UN vehicles and soldiers with different uniforms coming and going.

"Yes," Jenna replied, turning toward him. "The main international airport is in Goma. This is the closest to the location where we had our camp."

Azizi was waiting impatiently outside the building, barely able to keep himself from laughing hysterically from happiness to see his beloved once again. He was afraid he had to forget about her, or she'd forgotten about him.

His heart was beating fast in his chest, and his head felt light as time passed by. He saw the little airplane that was probably transporting Jenna and her friend landing a few minutes ago. He tried to remember how much time it took last time to clear immigration, so he could determine how long he had to wait before starting to fear they didn't make it to the plane and would arrive the day after.

He grabbed his mobile phone when at the same second he saw her appearing from the main door.

He couldn't stop his tears and ran toward her to hold her in his arms.

Jenna dropped all her luggage to run to him. She didn't realize how much she'd missed him until she saw him once again.

"Azizi!" she yelled, tears forming on her eyes.

"I have been missing you so much!" His voice trembling.

Before they realized it, their lips met in a tender kiss. That level of closeness melted Jenna's soul. *This is the man I need in my life.*

"Azizi, how could I have ever lived without you for all those months?" she said with a shaky voice, holding his hands tightly in hers to make sure her heart was not playing tricks on her, and that was not only a dream.

"I was wondering the same thing, but now you are here, and there is nothing more important to me."

They hugged as if they wanted to fuse their bodies.

"Ehm..." Mark coughed, trying to call their attention to the fact that they were not alone and perhaps it would have been better to start moving to the place where they were supposed to lodge, whether a hotel, a bungalow, or a tent.

Azizi glanced at him and broke into a bright smile. "Sorry. You must be Mark. I'm Azizi, and I'm going to escort you during your permanence here in DRC," he parted from Jenna and shook Mark's hand.

He went to help to grab their luggage. "Did you have a pleasant journey?"

"Yes, thanks. Although the last hour wasn't the most comfortable, I can't complain. Where are we going to stay?" Mark wondered.

Azizi opened the doors of the jeep to let them in. "I couldn't arrange for you the same bungalows as you had the last time," he said, glancing at Jenna. "But I could set up lodging in a close-by village. They are exactly of the same kind. Nothing fancy, but they have all the basic needs."

"Then I believe we should also stop somewhere to get some groceries, particularly for water supplies. I remember last time we were constantly drinking, and yet it was never enough."

330

Mark looked around at the new environment and wondered how he would be able to find Kaine in a place so vast and about which he knew absolutely nothing. He hesitated a moment before entering the jeep and noticed Azizi's AK-47. It was to be quite old and in rough shape, but he was sure it could still serve the original purpose without any trouble.

"That is to ensure your safety." Azizi acknowledged Mark's glance. "DRC is not a safe area, not only for tourists but for everyone."

Mark nodded. "I've read about the difficult situation in your country, and I should have expected you to carry a weapon with you all the time, particularly if you are escorting a couple of clueless travelers."

They started their journey in a weird silence. Azizi knew they were looking for Kaine, and by no means should he reveal his location. That was not only because this was the will of the witch doctor, but also because he knew Kaine had been cursed and he didn't want to put the lives of Mark and Jenna in danger.

Nevertheless, he had no idea where he should divert the search and considered all the possible places where he could bring them.

"I know you have met Dr. Martin before," Mark commenced, willing to break the silent curtain that formed as soon as they entered the car.

"Yes, I did. Although, I was mostly escorting the team of Jenna, who needed to reach vantage points to get to fly their drones," Azizi tried to explain, already warning of the possibility that they wouldn't find him.

He hated to lie. He had lived a whole childhood of lies, and all he wanted was to live in peace and honesty.

"I remember he was going with Dr. Murdock. Do you know where we can find him?" Jenna wondered. "Probably, he had seen him or has some clues about the last location where he had been seen."

"Hmmm..." Azizi mumbled. *How in the world am I going to handle this situation? Why did I agree to guide them?*

"I haven't seen him recently. He had been busy fetching new material for the school and had been at the village quite seldom. If I can spot him, I might tell him to come to see you, but I can't assure anything."

A light frown rippled her forehead as concern rose from the innermost recess of her soul. "Of course, don't you worry. We know that finding a person in this part of the country is like searching for a needle in a haystack. Moreover, we have no idea whether he had been kidnapped..."

"Oh please, don't mention it!" Mark begged. "If he had been taken as hostage, a request for a ransom would have already come to the embassy, I believe."

"I don't want to scare you, but in this case, they would have contacted his family, not you. But we can call them and ask whether there has been any news about an American citizen. This will eliminate one of the possibilities," Azizi tried to reason.

Mark felt hopeless. There were too many options involving Kaine's death, and he was not ready for such an option. Not so soon, at least.

He grabbed his head between his hands and swallowed the tears, too plentiful to be contained behind his eyes.

Jenna turned at him. She felt his pain and wondered how she would feel if something similar had happened to her. *What would I do if someone told me Azizi was nowhere to be found?*

She caressed Mark's hair. "We will find him, and we will bring him home safe and sound, even if it takes an entire lifetime to do this."

Mark sighed, wiping his tears away. He couldn't even speak, with a lump formed in his throat.

He drew a deep breath, trying to calm himself. *We still have no idea what happened to him; perhaps he is lost, and soon we will find him.*

He wasn't sure he believed it, but he needed to remain positive for Kaine's sake. He couldn't lose hope before they started.

*I hope the voice will come once again to help me. If it was telling the truth and could guide me to the place where Kaine is, then now it should be a piece of cake, as we are both in the same place.*

Mark shook his head at that thought. He couldn't trust something probably caused by a chemical imbalance in his brain.

Jenna turned her gaze to Azizi, who kept his eyes steady on the road, hoping to reach the village as soon as possible. "Azizi, do you have any idea where we can start from, besides calling the embassy and trying to get in touch with Dr. Murdock?"

"No, honestly, I don't. The only thing I know is the bungalows were temporary structures, and they have all been dismantled. This means Dr. Martin left at some point, but he might have thought of going somewhere else."

Jenna nodded, disappointed that one of her ideas was ruined. "I was thinking to go to the village and search for clues there in the bungalow area, but if you're telling me they've been dismantled..."

"I mean, I can bring you there, but I'm afraid there won't be anything useful for you to find," Azizi explained matter-of-factly, hoping she couldn't spot his lies.

After a seemingly endless journey, Mark and Jenna reached the village where they would be lodged. Mark smiled at the sight of the cabins destined for them.

"Have these been built expressly for us?" He wondered as he started to walk toward one of them to observe the structure more closely.

Azizi took Jenna's luggage and followed him to the bungalows. "These structures are quite easy to assemble and dissemble. You might notice the general standard is lower than what you might have in your country or you can find in any hotel around. We don't have strict regulations about security, but we at least know how to make things somehow working." Azizi gave a dismissive tilt of his head and left the luggage in front of one bungalow. "Come, I'll show you what I mean."

Mark followed, him curious to see how it would have been easy to assemble something like that and what kind of safety norms were sacrificed in the name of speed.

"Look here." Azizi pointed his finger at the electric wires coming from a hole in the wall. They reached a pole to be lifted to an elevated position. From there, they followed a bundled network of cables toward an old wooden cabin. "From every place, whether it is the shack or the house of a villager or a bungalow for guests, comes the bundles of the electric cables. They are all connected with the mainline, which crosses the main locations in the country." Azizi pointed to the trail of bundled wires that disappeared between the trees. "There are many times when a monkey or a bird cut the line. Yet we have learned the most critical points, so we can find and fix the problem within a couple of days. I know for you, this might seem like a long time, but we do not have the same monitoring systems as you have. We try to survive with what we got."

Mark nodded, observing the system they'd developed. It was something primitive, but with the scarce resources they had, it was a miracle that they were able to achieve so much.

"What about the water?"

"You mean running water?" Azizi wondered. "For that, we have wells, and we get the water delivered through pumps. Not everyone in the village has running water in the house, but the well is not far, so going to fetch it's not a big deal."

With another general glance, Mark nodded, satisfied at the amenities offered. "To whom should we pay for the bungalows?"

"If you don't mind, more than money, the people of the village would rather need some help. Whatever skills you want to put at the service of the community would be highly appreciated. If you can hunt or fish, you can join the men for a hunting trip, or you can assist them if they need to repair something. They will come to ask you, so you don't need to find a way to be helpful."

Jenna sighed. She felt slightly concerned about the time at their availability. "I'm not sure how we can be useful. Just like the previous time we were here, we are going to use most of our time trying to search for Kaine. We won't spend much time here in the village, so maybe we can agree on a compromise. What about if we are going to buy goods they need every time we are going away? They might give us a list of things to be purchased, and we can see what we can find with our budget."

A fat bluish and red lizard crossed the space between their legs. It stopped for a moment, and after having considered the three strangers, it did a couple of push-ups and left.

Mark observed it, amused. He wondered what kind of unknown animals he would see during his permanence.

"It's an Agama lizard. They don't bite you if you don't threaten them, but they are not poisonous," Azizi explained.

Mark chuckled as he watched it running away. "There will be so many things I will have the chance to see here. Yet, there is only one creature I wish to see as soon as possible alive and well: Kaine. I can't conceive of the possibility of having lost him..." He felt his heart aching at that thought.

Jenna rubbed his shoulder gently to console him, to make him understand he was not going to be alone in his quest.

"Well, I think it would be better if we place the luggage in the cabins, and we go to buy some water and do some groceries. There won't be anything in your bungalows, so we should hurry to the next town where we can find some shops," Azizi said hurriedly, wishing to be as far as possible from them, even if this meant being away from the woman he loved.

*I need to ask the shaman what I'm supposed to do from tomorrow on. They should understand I can't bring them from place to place without any direction.*

***

The sun began to set, when, finally, they returned to their camp. The shaman, like in the other communities protected by Akuna-Ra's power, had already started the fires in the center of the village and scrutinized the two strangers returning with Azizi.

"Good evening," the man said kindly as he approached them. "It's always a pleasure to have guests coming. Although you arrived early this afternoon, I wish to welcome you to our community. I have put candles in your bungalows, and I recommend you keep them burning during the night. Also, I suggest you do not leave your houses until sunrise; the spirits will be free, and it's not advisable to risk getting in their way."

Mark smiled. He wasn't a believer in the paranormal, but he was aware of the local practices, and *whether one believes or not, it's better not to take risks and do precisely as he said. Moreover, I think it would be quite disrespectful and rude not to follow the rules of the village.*

"Thank you, we will do as you say. I would like to express to you our gratitude for the kind hospitality, and I hope we will be able to repay you in equal measure," Mark replied.

Jenna was already familiar with the practice, and after a small chat and agreeing to meet Azizi the morning after at eleven, they both retired to their bungalows.

As he entered, Mark closed his eyes and inhaled deeply to get accustomed to the new environment. He wanted to register every different smell and noise in that place to make him feel more at home. *I'm not planning to remain here for a long time, but even if it's a question of a couple of days, I want to feel comfortable in this bungalow in the same way as I do back home.*

The scent coming first to his nostrils was the one of the wood with which the cabin was built, then the earthy smell of the mud used to create the roof, together with branches and straw. Everything was enticing and new to him.

"I understand now what Kaine meant when he described the place to me. He said there wasn't any sort of hotel in the area, and the living was quite basic. Yet, I can't say it's missing anything important."

He opened his eyes and walked to the kitchen. The modest furniture in the place didn't bother him, although he was used to a completely different style.

He took his time to observe everything, opening the closets to understand the spaces, and when he was satisfied, he started to place his groceries in order, together with the clothes and the rest of the luggage.

The bathroom was composed of a room where there was a tap for the water and a bucket to be filled. And the toilette was accessed by a small door leading to a sort of connected outhouse.

He recalled those types of dry toilettes from the times he used to go camping with his father; they were perhaps not the most comfortable choices, but they were far better than going outside. Despite this, the village took good care of the sanitation, as there weren't any foul smells coming from anywhere.

The air was quite hot and wondering about an AC system when, returning to the main room where the bed was, he noticed the fan on the ceiling. "That thing might save my life."

He switched it on and went to lie on the bed. Although he'd had only breakfast and lunch, he felt more tired than hungry and decided to try and fall asleep.

He closed his eyes and was ready to fall asleep when he remembered the recommendation of the shaman to keep the candles lit for the whole night.

With a slight groan, accompanied by a creak of the bed structure, he stood up and walked to the small dresser placed in front of the window. He lit the candle and peered outside.

The shaman was seated facing the fire, observing the flames burning. He regretted he didn't have a camera with him, as that image was simply spectacular.

The intense expression depicted in the shaman's eyes, the frown on his forehead, and the movements of his mouth as if he was reciting a spell or talking with the spirits were mesmerizing, together with the dancing of the flames.

Mark felt like he might have fallen in love with the place. Everything was far from the hassle of the city, and he started to reconsider his life.

A loud yawn escaped him, and he turned to the bed, ready to bid that day goodbye and hope for a better day the following one.

# CHAPTER 27

The old shaman smiled at Kaine. "Akuna-Ra was right. You have incredible potential and powers."

They went to sit by one of the fires burning for the night.

"You know," the man went on. "It doesn't matter whether you will stay here and continue my work in this village, or you will return home. Your gift and capabilities should be used wherever you are. You will always have to remember that you will be a door between the underworld and the world of the living. Wherever you are in the Universe, you will always have to be on alert as to who and what is going to pass through this door."

He pointed at Kaine's head, as he knew it was from there that all the powers came.

Kaine pondered what he'd said. He understood a shaman remained as such wherever he goes, and from that moment on, from the day he started his training to help Kaiphindi's tribe to return home, his life would never be the same.

"I still feel confused. If one day I would ever leave here, this also means that I will be alone to keep my door well-guarded. You won't be there helping me..."

The shaman chuckled, amused. "My son, you have always been alone. My presence here won't be of any help if your door remains unwatched. I can't guard against everything you let pass through you."

He then turned serious, and with a grave expression, he locked his eyes on Kaine's. "You need to believe in your powers and judgment. You need to trust yourself with your life because there isn't anyone who can fix such a mistake. If the wrong entity passes through you, you will be the only one who can return it to where it came from."

Kaine gasped, "How?"

"You will learn that; I'm not going to leave you untrained. If you are going to make mistakes that can cost other people dearly, I would consider it also my fault if I haven't trained you properly." The shaman patted Kaine's shoulder.

Regardless of that reassuring thought, Kaine still felt scared and wondered whether he was the right person for the task.

His eyes returned to observe the flames, when he suddenly thought he could see something in them.

He tried to get closer to get a sharper view, when he recalled it wasn't by getting nearer that he would better see what was going on, but preferably by opening his inner sight. He inhaled and exhaled slowly. Focusing on the blurred images, he thought he saw some human figures.

It was like someone was trying to warn him about the arrival of someone, but he couldn't understand what it meant. *Why should I be alerted if someone is arriving here in the village? People are coming and going. There isn't any sort of restriction, and it seems like those who can't be protected against my curse are not going to meet me.*

He closed his eyes, wondering whether this would be a better way to get a clearer picture or message.

In the beginning, there was only a foggy and blurred image, like he'd seen previously through the flames. He drew a deep breath and slowly exhaled to keep his mind focused and his heartbeat under control.

It took what it felt almost an eternity, but when he understood who arrived, his heart started racing in his chest as if it wanted to run away from him.

He opened his eyes and remained breathless for a second.

Terrified, with his hands trembling and his legs numb, he tried to run in the direction of the camp. He needed to talk to Akuna-Ra, and there was no time to waste.

He fell on the ground, unable to stand up.

A couple of hands tried to help him, and when he turned his gaze, he saw the shaman.

The shaman didn't say anything, and most likely he saw the same, or perhaps he already knew Mark and Jenna had arrived at a neighboring village, searching for him.

"This can't be true. They can't find me!" Kaine mumbled as his voice trembled more than the rest of his body. "I need to talk to Akuna-Ra..."

"She knows..." the shaman replied quietly.

"Did you know it too? Why haven't you told me anything? I can't see them, or they will die!" He talked frantically as he desperately struggled to stand up.

"They are not going to meet you, fear not. They are guided by Azizi, and he has been instructed on how to keep them away from here." The shaman locked his eyes on Kaine's and tried to calm him. "Nothing is going to happen to them."

Kaine closed his eyes and felt like he was almost fainting.

Very slowly, almost imperceptibly, his heart reached a regular pace. When his legs were once again able to support him, he gathered all the strength he had and stood up, still helped by the shaman.

"Why wasn't I informed about it?" Kaine wondered, still intending to go and consult Akuna-Ra.

The shaman invited him to go and have a seat beside him in front of the fire. There wasn't any hurry to talk to Akuna-Ra, mainly because he knew that recently, and in particular during the night, she was receiving Jason, more often than she'd ever used to.

He wasn't sure what the deal was between them and would have never believed a creature like Akuna-Ra would have been capable of human feelings like love.

"We kept this secret from you because you needed to concentrate entirely on your training. You had to clear your mind from any other worries in order to reach the right focus and develop the connection with the underworld," he explained, feeling the pain in Kaine's heart.

There was a long pause of silence between them. Kaine considered carefully what the shaman said, and he had to admit that they made a wise decision.

*Had I known about the arrival of Mark and Jenna, I would have thought only about them. Perhaps I would have tried to get in touch with them to let him know that I'm alive, but I need to complete this task before returning home.*

He shook his head and lowered his gaze down at his hands.

"Things have been changing so much and so fast."

He then turned his eyes to the shaman. "Can a shaman see the future?"

"It's a dangerous question, and I suggest you not go deeper into it," he reproached, knowing of the repercussions predicting one's destiny might have. "Nobody should know what the future holds, as this is not the way we are supposed to live our lives."

"Yeah, maybe you're right. I guess I need to gather my thoughts together. This vision shook my whole world," he admitted.

"Sometimes the visions we have can be scary, that's why we need first of all to learn about control." The shaman stood up and checked around the fires, walking to one which needed more wood, and added from a woodpile close by the fire.

He turned his glance. "This was a great teaching lesson from which you can gain a better understanding of yourself and how, from this moment on, you will manage your emotions."

He returned to sit beside Kaine, tracing random squiggles on the ground with the stick he carried in his hand.

Kaine started to feel tired. That vision drained him of all energy. *I'm wondering what Mark and Jenna are doing here. They shouldn't have remembered what has happened, and in their minds, there should have been the certainty that I'm missing.*

*What a fool. Mark would have never accepted the simple fact that I had gone missing without trying every road to get me back. They didn't take into account what love can do. They didn't consider a man in love would go to the end of the world to try and get back the loved one.*

With a slight smile on his face and a sudden warm feeling in his heart, he wished he could once again see the vision of his mother.

*At least a familiar figure, after all the threatening, would have been comforting. Yet as I know that Mark came to Africa because he couldn't agree to give up on me, it makes me feel like wanting to run to him.*

*If there would only be a possibility for us to communicate. If I could let him...*

"I have a request..." Kaine said, suddenly entwining his fingers and twisting them. "Would it ever be possible to have a message from me delivered to Mark? Can't I let him know the reason why I find myself trapped here?"

The shaman shivered at a request, which could give him more trouble than he wished for. "You still don't have any idea about who you are dealing with, do you? The only person who can grant any connection between you and the world you have left behind is Akuna-Ra. And don't start thinking she won't come to know; she already does, and I'm sure she doesn't like the direction of our chat. You are not supposed to connect with anyone else; your only focus should be on the learning process."

He averted his gaze from Kaine's questioning eyes. "If you need to ask for an exception, you need to deal with her; don't put other people in danger. This is not about you and your boyfriend, this is something which will have consequences on the whole village; the same I aim to protect."

Kaine's shoulders fell and his chin lowered to his chest. Only one second ago, he felt as if he had all the solutions to his problems, and now, they all disappeared with the name of Akuna-Ra.

*I wonder how Jason can love her. It must be a case of Stockholm Syndrome, whether he realizes it or not.*

345

***

Mark was asleep in his bungalow. The chirping noises of the night insects worked for him as a lullaby, and he was sleeping so deeply that he was dreaming.

Yet, he wasn't sure they were dreams, as everything felt too real. He thought he could hear Kaine's voice. He was talking with someone else, begging to have a message given to him.

His heart was gripped by a sharp pain like someone was stabbing him. Mark was certainly glad to know Kaine was still alive, but the hope to find him again became slimmer.

*But how can he know about me being in Africa looking for him? How can he know about Jenna and...*

With eyes opened wide, he sat up on his bed. "A dream, it was only a dream."

Paying attention to the noises of the night, he stood up. The candle was still burning on the dresser in front of the window, and the alluring dance of the flames made all the silhouettes in the room move to a whimsical melody.

Mesmerized by that dance he remained for a moment to and wondered whether he could return to sleep once he rehydrated himself.

Despite the fan, endlessly spinning on the ceiling, the humidity and heat didn't give any mercy.

"Yet, I slept pretty well until now, but since I noticed that I'm sweating and losing all my fluids, falling asleep is a mission impossible."

Keeping the light off and allowing the little candles to shine for the night, he grabbed the bottle of water and went to have a seat at the table.

The first gulp flowed down his throat like water in the desert. He pushed the glass away and drank directly from the bottle, convinced that soon he would have swallowed the whole two liters, so desperate was his thirst.

He stood up and went to peek out the window. The fires were burning brightly, and it seemed like the shaman was keeping himself busy, either with spells to protect his village or checking that the bonfires were fed like hungry beasts.

"It must not be an easy job, the one of a shaman. He stays up every night, watching over the good-night sleep of the villagers. They should be grateful for his service," Mark said aloud as he observed what was going on outside his bungalow.

Feeling the tiredness, his eyes met the small alarm clock he had with him; it was still early for the sun to greet a new day. He didn't feel sleepy, though and blamed the time difference for his difficulty in falling back to sleep.

His sight lowered to meet the dresser and opened the first drawer, where he kept the first-aid kit, including some sleeping pills. "I was sure I might have needed one of these, particularly during the first few days."

He took one pill and swallowed it without water. Being the capsule quite small there wasn't any need for water.

For a few moments, he held his breath before exhaling, he closed his eyes and inhaled deeply. From the second drawer, he grabbed a book he'd bought at the airport and walked to the bed, hoping the combination of the sleeping pill and reading would perform some kind of fast magic and put him back to sleep.

Falling asleep once again was easier than he thought and slept until someone knocking at his door the morning after, woke him up with a jolt. To his attempts of sitting up, the bed replied with a noisy, squeaky sound, in protest to his sudden moves.

"I'm coming!" he said as he put on his jeans.

The smiling face of Jenna greeted him. "Good morning!" She giggled amusedly as she saw the groggy expression on Mark's face.

"I know I look terrible when I wake up in the morning. Come in."

His hands ran through his hair trying to comb it, knowing that it must have been sticking up on his head like the spikes of a porcupine.

His hands moved to his chin, where the stubble probably added a dramatic touch to his overall image. "Before we start, you can make yourself comfortable as I neaten myself up."

Jenna glanced at him as he walked to the restroom, acknowledging how sexy he was, also with the hair sticking irregularly on his head, the stubble on his chin, and the grouchy expression in his eyes.

Shaking her head, she went to the kitchen and started to get busy preparing coffee for both. *I already had mine, but one more is always welcome, and besides, if we want to get ready by the time Azizi reaches us, we need to move.*

Like on a quest, she opened the cabinets to check for the groceries he'd bought to see what he had to make for breakfast. *We won't have time if he must prepare everything by himself.*

They wouldn't have been late for anything, but she hated to make people wait for her, and besides, if this meant letting Azizi wait, and having less time for each other, she was more than willing to even clean Mark's bungalow if necessary.

After half an hour, Mark returned, looking more like the god he used to look like. His perfectly shaped bare chest left Jenna speechless. "I have prepared something to eat and coffee."

She averted her glance from him, trying to sound unimpressed, but in reality, she would have eaten him with her eyes.

Mark noticed her expression and chuckled. "That was truly thoughtful of you, thank you. Please join me."

He walked to the dresser to get a clean shirt and then joined Jenna in the kitchen. "I'm wondering where we should start looking for Kaine. Last night I had a terrible nightmare about him being kept captive somewhere." He recalled the strange dream he had, as he took a seat at the table.

"We'd better ask Azizi if he has a better plan to find him." She took a loaf of bread and cut a slice. "This morning I called the embassy to find out if there has been any ransom request for the kidnapping of Kaine. They replied that thank God, it has been a long time since the last kidnapping, and anyway no one with that name. This should eliminate the possibility of a kidnapping."

Mark bit his lower lip as he sipped his coffee. At the first sip, his eyes opened wide. "Damn, that's strong coffee!" he exclaimed, shaking his head.

Jenna laughed at his sudden reaction. "I'm sorry, I'm used to extreme tastes, or I can't wake up. I might have forgotten that not everyone is as addicted as I am."

The noise of a jeep arriving in front of the bungalow attracted their attention. "This must be Azizi. You finish your breakfast; I'm going to tell him we're coming soon." Jenna jumped like a spring from the chair, feeling incredibly grateful for the prompt rescue offered by Azizi's arrival.

Mark remained glancing at the cup filled with pure poison and added some water and sugar to it in the hopes of making it taste milder. He took a sip and realized that it might have needed at least one liter of water to get to the levels an average person enjoys coffee. Nevertheless, he closed his nostrils with two fingers and gulped the whole contents of the cup.

With a disgusted grin, he ate something to cover up the awful taste left by that bitter and robust coffee, knowing that for the next ten years, he wouldn't be able to sleep again.

After placing the food back in the fridge and swiftly cleaning, he was ready to join Azizi and Jenna, who were waiting outside.

# CHAPTER 28

Kaine returned in the morning to the bungalow he shared with Jason. It was evident they wouldn't have trouble being roommates, since Jason was, most of the time, spending his nights at the camp, and Kaine was busy becoming a shaman.

He let himself collapse on the bed, tired and worn out. The bed protested with a dangerous noise that alerted Kaine's senses.

He hoped he didn't manage to damage the frame irreparably and went to check. As the structure was still looking solid, he returned to lie on it, being careful not to break anything.

He followed the movement of the fan on the ceiling, which was left turned on. "It's indeed a one of a kind experience to have the chance of being trained by the local shaman. In other circumstances, I would have killed to have had this chance. Yet, being forced to train under threat is not something I was keen to experience," he said aloud.

"I just hope I will be able to reach the level expected of me. And I hope it will happen quite soon."

He'd never asked anyone about what the training process would be and how much time he was supposed to spend on it.

Two months have passed since he'd started, and he felt like he hadn't made any progress.

With a long sigh, he turned himself on his side and closed his eyes. "I will have to remember to ask the shaman about it. Perhaps he has a better perception of the point I'm at and how much time he thinks it will require.

Without even thinking whether he felt tired or not, he fell immediately asleep.

*** 

Kaiphindi paced as she waited for the arrival of the shaman. Things were not going according to the plan, and she wanted to understand whether there was any way to fix the problems with the two strangers who had arrived to search for Kaine and how much time it might have required for Kaine to reach the point where he could help them.

Akuna-Ra was also summoned, and she was supposed to come together with the shaman. Yet, time was running too slowly, and they had not yet arrived to release her stress.

It was after about half an hour when she thought she couldn't wait any longer, when the curtain of the door opened, and Akuna-Ra appeared, followed by the shaman.

"My queen, I feel your restless soul." Akuna-Ra tilted her head, concerned, as she'd never seen her queen as agitated as she was.

"My soul sister," she commenced, relieved at seeing her and hoping for good news. "I don't know what might have gone wrong during the last year, but now, as we start considering resuming our journey, we find ourselves in a risky situation."

She went to sit on the throne in the middle of the room, grabbing her head gracefully between her hands.

Akuna-Ra walked toward her, hoping to give comfort to her soul. "The two intruders are not a threat to us. To be honest, they are still searching for Dr. Martin, and Azizi is doing a great job diverting their search far from us."

She held Kaiphindi in her arms, rocking her to make her feel protected and reassured that she would do everything for her and the whole tribe's sake.

"We all need to keep control of our emotions. Having the chance to use our feelings doesn't necessarily mean we must use them at all. Particularly now, we don't need them."

Her voice was unusually soft and gentle like the shaman had never heard, and he remained baffled at her attitude toward her queen.

"Akuna-Ra, my soul sister," Kaiphindi wept, resting her head on her arms. "We need to resume our journey, for it's not yet over, and perhaps we have lingered here for too long, almost forgetting our mission."

She parted from Akuna-Ra. "We relied on human evolution to understand the rest of the Universe, but we forgot that, at this point, the same development we took advantage of is becoming a trap."

With a deep sigh, Akuna-Ra walked away from her. "Then we need to plan carefully our way out. Their satellites are advanced, but we have at our availability more refined technology, which has progressed even further. We need to call back to us the rest of the team who has been deployed in different countries to observe and grow." She walked away from Kaiphindi with a wicked grin. "I warned you about the danger of human feelings. Some of them can be useful; others are doing nothing else but holding us back. We have seen the effect on the human population, and nothing good seems to come from them."

Kaiphindi's expression toughened, and her fists clenched. Akuna-Ra was right, and although admitting being wrong was not a problem, she was the one who suggested getting closer to the human race to understand them better.

*This was supposed to be just another part of the exploration, and she was right when she warned about the possible risks.*

"You are right, but now we need to start focusing on the preparation for our journey." She turned her eyes to the shaman who remained there at the entrance, almost fearing what was going to happen next. He was indeed in touch with the spirits, but Kaiphindi's tribe was far more powerful than any other entity in the underworld. Some of them obeyed their commands.

"Fear not." Kaiphindi smiled, sensing the concerns of the shaman. "We have no reason to harm any of the people of the village we are protecting. The deal between us will remain, and we will make sure you will remain protected for the rest of eternity."

The old shaman lowered his gaze, surprised by the ease with which she could read his mind, but felt reassured about the fact that they didn't have any intention of breaking the deal.

"Forgive my doubts, Kaiphindi. I might have misinterpreted your words..." he cautiously replied, remaining at the entrance.

"I summoned you because I need to know about Dr. Martin. Akuna-Ra assured me he has remarkable mental powers. Can you tell me more about what you have found out?"

"Dr. Martin has indeed a rare gift, compared to any human I've ever met. The only problem is that he is the first one to doubt his power. He either doesn't trust it, or he is scared. Either way, this can hold him back from developing to the point you need him."

His voice regained confidence, and as the threatening feeling disappeared, he walked closer to Kaiphindi and Akuna-Ra.

"Do you have any suggestions about how to vanquish his doubts?" Kaiphindi wondered, also glancing at Akuna-Ra, who perhaps might have some ideas.

"I personally have tried to explain to him that he needs to believe in his capabilities, but although a part of him wants desperately to be able to return home, the other is held by fear."

With a brief nod, Akuna-Ra peered at Kaiphindi and then the old shaman. "Bring him to me as soon as he wakes up. Tonight, he will have training with me, and I'm going to free his mind from all his fears and doubts."

Cringing at the thought of what she might have in mind to do, the old shaman backed up a couple of steps. "You don't mean hurting him..."

"Of course not. Why would I do something that might compromise our chance for a smooth resumption of our journey? It wouldn't make any sense."

There was a long pause of silence. Akuna-Ra started to consider the way she would approach the problem, while Kaiphindi wondered when the rest of the team she called back would finally return.

The old shaman, glad not to have raised the anger of Kaiphindi, but particularly of Akuna-Ra, started thinking that maybe that night, he might have also chosen the next candidate to become the next shaman. *If Kaine returns home, my village will soon remain without any shaman. I'm not eternal, and I have made a mistake in waiting for so long to choose the next one. The problem is that it should be one of my children, but I don't have any. Therefore, I need to select the potential candidates and ask the spirits who I should train.*

Kaiphindi went once again to sit on her throne and observed what was around her. "I suppose, then, there is nothing else but to wait, either for this evening when Dr. Martin will be brought in front of Akuna-Ra, and when the rest of the team has reached us.

"At that point, we will be ready to leave, and either we will continue our quest, or we will consider our mission completed."

With a light bow, Akuna-Ra and the shaman left Kaiphindi alone, and in silence, they walked together in the direction of Akuna-Ra's shack, which was on the far end of the camp, close to the path that led to the village.

As they reached the path, Akuna-Ra stopped. "Bring Dr. Martin to me. I will take care of the rest. I know you are wondering about the person you will have to choose as the next shaman. I can assure you will find one, and perhaps one of the best so far."

Without waiting for a reply from the shaman, she entered her shack, ready to communicate with the spirits. There was quite a lot to be done before departure, and she needed to focus on her duties.

She stared at her empty bed, where Jason had started to share every night. She sighed, knowing the advice she gave to Kaiphindi wasn't one she was following herself.

She felt drawn to Jason, and she had the impression that parting from him would be difficult, if not painful.

*You have to promise me that if I'm still alive on the day you leave, you will end my life...*

Those words, spoken ages ago by Jason, felt daunting. She wasn't intending on killing anyone, especially him. "Yet, it's also true that I will feel the same kind of sorrow in leaving him behind, and that's the reason why I'm trying to spend my time with him as much as possible." She walked to the center of the room where the fire kept burning and glancing through the flames, she felt her heart at peace.

She visualized once again their home, so far and different from Earth, yet so similar in many aspects. She smiled at the vision she had of it and recalled all the memories she had from the place she used to call home.

Immortality was the ultimate frontier for the human race, and they'd made incredible advances to extend their existence on this planet. Yet, they failed to understand the basic concept for immortality, and that was infertility. Generation, not creation, and even in such case, extremely controlled and balanced by destruction.

"They fail to understand the necessity for destruction, to avoid creation to overwhelm all the rest. That's another risk of humanity... losing their grip on balance and equilibrium. Death is seen as the ultimate sorrow, when it's just a balancing force, very much needed."

She peeked around her place, inhaling deeply the scent of the wood, of the earth, of the animal skins, and aromatic herbs she collected for her studies and magic.

She would have to collect some of those herbs and bring them to her home. Many of those were absolutely foreign to her people, and they could be beneficial. During her expedition, she had collected a significant variety of seeds, which had been kept in provisional containers to preserve them for an indefinite amount of time.

***

In the evening, Mark and Jenna returned from their exploration rounds a bit later than usual. Neither of them had much of anything to say, and perhaps that was the time for them to decide what to do.

She didn't want to suggest him that perhaps Kaine was nowhere to be found, and wherever he was, if he was still alive, it would take more time than originally planned to find him.

*I also need to decide whether to remain here and build my life with Azizi, try and bring him with me after our marriage, or... I have no idea what I'm supposed to do. One thing for sure is that my vacation is starting to reach an end, and if I want to keep my job, I need to return home and search for another arrangement, whether to work from abroad or something else...*

She looked at Mark, who was keeping his gaze lowered without even looking where he was going. It was like his legs were bringing him somewhere without any specific command from him.

"Mark..."

Her voice sounded too distant to reach him through the wall of his thoughts. But the slight frown at the corner of his mouth revealed the pain he was feeling. A pain she hoped never to experience in her life.

"It's one thing to experience the death of a loved one..." he started to whisper, almost talking to himself, barely acknowledging Jenna's presence. "When someone you love dies, it will be a matter of time, but eventually, you will find the strength to go on with your life. When that person goes missing, your soul is constantly tortured by the feeling of not having done enough. You will constantly think about whether he is still alive. Is he

358

suffering? Is he crying, wishing to be found? Does he feel betrayed by those who are giving up the search?"

Tears collected, dropping heavily like rain from his eyes, and then, there was nothing more he could add, and the sobs became louder.

Jenna held his hand, wishing she had something wise to say. *This is the time when, perhaps, it's better to remain silent and listen to him. I believe the only thing he needs now is to discharge the pain, rather than to listen to my nonsense.*

He couldn't stop crying. The pain started to become unbearable, and he had no idea what he was supposed to think, let alone what to do. He felt like his hands were chained, and there was no movement he could make that could have helped any of them. Though, he felt grateful for the silent support offered by Jenna.

After a few minutes of sobbing, he finally found the strength to raise his gaze at her. She offered him a napkin to wipe his tears.

"I believe you are also thinking that you should return home. Your work won't wait forever, and perhaps this is also something I should think about. Yet, I can't just..."

"I also have a decision to make, and that's whether to remain here forever with Azizi, or ask him whether he would like to come to live with me. Nevertheless, my time here is ticking low, and soon I will have to return, even if it's to announce my decision to leave forever for Africa," she admitted. "What about you? How much time do you have left of your vacation?"

Shaking his head, he grabbed his mobile phone, where he could check his calendar. "I have about two weeks left. Unless a miracle happens, I will have to leave without Kaine. This is going to be the most difficult decision I have ever made in my whole life."

Without saying anything further, they reached their bungalows, and with a last hug, Jenna said farewell to Mark for the night. "Try to sleep. Tomorrow we will think about what to do. We both need to see things clearly."

***

Kaine woke up after a long rest during the day. His sleep was cursed by nightmares, and all of them included Mark arranging for his funeral.

"I can't leave him with this pain," he said aloud as he stood up from his bed.

Suddenly, without even knocking at the door, the shaman entered the bungalow, anxious to bring him to Akuna-Ra's presence. He hoped she could conquer his doubts and open his mind to his capabilities.

Kaine remained for a second, baffled about that sudden intrusion and was almost going to complain, but the old man didn't give him a chance.

"Akuna-Ra wishes to have you at her presence," he urged, wanting him to get dressed and ready to leave.

"What's the hurry? Are we under attack?" Kaine tried to lighten up the situation with a joke, but the shaman was not in the mood, and his expression darkened.

"This is not the time and the place for jokes, my son. You should know better. When Akuna-Ra commands something, it's not wise to let her wait without a valid reason."

Kaine shook his head. *Sometimes I don't understand those people. I can't wait until I can put this incident behind me. Perhaps it's good that she asked me to see her. I need to ask her some questions about my future. That nightmare shook my nerves, and I need Mark to know that I'm not dead...*

He dressed as quickly as he could, as the old man followed his every move in anticipation.

"I'm ready; let's go."

They started to walk in silence, taking the secondary path that, through a small stretch of the forest, led to the camp where the tribe of Akuna-Ra was settled.

The sun was almost set, and the only light they could rely on was a torch the old shaman preventively brought with him. He was in a hurry to bring Kaine to the destination, as he would have been, otherwise, late to light up the fires to protect the villagers from the evil spirits that were roaming freely during the night.

"Please, wait, don't run!" Kaine said, running behind him, hoping not to get lost in the middle of the forest.

"The old man slowed his pace and stared at Kaine impatiently. "I need to return to the village before it's too late. The fires need to burn, and there is no other person who is going to do it besides me," he explained, resuming his run to the camp.

"I understand. We could have first lit the fires, and then I would have come to see Akuna-Ra. Certainly, she would have understood that this is a vital issue for the safety of the people she is protecting."

Kaine failed to understand all the hurry and impatience, but with a dismissive huff, he decided that an answer wouldn't have come, and many times, it was better not to question what he saw.

Finally, he could see the fires of the camp through the bushes of the forest. "I can go on my own. You just go and take care of the fires in the village. I will be back as soon as possible."

The old shaman glimpsed him gratefully and broke into a kind smile. "Thank you. I guess this is the best idea.

Anyway, you are expected, and you know how to find Akuna-Ra. Her shack is the first you will meet coming from this path."

He pointed in the direction with the torch he was holding in his hand.

# CHAPTER 29

As Kaine reached the shack, he took a deep breath and pleaded with every entity present in the forest to come and protect him from the eventual rage.

She came outside, sensing his arrival, and wondered about the missing shaman. "I was also waiting for the shaman to arrive with you," she sneered, crossing her arms over her chest.

"I asked him to return to the village. The fires were not burning, and it would have been a risk for the villagers having the place left unprotected."

As he explained to her the reason why the shaman was not with him, he felt ridiculous. *If any of the people I know could hear what I said, they would think I've lost my mind. What's worse is that they would be right, as I'm not sure whether evil spirits in fact exist, or if they can be scared so easily by the light of a bonfire.*

"At this point, you should have more faith in the powers of the forces governing the underworld. You have witnessed their presence and their powers. Yet, you still feel skeptical about them," Akuna-Ra replied to his thoughts. She turned her back to him and walked back inside the shack, expecting him to follow her.

Knowing that complaining would have been utterly useless, if not dangerous, he followed her. Inside, the fire burned brighter, and the flames danced restlessly like hungry beasts in a cage ready to strike and attack their first prey.

Kaine observed them, more fascinated than afraid. He was still sure there was something that intended to protect him. That didn't necessarily mean Akuna-Ra or any member of the tribe; there was something or someone from the underworld who tried to keep the beast at bay.

"Speaking with the shaman this morning, I understood that your power is held back by your fear and doubts." She took a seat in front of the fire and invited him with an elegant gesture to sit down.

"I asked you here because I would like to understand better the reason for your doubts and to help you to overcome them. I can't yet say whether it's doubt or fear, but I'm soon going to find out, and I will help you to open your mind and soul to the acceptance and understanding of your powers."

Kaine remained silent. The tone Akuna-Ra used was quiet, and that made him feel more alert, as he'd never heard her so calm. There had always been that little trembling in her voice that betrayed her real state of mind. He was not a psychologist, but he could recognize when a person was about to explode with rage.

"I have no idea either. But there is something I needed to ask you, and perhaps, since I'm sure you have already read my mind, you might already give me an answer..."

She narrowed her eyes, and her facial features toughened. "Don't be insolent."

Her voice thundered inside the shack, but he was wondering whether this could be only his perception biased by his feelings.

"Then, I will ask you. What is the hurry? Why did you need to see me right away?" Kaine wondered as if she wasn't able to read his mind.

"This is a question you might easily answer yourself. You know perfectly well that we are planning to resume our journey, and we need all possible help to make us invisible, not only to the radars and the satellites but also to the population. We will leave soon, as we fear that the more we linger, the more difficult it might become to elude all the surveillance your people put on the planet and all around it. We would like to avoid a dramatic exit."

Kaine considered what she said, and he had to admit that she had a point, but there was more, and he needed to know what her intentions were with Mark and Jenna.

"So, you will release me from the curse...?"

"Your curse will be taken away as soon as we can leave, don't you worry, and so will the one upon Jason."

He relaxed on the seat in front of the fire. It was clear that she had no ill intentions, and she seemed cooperative in answering his questions. "I know Mark and Jenna came to search for me. What are your intentions for them? What is going to happen?"

A smile appeared on her face as she averted her face away from the fire, looking around herself. "I don't have any reason to harm them, if this is what you mean. They will soon leave, believing you are dead..."

"But this is even worse! Please!" Kaine urged, raising his voice.

"I warn you for the last time to avoid raising your voice with me. You are not in the position to set conditions."

Her eyes locked on his, and the fire raged inside them. He backed up at the imminent threat as the hair on his neck rose, and a cold shiver ran along his spine.

"I'm begging you, don't let them go without the reassurance or hope that I'm still alive. They will be waiting for me at home, but with a renewed hope to see me once again in the near future."

Akuna-Ra pursed her lips. She was indeed considering accepting the request, as it wouldn't have made a big difference.

*As a matter of fact, they could also reach him, and I could lift the curse upon him. So far, he has been willing to redeem himself, and perhaps he was honest when claiming that he didn't mean to tell anyone who could have had the power, or the intention to find out more and reveal our existence to the whole world. Anyway, this is a decision for Kaiphindi, but I might at least make sure that they won't leave until their fate is decided.*

"I need to speak about it with Kaiphindi. This decision isn't completely up to me, and the risks involved need to be addressed to her. She is our leader, and the last word on many things is up to her. We will let you know about our final decision."

With his heart filled with hope, his expression opened up into a bright smile. "Thanks." He couldn't find any other words at that moment because there wasn't anything more than just a promise to reconsider their decision. Yet nothing was going to happen soon.

"But now..." Her tone became grave once again. "We need to focus on sharpening your powers and suppressing your doubts." She stood up and went to a corner of the shack, one of those that generally would have remained in the shade, like the place where she supposedly used to sleep.

366

She returned, holding a wooden cup. "Drink," she ordered.

Kaine took the cup in his hands and studied the contents suspiciously. In a normal situation, he wouldn't have questioned a friend offering him something, but Akuna-Ra was not a friend, and that might have not been just a drink.

He peeked at her as she waited for him to drink the contents.

He smelled the fluid in the bowl, and although there was not a definite scent coming from it, he felt confused and suspicious.

"It's not poison and will not kill you. It will allow your soul to trust your instincts."

Hesitatingly, he brought the cup to his lips. *Oh, fuck it.* With a single gulp, he drank the entire contents.

The cup fell from his hands, as he could no longer hold it. The whole room spun around him, and he felt his heart racing in his chest. From the flames of the fire burning in the middle of the room, demons took shape, dancing wildly around the room. Flames engulfed his body, and he felt his soul transported far away.

It was a matter of undefined time. He couldn't understand where he was brought, or how it could be that the flames dancing on his skin didn't burn him. They penetrated through each pore, reaching his soul.

Gradually, he realized that he was the fire and the fire was him. His known human shape was gone, and together with the flames, his body could divide and spread to the whole universe. He felt raging inside as the stars and planets grew farther and farther away.

As the Universe he knew seemed to be too far away to even be seen, everything became dark. He had the same feeling of falling indefinitely, until he reached what supposedly was the bottom of wherever he was dropping through with a heavy thump. The darkness was complete, and fear grew in his heart. He tried to call out.

Yet, no sound came from his mouth, and nothing could be heard around him. *Where am I? Am I even still alive?*

He tried to reach his face with his hand, wondering whether he had regained his human form. At the first touch, it appeared as if he was himself once again, but he needed to know where he had been brought, whether he was still in the shack of Akuna-Ra or somewhere else.

The sound of his heartbeat comforted him and he closed his eyes to focus on it. It was the only certainty he had left in that place.

He was alive, indeed, and he needed to get a grip on his emotions.

When he finally opened his eyes, he could see once again, and he was back in the shack where Akuna-Ra stood in front of him.

"I told you, you wouldn't have died."

"What has happened?"

"The spirits have been summoned once again. Now you will have to face your fears and show what have you learned during this period you've spent with the shaman. They are coming for you, and you will be put to the test. You certainly know what this means."

Her voice was steady, and soon the whole forest was shaken by a strong wind.

"I-I'm not ready... I don't..." he mumbled. From the fire, the flames gathered, and evil eyes glanced at Kaine, still sitting on the floor.

Akuna-Ra slowly walked back toward the exit of the shack, ready to leave him alone. *There is only one way to learn to control the spirits and gain control of the gates between the underworld and the one of the living. This is through fear. Either you are going to control them, or you are going to succumb.*

Kaine kept his eyes steady on the fire taking shape and didn't notice Akuna-Ra had left the shack, walking to Kaiphindi. Her power was strong enough to take care of the situation if Kaine lost control. "He won't. I can feel it."

She turned one more time at her shack, and since the light of the fire began to pulse at a regular pace, she believed Kaine understood the meaning of the training, finally, and was able to control those forces he vehemently struggled to recognize as real.

*This is the hard way to learn when you have to control and fight for your life and the lives of the people you care for.*

She turned her shoulders and resumed her walk to Kaiphindi.

"I understood that Dr. Martin would be spending the night with you, training to overcome the obstacles standing between his potential and his fear." Kaiphindi was certainly not expecting to see Akuna-Ra coming alone so early.

"Oh, I summoned the spirits, and they are testing him; he will be on his own."

Open-mouthed, Kaiphindi ran outside, looking in the direction of Akuna-Ra's shack. She wasn't joking, and every single entity had gathered to test Kaine.

Nevertheless, the silence and the apparent calm surrounding the shack revealed that, once again, there wasn't any reason to doubt Akuna-Ra's judgment.

"You knew it..." Kaiphindi turned her glance to Akuna-Ra.

"I know everything I need to know, my queen; you should be aware of that. There was certainly a risk involved, and in that case, we would have, sadly, lost him. However, I could see through his soul this evening. He is indeed a one of a kind human being, and it's a pity we can't bring anyone with us."

She sounded almost sad to Kaiphindi's ears, and perhaps she knew that with the last sentence, she didn't necessarily mean Kaine, but Jason.

"As you also know, there is always the chance to bring him with us..."

Akuna-Ra turned her gaze to Kaiphindi, wondering whether she understood what she meant.

"I have a question for you." Akuna-Ra changed the topic of the discussion she didn't want to engage in. "Dr. Martin wondered whether we could let the people who came to search for him know about him being still alive. I was also reconsidering to lift the curse and let him meet them. As we are approaching our departure, their knowledge about us won't make any difference once we are far away. At that point, even the whole world could know about us, as we would be already far away, leaving absolutely no trace of our passage."

"Hmmm, we still don't have any idea about the time required for our leave. If we let them here, they might not be able to leave the place until we are ready. Do you think it would be a better solution than letting them go with the knowledge that Dr. Martin is probably dead?" Kaiphindi replied, inviting her to come inside her hut.

"I was also thinking the same, but Dr. Martin was insisting on having the latter option left aside. I understand he cares for them, and since they haven't done anything wrong to our people, it might seem unfair to punish them."

Kaiphindi walked to her throne and took a seat, creasing her forehead, deeply immersed in considering all the possibilities available.

*Indeed, they shouldn't suffer for the fault of Dr. Kaine, and he also seems to have done a lot to redeem himself from the curse. I need to think about it calmly. I can't answer right away.*

"I understand," Akuna-Ra replied, hearing her thoughts. "I came here to inform you about his request, not to have an answer right away."

Turning her gaze and attention toward her shack, she smiled. "I'd better return to see how Dr. Martin is doing. As I can't feel any sign of destruction, it might be that he was not just able to control them, but also to send them back to the underworld... I'm impressed."

Without waiting for an answer, Akuna-Ra left Kaiphindi, knowing that she would be busy for the rest of the night, finding a compromise to bring together the safety of their team and the need for Dr. Martin to reassure his loved ones.

When she reached the shack, Kaine lay unconscious on the floor in front of the fire which burned quietly in the middle of the room.

She crouched down to him and gently shook him to wake up. "Dr. Martin..." she called.

With a sudden jolt, Kaine woke up and looked around himself. "Did...Did they...Did I..."

"Yes, they have been sent back, and you controlled them. From this moment on, you should never doubt your powers, not for a single second." She stood up from the ground, expecting Kaine to do the same.

"I barely remembered what happened, and I have no idea what I did to control them. The only thing I can recall is that I felt as if I were the fire; it felt like a part of my own being. Although, I wasn't even sure I was still in human form. It all resembles a bizarre nightmare..." he said, struggling to stand up.

Akuna-Ra helped him to stand, scrutinizing him and his deepest thoughts. She felt his confusion and that he was still shaken by the experience, but the doubts had, finally, faded away.

The sun started to rise, and the shadows of the night were less frightening as they withdrew to the deepest parts of the forest.

"I believe what is holding me back the most is the cultural environment I was grown into. Back home we don't accept the existence of paranormal activity. What you see is what there is, and if something can't be proven, it might be a good reason to see a psychiatrist." Kaine tried avoiding looking at Akuna-Ra's judging eyes. She was the most controversial figure he'd ever met in his whole life.

*At times she seems willing to kill anyone, being the perfect killing machine. Yet, there are times when she reminds me of a demanding teacher, using all her tricks to give a lesson.*

"It all depends on who I have to deal with, Dr. Martin." Her voice coming to answer his thoughts surprised him in the silence of the shack, interrupted only by the crackling of the fire.

"You see, I allow only selected people to get to know our culture. I'm not infallible, as many of you have an incredible gift in deception. Nevertheless, when I see potential, just like in you and Jason, I prefer to give a punishment that will teach a lesson, bringing out the potential hidden within."

He turned his eyes at her, rubbing his chin. "I understand the potential you wanted to bring out in me, but I can't understand what you needed from Jason..."

Akuna-Ra shook her head. "I didn't need anything from him, but he needed something from the bottom of his soul. He came here as a young researcher, dreaming of greatness, careless and thoughtless. The only goal in his mind was glory and fame. When I cursed him to remain in these forests, it was to teach him about something he had inside: kindness, selflessness, and patience."

She smiled as she recalled the times Jason was allowed to meet them, and undeniably she felt attracted by that handsome man.

"He had no idea who he was, and when he started to live with the villagers, knowing there wouldn't be another life for him, he started to understand. Being a teacher to the children of the community wasn't something requested. Nobody asked him to do it. It came from his heart. He saw them and understood their struggles. He offered them a future, a chance...That was the lesson he needed to learn; he needed to find his heart, where before there was only greed."

"Others..." Her face toughened, and her nostrils dilated as her expression darkened with pure anger. "Others came here only to betray, and they found solely demise, which was exactly what they deserved."

She turned her back to Kaine and went to the fireplace. "We arrived here without the intention of staying for such a long time. We were supposed to gather information about this planet and leave, something that generally takes less than a month. Nevertheless, we decided to remain, and we got to study all the species populating your planet."

Kaine smiled, fascinated by the story she told, and wondered whether all the questions he had in his soul would ever be answered.

Akuna-Ra resumed her story without averting her eyes from the fire. "They were all unknown to us, and this was the reason for our lingering here. We saw you developing and growing, we learned your language and, to a few, we gave a unique opportunity to get to know life from other planets, together with our knowledge and heritage. Some benefitted by the fair exchange, others wanted only to take advantage. We wanted your people to thrive and learn something about the complicated environment you live in. Both the visible and invisible."

"Do you connect with the underworld powers on your planet?"

"As you may guess, yes. We have a strong connection with the invisible forces governing the equilibrium between life and death. You had that connection once, but preferred to ignore it." The eyes of Akuna-Ra pierced Kaine like sharp blades, and he felt naked in front of her.

"One question, though," Kaine dared, feeling his heart racing and the adrenaline rushing in his blood. "Where is your spaceship?" He felt he was the stupidest person in the world to ask. It felt like they should have something more or different than a spaceship. *Well, the whole word sounds ridiculous when it's not connected to a sci-fi movie.*

Akuna-Ra laughed, not because of the question, which was quite a legit one, but at his embarrassment to talk about it.

"What's so funny?" Kaine wondered.

"You are in the spaceship. Likewise, many others come and go every time you reach our camp."

He opened his mouth without having anything to say. *How could it be? There is nothing else but the camp.*

Akuna-Ra stood up from her place in front of the fire. "Come with me."

She turned her back to him and walked outside the shack, expecting Kaine to follow without questioning her.

# CHAPTER 30

As he followed Akuna-Ra through the camp, he tried to observe every detail, trying to spot something that made some sense to his eyes. That certain detail in a picture that remains hidden the whole time, but once you spot it, everything makes sense.

Yet for as carefully as he was glancing around, at the people, the huts, the trees surrounding the clearance, nothing unusual appeared to his eyes.

"It's useless to try to spot the ship. Until we want you to see it, you won't," she replied, guessing his behavior.

They soon reached the hut of Kaiphindi. She was returning there and was not alone. Together with her, there was a group of at least ten men and women.

"Akuna-Ra, we need to talk," she urged. "Dr. Martin, we need to dismiss you, and you can return for tonight's training if Akuna-Ra considers it necessary."

His expectations dropped. He felt so close to seeing a real spaceship, and in a matter of seconds, he was dismissed. His shoulders dropped, and lowering his head, he turned his shoulders, not even waiting for any instructions from Akuna-Ra.

*She will send someone to call me if she needs me. To be honest, I'm also starting to feel tired. I have no idea how they are going to recharge their brains, but if I don't get some rest soon, I might drop down right here in the middle of the yard.*

Akuna-Ra felt his disappointment, but there was something more important to take care of right now than allowing him to see their technology. Now it was time to plan their departure, and nothing was more important than that.

*** 

Kaine reached the bungalow he shared with Jason.

"Good morning!" Jason greeted, seeing him returning from the camp. "You look like a zombie. Is there anything else bothering you besides the long night you spent with Akuna-Ra?"

Kaine's words were barely understandable; he simply grunted something Jason doubted had any sort of meaning, besides "goodnight."

With a smirk, Jason nodded and walked away to another large building, where he had a school for the children. He wondered whether Kaine would ever return home, once, and if, there was an end to his punishment.

*Another teacher could be useful here. We could organize classes, not only for children, but also for people of all ages who need to know at least how to read and write.*

Kaine didn't bother undressing, and let his body collapse on his bed. Although he felt drained of all energy, after the night he'd spent at the camp, he couldn't fall asleep.

It wasn't because of the heat, or the humidity of the rain forest. So many thoughts in his mind prevented him from falling asleep. The first one was, of course, Mark. Knowing he was so close to almost be able to touch him, yet so far; knowing that with a single glare he could kill him.

*Soon he will also decide to leave and forget about me. How can I stop him? How can I let him know I'm alive, but I need to make up for a terrible mistake I have made?*

He turned on his back, still keeping his eyes shut. He focused his thoughts on Mark, wishing from the deepest part of his heart to make him stay, at least until there was an answer from Kaiphindi, who was too busy to take care of his request.

Behind his closed eyes, he could visualize the bungalow where Mark was. He didn't know whether he was actually seeing him, or it was a vision. Wherever he was, the tears in his eyes as he was preparing his luggage were real and brought him an endless sense of despair.

"Please, Mark, don't leave. I'm not dead," he said aloud, as his voice trembled with the first tears welling from his soul.

*** 

Mark was in his room, preparing to return home, where he needed to go back to his workplace. There were no longer any excuses to keep him there.

He was heartbroken and felt hopeless to find Kaine alive. "Whoever kept him prisoner, he might have already killed him, or perhaps he died in the forest, attacked by some sort of animal..."

It was just as he started to close his suitcase, when he thought he heard Kaine's voice. He remained as still as possible, not even breathing, assuming what he'd heard was a voice coming from his imagination, from a ghost, or something else he couldn't even fathom.

"K-Kaine?"

The voice came once again to his ears, like a whisper carried by the breeze. "Don't leave, please..."

He heard it again.

"What am I supposed to do then? Where should I search? How long should I wait?" he wept, aware of the fact that he was probably going insane if he was starting to hear voices in his head.

Nevertheless, the voice was not coming from his head; it was carried by the wind, and it came distinctly to his ears. His brain screamed to ignore it and leave as soon as possible. And, eventually, also pay a visit to a psychiatrist, who would probably consider the trauma of the loss of his loved one as the main cause for his hallucinations, and would prescribe him some pills that would take away all the pain and voices.

Then there was his heart, which yelled at him to ignore what the brain was saying because no psychiatrist could know better than him that Kaine was indeed alive. He was perhaps lost in a place where strange things appeared to happen, but still alive.

Mark sat down on the bed, grabbing his head between his hands as if it was going to explode. He remained for a moment there, cursed by thousands of thoughts and doubts to which he couldn't give any answer.

Then, suddenly he raised his head. "If it's true and magic exists in this place, then my only hope lies in the words of the shaman."

He stood up and rushed outside the bungalow, determined to find out where he could find him and to get some answers. *He might not know where Kaine is or where*

*I can search for him, but certainly, he can be more helpful than returning home, giving up on Kaine. Fuck! I'm not going to give up on him.*

He didn't know where he could find the shaman; the only thing he knew was that every night he would guard the bonfires in the village to keep the evil spirits at bay.

He saw one woman coming out from a hut, carrying a large empty basket.

"Ma'am!"

The woman turned her eyes at him, wondering what he was looking for. Despair filled his eyes and she wondered whether he was drunk.

Nevertheless, as she knew he was a guest, she smiled at him. "Good morning, Mzungu! What are you looking for?"

"Do you know where I can find the shaman? The man who takes care of the fires at night?" he asked, wondering whether he was even using the right term.

The woman pointed at one hut at the end of the village. "You can find him there. Are you ill?"

"No, but I desperately need advice, and I know there isn't any other person who can help me more than him. Thank you!"

He started to hurry toward the hut she pointed at. In front of the door, he hesitated, wondering how he would introduce his question.

"Come in," said a voice from inside.

Gingerly peeking from the door, still questioning whether he'd seen him coming or heard someone arriving, he said, "Hello, I... May I have a chat with you?"

Mark felt guilty for bothering him when he probably was ready to go to sleep after a whole night of checking the fires.

The old man appeared from a darker corner of the house. "I wouldn't have invited you in if I thought you were disturbing. Please, sit down."

They both sat on a bench made out of logs, as Mark tried to find the right words to tell him what was bothering his mind.

"I was preparing my suitcase, as we are ready to leave. We reached here, hoping to find where Kaine is, but although we have been looking everywhere possible, Kaine seemed to have disappeared from the face of the earth."

The old shaman simply nodded without answering. He knew perfectly where Kaine was, and he was proud of Azizi for keeping the secret, but he also felt sorry for a man who was going to mourn a person dear to him. *I wish I could help him and tell him not to leave, but I had no answers from Akuna-Ra, and I can't risk a curse falling on the people of my village for not honoring my word.*

Mark lowered his eyes at his hands, as he twisted his fingers, grabbed by the biggest indecision in his entire life. "Something has happened there in my bungalow, today. Perhaps you will think I'm crazy and I need to see a psychiatrist, but I distinctly heard Kaine's voice telling me not to leave yet."

He raised his eyes to meet the shaman's, hoping to find an answer to his questions. "My question is, should I believe that he was talking to me? Was it something I imagined because I desperately want him to be alive and well? Then before I came here, there was a voice telling me Kaine had been taken and brought against his will back

381

to Africa, but I can't even remember his return. I'm afraid I'm going crazy."

The old shaman's heart ached at the feeling of the pain in Mark's heart. He grabbed Mark's hand and held it tightly in his own.

"My son, this forest has many eyes and many hearts. If you can hear the voices of the spirits begging you to take a different path than the one you were going to take, then you need to listen to them. If they say you need to stay, then you will have to postpone your departure. They don't contact people for no reason at all."

Mark held the shaman's hand, feeling like it was the only thing keeping him from falling into a deeper abyss. He was his only hope.

"Do you think Kaine is still alive somewhere?"

"I don't know; the spirits do."

He couldn't tell him he knew the voices were right, and perhaps Kaine was able to develop the power to communicate with Mark.

Having someone ready to listen to him without judging or considering him crazy, was relieving. There was, at least one person in the world who believed him and considered it plausible the possibility that Kaine or the spirits, got in touch with him.

"Then, I will listen to what they suggest, and I will remain here if you don't have any objections to it." Mark stood up, ready to leave the shaman to his deserved rest. "You can ask me for whatever service. I will help whenever and however I can like I've done so far."

"There are no strangers in this village, and everybody is family to us. You and Azizi's friend are more than welcome to stay for as long as you wish. This is also your family." Creasing his face into a broad smile, the shaman stood up, patting Mark's shoulder.

"Thank you," Tears of gratitude blurred his sight.

As he returned to his bungalow, Jenna called him, coming from a road leading out of the village. "Mark!" she called, starting to run toward him.

"Mark, listen, about our return to the States..." she commenced.

"I'm not going back; not yet, at least."

"Really? I thought you needed to be back at work this week." She wanted to tell him she made the final decision to remain there and to marry Azizi, but she was baffled by Mark's decision to remain too.

"I know, but as strange as it might sound, and I know you will think I'm crazy, but it doesn't matter. I heard Kaine's voice begging me not to leave yet. I wasn't sleeping. I heard him when I was preparing the suitcase."

She lowered her gaze. "I don't know what to say, and had I never visited this place, I might have thought you were completely insane. However, this place seems out of this world, and strange things happen regularly."

Her eyes toured the surroundings of the village, as life went on apparently following a routine. "Take, for example, the shaman of the village. I have seen many tribes around the world, and we have studied them thoroughly. However, none of them seemed to be so obsessed with keeping the lights on during the night. I understand the fear of wild animals, but we're not talking of this..."

She shook her head, biting her lower lip. "I can't explain. There is a part of me that feels the need to run away and as far as possible from this village. Another part is completely fascinated by them, not to mention I have fallen in love with Azizi."

"So, are we both remaining here?" Mark questioned as if to ask for a confirmation of their decision.

She didn't reply. She simply nodded, feeling also afraid of the consequences.

***

Certainly, Kaine couldn't see what was going on with Mark and Jenna, but something gave him the certainty that they would remain a little longer there in Africa. He wasn't sure whether their decision had anything to do with him pleading for Mark not to leave yet.

With a smile on his lips, he closed his eyes and fell asleep almost immediately, hoping the departure of Akuna-Ra and her people would arrive soon, so he could be allowed to return to his life with Mark.

***

There was a long pause of silence as the whole tribe collected at the center of the camp. The tension was high, as never before had their leaving been so close.

So many things still needed to be taken care of, starting with the tests for the engines, the eventual repairs, time and climate might have caused, and the modality of departure.

Kaiphindi considered her surroundings and, when she was sure that everyone was present and she had their attention, she started to talk. "We have been waiting for too long, taking advantage of the humans' development, without considering the downside of this vantage, which is digging ourselves a trap."

"Captain," Yosin interrupted, feeling that there was more than having fallen into a trap. "It is true, and we

384

shouldn't have waited such a long period, but together with the evolution of humanity, we have developed ourselves too, carrying out independent research and improving our technology. We can say our race is far more advanced than the human's, and for this reason, we should put into practice what we have learned."

Kaiphindi smiled. "This was also the reason why I have summoned you all here today. We all need to understand what kind of development we are talking about. Your team, Yosin, followed the scientific path; meanwhile, our Akuna-Ra pursued the paranormal lead." She paused to gather her thoughts, and when she was finally ready, as the rest of her people maintained an almost religious silence, she went on explaining her plan, hoping there wasn't much of anything to improve.

"We have found a few individuals among the human race who hold incredible mental powers. They can't simply communicate with the spiritual entities but can also create a bridge to control the minds of other human beings. In practice, our ship will at least be undetected by the eyes of humanity, thanks to the abilities of those external cooperators."

Yosin smiled, excited about the prospect of resuming their journey. "Our system can easily jam the radars to make sure they won't reveal the presence of our spaceship leaving the planet. However..."

His expression darkened.

"We have no idea about the conditions of our ship, and before singing our success, we will need to make sure that everything is going to work smoothly."

"But then, this means only one thing, that we need to start working on testing everything we have, and get ready for the departure," Akuna-Ra intervened.

"In theory, this is exactly what we need, but we will first need to assess the condition of the spaceship..." Yosin's eyebrows knitted together.

With a brief nod, Kaiphindi acknowledged the situation. "Then I suppose we all know what to do, and I suggest you all start right away."

Kaiphindi dismissed the team and everyone started to organize their work, taking care of every detail to be brought together for departure day. There wasn't yet a specified countdown, but they all felt the pressure.

Akuna-Ra observed the group dispersing to their duties and remained alone with Kaiphindi. "What would be the next target?" she wondered.

With a puzzled expression, Kaiphindi glanced at Akuna-Ra.

"I mean, are we heading back home, or is there another planet to reach? For how long are we supposed to explore the Universe?" She didn't want to admit it, but she'd started to find their expedition frustrating. *If time is not a question, it doesn't mean my heart doesn't long for the place I have left behind.*

"I thought I would have never said it, but I'm missing home," Akuna-Ra added, glancing at the blue sky.

Walking toward her, Kaiphindi grabbed her hand and held it tightly in hers. "We are all feeling homesick, and as soon as we can resume our quest, we will also be able to re-establish our connection with the base. You know we can't do this here. Every message can be traced by the recording systems of the earthlings. We need to have patience; there is only one way to have the chance to resume our journey home, and that is to leave this planet as soon as possible."

"I miss it too..." Kaiphindi added with a whisper.

In the evening, Mark called his supervisor. He didn't know what he was supposed to tell her, but whatever came to his mind, whether an excuse for his delayed return or presenting his resignation, he needed to inform her.

He stared at his mobile phone for a long time, figuring out in his mind the best way to approach the topic. He was not an irreplaceable worker in the lab, and he was sure the only way to solve the situation, from the point of view of his employer, would be that of letting him go and searching for another employee to fill his position.

"I was waiting for your call," Ms. Ridgewell, Mark's supervisor, replied when she heard Mark's voice.

"I know, and you were also expecting me to call you from the airport, confirming my imminent departure." Mark's heart raced, and his hands started to dampen with sweat. The telephone became insanely hot, to the point he was close to throwing it away. "There has been a problem which might delay my departure of about a month."

The deadly silence on the other side of the line told him that Ms. Ridgewell was on the verge of exploding. "Mr. Donovan, I'm afraid I will need more information about the problem keeping you from returning from your vacation."

"I understand. As you know, I came to Africa, not for a holiday, but to find a missing person." He wanted to clarify that point once again, as it wasn't fully clear to his employer. "Although you can say this is something I should leave to the Police, I would like you to remember that the political situation in this part of the world is not settled, and finding a person might not be what the Police is interested in, particularly since there are no leads whatsoever."

He could not tell her that the reason why he came to Africa to search for his boyfriend, was because a voice told him to do so.

He was sure that by the time he returned home, he wouldn't be simply unemployed; he would be locked down in an asylum.

*Nobody else but Jenna,* Kaine *and me can understand the meaning of having a voice guiding you when you're here.*

"I would appreciate it if I could have one month more. You can quit paying my salary and resume it when I get back to the Lab," Mark proposed. "Although, I wouldn't blame you if you need to fire me and find someone who can be available to actually work starting from now."

Deep in his soul, he hoped to get fired, to gain the freedom to remain there in Africa for as long as it was required.

Ms. Ridgewell exhaled loudly. The news arrived unexpectedly, and she needed some time to decide, not to mention she should also talk with her supervisor.

"Mr. Donovan, I will need some time to give you an answer about whether you are going to keep your job here or not. I will bring your question to the Director and will get back to you as soon as possible. Since you are staying there in Africa for another month, I don't think you will be in a particular hurry to get an answer from us."

Her tone was impatient; he knew she would have a hard time explaining the situation to her Director.

"I understand your position and I'm ready to accept any decision you make. I want to make sure that..." His voice started to flicker. He inhaled deeply and held his breath until he could keep the tears at bay. "I'm sure you understand the situation I'm in... I can't return if Kaine is still missing in the middle of nowhere. I need to at least have evidence of his..." He could not continue the sentence. He wasn't ready to accept his death.

Ms. Ridgewell nodded and hoped she could find a good compromise that would satisfy everybody. "I will try my best to give the most complete description of your situation to the Director. For the moment, there is nothing you can do but to wait."

"I appreciate your help, Ms. Ridgewell. I will be waiting for your reply. Thank you once again, and I hope to see you soon."

"So do I..." she replied, ending the conversation.

# CHAPTER 31

After one month of frantic preparations, calibrations, repairing, and training, the team could finally anticipate leaving the blue planet.

The access to the camp was restricted only to the shamans of the villages, therefore, Jason was not allowed to reach them. Concerning Kaine, he could only go for his training, which started to be coupled with the other shamans.

Jason was at Omar's bar and, although everything seemed to be business as usual, as he knew, there was something different. He stared at the place through the glass filled with whiskey and wondered if it was because the departure of the 'lost tribe' was imminent. He felt like his brain was going to soon explode, and that was the reason for him to be at the bar. There was nothing like a good dose of alcohol to keep him from insanity.

*I wonder whether she will take my request seriously about killing me the day she leaves. I'm not afraid of dying. And, certainly, whatever life is left for me to live without her, is not appealing me at all.*

He sipped the whiskey and, for the first time in his life, he found the taste unappealing, almost bland and unsatisfying. He studied the bottle to check whether it was a different brand.

Omar observed him for a long time; he had never seen Jason as restless as at that moment. "Boss, is there anything I can help you with?"

Jason turned his face to Omar behind the bar counter. He didn't know what he was supposed to say. *Can he help? Can anybody help when I have no idea what's wrong?*

"Are you sure this is the same whiskey I usually drink?" Jason asked, raising the glass toward Omar.

"Why? Of course, it's the same..."

Jason lowered his eyes back to the table. He gulped the liquid and stood up.

Something was definitely wrong and perhaps it was the restricted access to the camp, and hence to Akuna-Ra. His nights suddenly felt lonely and the days worthless if he couldn't see her. Also teaching, which generally put him in a good mood, giving him a sense of worth, lost all meaning.

Restlessness grabbed his heart, like a beast with clawed hands was holding it, squeezing tighter and tighter.

He reached his bungalow at about dinner time. Likewise every evening, he lit the candles in the bedroom and kitchen determined to prepare something to eat. He wasn't in the mood to cook anything.

"To be honest, I don't feel like I want to eat at all, but since it's something I must do, I'll make something easy."

Listlessly, he prepared himself a couple of sandwiches and poured a glass of water.

As he ate, he looked at the flame of the candle, dancing like it was playing with the draft coming from the door. For a while, he followed it as it seemed to invite him to play with them.

A smile appeared on his face, as if the little blaze understood his feelings and wanted to dance for him, cheering up his soul.

"Thank you," he said, not sure why he was thanking a flame, or perhaps one of the benign spirits that populated the forest.

Recalling the experience, he had at the bar with the whiskey offered, he stood up, curious to see whether it was only a problem with the bottle Omar had, or if it was a question concerning him and his perception of tastes and flavors.

He poured a glass and brought it to his nose, deeply inhaling the aroma. The smoky bouquet gave him a wider smile. *I might be lost in the middle of nothing without any steady income, but I have never felt as rich as I feel now.*

He toured visually the wooden bungalow where he was living. "Not a mansion, not a car, not any fancy restaurants or meals. Yet, nobody I have ever known who had a lot of money could dream of the same amount of freedom I'm enjoying here."

He sipped the whiskey and started to chuckle. "I have never felt so free and happy in my life. Akuna-Ra is a genius, and this punishment, this curse, now feels more like a blessing."

He filled the glass again and walked to the bedroom, to the window, from where he could have a glimpse of the yard where the shaman was keeping the fires alive.

Nevertheless, all the shamans were busy at the tribe, and the critical task to keep the village safe from the evil spirits was given to their young trainees.

Jason didn't know what was going on with the other trainees of the shamans, but the one who was in charge of caring about the bonfires appeared to have the situation under control.

"At least he seems to know the spells, and that is, to me, quite impressive," he said observing the young man.

He remained for some time to observe all his movements when a loud yawn informed him the time was late. He lazily undressed and, watching the fan on the ceiling, he fell asleep, mesmerized by that slight buzz and the dancing of the shadows.

Mark, instead, couldn't find any sleep. Another month had already passed and although he got the chance to leave his job temporarily, to have his position reconsidered once he would return home, he couldn't stand the feeling of being so close to Kaine, yet so far. It was like a mirage in the desert; he could see it but couldn't grab it.

"Kaine..." He stood from his bed, walked to the window, and observed the fires burning.

He closed his eyes and tried to focus his thoughts on Kaine. *Where are you? Why can't I hear your voice anymore?*

He remained silent, breathing as slow as possible to avoid making any sound that could have covered the finest noise. He needed to listen and to have an answer.

The words of the shaman about listening to what the voices of the forest say began to haunt him; he needed more.

From afar, he could hear some noises. It was the first time he'd noticed something different than the night-chirping of the insects and night creatures in the forest. They sounded like drums.

He didn't open his eyes, for fear of breaking that sort of connection with the drumming noise. The pounding was regular, but unlike anything he'd heard coming from the drums of other tribes. He would have said it sounded like something electronically reproduced, as there was something unnatural them.

The light breeze blew in his direction, bringing a slight relief from the oppressive heat and moisture of the air. His heart started to pound together with the drums when...

BAM!

A loud noise like someone wanted to tear the door down forced him to open his eyes.

A scream escaped his mouth, as a release from the fright he experienced.

Almost frozen between the two ticks of a clock, he remained to stare at the door, wondering whether whatever was on the other side would consider tearing it down or not.

BAM!

Another loud bang echoed in the room. Stiffening his lips, ready to face whatever was out there, he went to open the door and saw the shaman in his ceremonial mask followed by two large men, who he recognized as warriors, standing in front of him.

The dark figures resembled in his mind the imagery of demons he'd been taught as a child, and instinctually he backed up a couple of steps.

"You need to follow us," the shaman said.

Without giving him time to answer, he was grabbed promptly by the two warriors and his eyes covered by a rough piece of fabric tied around his head.

His heart started to pound; the friendliness he had experienced until then resembled a fading memory, and he feared he was being brought to his final demise.

He had no breath left to walk, and as odd as it might have sounded, the way the two warriors forcibly carried him by the arms was the only thing preventing him from falling.

Blindfolded, a sense of fear overwhelmed him; tears damped the cloth that blinded his eyes and soon they streamed down his face. His body shook at every further step they took, as they brought him nearer to what he believed would be his doom.

Something he noticed was the drumming sound which got closer, giving him at least an idea about the direction they were bringing him to. *Were those drums for me? Should I have run away as soon as I could hear them?*

They suddenly stopped their march and without saying a word they removed the blindfold from his eyes.

He looked around him, wondering what kind of place he was brought to. Seemingly it was another camp where one of the local tribes established their territory. Some of the people there were wearing western-style dresses, jeans, t-shirts, and others were instead more traditionally dressed.

A slender, tall woman approached him. Her dark skin was decorated with white designs on her body, and suddenly it brought to his memory the image Kaine showed him on his computer before he left for Africa. He was wondering whether she was belonging to the same tribe, as she couldn't be the same person. That picture was supposed to be quite old, considering the resolution.

Something fascinating him was her eyes, those amber-colored eyes, so bright and shining as if they possessed a light all their own. He'd never seen anything like it and couldn't take his gaze off of them.

"Mr. Donovan, we have been informed about your arrival, and there has been quite a debate about whether to let you come here or not," she commenced.

"I'm not a researcher; I didn't come here to get in touch with any tribe..."

"SILENCE!" she thundered.

An unspeakable pain surprised Mark, forcing him to his knees, unable to scream out loud. It was like his whole body started to cramp, muscles tightening up and bones twisting away from their positions.

"You speak when I ask you something, not before." She grinned.

Mark barely managed to nod, and immediately the pain disappeared as if he woke up from a nightmare. He wondered whether she was the cause of it; something in her eyes confirmed his fears, and told him this was only a foretaste of what she was capable of.

"I know why you came here, and I suppose the best person who can explain the reason why you need to take the first plane and return to the place you came from is the one you came to search for."

At a swift gesture of her hand, a man who stood at her side moved away without saying a word. After a few moments, the same man returned, bringing another man who was also blindfolded.

It didn't take him more than a couple of seconds to recognize the silhouette of the only man he loved – Kaine.

Just like in a trance, feeling his head light and his heart full of insane happiness, Mark stood up, hoping he would be able to stand and walk toward him.

When he was close enough, he tried to remove the blindfold, but Kaine stopped him, holding his hands in his own. "Mark, is this really you?"

His voice trembled and the first tears appeared from beneath the cloth.

"Kaine, I thought you were dead. When I heard the voice telling me you had been taken back to Africa, I couldn't refrain from coming. I needed to have you back at any cost, regardless of whether I had to return to bring your corpse, or with you alive. I would have gone to the end of the world to get you."

Kaine thought he could die, as now he was once again happy, and if his life had to be terminated in the arms of his beloved, then he had nothing more to ask in his life.

"Mark, there is something you need to know about the reason why I'm here, and also the reason why you will have to return home and wait for me there," Kaine started to explain. He felt quite grateful for the blindfold because he was sure that if he could have looked into Mark's eyes, he wouldn't have been able to ask him to leave.

It was difficult enough to do so from behind that curtain.

"Before I left this tribe, I made a promise. I should never have talked about them with anyone, as their secret was vital to be kept. I foolishly thought that talking to you wouldn't have been considered breaking the vow... I was wrong." He lowered his head as if to glance at their hands holding each other.

"The day after, I found Akuna-Ra in the house, and she put a curse on me. Whoever I would have stared at would have died soon. I thought it was only a nightmare. Though, when I was drinking my morning coffee, I watched out of the window of the kitchen. There was a young girl who was walking down the street..."

His breath turned heavier and heavier as he recalled the way the girl died; the way he killed her.

Soon tears started once again to wet the rough fabric, and he sobbed desperately at that hurtful memory.

Mark held him tightly to himself. "Is this the reason why you are blindfolded now?" he murmured in his ear. He caressed the back of Kaine's head to soothe his pain, as slowly he felt Kaine's body relaxing and his sobs subsiding.

"I was brought here to pay for my stupidity, and the reason why they wanted me here is my ability to communicate with the spirits."

When he felt calmer, he parted from Mark and explained to him why they needed his abilities including their identity and alien origin.

"Will you go back home, once you... they..."

"Yes," Akuna-Ra interrupted him briskly. "Once we leave, the curse will be lifted and he will be free to return home, if this is what he wants."

Mark gave her a freezing glance. He didn't like her, but he knew he had to act wiser if he didn't want to experience more of her powers.

"Can't I remain here waiting for you? We might return home together..." Mark wasn't planning on leaving without him. As he knew he was alive, there wouldn't be any reason for him to go back. He needed to be there with him.

"You will need to go back to your job. They won't wait for you for eternity, and I believe you have already stretched your available time off. Am I wrong?" Kaine wondered.

"I can stay for as long as necessary. I got the confirmation from my supervisor and I have been temporarily suspended. My position will be reconsidered once I return, so I don't have any deadline anymore," Mark explained. Then glancing at Akuna-Ra, he asked, "How long will it take for you to leave?"

Akuna-Ra didn't know what to answer; it could have been a matter of days as much as it might have taken another year. This was a question concerning the whole team and was not up to her to know everything.

"It will take another month." A voice resounded from beyond Akuna-Ra's shoulders and another female figure appeared.

She was, perhaps, the most beautiful woman he'd ever seen, although he had to admit Akuna-Ra also had an uncommon beauty.

"I must apologize for my delay to the meeting," she said sarcastically, giving a severe glance at Akuna-Ra. "Allow me to introduce myself. My name is Kaiphindi, and I lead the expedition that brought my people here. Akuna-Ra is my right arm and a trusted friend. In my opinion, your return home might be appropriate.

Nevertheless, we need to make sure you won't say a word, so I'd prefer you won't be allowed to go anywhere else."

Her tone of voice was calm, but in the background, a nervous shake stirred the quiet of her tone of voice. *It might be the fact of having an intruder in the tribe, or perhaps it's the approaching of the day of their departure.*

"I don't mean any harm to your people, but I agree to stay here and wait to leave together with Kaine," he replied. "I have no idea how to reach the camp, so once I return to my bungalow, this place will remain unknown to me."

Kaine sighed. He began to feel torn between the desire to go back home and the intriguing chance of becoming the next shaman of the tribe. That was an honor never allowed to strangers. Only the shaman's son was supposed to continue the tradition of the protection and connection with the spirits. For him, being chosen to be the next shaman was a privilege he knew he would have regretted having denied. *I wish I could have a clearer mind to decide what would be better to do, but he might be right and remaining here would make things easier.*

Kaine turned his head as if to watch around himself. "I would like to have the chance to talk with Mark in private."

Kaiphindi peered at Akuna-Ra and Okumi, signaling them to give them some privacy.

"Mark," he said when they were alone, "So many things have happened since I got lost here, and I need to understand their meaning. My only wish is to spend the rest of my eternity with you, but there are also other things I need to consider."

Mark listened to what Kaine was saying and with every word, he feared he was going to dump him. "Are you trying to find a way to say it's over?" His voice trembled and he felt as if he made a big mistake in coming to find him.

"No, I want to live my life with you. It has been a nightmare not having the chance to call you or let you know about the changes that have happened in my life."

There was a small pause of silence between them when Kaine tried to recall his thoughts and find the best way to explain his feelings.

"Yet as much as I have been in touch with them and the other villages around this camp," he continued, "I had the chance to discover something more about me and the Universe surrounding us. This brought me to develop some skills that were dormant in me, and based on those powers, I have been asked to become the next shaman of the tribe."

With a long sigh, Mark closed his eyes and allowed his thoughts to run freely. He hoped in that way, a steady one would reach him, allowing him to see things clearly.

He opened his eyes and observed Kaine, who didn't move, waiting for his answer.

"So, you are considering remaining here and becoming a shaman... Where do I fit in this vision?" His heart sank fearing Kaine was eventually thinking about leaving everything behind. He felt abandoned and betrayed.

"What about the shaman's husband?" Kaine proposed and searched for Mark's hands. "Will you marry me?"

His proposal came to Mark's ears like a blast and he remained dumbfounded at its unexpected arrival.

"Kaine-"

He had no words to say. His mind went blank. Only one second ago he was sure there was no place for him in Kaine's life, then... Everything changed, and he proposed to him to get married.

"I have no idea how I'm going to reply. Certainly, I would love to marry you, and there is nothing in my life that makes me happier than being with you. Though, what am I going to do here?" Mark held Kaine by his shoulders. He hoped he could understand that whether, for him, this would be the chance of a lifetime, for a chemist employed in a pharmaceutical laboratory, he couldn't see any career or hobby in sight.

"You are a chemist, aren't you?"

Mark shook his head with a hopeless grin. "Yes, but-"

"You have no idea about the potential for medications to be found in this forest. All you need is to have a small lab. The company you are working for could organize it if they are interested in new finds in the pharmaceutical field. Or... You can be the medicine man... There is a huge need here for everything."

Mark thought for a moment. He knew every single medication comes from the combination of compounds found in nature, and he had to admit feeling fascinated by the possibility to research new active constituents in that wonderful environment.

*It has potential, indeed and I wonder why I haven't thought about it too.*

He reached Kaine's lips and fused them into a tender kiss. It was as if it had been years since the last time they touched, and yet it also seemed to him like the first time they'd ever kissed.

Kaine felt their hearts beating in unison. He could sense Mark's heart pounding from his lips, pumping faster and faster as passion took over and his kisses became more passionate and demanding. He wished he'd never been cursed and could have the chance to bring him to the bungalow and spend the whole night experiencing once again what they thought they'd lost forever.

"I need you," Kaine whispered through the kisses.

Mark parted from him and understood this was the time when a decision was to be made, knowing that a simple answer wasn't to be sought in one minute.

"I want to marry you right away, and it doesn't matter whether you will be forced to keep your eyes blindfolded. I would marry you even if you had to wear a spacesuit for the rest of your life."

Kaine laughed and exhaled in relief as if a stone had fallen from his shoulders. Then his expression turned grave once again. "Mark, we need to wait before we can be together once and for all. All I ask of you is to have patience. If you want to set up a new life for us, we will need to settle everything back home. We can ask Kaiphindi to allow you to return and settle everything."

"Yes, you're right. There are plenty of things to set up before we can move, and since you're not going to leave this place, I might take care of them." He brought Kaine's hands to his lips and kissed them tenderly.

"Remember, though..." Kaine said before parting from him, allowing Okumi to bring him back to his bungalow. "Thou shalt never tell... about what you saw here. Not a single word, or else..."

# EPILOGUE

The sun rose on a bright morning. The shadows of the night slowly withdrew from the kitchen where Jason spent the whole night thinking and drinking whiskey. The time for Akuna-Ra and the tribe to leave arrived, and he hadn't heard anything from any of them. He felt dismissed and discarded like an obsolete object, something that brings more shame than shine. Like an old toy that turned out to be useless and no longer entertaining.

And the worst of all, he felt that way too. He knew he should have stood up to go claim his place, or at least to demand the promise to be kept and be gone as soon as possible.

"I should kill myself, and be a man for once in my pathetic lifetime and get out of this world for good," he mumbled with the short breath he was left after a whole night spent feeling miserable.

He tried to stand up, but his legs failed him, and he fell on the floor together with the now empty bottle. He felt like the entire world was collapsing on his head, and there was nothing in his power to stop it. He leaned with his shoulders against the counter of the kitchen and, grabbing his head between his hands, he started sobbing desperately.

*Why can't I be brave enough and kill myself? Why am I such a coward? It shouldn't surprise me she told me it wasn't possible for me to go with them. What kind of use could they ever have for a loser like me?*

As tears streamed out of his soul, draining him of all the energy he had left, he didn't notice the door opening and the one who, with silent footsteps, arrived in front of him.

"It has never been because of cowardice or strength," she said.

Surprised, he raised his head from between his hands. Her figure, blurred by the tears against the first light of the day, seemed like a dream. He wondered whether he was still awake or if he'd fallen asleep on the floor of the kitchen.

He remained silent.

She crouched in front of him. "What is going on in your life to make you feel so pitiful?"

He shook his head. "It's human shit called love. We should have never invented it. Better to be cold, calculating, and more machine-like. It burns like hell, regardless of how much alcohol I drink to drown it."

"I see..." She stood up, glancing at the empty bottle, which fell on the floor and offered him a hand to stand up.

"We are preparing to leave... Everything is ready and tonight we will resume our journey."

With a groan expressing the pain he was feeling all over his body, he stood up, grimacing. "Why should this interest me, unless you are going to grant my request..."

"...and kill you?" she wondered, failing still to understand the drama humans were able to create. Nevertheless, she felt fascinated by the power of their feelings, and had to admit she would have badly missed Jason's presence.

He still felt dizzy from the alcohol he'd drank during the night, but the thought that he was going to live his last day made him sober up faster than he could ever hope.

"Yes..." He wasn't sure he wanted to die anymore, but he was certain he didn't want to live without her.

He stopped for a second, and like waking up from a nightmare, he glanced around himself as soon as they were out of his bungalow.

There was a strange silence around, and he considered it weird that he couldn't see any of the people of the village around. "Where are all the others? Why is it all so silent?"

"With us leaving, they are all wondering whether they could continue to benefit from the same sort of protection we have offered. While we were here, rebels, warlords, and all sorts of intruders were kept far away. Now, as we are going to leave, who will protect them?" she replied looking in his eyes.

Jason considered the feelings of the villagers, and perhaps the feeling of betrayal which might have germinated in their souls. "Yes, who is going to take care of them...?" he repeated almost mechanically, refusing to move another step.

"You might ask the new shaman and the medicine man..." she replied matter-of-factly. "Kaine is the new shaman after Mandawi."

"The kid is full of surprises," Jason pondered, almost talking to himself. "Why didn't Okumi come to bring me to your presence? You have never come to my bungalow." A strange impression that she was up to something flashed in his mind, and generally, when it happened, it was nothing good.

"Maybe we aren't different, after all," she commenced, not understanding what she was going to tell him or what would be the consequences of her decision. "Perhaps it's also true and I began to understand what the spirits tried to tell me for all those centuries and the reason why you have been brought to me."

With an amused smile, she averted her gaze from him. "I know there will be many things about this planet I would miss, but their memory will keep them alive in my heart. Yet there is something I can't keep alive with the simple memory: that human shit called love."

With a catlike swiftness, she turned around, extracted a machete from her belt, and swung it in the air, stopping just a touch away from Jason's throat.

Jason's heart stopped for a second at the threatening feeling of the cold blade against his skin, and he remained frozen in the same position, unable to move any further.

"Your wish to die will be granted right away, but you might also consider the chance to leave with us. It has never happened, and I can't ensure you might survive, but the odds might be in your favor."

It took a couple of moments for Jason to register what she said and interpret the meaning of her words.

Slowly, he raised his hand to the blade and pushed it away from his throat. The machete fell on the ground as their lips touched in a passionate kiss. For the first time since he met Akuna-Ra, he felt something different in the way she held him. It was passion, affection...love.

*That human shit called love. It forces you to make the wrong decisions, but in the end, dying by trying is better than dying for nothing.*

*They came from far away; they came to discover and understand the Universe. On Earth, they found more than they could imagine, and for the earthlings they got in touch with, they were a blessing. Yet, they also discovered something more about their nature and learned to embrace and appreciate the differences. They brought together with them the knowledge of something even worth dying for.*

# ABOUT THE AUTHOR

P. J. Mann is, first of all, a traveler who cannot live without having a flight ticket to the next destination. her wanderings brought her to meet new people, cultures, and places from where she gets the inspiration for her novels. She doesn't like to restrict her stories to a particular genre, although she prefers crime stories to which she adds her personal twists of introspection, proposing an alternative point of view to the many issues of life.

Learn more about me at:

https://pjmannauthor.com/

## ONE MORE THING

If you enjoyed this book, I'd be very grateful if you'd post a short review on Amazon. Your support really does make a difference.

Printed in Great Britain
by Amazon

87215971R00243